PRAISE FOR NAT

'A significant new voice in Women

'Thought-provoking, emotionally intelligent.'

UN
PLANNED

ALSO BY NATALIE K MARTIN

UN
PLANNED

Natalie K Martin

Text copyright © 2022 by Natalie K Martin
All rights reserved.

Published by Lake Union Publishing, Seattle

www.apub.com

Amazon, the Amazon logo, and Lake Union Publishing are trademarks of Amazon.com, Inc., or its affiliates.

ISBN-13: 9781542034647
ISBN-10: 1542034647

Cover design by Liron Gilenberg

Printed in the United States of America

For my mum, her mum and all the mums

Chapter One

'Do you want to keep it?'

A frown carves into my face and my eyes narrow as I look across the sofa at Sam. 'Are you serious?'

The face looking back at me is the last one I've seen at night and the first I've seen in the morning for almost eleven years. But this is the first time I've seen it this pale, drained of blood and dumbfounded.

'I don't know, Zoe. I mean . . . you're *pregnant?*' Sam looks at the test lying on the grey material of the sofa between us. 'How? You're on the pill.'

I shrug, holding my shoulders up to my ears. 'I don't know. Maybe it was the food poisoning.'

I grimace, remembering the outcome of my first, and what will definitely be my last, try of oysters. I'd ended up in bed with a fever and a stomach that wouldn't hold onto anything for more than two minutes for days. I hadn't even bothered to take the pill because what was the point when I'd only throw it up again? We should've used condoms until I was sure that we were protected. I know that now.

Sam turns to look out at the balcony. The sky is covered with paintbrush strokes of orange-tinted clouds and, despite it being hot and humid outside, the climate-controlled air in our apartment is cold on my skin.

'It's not April Fool's, is it?' he jokes, turning back to look at me with a weak smile.

I tilt my head to one side. 'Two months too early.'

'It was worth a try.' He heaves a sigh that sounds like it should come with him rolling his sleeves up. 'So, what do we do now?'

We. I like that. Optimism flickers in my chest, replacing the doubt that's set in since I took the test two days ago. It's been agonising, waiting for him to come home from a photoshoot in Melbourne, but *we* is good. *We* has possibilities.

'Well, it's bloody terrifying,' I reply with a little laugh. 'I mean, it'll be a huge change, for both of us. But it could also be pretty cool, too.'

Sam looks at me as if I've spoken in a language he doesn't understand before looking around the room, shaking his head. I get it. He's ten years older than me and becoming a dad at forty-eight wasn't in his life plan. He's probably thinking about the disruption that will inevitably follow. Our eighth-floor Sydney apartment isn't exactly child-friendly with its hard, tiled floors, white walls and a downstairs neighbour who pulls all-night raves most weekends.

'Zo,' he says slowly, dragging my name out with his Australian drawl, 'we said we didn't want kids. We planned to travel wherever we wanted, whenever we wanted instead of being tied down. Remember?'

'I know,' I nod. 'But it's not like we're bouncing around from guesthouse to guesthouse anymore. To be honest, I thought you were enjoying being back so much that you wanted to stay.'

Sam shakes his head. 'We were only just talking about Mexico a few weeks ago.'

I bite my lip to hold myself back. We signed the lease on our apartment five months ago, and from the way he's been talking,

Sydney's in his future plans for at least another year. And even though we *have* just had a conversation about going to Mexico, it had been about attaching a couple of weeks onto a photoshoot he might be being booked for. Not as somewhere to move to.

'It would be Mexico, not Mars,' I say instead, and reach out to take his hand in mine.

His palm is clammy and his grip is firm. I have the feeling that he's holding on for dear life, so I throw him a smile, despite the hammering in my chest. When I'd read the result I'd felt a huge wave of fear and doubt so big, I'd actually thrown up from the shock. I hadn't noticed anything was wrong until I'd happened to look at my period tracking app and saw that I was late. I've had time over the last two days to get used to the idea though, and even though it's not planned, I know we'll make good parents.

'Look, I've had a couple of days to let it sink in,' I say, giving his hand a reassuring squeeze. 'Maybe you just need some time to get used to it? It could be the next adventure in our story.'

'But I don't want that kind of adventure.' The skin between his eyebrows wrinkles as he looks back at me. 'I don't want to sound like a dick, Zo . . . but when I told you I didn't want kids, I meant it. I thought you did too?'

'I did. But it was hypothetical back then. Now, it's real.'

'Exactly.'

Despite the heat, goosebumps erupt across my bare arms and my throat dries. I let go of his hand to reach for my glass of water before gulping a swig down.

'So, you want me to get rid of it?' I ask evenly, unable to bring myself to face him.

It doesn't matter what his answer is. I already know from the violent lurch of my stomach as I say the words that it isn't something I could bring myself to do. Sam gets up from the sofa and rakes a hand through his short, sandy blonde hair.

3

'That's not fair, Zoe. I didn't say that.'

'You just said you don't want a baby, so what else can you possibly mean?'

'I want *this*.' He sweeps his hand to gesture to the space around us. 'I don't want to lose the freedom we have.'

'The freedom *we* have, or the freedom *you* have?'

'What's that supposed to mean?'

'Well, a normal relationship is already a stretch for you. A kid on top must sound like a prison sentence.'

'I'm committed to you, Zoe. I always have been, you know that. Our relationship means more to me than anything else.'

'Does it?' I ask, feeling bitterness rise in my throat.

'Yes, it does. Which is why I don't want to bring a kid into it.'

I scrub my hands across my face and sigh. 'So, you *do* want me to have an abortion.'

'Do I even have a choice? It's *your* body.'

'And it's *your* baby.'

Sam tilts his head back with a sigh before looking at me with a long shrug. 'God, this is so fucked. If I say do it, I'll feel like a chauvinistic, controlling prick. And if I say *don't* do it . . .'

He visibly shudders. That's how much the idea of having a child repulses him. I want to be angry, but I can't even blame him for his less than enthusiastic response because he *had* told me right from the start that he didn't want kids. It isn't that he's not good with children either, because he is. He has two nephews he dotes on, and he's that guy who women look at and say, *he'll make a great dad one day.* Sam loves children. He just doesn't want any of his own. He doesn't want the sleepless nights, messy nappies and dwindling sex life. Although, the effect on our sex life would most likely be felt more on my side than his.

Our relationship is, as he calls it, monogamous-ish. It was his idea, and I suppose he was being pragmatic and honest, even if it felt brutal at the time. He'd made it clear that he loved me, but after a decade with just one person, he couldn't hide that he was attracted to other people and neither did he want to. To say it had been a shock would be putting it lightly. It had hurt to hear it. But it had sounded like a kind of insurance policy. Men cheat. I'd already learned that the hard way. At least with an open relationship, I'd know about it. It hasn't been easy.

I'd read books and tried to understand why it might be a good thing for us. There were people in open relationships who wanted to know every detail of the people their partners dated or slept with, but I'd known straight away that wouldn't be me. The first time Sam went on a date, I'd distracted myself with work. The second time he went out, he'd messaged to say he wouldn't be home and I'd barely slept. It had taken a solid week before I could face the idea of having sex with him again. He's slept with three other women and it's been far from easy but I'd told myself it was something he needed to get out of his system to feel able to truly settle down.

'Can't this just be enough?' Sam asks.

I honestly don't know if it can. It always had been. Life on the road with little more than our backpacks between us had been enough in South Africa and Zanzibar, in Bali and Rome, and every place we've been in-between. Maybe I'm going mad. Can it really be possible that peeing on a stick has torn through all of that?

Sam blows out a big breath and runs his hands through his hair again. 'Look, I'm really tired. I can't take all this in right now. You're right. You've had a couple days' head start. Maybe I just need to wrap my mind around it.'

It's not decisive, but it's fair, and for the rest of the evening we avoid the subject completely. It feels like a normal Wednesday night, with pasta for dinner in front of the television. Normal except the only glass of wine on the table is Sam's and, instead of cuddling, we're at opposite ends of the sofa.

The next morning, I'm sitting in a coffee shop with my friend, Adele, and have just told her the news.

'So, what are you going to do?' she asks.

'I don't know yet. Wait it out, I suppose.'

I haven't told anyone else yet. For some reason, telling Adele, who I've only known a few weeks, feels easier than telling my family and friends back in England. Adele barely knows Sam. They've met twice, maybe three times, when we've sat and worked in a cafe he goes into for lunch now and again. Ours is a fledgling friendship based on the fact that we're both self-employed expats – her in coaching and me in graphic and web design. Today had been a scheduled co-working date in a cafe equidistant from our apartments but, so far, our laptops have remained firmly closed. I sigh, looking down into my milky flat white and wonder if I'm even allowed to drink coffee anymore. I take a sip anyway. After a night of tossing and turning with weird dreams, I need the caffeine.

'Would you really have a termination if he wanted you to?' Adele asks, her blue eyes widening. 'I mean, could you imagine staying with him if you did?'

'Good question.' I shake my head. 'And I honestly don't know the answer.'

There are some things in a relationship you can sweep under the proverbial carpet, like the small annoyances that wind you up now and again – the wet towels on the bed and the way sport takes over your social calendar when the football season starts. And then there are things that are harder to ignore, but can be worked on with effort, like when your partner wants to feel free to follow through on attractions to other women and even wants you to do the same – even if it isn't really what you're into. But then, there's something like this. Something huge, and fundamental. Something that has everything to do with your relationship and at the same time, feels completely separate. Could I really imagine waking up to Sam every day, kissing him, sleeping with him, *living* with him, if I had a termination at his request? I don't know if I'd be a big enough person not to hate him, but from the way my body feels right now, I can't say I'd like him all that much.

I shake my head again. 'I don't think so, no.'

Adele nods with understanding from her seat next to mine and my stomach feels like its leaping from one side of my body to the other. If I can't imagine having a termination and still staying with Sam, and he can't imagine having a baby, then it really only leaves one option.

'Will you move back home?'

I laugh to myself at Adele's choice of words. I'm enjoying being here in Sydney. My visa application is in progress and finally, after sharing the spare room in Sam's family home since we arrived, we've found an apartment we can actually afford *and* looks nice. Sam has a circle of friends he's known since the year dot and I love the lifestyle here. It's about as far away from the streets of Peckham as you can get, both literally and figuratively. But it's never felt like home.

I nod slowly. 'Yeah, I think so. What would be the point in staying otherwise? Being alone with a baby miles away from anyone who cares?'

'I care.'

'You know what I mean,' I reply with an apologetic smile. 'I'm grateful for you, I really am. But seriously, what would I be staying for?'

'I hear you. I'd probably feel the same in your situation. But you never know, he might get over the shock and come around. I mean, stranger things have happened, right?'

'They have,' I reply.

An unconventional life of moving from place to place, the blurring of lines where monogamy used to be, and now getting pregnant thanks to a case of food poisoning. If there's such a thing as a quota for strangeness in a relationship, I'm not sure how much of ours has been used up already.

Chapter Two

'I'm coming, I'm coming,' I say, quickly sliding an earring through my ear.

Sam sighs with the kind of exasperation that can only come from being with somebody for so long. 'Why do you always leave getting ready to the last minute?'

'Because I was working and lost track of time.' I puff my cheeks out and check my reflection in the mirror propped up against the wall. 'How do I look?'

His eyes flick down to my belly and I wonder if he's thinking about the DNA and cells that are multiplying inside. I've made an intentional effort to dress up tonight and this feels like the first time he's looked at me properly since I told him about the baby. Sam looks at the plunging V-neck of my dress that goes right down to the bottom of my breastbone.

'Good,' he says. 'Great, actually.'

I smile. 'It's not too much?'

He shakes his head and I adjust the delicate lace hem skirting the tops of my knees. I'd bought this dress aeons ago but this is the first time I've had a chance to wear it, and now with the way things are, it might be the last. Sam scoops up his wallet from the chest of drawers next to me, sending a whiff of aftershave my way and I react with a quick, sharp exhale through my nose.

'Jeez, Sam. Did you use the whole bottle?'

He looks back at me. 'Like it?'

'Maybe, if there were less of it.'

'Tough,' Sam replies with a shrug. 'I don't have time to sort it now, we're late enough as it is.'

I roll my eyes. It isn't the most scintillating of conversations we've ever had, but it's normal. It's two people who've spent years together and have come to know each other's foibles, like the fact that I nearly always lose track of time while working and end up in a flap when we've got evening plans, or the fact that Sam's never been able to accurately dose anything, whether it's aftershave or freehand gin and tonics. The normality of it lands warmly in my chest and, as I take one last look in the mirror, I tell myself that things really might be okay.

My heels clack loudly on the floor as we make our way along the corridor, down the stairs and out onto the street. The summer air feels as hot in the early evening as it did earlier this afternoon, and the contrast between our air-conditioned apartment and this feels like walking into a wall of heat. I hold my clutch bag in one hand while automatically reaching for Sam's with the other.

I turn to look at him. 'So, remind me again, Pete's new girl-friend is called—?'

'Laura.'

'Right.'

It's been a while since I've come with him to one of Pete's drinks. He's one of Sam's oldest friends and the director of an advertising agency. Technically, Sam's a freelance photographer, but in reality, most of the jobs that have been coming in since we moved here are either directly or indirectly through Pete.

'And Jenny won't be there?' I ask.

'Why should she be?' Sam replies, as if I've just asked the dumbest question on earth.

'I don't know. Because she was just as big a part of that agency as he is?'

'Not officially.'

I shake my head as we cross the street. Official or not, the way Jenny got pushed out has always felt undeniably wrong to me. She was always really friendly and welcoming – the only one from that crowd I'd liked – if I'm honest. She was also the one who'd start ordering shots and tip the night from civilised after-work drinks to a full-on bender. I wonder if it'll be a tamer affair without her.

'Laura's nice,' Sam says once we're on the other side of the road. 'I know you don't agree with how they got together, but you'll like her.'

'He was married, Sam.'

'And unhappy.'

'So that makes it okay?'

'Did I say that?' Sam replies defensively. 'I'm just saying, Laura's a nice person. Pete and Jenny had issues for years.'

'That doesn't condone cheating,' I reply, feeling the familiar prickle of irritation under my skin.

'No, it doesn't. But it happens.' He squeezes my hand. 'Except to us.'

He says it as if we're somehow better than everyone else, but I'm not so sure. The only difference between me and Jenny is that she didn't know her husband had been sleeping with someone else behind her back. They say it's the lying that makes it worse and, until Sam and I became open, I would have agreed. But honestly, I'm not sure that knowing actually makes it any easier.

We get to the bar and I tell myself that tonight should be about fun. Things are tense enough as it is and a fun night together will go a long way to showing Sam that we can still live the life we have, even with a child. Raucous laughter pours through the doors as we step in inside. Judging from the looks of it, I'd say Pete and the rest are already a few drinks in.

I'd assumed that anyone replacing Pete's wife would be as glamorous as she'd been, if not more, but I'm introduced to a small, almost mouse-like woman whose big brown eyes make her look like a deer caught in a pair of headlights. Her make-up is sensible, her hair is sensible, and her plain, black, shin-length dress is sensible. She's the complete opposite of Jenny, and I can't imagine her being anyone's Other Woman. We're brought straight into the fold with a shot of tequila each, which I discreetly pour into an empty glass on the bar while everyone else downs theirs. Jenny or no Jenny, it looks like tonight will be as messy as always.

I order a beer for Sam and a spirit-free margarita for me. I watch the bartender as he lights a sprig of thyme on fire, catches the smoke in a glass and covers it with a coaster. They take making cocktails seriously here, which is why it's always so busy. It's a bit posey, but the showmanship is worth it. The drinks here are probably the best I've had since arriving in Sydney. I turn from the bar and see that the group have moved to a high, standing table by the window. Sam is talking to one of the women and, when I hand him his beer, he looks surprised to see me for a moment. I look at the woman he's talking to and lift a hand in a small wave.

'Hi, I'm Zoe.'

'Ah, so *you're* Zoe,' she replies. 'I've heard a lot about you.'

I can see from the way her eyes narrow slightly that she's thinking, *Really? That's Sam's girlfriend?* She's probably looking at the way Sam's white shirt clings to his muscular body, bringing out the tan of his skin and the dark trousers that fit snug against his legs. And then she's probably looking at me and seeing my soft body, thick thighs and Cardi-B-worthy bum. All of which will probably only get bigger over the next nine months.

'This is Charlotte, the new creative director,' Sam explains and turns towards her. 'You joined, what, a few weeks ago?'

'December. The week of the Christmas party, remember?'

The skin round Sam's collar flushes red and he quickly glances over at me. 'Oh, God. Yeah. That.'

'I should probably apologise for the state he got into,' Charlotte says, quickly placing a hand on my arm. 'I hate to think of you having to nurse him because of me.'

I remember Sam stumbling through the door at almost ten a.m. the following morning, looking like he'd been dragged through a row of bushes backwards and collapsing on the sofa for the rest of the day. In all our years together, I can count on one hand the number of times he's been that wasted.

'Oh, he's a big boy,' I reply lightly. 'He knows how to look after himself.'

'You're not wrong there.'

Sam shifts on his feet next to me and my face flames. I know, I just *know*, that something is going on between them. It takes every ounce of will I have to keep my face neutral. I am supposed to be okay with this, after all. Sam is technically allowed to flirt with whoever he wants, but it's one thing to know it's happening and quite another to see it.

'I'd better go mingle,' Charlotte says, turning to put her glass on the table. 'See you in a bit.'

'What was that about?' I ask once she's gone.

'What do you mean?'

'Is there something going on between you two?'

'No.'

'But you want it to?'

'Come on, Zoe, let's not do this tonight. Can't we just have fun, for once?'

'Not unless you think my idea of fun is standing here, pretending not to notice or care about you flirting with some other woman.' I shake my head. 'Jesus, Sam. I'm pregnant, in case you've forgotten.'

'No, I haven't, but I bloody wish I could,' he mutters into his glass.

Tears sting my eyes as I look at him. The sense of normality I'd felt in the apartment earlier, the ease and everyday-ness of it all was just my imagination. Sam's simply been pretending. I look at him and shake my head as I realise he isn't going to change his mind. He never was.

'I'm leaving,' I say, putting my glass down on the table. 'Enjoy your night out.'

◆ ◆ ◆

I spend the next few hours on the sofa in front of the television, mindlessly looking at the screen. Nina told me this would happen. The urge to pick up my phone and call her is so strong. I'm craving the familiarity of my best friend, someone who's known me since we were kids and feels like family. But I don't. She's not the type to say *I told you so.* At least, not straight away. But she *had* told me.

'You can't agree to this if it's not what you really want. It'll only make you unhappy in the end.'

She'd said this so clearly when I'd told her about Sam's idea to be monogamous-*ish*. All I'd wanted was Sam and I'd have done anything to keep him. I'd needed him. But, as I sit here in our apartment surrounded by the possessions we've filled it with after years of nomadic life, I find myself questioning what I've always thought. Being willing to do anything for someone is a lot. Much more than I feel able to give. And I've reached my limit. If you'd have asked me to imagine what the end of an eleven-year relationship would feel like, I'd have said, *dramatic*. But it just feels sad.

By the time Sam comes home, my cheeks have been scorched by a trail of silent tears. He stands against the counters that divide the kitchen from the living room and I look at the clock. It's barely past midnight.

'You're home early,' I say.

'Wasn't in the mood.'

Our eyes meet and he pauses for a moment, as if he's deciding whether to come into the living room or stay where he is. And even though I know the outcome of this conversation, my chest still constricts tightly around my heart.

He rubs the back of his neck with his hand. 'I'm sorry about earlier. I swear there's nothing going on with Charlotte but still . . . I was a dick. This whole baby thing is a big deal.'

'Yeah,' I nod. 'It is.'

'I just . . .' He sighs and pulls out one of the stools at the counter to sit down. 'I don't know how you can be so sure you want it.'

His eyes search mine and, despite my anger, I can see that he's really trying to understand.

'I can't really explain it,' I shrug. 'It just feels like the right thing to do. I know it seems crazy to you, but for me, everything's changed now. It feels like a priority that our life needs to shift around for.'

'See that's the thing,' he says. 'I know it sounds selfish, Zoe, but I don't *want* to have to change my priorities. I've seen what having kids does to people. Look at my sister. She's half the person she used to be. I don't want a complicated life and kids are complicated.'

'Our lives already *are* complicated, Sam. How many girlfriends have to ask their boyfriends if they might be shagging the woman

15

she's just been introduced to?' I shake my head. 'I should never have agreed to this whole thing.'

'But why are you only just saying this now? You never said anything about having a problem with it before and it works both ways.'

'I've never needed anyone else.'

'So why did you agree to it?' he replies, his strained voice rising.

'It was a compromise. That's what happens in relationships.'

Sam drops his head back and sighs. I stay perfectly still, my arm protectively guarding the new life growing under my skin while a weight sinks deep into my chest. Neither of us speak. I guess there isn't any need to. He looks at me and the tears in his eyes are just like mine – holding eleven years and four months of a life together in them.

'I'm sorry, Zo,' he says.

'I know.' I nod. 'Me too.'

Chapter Three

Thirty-six hours later, I find myself sitting on the single bed in my childhood bedroom with a towel wrapped around my body. Beads of London water sit on my skin after a long, hot shower – the very first thing I do after travelling for hours on end. Even with all of the planes I've been on and time zones I've crisscrossed over the years, it's still a strange feeling to fly from one country to another. I find it surreal that, one minute, I was in the heat of a Sydney summer and just a hop, skip and jump later, I'm back here, in my old bedroom at the tail end of an English winter. I hadn't told Mum that I was coming. I didn't want to tell her what had happened over the phone. I'd pictured coming back and surprising her while she was watching TV or cooking, but when I'd unlocked the front door, I'd found the flat empty.

I dig out a pair of leggings and a t-shirt from my luggage and, once I'm dressed, I pick up my phone to take a selfie. I make sure to get the distinctive yellow wallpaper in behind me before firing it off in a message to Nina.

Nina: SHUT UP! Are you back???!!

I grin at the reply that comes in an instant and before I can finish typing out my reply, the phone rings in my hand.

'Whaaat?' Nina screeches down the phone and I laugh as I hold the phone away from my ear to save my eardrum. 'You're back? Since when?'

'Since about an hour ago.'

'What are you *doing* here? Your mum didn't say anything when I saw her earlier,' Nina replies with her characteristic speed.

'That's because she doesn't know,' I confess. 'Where did you see her? Do you know where she is?'

'She was at the bus stop. I didn't ask where she was going.'

I can picture Nina talking not just with her mouth, but with her hands as well. She's always been larger than life with her expressions. We met on the first day of the primary school term in Year Three and have been best friends ever since. Our mums were best friends too and had stayed that way right up until Nina's mum died a few years ago.

'So how long do we have you for this time?' Nina asks.

I run a hand over crinkles in the bed sheets. 'Forever. Maybe.'

'What do you mean, *forever*?'

I get up and crawl to the other end of the bed where I can look out of the window. It's exactly as weather in London should be at the end of February – grey and wet, with heavy clouds dominating the sky.

'Is Sam with you?'

'No . . . We split up,' I say, the words feeling alien coming from my mouth. 'He's still in Sydney.'

'Bloody hell,' Nina replies and I can practically see her pierced eyebrows raising towards her hairline. 'What happened?'

'Can we meet up? It'll be easier to tell you everything in person and I can't wait to hug you.'

'Me too. But I'm fully booked today and my last appointment's a late one.'

'You're always in demand,' I reply with a smile.

'I know. That's what tattooing footballers does for you.'

Nina says it in an almost dismissive way, but I know how proud she is. One of her clients is an old schoolmate of ours who's been making waves as a footballer, first playing for Luton, then Tottenham Hotspur, and last year he'd played for England. He'd posted a photo of the tattoo Nina had done on his leg, tagging her studio's account in it and she's been pretty much booked out ever since.

'I've got an hour free at lunchtime tomorrow?' Nina suggests. 'But you have to tell me what's happening now. There's no way I'm waiting until then to hear what's going on.'

This isn't how I'd pictured telling my very best friend that she was about to fulfil the pact we'd made once about being godmothers to each other's children.

'I'm pregnant.'

Nina takes a dramatic intake of breath on the other end of the phone. 'No! Really?'

'Really,' I reply, watching a pigeon pecking the ground outside.

'So why've you split up? It is his, right?'

'No, it's some surfer dude I met on the beach called Bob. Of course it's Sam's. Who else's would it be?'

'I don't know. Maybe you'd decided to say *screw it* and go do what he's been doing too?'

'Just, let's not go there.' I groan and move away from the window and the greyness outside to sit with my back against the wall. 'It's nothing like that. We'd agreed no kids.'

'Okay, but you're actually pregnant now.'

'I know. But he's sticking to it.'

'Seriously? What a dick,' Nina replies, her loyalty as strong as ever. 'He can't just leave you to bring up a child alone.'

'He isn't. I decided to leave.'

Nina sighs. 'Oh, crap. I think that's my twelve o'clock having a smoke outside, I have to go. Let's meet up tomorrow?'

'Sure. But don't say anything to anyone, Nina. Not until I've told Mum.'

'I won't. I promise. And Zo? As much as I think it's a dick move from Sam, I'm bloody *stoked* you're back. And I'm going to be an aunt!'

A smile stretches across my face. 'I've missed you.'

'I've missed you too. Gotta go. I'll text you about tomorrow. Love you.'

She blows a kiss down the phone and I picture her behind the counter in her studio with her arms covered in tattoos and bright, almost neon pink hair. We message each other most days and are as close as we've always been, but still. Being back and knowing I've got my closest people around is only going make the next nine months feel a lot easier to deal with.

◆ ◆ ◆

A few hours and a nap later, I close the oven door on a tray full of almost-cooked chicken drumsticks. I have no idea when Mum will be back but I figure she'll be happy to not have to cook. My stomach growls ferociously at the scent of aromatic spices filling the kitchen. Aside from aeroplane food, I've only had an avocado and hummus bagel on the train. It growls again and the thought that I'm going to be eating for two for several months pings into my head. I put a hand across my tummy. It's never been flat, despite all the crunches and diets I've put myself through over the years. There's always been a bulge I've never been able to shift. I'm embarrassed to admit, but I've always held a bit of a grudge about it and knowing that my body will change as the months go by isn't exactly filling me with joy, despite wanting the baby.

I hear the sound of the lift doors pinging open outside the kitchen window and go to the front door to look through the spy-hole. It's Mum, and I throw the door open before she has a chance to put her key in the lock. She stands there with the key in her hand, suspended in mid-air with a look of confusion on her face that makes me grin.

'Hi, Mum.'

'Zoe?'

She shakes her head as if she's trying to make sense of what's happening before reaching out for a stunned hug. It's only been a few months since I was last here, but I swear she's gotten smaller, even since then. I hold her close and she laughs as the shock wears off.

'What are you doing here?' Mum leans back, holding me at arm's length to get a proper look at me. 'When did you get back?'

'A few hours ago.'

I've managed to hold everything together, until now. Even while I was packing my things with Sam right there next to me, I'd kept the tears inside, and when the plane had taken off, all I'd felt was numb. But now that I'm here, standing in front of Mum, a ball has wedged itself into my throat.

'Come on, let's get inside, we don't need the whole block to get involved,' Mum says, bustling me through the hallway towards the kitchen. 'You've cooked?'

I nod and take bags of shopping from her. 'Hope you're hungry.'

'If you'd have told me you were coming, I'd have made something.'

'I wanted it to be a surprise.'

'Well, you did that. You almost gave me a heart attack yanking the door open like that.'

'Better than waiting inside and having you think I was a burglar.'

Mum nods in agreement and takes off her ankle-length puffy coat. The ball eases back down my throat a little. The familiarity of my surroundings feels more established now that she's here. I'm not tall, but I'm a whole head higher than she is now. Still, she looks good for her age. She'd been a young mum, having me when she was twenty-two, and her smooth, brown skin disguises her sixty years, especially when her cheeks widen into a smile. Her hair is hidden by a weave in the same style she's worn for years and she's put on a little weight, despite repeated warnings from her doctor about her blood pressure.

I unpack one of the shopping bags and grin, taking out a small, dark loaf. 'Ooh, bun.'

'There's cheese in the fridge if you want it.'

There are certain things I've missed about home and they're mostly food, especially the things that were a staple part of my Jamaican upbringing. I literally feel my mouth watering in anticipation of a thick slice of cinnamon-and-ginger spiced bun with a decent layer of butter, topped with a thick slice of cheddar. Instead, I leave the loaf alone, deciding to save it for after dinner instead.

As I put the shopping away, I notice a vase of fresh flowers on the table. They're beautiful, and absolutely not the cheap, supermarket bought kind either.

'Those are nice,' I say. 'Since when did you start buying flowers?'
'I didn't.'

I'm intrigued and wait for her to elaborate, but she doesn't. I raise my eyebrows, puzzled. The only flowers I ever saw in our flat growing up were synthetic ones. We weren't exactly poor, but fresh flowers were simply a luxury that didn't belong in our single-parent household.

Mum looks at me with inquisitive eyes. 'I'm really happy you're here, but something's wrong, isn't it? You've never just come home unannounced before.'

'I missed the food.'

It's a weak joke, but it helps to take away the worried look on Mum's face for a moment. It's the same look I'd seen when I'd told her I'd decided to basically ignore the law degree I'd worked so hard for to go full time with my side hustle of designing websites.

'You came all this way for bun and cheese?'

'I'm pregnant.'

I blurt the words out for the second time that day and Mum's mouth opens wide as her jaw drops.

'Surprise.' I pull my lips into a small smile, feeling tears tickling the backs of my eyes. 'You're going to be a grandma.'

Mum laughs and claps her hands together. 'Zoe, that's amazing.'

After being with Sam for so many years, I know she's been waiting with bated breath for an engagement announcement, followed by a baby one. Over the years, her hints have become less and less subtle to the point where she'd said outright once, *Zoe, I want to become a grandmother before I die.* I hadn't told her about mine and Sam's agreement to skip having children – maybe because, deep down, I'd secretly hoped it might happen. Mum hugs me tightly and for a moment, I feel immensely proud for giving her what's she's been waiting for for so long. But then the tears that have been building behind my eyes fall and I can't help the sob that escapes my lips in a hiccup.

'Hey,' Mum says, sitting me down on one of the chairs around the table. 'What's with the tears?'

I drop my head to look down at the floor, feeling the fat droplets being pulled from my eyes. 'Sam doesn't want the baby.'

'Oh . . .'

There it is – the harsh truth. This time though, it doesn't feel distant or detached. It feels gut-wrenchingly real, and the warmth of Mum's hand on my knee only seems to intensify it.

'Maybe he's just in shock.'

'No. He really doesn't want it,' I sniff through a stuffed nose, watching the pool of tears gather on the blue linoleum floor. 'I've left him.'

I'd felt so strong when I'd decided to keep the baby. So determined. But now, I'm not so sure. Sam's been my best friend for over a decade. We'd planned a whole life together, shared hopes and dreams. And now I'm in my mum's kitchen in Peckham, feeling like I might have just made the biggest mistake of my life by leaving the man I thought I'd grow old with. My stomach turns as a wave of doubt rolls in my belly.

'How far along are you?'

I shrug, swiping at the wetness of my cheeks with my palms. 'I don't know. I haven't been to the doctor's yet but I think about five weeks.'

'First thing tomorrow, we'll get you re-registered at the doctor's.'

'What if I've made a mistake leaving him?' A fresh bout of tears burn down my cheeks. 'We were supposed to have a life together. And now I've thrown it all away.'

I replay the argument with Sam in my mind and remembering his words hurts. They sting, right in my chest, and it's not just down to disappointment. There's also a feeling of not being wanted. I know it's silly, but Sam rejecting the baby feels like an extension of rejecting me.

'I don't think I can do this alone.'

'I don't think anyone does,' Mum says. 'But just because a man's there when you give birth, doesn't mean he always will be. They're not forced to stick around. Look at your dad.'

'But didn't you hate having to do it all by yourself?'

Things changed after my parents divorced when I was fourteen. We moved from a three-bedroom semi to this social housing block and Mum had given up her degree at the Open University to work full time instead. The food in the cupboards changed from named brands to discounted ones, and I went on free school dinners. It felt like our lives had literally changed overnight.

'I had help,' Mum replies. 'I had family and friends, just like you do. We're all here for you, Zoe. Besides for the next nine months, you'll have your baby *with* you. It's just about the closest you can ever get to a person. You're far from alone.'

I pick at the skin on the side of my thumb. I hadn't really thought about it like that.

'And trust me,' Mum says with a lighter tone, 'after a few sleepless nights you'll be begging for some alone time.'

The timer on the oven beeps and Mum gets up to check on the chicken, shooing at me to stay in my seat. I've already made a huge life change to accommodate this unknown being growing inside of me and I'm under no illusions. I know there's going to be a whole lot more coming, which is precisely the reason Sam doesn't want to be involved. Even at this early stage, I know it'll mean sacrificing more than just my relationship. At some point in my twenties, I'd had the realisation that my mum wasn't just my mum. She was also her own person with her own hopes and dreams and wishes – some of which would have been completely dashed, first with pregnancy and again with the divorce.

'But isn't it hard being a single mum?'

'Well, you were already grown when we divorced. It would probably have been different had you been younger. But yes, sometimes it was hard.' She pulls on her floral oven gloves and thinks about it for a second. 'Sometimes. I know it's scary right now, but you will be incredible, Zo. And who knows, maybe Sam will change his mind before he misses out on it all.'

Mum opens the oven and the aroma of cumin and garam masala fills the kitchen. The seasoning mix is one that's been imprinted on me since childhood. I let her words land like a force of calm in my mind because I know with absolute certainty that I agree.

I'd rather do it alone, than not at all.

Chapter Four

The next day, I burrow my nose into the shawl around my neck as I walk past a stall with fresh fish resting on beds of ice. The smell is overwhelming, just like the cloying scent of someone's perfume on the bus. It had been so bad, I'd had to get off a few stops early or risk throwing up. Surely it can't be morning sickness already? Maybe that's why Sam's aftershave had been so overpowering the night of Pete's drinks.

'One sec!' Nina calls from a room at the back of the small space.

The walls are covered with tattoo designs and photos of freshly inked skin, and an array of body jewellery glistens under a glass counter.

'Eek! I can't believe you're back!' My larger-than-life bestie bursts through the doorway and gathers me up in a hug. 'With a bloody baby, too.'

'I know. Takes bringing a souvenir back with you to a whole new level, doesn't it?' I grin widely and look around at the studio. 'This place looks amazing, Neens.'

'Right?' She grins back and puts a hand on one of her hips. 'Things were getting out of hand after Coleman tagged me in that photo. I couldn't breathe for all the testosterone. So I decided a little rebrand was in order. The world doesn't need another macho tattoo studio anyway.'

'You trendsetter, you,' I joke, but it truly is a gorgeous space.

The standard black, white and wood look that once said it was a tattoo studio has been replaced by a palette of pastels with neon highlights. A variety of lush, green plants are placed in the corners and hang from the ceiling. It looks like the kind of place where you'd meet your friends for a chai latte and gluten-free carrot cupcake for a post-date debrief. Maybe it helps to distract you from the pain you're about to be subjected to when you went from this comfortable waiting area to the privacy of Nina's back room.

'You're looking good,' I say, tugging on a lock of Nina's jaw length, pink hair.

'Thanks. I've been weight training.'

She flexes her bicep, showing off the bright-orange snake wrapped around her white skin. Her corduroy dungarees are turned up to above ankle-length and, as always, she's wearing two different Converse on her feet – one black, one white. Nina's always stood out. She was the tallest in our class, even back in Year Three, and had stayed that way all through secondary and college. She has elfin features that, combined with her height, made her a target at school. And when *The Lord of the Rings* came out, she'd been nick-named Arwen or, simply, Elf. She'd decided early on to embrace her uniqueness and make it cool. It's something I've always admired about her.

'And you have enormous boobs. As if they weren't big enough already,' she says with a laugh and a hint of envy.

I put my hands on top of my breasts and shake my head. 'I swear they weren't this big yesterday.'

'I have something for you,' Nina replies, reaching behind the counter as I sit on the velvety, peach-coloured sofa.

She hands over a thick, paper bag and I pull out a spiral-bound journal with a beautifully illustrated pregnant woman on the cover.

'It's gorgeous,' I grin, running my hands over the golden letters.

'There's loads of stuff inside, week-by-week guides and all that.'

'I love it. Thanks, Neens.'

'Oh, please. I'm so excited about this, anyone would think it were me having the baby,' she replies with a laugh. 'So how are you feeling?'

'Fine, mostly. A bit queasy this morning but otherwise fine.'

'And what about Sam?' She switches on the kettle that is standing on a brass art deco style bar cart. 'What happened?'

'How long have you got?' I grimace.

I flick through the journal and see a page where I'm supposed to write down the reaction to my pregnancy reveal. There's no way I'll be writing the story I'm telling Nina now.

'He was never good enough for you,' Nina says in a matter-of-fact way once I've finished.

'Don't sugar-coat your feelings will you, Neens?'

'Still, I'd never have thought he'd do something like this.'

I sigh. 'To be fair, it was my choice to leave.'

'Doesn't sound like he gave you much of one to start with.'

Nina's face is etched with disapproval. After introducing her to Sam all those years ago, I'd been excited for the next-day-debrief. Until Nina had immediately said she didn't like him, much less trust him. He'd been tolerated at best. At least now, she doesn't have to pretend to like him anymore and, I have to admit, there's a part of me that's secretly relieved not to have a sad reaction to the break-up news. It's hard enough as it is without knowing other people are disappointed about it too.

'Yeah, well.' I look back down and flip through the pages of the journal again. 'It is what it is.'

'What did your mum say?'

'She's excited, of course,' I smile. 'I know there's a part of her that wishes there'd been a wedding to go with it, but she's already talking about turning my old room into a nursery.'

'She doesn't waste any time, does she?' Nina laughs.

'Right now, I'm just trying to let my body catch up with the fact that I've flown halfway across the world.' I yawn loudly. 'I'm shattered. Some idiots decided to race up and down the whole street last night.'

'You're always welcome to come stay at mine.'

Nina lives in a little one-bedroom flat in Elephant and Castle. It's just as busy, but at least her road has a speed camera on it.

'Thanks, but I'll stay at Mum's for now. I kind of feel like I need the home comforts for a bit, and it'll be nice to spend some time together.'

'Well, just know that rental prices aren't what they used to be,' Nina says, pulling a face. 'Not even around here.'

'I bet.'

The idea of renting a flat alone in London feels bonkers. Rents have never been cheap, but I don't even want to think about how expensive it must be around here now. Every time I come back, the place I've known all my life seems to be getting facelifts quicker than an ageing Hollywood actress. Fancy coffee shops, yoga studios and bicycle repair shops have sprung up everywhere. A few years ago, you wouldn't have even been able to pay people to move or set up businesses here. Truthfully, I don't mind it, to a point. I'm partial to a decent cappuccino with fairtrade, organic coffee instead of a cup of instant granules that I could make at home. But still, there's a hint of satisfaction in me that the streets are still a bit grimy, and that the pound shop that's been on the corner of the high street since forever is still there, withstanding the slow creep of gentrification.

'I'll keep my ears open for you if I hear of anything,' Nina says, making her way up to stand. 'I'm going to grab a falafel wrap from over the road, do you want one?'

I grimace at the thought of food and shake my head. 'Think I'll stick with the tea.'

As Nina pulls on her denim jacket and leaves, I take a pen from a copper mug on the low table next to me and open the journal. It's just like Nina to gift something like this. She's one of those people who always seem to know the right thing to get for a birthday or Christmas, unlike me, who leaves things to the last minute and gets stressed by it. The paper inside is thick and smooth, and the ballpoint glides across it easily as I write.

◆ ◆ ◆

Pregnancy Journal
Pregnancy week: Six
You're the size of a: Lentil
Today, I feel: Anxious

Hello, little one. I'm your mum . . .
Well, you'll get to know me a lot more over the next few months, but we've got to start some-where! So I'm your mum, Zoe. Right now, I'm thirty-eight which, on one hand feels a little old but on the other, nowhere near old enough.

Until yesterday, I lived in Sydney, with your dad, Sam. I promise to tell you about him at some point but, right now, he's still there. I'm (or, I guess I should say, we're) in London which isn't quite so warm or beautiful right now, but is spe-cial in its own way. So far, everyone here is ecstatic to meet you. Myself included. And, thanks to your aunt Nina, you'll be able to read back on the first nine months of your life.

I'm going to be honest with you: I have no idea what I'm doing and I'm fairly terrified about this. But it's a journey we're on together, right? I'm sure we'll find our way.

Zoe

x

Chapter Five

For what feels like the millionth time that day, I yawn loudly, feeling it dredge up from my feet.

'God,' I groan. 'Tell me this tiredness gets better.'

'It gets better,' Mum replies. 'And stop taking the Lord's name in vain.'

I roll my eyes and follow her through to the shared garden of Nina's flat. I've only been home a few days and somehow I seem to have regressed to teenage mode. If it was anyone else but Nina, I would have sent an apologetic text and spent the afternoon in bed, but it isn't anyone else, and this isn't just any barbecue. It's the continuation of the birthday get-together that Debbie – Nina and Jude's mum – used to throw every year. They've been a staple of my childhood memories since I can remember. As a kid, it was about being able to take full advantage of the overabundance of sweets and desserts and, as a teenager, it was about sneaking some of the seventy per cent overproof rum from the table. Even when Debbie died five years ago, there wasn't a pause. The March barbecue is an institution and this year it looks altogether less wild, but no less busy.

A gazebo covers the table laden with food, eighties pop hits are playing from a speaker, the unmistakable scent of barbecue is in the air and it has just the same vibe as it did in the garden of Debbie's house. The sun is shining as the weather plays ball for another year. Somehow, these barbecue Saturdays have almost always managed to escape the rain. I nod hellos at people as we make our way to the gazebo where Mum offloads the pot of curried goat she made this morning and I fill a paper cup with a glass of juice.

'Oh, there's Heidi,' Mum says, looking over my shoulder. 'I'm just going to go and say hello.'

'Yeah, sure,' I reply.

I stifle yet another yawn as Nina comes out from the apartment block looking as summery as she ever gets in a pair of cut-offs and a t-shirt. I watch her as she picks her way through the garden, stopping now and then to say hello to her guests. She looks just like her mum. Tall and willowy with a smile that sometimes feels too wide for her face.

The weather can't seem to make its mind up. This past week has oscillated between cold wintery gusts of wind, and surprisingly hot bouts of sunshine. This might be the first touch of sunlight I've had since leaving Sydney and my mind swaps the image of the South-East London garden I'm in for my favourite patch of beach. I miss the water. Maybe more than the city itself. I've always loved the sea and a pang of longing tugs in my belly.

Sam hasn't messaged since I left. Not once. Not even to see if I made it back okay. It's as if I've flown not just from the city, but also from his existence. He'd said our relationship was the most important thing in his life. He'd said he still loved me. Even as we'd been breaking up, the love had still been there. I'd felt it, I'm sure of it. I'd be lying if I said it didn't hurt to have no word from him since.

'Earth to Zoe.'

I blink as Nina clips her fingers in front of my face. I hadn't even noticed that she'd come over.

'Sorry,' I reply, shaking my head. 'I was miles away.'

'Are you alright?' She wraps me in a hug before looking at me with concern. 'You look awful.'

'Gee, thanks.'

'Still not sleeping?'

'Those idiot racers are still at it.'

'There I was thinking you'd had a wild night of partying.'

I snort. 'That isn't too far off from how I feel.'

Nobody had told me that the first bit of pregnancy would feel like a hangover. Nausea – thankfully no vomiting yet – and an aversion to food means I'll probably have to give the buffet today a miss and be content with nibbling on a carrot or something instead. But it's the tiredness that's killing me. I can't remember ever being so exhausted, even though I'm not doing much. True, I'm trying to process the sudden collapse of my relationship and life in general but still, the tiredness is a surprise. On the plus side, it's meant I haven't spent all my time crying my eyes out like with other break-ups, because I spend all day sleeping. I've only opened my laptop once, and I'm in danger of getting behind on my current workload and delivering the websites I'm building for my clients late. Which then spirals into questions of how I'm ever going to be able to pay for a baby and all the things it needs and only exhausts me even more.

I spot Mum over in the corner with a man I don't know and nod towards them. 'Who's that with Mum?'

Nina cranes her neck to look in their direction with a little laugh. 'Barry? You've met him before; he was a friend of Mum's.'

We both watch my mum laughing at whatever it is he's saying, with her head cocked to one side. She gently puts a hand on his chest and I widen my eyes. 'Oh my God. Does my mum have a boyfriend?'

Nina shrugs. 'They could just be friends.'

'Since when does Mum do male friends?' I raise an eyebrow. Since my parents divorced, there hasn't even been a *hint* of the masculine around the house.

'Don't tell me you don't approve?'

'Are you kidding? You know I've always thought it was sad she's stayed alone all these years. I think it's great.'

Before Nina can reply, a pair of large hands clamp down on her shoulders from behind and she shrieks, spilling most of her drink down her chest. We both turn to see her brother, Jude, and she swears.

'Nice one, idiot. My t-shirt's soaked now.' Nina rolls her eyes. 'Don't you ever grow up?'

'Nope,' he grins.

'I'm going to kill you once I get changed.'

'Promises, promises,' he replies with a laugh.

She swears again before stalking away and I hide a giggle, looking up at Jude.

'Well, that wasn't very nice now, was it?'

'It wasn't on purpose, but don't tell her that.' Jude grins back, showing off the genetic dimple he shares with Nina in his cheek. 'I'd heard you were back but I had to see it to believe it. It's been forever.'

'It has,' I reply, tiptoeing as he hugs me hello.

How many years has it been since we've seen each other in person? I think back. I'm pretty sure the last time was just before his break-up, so it must be five or six years. His fiancée had left him a few weeks before their wedding for a colleague. He'd worked abroad after that and we'd always just missed each other when I'd come back. Apart from the odd message here and there, we'd all but lost contact.

'You look good,' Jude says. 'Considering.'

'Wow, your charisma skills are off the charts.' I roll my eyes. 'I think the women of South London are safe tonight.'

I've had to buy new tops to accommodate my already swollen breasts and have swapped the leggings and hoodie combo I've been living in since I came back for a black tank top with a pair of jeans, tucked into my favourite biker-style boots. It's pretty much a carbon copy of the clothes I always used to wear before living in a tropical climate.

Jude laughs back, opening his bottle of beer with a lighter. 'Seriously, though. Congratulations.'

He taps my glass with the bottom of his bottle and I twiddle my fingers in my hair. 'Thanks. Still feels a bit weird.'

'I bet.'

He squints his brown eyes as the sun peeks out from behind a cloud and I feel a little burst of affection. He's two years younger than Nina and I, so I've known him almost his whole life. Despite the six feet something in height and broad shoulders he's grown into, I can still see bits of the teenager he'd been.

'How've you been?' I ask. 'Are you still working in Spain?'

He shakes his head. 'No, I'm back for good and totally backed up with work these days.'

'That's great.'

'Yeah, it is. I'll probably have to get a second pair of hands soon.'

'Looks like I'm not the only one with growing responsibilities,' I reply with a grin.

'Ehhhh, I'm not sure I'm ready for that mountain of responsibility,' he laughs back. 'Are you freaking out yet?'

'Not really. I mean, if I sit and think about it for too long then, yes. But right now I'm just going slow. One day at a time.'

'It's early days,' he says knowingly.

'Exactly,' I reply.

It's all still very precarious and strange thoughts have been popping into my head since yesterday about things going wrong. Like, what would happen if I lost the baby and whether it would've been a waste, leaving Sam if that happened.

'Still, rather you than me,' Jude says.

'Not quite ready to settle down then?'

He shrugs and lifts his lips into a lazy smile. 'If things had gone differently, I'd be way ahead of you by now.'

'True.'

'But I'm not and, well . . .' He shrugs again. 'There's too much stuff I haven't done yet.'

'It's a baby, not a death sentence,' I reply. 'You sound just like Sam.'

'Never. I'd never leave my girlfriend to do it singlehandedly. But I can understand the reluctance. I mean, there must be stuff you're sad about giving up? Booze for example,' he says, pointing to my glass. 'You should make a bucket list.'

'Ten things to do before you become a mum, kind of thing?' I laugh. 'I don't know what I'd put on it. It feels like I've done a lot already.'

The main thing that Sam had objected to about the baby was the only obvious thing I can think of: travel. I've done plenty of that and it's not like I never plan on using my passport once the baby's here. I spot Nina walking back over wearing a fresh t-shirt and raise my eyebrows.

'Heads up, she's coming back,' I warn.

She stands right next to Jude, flicks her hair behind her shoulder and looks at him. 'Give me that.'

She grabs his bottle and takes an overly long swig. As well as sharing dimples, they also share the height that their mum had always said was from Scandinavian ancestry. But where Nina has milky white skin and almost straight, glossy hair, Jude gets his light-brown skin from his dad's Jamaican roots. He wraps an arm around Nina and pulls her in for a reluctant hug while she rolls her eyes playfully.

'Did you tell her about the flat?' Nina asks.

'No.'

'What flat?' I ask, my interest piqued.

'Jude's working on a new block by the Common and he might be able to talk to the landlord for you.'

'Did I say that, though?' He shakes his head, dropping his arm from her shoulder.

'More or less,' Nina replies. 'He'll need to rent it to *someone*.'

'I'm a carpenter, not an estate agent.'

'You've basically mafia'd the place already.'

I hide a smile by drinking my fruit punch. Nina can be like a steamroller sometimes.

'He's got all of his mates on the job, Zo – the plumber, electrician, decorators. It's like a gang of Jude and his friends.' Nina twists her neck to look at him. 'All you have to do is tell him one of your best friends needs a place and I guarantee, he'll do it.'

Jude catches my eyes with his and gives them an apologetic smile. 'I'll try. But I'm not promising anything.'

'Thanks, Jude,' I reply. 'I appreciate it.'

Being at Mum's is providing me with a soft cushion to land and it's been really nice to spend so much time with her again. But I also know there's a limit to how much I'm able to take. Apart from me falling back into petulant teenager mode, Mum has her own way of doing things around the house, and being back in the bedroom I'd spent the second half of my childhood in is as disconcerting as it is comforting. The walls are still the same golden yellow they've always been, but the posters and pictures have gone. And the bookshelf is still stacked with my favourites – Judy Blume when I was younger and Jane Green as I got older – but the furniture has changed, and a small workstation has been put in where Mum makes little toys from felt for a local playgroup. It feels like being in a strange no man's land and I have to admit there's a flicker of excitement in my belly at the prospect of having my own space. It would be the first time in my life that I've ever lived alone; at least it would be until the baby came along. Maybe that could be the first thing on my list: *live alone.*

'What do you say we go for a drink after this? A new family's just moved in downstairs and I said it wouldn't go on too late tonight,' Nina suggests. 'There's a bar in Brixton with amazing alcohol-free cocktails.'

'Can't,' Jude says. 'I've got a date.'

'Another one? I'm surprised there are even any women left, or have you crossed over to the other side of the river now?'

Jude rolls his eyes as I laugh. 'I'm out, too. I might even have to bow out of this before the oldies do.'

'And you say there's nothing you won't miss,' Jude says, raising an eyebrow.

I shake my head. 'The only thing I'm missing right now is my energy and being able to stay awake past seven p.m. But if I think of anything else, I'll let you know.'

Chapter Six

I turn my phone over and over again in my hand as I wait for the lift doors to ping open. The air in the corridor carries a smell of disinfectant that can probably be recognised the world over. I'd come into contact with a poisonous caterpillar in Sri Lanka once, and huge welts had erupted all down my back and legs. The hospital had smelled pretty much like this one and the antihistamine injection I'd had in my bum had been shockingly painful. Sam had waited on me hand and foot for that entire day.

I still haven't heard from him. Nothing. Nada. Zilch. The man who'd panicked and ran outside to flag down a tuk-tuk to rush me to the hospital because of a caterpillar wasn't with me for my first antenatal appointment. It feels surreal that our lives are no longer intertwined, despite him being the father of the baby I'm carrying. I know I shouldn't be disappointed – he'd been clear enough about where he stood – but I am. I'd hoped he would've at least replied to my message this morning, if only out of curiosity if nothing else.

The lift doors ping open and I step inside, avoiding the eyes of the man with a distinctively bald head and almost grey skin. I've never really worried about all the things that can go wrong in life before, but now it's different. The midwife had taken my blood to check for sickle cell disease, told me about my elevated risk of age-related pregnancy complications and given me a pamphlet load of advice about lifestyle. For the first time since taking the test, I really understood that I'm not just pregnant. I'm responsible for the growing of another human being. Me, who's never even had a pet before. Not even a goldfish. I blow out a trembling breath as the thought hits me that I really have no idea what hell I'm doing.

By the time I step out of the lift and walk briskly to the exit, my mind is tumbling over itself with doubts. Rain falls as I pop open my umbrella and make my way to the bus stop. The sunshine that had stuck around for a couple of days after the barbecue was now well and truly gone. I feel about as miserable as the grey sky and it isn't helped by the coffee craving gnawing at me as I pull out my phone again.

Zoe: Just finished with the midwife – first scan is in 2 weeks. It's really real. I'm bricking it.

I chew the inside of my lip at the thought of seeing the baby on a screen and hearing its heartbeat at my ten-week scan. It's scary as hell, but the fear is interrupted by flickers of excitement and I shake my head a little. There are so many emotions rattling around inside of me, it's hard to keep up.

Nina: Of course it's real lol. Want me to come with? I can try and move appts if you need x

Zoe: Thanks hun. I guess I'll ask Mum, though. Still good for a movie later? I promise I'll try to stay awake!

Nina: Sure thing. We can order some food in too and put some face masks on. Have to get ready for client now, chat later xx

I smile, putting the phone away. Despite the abrupt change from Sydney to London, it feels nice to have so easily slotted back into things. In some ways it's almost like I'd never left and a large part of that is down to the fact that Nina is currently single. She's never been the type to forget her friends when she's in a relationship, but I know it wouldn't have been so easy if she were still with her ex. There's a certain exclusivity that comes with being a couple and I'd hate to feel like I was intruding.

When the bus comes, I sit downstairs, right at the back where the engine has warmed the seats and take out the pamphlets the midwife gave me. The passing aroma of someone's coffee flames that craving again so strongly, I can almost taste it in my mouth. The advice is that a little coffee is fine, but it would be pointless anyway. The smell of it is one thing, but the taste is another entirely. The sip I'd had two days ago had left me nauseous, and yesterday it had given me my first true experience of morning sickness. It's not something I'm keen to repeat, no matter how good coffee beans smell.

I take out my phone again to search for Jude's number.

Zoe: I know something I'll miss . . . coffee :-/

I put the phone away before taking it back out again and adding, *and mayo*.

On the plus side, the list of things to avoid isn't quite as long as I'd expected. It was simply a case of testing whether I could tolerate them. A heavily pregnant woman gets onto the bus with a toddler in tow. I can't take my eyes off her as she sits on the seat directly opposite mine. I stare at her protruding bump and feel a shiver of fear. How is it possible for a human belly to stretch that far out? I look up and she catches my eye. My cheeks flame as I hear my mum's chiding voice in my head reminding me that it's rude

43

to stare, especially because I have a face that's unable to hide what I'm thinking. The woman's eyes flick down to the pamphlet in my hands and she looks at me as if to say, you've got this. It feels nice to receive, even if right now it doesn't feel entirely true.

◆　◆　◆

'I'm telling you, her belly was massive,' I say to Nina later that evening.

'Well, duh. It's not like you've never seen a pregnant woman before.'

'No, but let me tell you, when it's happening to you, you look at them in a whole new way. I swear, I've never seen so many pregnant women in one go before.'

I lean against the velvety arm of the sofa – a dark-green version of the one in the tattoo studio. Nina's flat is a mesh of boudoir meets Boss Babe, with plants in every corner, shiny metallic furniture accents and texture upon texture.

'Maybe it's like when you've decided to buy a new car and suddenly, everyone else seems to have that exact make and model,' Nina says.

She steps around the counter that divides her open-plan kitchen from the living room with a big bowl of popcorn in her hands, and my sensitive nose catches the scent of melted butter.

'God, what am I doing?' I groan. 'I must be mad to actually be doing this.'

'Well, you wouldn't be the first,' Nina replies, sinking into the sofa next to me. 'I do have to admit though, I'm glad you're doing it before me. Can you imagine if I'd have had one with Dan? He would have been the worst dad in the world.'

'That's because he was a cokehead,' I point out.

Nina sighs, rooting in a box next to the sofa. 'Never again.'

From the outside, it had looked like insanity when she'd walked out of a six-year relationship on what seemed like a whim from the outside. I was the only one who knew what had really been going on – the mountain of debt he'd accumulated and the money he'd been draining from Nina to pay for his habit, not to mention the weekends spent with friends getting wasted. By the time she'd left him, she'd become a tired, dimmer version of herself. The change after their break-up spoke volumes. She'd left the tattoo studio she'd been working in and set up on her own, building a thriving business. She looked better than she had in years and had taken out a mortgage to buy this gorgeous little flat.

'So,' Nina says with a theatrical flourish and presenting me with a small box, 'I thought we could do a little card pull.'

'*You* have tarot cards?' I raise a sceptical eyebrow. 'Since when?'

I'm not sure I believe in all that stuff, mainly because my Jamaican Christian upbringing has engraved it onto my brain that cards and crystals and anything of the sort is basically an invitation to the devil.

'They were a gift,' Nina replies, 'and actually, they're pretty fun.'

'Have they predicted that you'll meet a tall, dark and handsome stranger?'

'They're oracle cards, not tarot. And there's already a tall, not-so-dark stranger on the horizon.'

I nudge Nina with my foot. 'And you didn't tell me?'

'I was going to. His name's Luke and I've spent a total of about ten hours working on his body already.'

'*And?*'

'Hot,' Nina laughs, tucking a strand of her pink hair behind a multiple-pierced ear. 'With great tattoos.'

'Obviously,' I grin. 'How long have you been seeing him?'

'We've been texting every day for a while and we've got a proper date this weekend.'

'Well, just make sure you use protection, or you'll be right here with me,' I reply, patting my belly.

We both laugh as Nina shuffles the cards and I take a piece of popcorn and tentatively drop it into my mouth. The saltiness settles on my tongue with surprising satisfaction and I immediately take another.

'So how does it work?' I ask, nodding to the cards.

'You just ask a question and then see what card you get.'

'What if I don't have a specific question in mind?'

Nina shrugs and hands me the deck. 'Then maybe just take one out and see what it says.'

I take the cards and shuffle them. They're surprisingly thick, embossed on one side and coated around the edges with shimmering gold colour. I'm dubious. How could a pack of cards possibly know what was going on in my life? They're like horoscopes – things I could probably read into and make applicable, no matter what.

'Alright,' I say with a sceptical sigh. 'What do I need to know about my pregnancy and this part of my life?'

'Ooh.' Nina takes a handful of popcorn from the bowl and nods. 'Good question.'

I pull a card at random and raise my eyebrows. There's a single word printed in block capitals underneath an ethereal, kaleidoscope-style picture of a woman. I flip the card around to show Nina.

'*Yes*,' I say. 'What is that supposed to mean?'

Nina flips through the little book that comes with the deck and shrugs. 'It means, yes.'

'It doesn't say anything more than that?'

'*Just say yes.* That's all.'

I hand her the cards and take more popcorn. 'It doesn't even make sense with the question I asked.'

'Maybe it's not supposed to be so obvious. Maybe it's like guidance for what's to come.'

'I've already said yes to becoming a mum. What else is there?'

'Maybe you'll meet your own tall, dark and handsome stranger,' Nina laughs. 'Or maybe it's a challenge. Like in *Yes Man*. Maybe you should say yes to everything until the baby is born.'

'That was a film, and from what I remember, he got himself into a whole lot of trouble,' I reply.

'Actually, it's a memoir and, from what *I* remember, there was a happy ending in both.' Nina sits up excitedly, crossing her legs underneath her. 'Seriously though, it could be kind of cool. Who knows what could happen?'

'Please,' I snort dismissively.

'Why not?'

'Because who knows what would happen, or where I'd end up?'

'*Exactly.*'

I shake my head. 'Neens, I'm pregnant. I can't be that reckless.'

'Okay, that's a fair point. But what if it wasn't for the whole pregnancy? What if it was only for six months? Or one month?'

I look at her sceptically. 'Would *you* do it?'

'Hell yes I would. But I didn't pull the card,' Nina grins. 'You know, the more I think about it, the more I think it could be good for you. You're on the precipice of a whole new life. What better time to try new things? Maybe you could add it to the list you and Jude were talking about?'

I snicker. 'That was more about the things I'll miss, like mayo and coffee. It feels kind of lame to have a regret list. It's so negative. I mean, I might be terrified but I *do* want this baby.'

'So let's make it a positive list. Hang on,' Nina says, getting up off the sofa. She disappears into her bedroom and comes back again with a notepad in her hands. 'Let's make a bucket list.'

'Aren't those for people who are dying? Besides, I've done heaps of stuff already. I've travelled, I've been up close and personal with a shark . . .'

'You've never sky-dived.'

'Nor will I ever.' I wrinkle my nose. 'Pregnant or not.'

'Cheers to that,' Nina laughs. 'Alright. So, what are some things you haven't done that feel important before you become a mum?'

I look out of the window and scrunch my face into a frown. 'I don't know, normal stuff I guess . . . putting down proper roots instead of living from a backpack? I've never lived alone before.'

'So, find a flat and live alone, that's perfect,' Nina says with a smile, writing it down. 'Not to mention practical.'

'If I become a millionaire maybe,' I reply, pulling a face. 'At this rate I'll have to work right until my due date and straight after, too.'

My eyes almost popped out of my head at the rental prices I'd seen online the previous day.

'Jude still hasn't been in touch about that flat?' Nina asks and I shake my head.

'It was always going to be a long shot. And even if he does manage it, I'll still have to kit it out with furniture and that's *before* needing things for the baby.'

'What about Sam? Shouldn't he be helping out?'

I brush the question away with a wave of my hand because there's still been no word from Sam about anything, let alone child support.

'I'm going to have to look at ways to increase my income. Raise my rates, maybe.'

'Let's put that down too then.'

My prices have stayed the same for a long time. It had always been enough, especially in Asia, where pounds stretched way further than they do here. Sydney was more expensive of course, but

I'd been sharing everything with Sam. Now I'm on my own, I really need to figure out a way to build a nest egg.

'What else?' Nina prompts.

'I'd love to go to a spa for the day. A proper one.'

She raises an eyebrow. 'You know they cost the earth, right?'

'I know, I know. It sounds ridiculous considering what I've just said about money, but let's face it, there'll probably be no time to shave my legs let alone chill out in a spa all day once the baby comes.'

'Fair enough,' she concedes. 'Next?'

I blow a raspberry and look at the collage of framed photos on the wall behind the television. One of them was taken at the Benicàssim festival a few years ago. I'd so badly wanted to go with them but work had clashed.

'Go to a festival?' I venture. 'I still haven't been to one.'

'We've been to plenty,' Nina replies with a frown.

'Not a day thing. A weekend one, like Glastonbury or something.'

'I think you've missed the boat with that for this year, but I'm sure there'll be something still bookable.'

Nina writes it down and I smile. This feels better than making a list of the things I can't do. It feels far more empowering.

'Awesome. What else?'

I puff the air in my cheeks while my mind searches for more list entries.

'Make a fire from scratch.'

'Really?' Nina laughs, shaking her head.

'It's a survival skill I probably should know if I'm going to be a mum. I probably should learn how to bake too.'

Nina snorts. 'Are you planning on moving to the countryside to pick wild garlic and bake loaves of bread every day?'

I stick my tongue out at her. 'No. But I'll probably have to cut back on coffee and cake trips to cafes, so I'd better start learning how to make them myself.'

'I love it. Other people want globetrotting and unforgettable experiences . . . and you want to learn to bake a cake and make a fire.'

'Not very sexy, is it?' I laugh.

'The Un-Sexy Bucket List. I think it's great.' Nina makes a note on the pad. 'Okay, anything else?'

I look down at my stomach. The memory of that woman with the huge belly on the bus is still etched into my mind. I'm about forty per cent excited and sixty per cent terrified about the same happening to me. And I'm not even letting myself think about what it might look like afterwards. But I also know that being scared of it won't stop it from happening and, in a way, I don't wish to. I feel like I want to do something to make the experience of growing a humongous bump something to look forward to in and of itself.

'I think I'd like to do something with my belly,' I say. 'To make peace with the fact that it'll probably never look the same again.'

'You mean like a Demi Moore shoot? Ooh, or a plaster cast, that could be cool.'

I nod. 'Yeah, something like that.'

'This is *so* good. See? All of this came from saying yes,' Nina says triumphantly.

'Maybe, but I am *not* going to start saying yes to *everything*,' I insist. 'No way.'

'You don't have to. But simply saying yes to more? You never know what might happen.'

I laugh again, shaking my head. 'Fine, okay. I'll say yes to more then.'

I'm not about to commit to signing my whole life away on the whim of a randomly pulled oracle card, but saying yes to a few more things than usual? That I can do.

◆　◆　◆

Pregnancy week: Eight
You're the size of a: Kidney bean
Today, I feel: Giddy

Hello, Little One . . .
So, it appears you're a fan of popcorn! Thanks for letting me eat and enjoy them :)

Today was our first official antenatal appointment and my first introduction to midwives. Funny how there are whole professions out there that you know nothing about until you need them. I wonder what you'll become when you're older? I'm a web designer (not the most glamorous of jobs but it's creative and fun) and your dad's a photographer, so you might be the creative type too. I wonder if you'll be a thrill-seeker or someone who likes to play it safe? And speaking of . . .

Your aunt Nina challenged me to say yes to opportunities more over the next few months. I have to admit, I am someone who tends to say no first. In fact, finding out I was pregnant might have been the first time I remember being so firm with a yes. Saying it more could be fun, right? Of course, I won't do anything silly. After the midwife appointment, I realised there's a whole lot involved in growing a human.

So, I want to make a deal with you: I'll do my best to keep you well fed, warm and safe, and you just concentrate on growing.

Sound good?

Love, Zoe

xx

Chapter Seven

ZOE, AGE 14

Zoe quietly closed the front door behind her and carefully dropped her keys back into her bag. The kitchen door was closed, but she could hear the muted sounds of her parents' voices through the thick wood. She went upstairs to her bedroom, her feet treading softly on the carpet. The urge to fall into her unmade bed was strong, but it was nothing compared to the excruciating cramps radiating across her belly and down her legs. Zoe slid open the top drawer in her chest, took out a fresh pair of knickers and grabbed the jeans she'd thrown onto the floor the previous night before going to the bathroom.

Her period had started today, right in the middle of chemistry class. They'd been learning about crystallisation when she'd felt a sharp twinge in her belly and had to be excused. It had been fine at first. She'd been carrying a pad in her bag for months in anticipation and had been more or less prepared. But it had got worse after lunch and the pad wasn't thick enough. Zoe untied her school jumper from around her waist and twisted her skirt around. Embarrassment flooded her body as she looked at the dark stain. At least her skirt was black, so the blood wasn't easy to see. She undressed, peeling off her tights and underwear and freshened up. It was the strangest thing. She was the last in her group of friends to start her period and had been eagerly awaiting its arrival for the last year. She was sure something magical would happen when she finally became a woman but, now that it was here, a part of her wished it would go away again. The cramps she'd had all afternoon were new and uncomfortable and were making her feel a little sick.

'Zoe?'

She opened the bathroom door to see her mum halfway up the stairs.

'When did you get back?' she asked.

'A few minutes ago.'

'What's that?' Janet frowned at the bundle in her hands.

'Laundry. I was going to put a wash on.'

'Since when do you do your own washing?' A frown of concern deepened on her mum's face. 'Are you okay?'

Zoe hesitated. She knew her mum wouldn't buy a lie, but a part of her felt embarrassed about admitting to bleeding through her clothes.

'I got my period today.'

'Oh, is that all?' A relieved smile set onto my mum's face as she climbed the rest of the stairs. 'How are you feeling?'

Zoe shrugged. 'A bit sick.'

'It'll get better. It's always worse at the beginning.' Her mum reached out for the bundle of clothes. 'There are pads in the bathroom and paracetamol if you need.'

Zoe handed her school uniform over. Was that it? It was silly to have expected anything dramatic, but her shoulders deflated a little. Carmen, one of the girls in her class, had been thrown a party when she started her period. Zoe had spent the afternoon in the big shed at the bottom of Carmen's garden with candles and chocolates, while her hippie mum spoke about the blessing of a girl's first period. It had been nice, but weird. She'd known there'd be nothing like that happening when her own time came, but still. She'd been told she would become a woman when she got it and, as far as she could see, the only thing that had changed was that today her belly felt fat and painful, whereas it hadn't yesterday.

'I'm going to lie down for a bit,' Zoe said.

'We need to talk to you first,' her mum replied. 'Your dad's waiting for you downstairs.'

'Can't we do it later? I'm really tired.'

'No, we need to do it now.'

Zoe groaned. 'But I feel sick.'

'Zoe, can you please just go downstairs.'

Her mum's voice was stern and had that tone to it that said there'd be no negotiating. Zoe rolled her eyes. Surely it couldn't be so important that it couldn't wait an hour? She went downstairs, huffing quietly to herself as she went.

'Hey, Dad,' she said with a yawn as she opened the fridge door.

'Hi, love. How was school?'

'Fine.' Zoe pulled out a Tupperware box filled with tuna and mayonnaise that her mum had made yesterday.

She took the tub and a bag of sliced bread to the kitchen table where she sat in the chair opposite her dad. He must've just come from work, because he was wearing his blue polo shirt uniform and still had the faintest hint of chlorine on his skin. As a kid, she'd been obsessed with *The Little Mermaid* but terrified of water, so her dad had told her he was part merman, making her part mermaid. He'd convinced her that nothing bad would happen if she tried to swim. If anyone knew, it ought to be him because he spent all day in the water, teaching swimming lessons at the local leisure centre. She'd been devastated when she'd learned he was only human a few years later, partly because it meant she was too. At least she was a strong swimmer now.

'Use a plate, Zo,' he said as she started to prepare her sandwich directly on the table.

She managed to stop her eyes from rolling in protest as she got a plate from the cupboard. With her sandwich made, Zoe took a big bite just as her mum came in with the basket of laundry. Her dad rearranged himself in his chair with a sigh and, she wasn't sure why, but the feeling in the room had changed. Zoe looked at her dad who was looking at nothing, and then to her mum who quietly loaded the washing machine. Zoe put the rest of her sandwich back on her plate.

'What's going on?' she asked, but she wasn't sure she really wanted to know.

Her mum stood up and leaned against the counter, crossing her arms. Zoe wasn't sure if she was angry or upset, or both. She racked her brain to remember if she'd done anything in the last couple of days. She'd shared a cigarette with Nina on the way home from school yesterday but she was sure she'd got rid of the smell. And she'd been getting good marks lately, so it couldn't be that.

'Are you going to tell her or should I?' her mum asked, looking directly at her dad.

Zoe's dad rubbed one of his eyes with a sigh before dragging his hand down over his mouth.

An awful feeling pulled in the pit of her stomach, and she was sure it had nothing to do with her period.

'There's no easy way to say this, Zoe. But your mum and I . . .' He stopped and looked across the kitchen at her mum and lowered his eyes. 'Well, I'm going to move out.'

'What? Zoe shook her head. 'Why?'

Her mum turned away and started putting the cups that had been drying on the rack away. Zoe could've sworn she was trying not to cry. She looked back at her dad but his face was unreadable.

'Are you getting a divorce?'

'I don't know.'

'But I don't understand. Everything's been fine, hasn't it?'

'It's not that simple, Zo,' he said, shaking his head. 'There are things that . . . It's not that simple.'

From what she'd heard from friends with parents who'd split up, there'd usually been a whole lot of arguing in the lead up. That hadn't been happening, at least not that she knew. Everything had seemed normal, except that her dad hadn't been around much lately. He always seemed to be working. He looked upset, and even though she couldn't see her mum's face, Zoe knew she was too. So why were they splitting up?

'When are you going?' she asked.

'Today,' her mum said, turning back around and fixing him with an icy glare.

Zoe's mum had the ability to make her stop misbehaving with just a single look of warning. She could look fierce sometimes. But this was a look Zoe had never seen before. Her eyes were blazing but her face was set like stone.

'As soon as I'm settled I'll send some train fare for you to visit.'

'Train fare? Where are you going?' Zoe asked, completely confused. She had an under-sixteen bus pass which meant she could go practically anywhere in London.

'Coventry.'

She blinked and looked from parent to parent. None of this made sense. What the hell was he going to do in Coventry? They had no family there and it was miles away.

'I don't understand.'

'It's complicated, Zo,' her dad said – adult speak for, you're too young to know.

A flash of anger boiled in her belly. They were treating her like a kid, something she hated. She shook her head as the anger built a film of tears over her eyes. She didn't need to know the details, but surely she had a right to know more than this?

'I'm sorry, Zoe.' Her dad got up from the table and went through the door to the living room.

Zoe's stomach turned. He'd already packed. A suitcase and a duffel bag were next to the sofa and he picked them up without a backward glance.

'Dad, wait.' She got up from the table and went after him. 'Don't go.'

'I'll be in touch, okay?' He avoided her eyes but dropped a kiss on the crown of her head before opening the front door.

Zoe looked behind her, waiting for her mum to come and stop him, but she didn't. Her dad walked out of their house and opened the door to his silver Triumph. Her tears rolled over her cheeks as her belly twinged with another cramp, and Zoe watched her dad drive away.

◆ ◆ ◆

I flush the toilet and sit with my back against the bathtub, wiping the back of my hand across my mouth. The aversion to the smell of coffee and cornflakes, I can handle. Even the nausea that's been hitting me in waves has been fine since I worked out that nibbling on a biscuit or piece of toast straight after waking helped. But this morning, I'd woken up with a mouthful of saliva and a throat coated in phlegm that no amount of coughing could budge. Even now, after vomiting, it's still there.

I open the door on the mirrored cabinet and take out a new tube of toothpaste. At least I won't be having a period for a while now. I'd met a woman on Bali once who worked as a period coach and told me that hating my period was like hating myself. It was easy for her to say. They've always been painful and heavy – a

58

nuisance, right from the start. As I brush my teeth, I remember that bus journey home from school and the embarrassment about leaking through my pad. And of course, there was the memory of what had come after. It was no wonder I hated them – they'd come on one of the worst days of my childhood. It sounds silly to say it as a thirty-eight-year-old adult, but over the years I've wondered whether if my period had come on another day, my parents might still be together.

After brushing my teeth, I wrap myself in my dressing gown and shuffle into the kitchen.

Mum looks up at me from her seat at the table with a sad smile of empathy. 'I've made you some ginger tea.'

I lift the lid on a pot of water with chunks of fresh ginger that smells as if it's been brewing for hours. 'Thanks. I hope it helps, I've got some really nasty phlegm going on. Why doesn't anyone ever talk about *that*?'

Everyone knew about morning sickness, but not this. Maybe I've just got a cold. I wouldn't be surprised if I have. London seems to have gone through all four seasons since I've been back.

Mum crunches on a slice of her brown toast. 'One of the girls at work had that. She was hacking away so bad I had to move her off the shop floor. It can happen.'

'Fabulous,' I reply with a sarcastic smile. I'd rather take the cold. 'What time do you finish today?'

'Eight, I hope.'

'Should I make us some dinner?'

'Not for me, I'm going out.'

I raise my eyebrows. 'For dinner?'

Mum laughs. 'Is that so strange?'

Actually, it is, but I don't say as much. Instead, I simply shrug and shake my head. Mum never eats out, mainly because she doesn't trust the hygiene in restaurants. When she *does* go somewhere for dinner, it's almost always a Jamaican restaurant where she knows everything on the menu anyway. I take my oversized mug of tea and sit at the kitchen table. It's hard to say if Mum looks any more dressed up than she usually does. She's a section manager at a department store so the blouse and dark skirt she's wearing could just be for work.

'Are you going with that guy from the barbecue?' I ask nonchalantly. 'What was his name again? Barry, wasn't it?'

'Would it be a problem if I were?'

I laugh a little and shake my head. 'Of course not. He seemed really nice.'

'He is.'

Mum smiles a little before eating the last bit of her toast, and I can't help but smile too. It's nice to see her happy. We're not the mother and daughter type who talk about love, sex and relationships. In fact, telling her I was pregnant might be the only time I've ever mentioned anything about sex at all to her, even if it was just by proxy.

'So, are you two dating?' I venture.

'Well, I think we're a bit old to call it that. We're spending time together.'

I nod knowingly and leave it at that, holding the cup under my nose to take a sniff of the tea. The scent of ginger is a familiar one from my childhood. It brings back good memories, like the smell of bulla cake we'd buy every Saturday at the bakery, as well as painful ones, like the memory of the ginger sweets Dad always had with him. I take a tentative sip, hoping it'll wash away the thickness clogging my throat as Mum gets up from the table.

'Do you think I should tell Dad?' I ask. 'About the baby.'

'I don't know,' Mum replies.

She doesn't even miss a beat as she rinses her cup and plate in the sink. We hardly ever speak about him. We don't have much reason to. After he moved to Coventry, I only saw him a handful of times.

'Are you in touch with him?' Mum asks, wiping her hands on a tea towel.

'No. I thought I could reach out on Facebook or something.'

Her face is neutral, but I can feel traces of the twenty-four-year-old hurt in there. As an adult with my own experiences of relationships and heartbreak, I can understand it.

'What do you think?' I prompt. 'Would you want to know, if you were him?'

'Well, I wouldn't be him to start with.' Mum hangs the tea towel on its hook. She'd said it in a light, jokey way, but there was an undertone of acidity to it. 'But if I were about to become a grandparent, of course I'd want to know.'

He might be a granddad already anyway. And if I've just thought that I'm sure Mum has too. She just has the decency not to say it. Even to this day, she's never bad-mouthed him, despite the fact that instead of moving into a crappy bedsit in Coventry like I'd imagined, he'd actually moved in with the woman he'd been seeing for months.

I shrug, suddenly irritated by the reality of why he'd left. 'It was just an idea. I'll think about it.'

'You do that,' Mum replies with a neutral smile.

I sip on my tea, grateful that it seems to be helping against the mucus plug in my throat. I don't think about Dad often. Once I found out the truth behind their split, I hadn't wanted to. I'd been too angry. Because of him, we'd had to move from our three-bed semi to a council flat on an estate that wasn't exactly dodgy, but a far cry from the quiet street we'd lived on before. For the first year, he'd called and sent a birthday card through the post. But after that, contact petered out. First with him, and then with his whole side of the family. He'd had a new baby and seemingly been so distracted by it that he'd forgotten about the child he already had.

I go up to my room and climb back into bed, taking my phone with me. I open the message thread with Sam that spans back years and my throat closes when I opened the media folder. The screen fills with all the pictures we've shared – sunsets and beaches, selfies and random things we sent to each other. He *still* hasn't contacted me and he's changed his settings so I can't see when he's last been online. The rejection punching me right in my solar plexus feels familiar. I'd felt the same crushing feeling when my sixteenth birthday had come and gone without any word from Dad.

I've just realised that two major life milestones have been tainted by the rejection of the most important man in my life at the time. First Dad, and now Sam. I don't need a psychology degree to see the significance. Instead, I sigh and put my phone away before laying down and pulling the duvet back over my head.

◆ ◆ ◆

Pregnancy week: Ten
You're the size of a: Strawberry
Today, I feel: Amazed
Hello, Little One . . .
I saw you today! What a surreal experience, seeing your little fuzziness float around on a screen like that. I know you're real, but actually seeing you, hearing your heartbeat . . . just amazing. Mum cried (I guessed she would) and I just stared at the screen, fascinated. You've got arms and legs and a whole life going on in there!

Are you a boy or a girl? What will your name be? And will you look like me, or your dad? I

62

know I've been a bit grumpy these last couple of weeks (not helped by caffeine withdrawal) but I am so excited now.

This won't make much sense to you right now, but just know that even though you weren't planned, you're so, so welcome here.

Love, Zoe

xx

Chapter Eight

I can't stop staring at the blurry, bean-like shape on the picture I brought home from the hospital. My eyes are drawn to it like a magnet with a heady mix of incredible awe and absolute terror. Since coming back to England, I feel like I've been running the whole gamut of emotions. Now it's gone into overdrive.

To say I felt fed up this morning would be an understatement. I'd felt sick, my mouth had waterfall levels of saliva and the phlegm plug was still there. I'd felt pissed off, and then guilty for feeling that way at all. The elastic on my knickers had dug into my waist thanks to the weight I've put on around my belly and, to top it off, I'd woken up knowing that I'd have to go to my appointment with Mum, like a sad, lonely singleton, instead of with Sam. My mood was nothing less than absolutely foul. But then, the nurse had put ice-cold jelly on my belly, glided a wand over it and the screen had flickered into life.

It was only when the pulsing sound of the baby's heartbeat echoed around the room that I realised I'd been holding my breath. The nurse had said that everything looked fine and the heavy feelings of frustration I'd been carrying came out with more than a few tears of relief. Until today, the baby had been this abstract thing that I knew existed, but still somehow wasn't one hundred per cent real. Now it is. I've seen it. I've heard it.

◆ ◆ ◆

'It's real,' I say out loud, with a jolt of nerves. 'A few more months and I'll have a baby.'

'Will you send a picture of the scan to Sam?' Mum asks.

'I don't know,' I mumble. 'I'm not sure there's much point.'

'Maybe seeing actual, tangible evidence that it's real might jolt him into action,' Nina points out. She came straight over after work with boxes of chicken and chips to see the picture from the scan, and it's been pretty much the only topic of conversation.

My body is fizzing with excitement having actually seen and heard my baby, but the underlying sense of panic is still there. I'm really doing this – alone. And I know I've got Mum and Nina by my side, but at the end of the day, I'll still be a single mum. I think back to the night when Sam had told me he didn't want kids all those years ago. Had I really meant it when I'd agreed? I try to remember the way I'd felt when he'd said it, but it feels like looking back at a memory of someone else.

Meeting Sam had been a breath of fresh air, with his straight-talking, *what you see is what you get* attitude. I trusted him straight away, which was saying a *lot* considering that the relationship before him had ended with a battered heart and a vow never to trust a man again. But I *did* trust Sam. He was ten years older than me and felt solid. Like a real man, who wasn't pussyfooting around and playing the field. Everything he said and did was with integrity. It always has been, even when he'd asked to open our relationship it had come from a place of honesty. I'd fallen for him quickly, despite trying not to in an effort to protect a heart that had only just started piecing itself back together again. The fierceness of my *yes* to this baby makes me wonder if I'd agreed not to have children just to keep him. Had I agreed to it because I'd been scared he'd leave if I didn't, and go on to find somebody who would?

Sadness makes my body droop. I feel sad that he's missed the strange awesomeness of this day. I feel sad for *him*, because even though this is terrifying the life out of me, the scan today has cemented my decision. Will sending a photo have the same impact on Sam?

'You know we'll have to send a copy of the scan to your nan,' Mum says. 'She won't know how to open the picture on WhatsApp.'

The thought of my almost eighty-five-year-old grandmother using a smartphone makes me smile.

'Speaking of,' Mum continues, 'we're still going to do the barrel shopping this weekend, right?'

I nod. I'd been half asleep on the sofa when I'd agreed to it yesterday. I've always hated barrel shopping, even as a kid. Because the price of groceries are so high in Jamaica, it's normal for families in here in the UK to fill barrels with everything from flour and rice to bubble bath and children's toys, and send them over by ship. The shopping process could take days and I haven't had energy for much beyond moving from the living room to the bedroom, but I'll only feel bad if Mum were to try and lug everything back home by herself.

'Should we pop the champers?' Nina asks, opening up the fridge.

It's really only sparkling grape juice, but it looks just like the real thing when it's poured out.

'I propose a toast,' Nina says, passing the glasses out. 'To new life, and new beginnings.'

I smile as we clink our glasses, but the feeling of sadness still lingers in my chest. As Mum and Nina chat, I take my phone from the table and open the photograph of the scan I'd taken earlier.

Zoe: This happened today . . . thought you might like to see it. I know you said you're not interested, but it's pretty cool. Miss you. x

I pause before pressing send. Am I allowed to say I miss him? And do I, or am I just feeling nostalgic and sad? If I really missed him, surely I'd have spent these last few weeks in a heartbroken mess? And does any of that even matter? I furrow my eyebrows as I try to navigate the strange void that's opened up in a place where certainty and instinct used to be and look at the picture again. When my baby gets older and inevitably asks about Sam, what will I say? Surely it would be better to be able to put a hand on my heart and honestly say I'd tried to involve him? I think back to the oracle card I pulled at Nina's house.

Yes.

And without thinking about it any further, I press send.

◆ ◆ ◆

That Saturday, I hold back a sigh and pray to all that's holy to extend my patience as Mum shakes her head disapprovingly at the tub of conditioner in her hand.

'*Seven* eighty?' Mum says, her voice loud enough to reach the ears of the Indian man behind the counter. 'It's a disgrace. I'm not paying that much, they can forget it.'

'Mum,' I groan. 'It costs exactly the same as in the last shop.'

'Exactly. They all have the same owner anyway.'

'Well, why don't you just get some from work instead?'

'You know as well as I do that our hair isn't catered for in the mass market, Zoe.'

I do have to grudgingly agree with that. It's always been a point of frustration. It's not as if Black people don't shop at regular supermarkets or department stores. Make-up, yes – because everyone can wear Fenty. But chemical relaxers, pomades and conditioner for kinky curls? That's considered too fringe. It would be so much more convenient to be able to sling a bottle of shampoo and conditioner into the trolley along with the rest of the groceries than having to traipse around specialist hair shops instead.

'We'll go back to the first shop,' Mum says and I shake my head, taking the tub.

'No way. I'll get them.'

'They're a pound cheaper back there.'

'Mum, I need the toilet and if I have to go into one more hair shop today, I'll lose it,' I reply firmly. 'How many does she need?'

'Six.'

'*Six?*' I shake my head. 'Why does Nan need six nine-hundred mil tubs of conditioner?'

'Two are for Sister Denise.'

I just about manage to stop my eyes from rolling – one of Mum's pet hates, along with bad language. This is the thing with barrel shopping. What starts as a reasonable list of things to send back explodes with extras for extended family and church members. I take an equal number of matching shampoos and put them on the counter.

'She doesn't need shampoo,' Mum says. 'They use regular ones, it's the conditioner that's important.'

'Then consider it a gift.'

'You need to be saving your money now, Zoe.'

'I know, but like I said, it's a gift. Besides, it's not like I don't earn more than Nan's pension.'

I hate the idea of my family struggling with money. Maybe it's a consequence of our household income being so dramatically reduced after my parents divorced. My nan had still lived in London at the time and had filled the gaps in income when

Mum's salary hadn't been quite enough. I understood why my nan had moved back to Jamaica – we're cut from similar cloth when it comes to an intolerance for cold weather – but the reality is, it's an expensive country to live in on an ex-care home assistant's pension. I know that for my nan, every penny counts, and the things we've bought so far today are the basics needed for life – rice, pasta, baked beans and toothpaste. They're things I never have to think twice about when buying for myself. And besides, it feels good to give something back.

Still, Mum's not wrong. The last-minute flight back was expensive, and while I've got some clients for the next couple of months, they'd booked with me before I put my prices up. I've started actually looking at the cost of things I'll need in shops and it's eye-watering. At this rate I'll have to become one of those mums who uses towel nappies and breastfeeds to save money. Sam hadn't said anything about providing child support. He's never been a stingy guy, but would he really financially support a child he doesn't want? Judging by his silence after I'd sent the scan photo, I'm not so sure. It's hard not to feel disappointed by him and his wall of silence as I take my credit card from my purse. At least I can say I've tried.

With everything stuffed into our canvas shopping bags, Mum and I make our way back to the Zipcar for the umpteenth time that day. It's mid-afternoon and Rye Lane is heaving. As much as I wish it could be normal for big chain supermarkets to stock Afro hair products, it would probably see the end of the high street here as I know it. It's already changing piece by piece, but some things seem determined to stay the same, like the huge indoor market that's been here for as long as I can remember, with stacks of plastic chairs, rolls of fabric, and enormous stainless steel cooking pot sets standing on the pavement. Or the countless food shops selling yams, breadfruit and green bananas.

'I was thinking of having Barry over for dinner tomorrow,' Mum says. 'Are you planning on going anywhere?'

'Is that your way of asking me to make myself scarce?' I reply as we weave our way through a cluster of people waiting at the bus stop.

'No, of course not,' she replies quickly and I laugh.

'I was joking. Things are getting serious with you two then? You're seeing him a lot.'

'Yes, I suppose they are.' She smiles a little before stopping abruptly outside a small mobile phone repair shop. 'Oh, wait a second. Mum needs a new charger.'

I drop my bags onto the grimy pavement as she disappears inside. Mum's changed over these last few weeks. She hums as she cooks now and seems lighter. Barry is clearly good for her and even though she doesn't talk about him all that much, I can tell by her smile that she's in love. Between her and Nina being in the first flushes of it, and the protective – if terrifying – love I'm already feeling for the baby, there's a whole lot of oxytocin around me right now. It makes me smile before the smell of dried fish from the African grocery shop next door brings my feet back to the ground with a bump.

'Oh my God, Zoe?' a woman with a pushchair stops in front of me and I frown for a second before my brain kicks into gear. 'Lisa? Wow, I didn't recognise you for a second.'

We both laugh and hug. Lisa had lived with Steph, an old friend of mine and Nina's, while we'd been at university.

'Gosh you look amazing,' I say, taking in her flawless skin and the colourful scarf holding her curls up high on her head. 'How are you?'

'If you call sleep deprived amazing,' Lisa laughs again. 'I can't remember what a full night's sleep looks like.'

I peer into the pushchair and my heart melts into a puddle at the big pair of brown eyes staring back at me, framed by a deliciously chubby face.

'She's adorable,' I smile, feeling a flicker of nerves and excitement that I'll have one of these myself soon. 'How's mum-life?'

'Tiring.' Lisa wheels the pram closer to the shop to make space for the people walking past. 'Thank God for hair scarfs and casual wear being a thing. If it weren't for Shaun I'd probably spend all day in my pyjamas.'

Lisa looks far from casual, with a fluffy pink jumper over dusky grey leggings. Sure, she looks a bit tired around the eyes, but otherwise, she looks amazing. I can only hope I look as good when the time comes, especially because I won't have a Shaun of my own to help.

'Sounds tough.'

'It is. But it's so worth it,' Lisa continues. 'I wouldn't change it even if I could. And what about you, how are you doing? Aren't you living somewhere warm and gorgeous these days?'

'I was living in Sydney,' I reply breezily. 'I got back a few weeks ago.'

'Oh, I've always wanted to go to Australia. I made it to New Zealand but not Australia, how weird is that?'

'And look at us both, back to where we started in south London.'

'We actually moved to York last year. We're just here to visit a few friends and I like to do some comfort shopping,' Lisa says, gesturing to the basket under the pram that is filled with plantains, mangoes and chow-chow.

'I'm here for the foreseeable,' I reply before letting out a little laugh. 'Actually, I'm pregnant. That's why I came back.'

A smile spreads across Lisa's face. 'Aw, congratulations and welcome to the club. How far along are you?'

'Ten weeks.'

'How are you feeling?'

'Meh.' I scrunch my nose. 'Exhausted and a bit yuck, but happy.'

'I know the feeling well,' Lisa replies as her baby starts to cry. 'But it does get better after the first trimester.'

'Any secret tips I should know about?'

'Yoga and as much sleep as you can manage to stock up,' Lisa winks. 'You'll be fine. I had so much anxiety about the whole thing and had to keep reminding myself that women have been doing this since the dawn of time. As long as you've got people around you who care, you'll be fine.'

'True,' I nod, taking her sage advice.

'So how's Steph?' Lisa asks. 'I haven't heard from her in years.'

I swallow the unease that hearing her name brings and shrug. 'No idea. We haven't spoken for a while either.'

'Really? You three were always together.'

'Yeah, well.' I smile sympathetically as the cries from the pram get louder.

Lisa groans apologetically. 'I guess that's my cue to go before things get crazy. It was really nice bumping into you, Zoe. Take care of yourself.'

'I will,' I reply, just about managing to not to wince as the cries reach extreme decibel levels.

We quickly hug goodbye and I watch her head off down the street. A memory of Steph pops into my mind, and how the flat she'd shared with Lisa had been *the* place to be at the weekends. Their parties had been legendary. The randomness of Lisa and I being on the same section of street at the same time, after so many years, makes me smile. Especially because she's a new mum. And she seemed to be doing well enough. If she can do it, then I'm sure I can too.

A wave of optimism washes over me. It's amazing how a few minutes chatting with someone I haven't seen since secondary school is more comforting than an hour with most of the people I'd spent my time with back in Sydney. I look down the street. It's tired and dreary, with litter gathered in corners and graffiti scrawled on walls. But, it's home.

Chapter Nine

'So, I know it's not the place we spoke about at the barbecue, but I think you'll like it,' Jude says, stopping the van and pulling up the handbrake.

I look out of the window with a frown. When Jude had called an hour ago for a spontaneous viewing, I'd pictured looking at a new building, with glistening surfaces and freshly painted walls. Instead, I'm looking at an ancient double-storey building with tatty windows, above a dental surgery on a busy high street.

'Really?' I look at him with a face full of scepticism.

'Really.' His eyes glint with amusement. 'Trust me, I think this place is much more you.'

'If you say so,' I reply with a sing-song voice and hop out of the van.

My phone falls from my hands and onto the floor, and after picking it back up, my head thickens as if it's been stuffed with cotton wool. I stand with my hand against the van's bonnet and blink.

'Are you alright?' Jude asks.

His hand feels steady on my shoulder as I swallow down a bout of nausea.

'Yeah.' I blow out a slow puff of air. 'I just stood up too quickly.'

'There I was thinking you were swooning over my property scouting skills,' he chuckles and holds out his elbow. 'Come on then. Can't have you falling at my feet, people will talk.'

'Then let's not give them anything to talk about,' I reply, raising my eyebrows and pushing his elbow playfully away. 'Honestly, I'm fine. Just lightheaded.'

'Did you have breakfast?'

I shake my head as we walk towards the door at the side of the dentist's.

'I'd just woken up when you messaged. You didn't exactly leave much time.'

'Yeah, sorry for the last-minute hectic,' he replies with an apologetic smile. 'There's only a small window of time to see it today before we start ripping things out and everything gets messy.'

'It's fine,' I say as he pushes a key into the lock. 'You can buy me a bacon butty afterwards to make up for it.'

He laughs. 'Deal.'

Jude pushes the door open and I lift my eyebrows, looking at a set of narrow stairs covered with a carpet that's so threadbare, I can almost see through it.

'Really, Jude? What about me says this would be my style?'

'You were into the whole grunge thing back at school weren't you? Nirvana and Anna in Chains and all that,' he replies, challenging me with his eyes.

'Alice in Chains. When I was thirteen and for all of five minutes.'

He shakes his head and steps through the doorway. 'Look first, judge later.'

I mimic him with a laugh. 'Okay, okay. I'm sure you wouldn't show me something awful. You'd have your sister to deal with if you did.'

Jude laughs back as we make our way up the stairs. The weak light overhead does nothing to brighten up the drab and scuffed beige walls. The air is musty and the memory of running down stairs as narrow as this with my heart breaking makes my throat tighten. I take a packet of mints from my bag and pop one into my mouth as Jude opens a second door that's stuck and apparently as unenthusiastic about the idea of us entering as I am.

'The door will be replaced, the wood's swollen,' he explains, giving it a final shove before it gives way.

I step into a sad-looking L-shaped room, with a faded swirly carpet and an abandoned sofa that looks like it's been here since the seventies. A single orange curtain hangs at the window and an old sideboard is wedged into one of the corners.

'So, what do you think?' Jude asks with a grin.

'Honestly?' I reply, sucking on my mint. 'It needs a lot of work. And that's me being polite.'

'Yeah, but it's got heaps of potential.'

The swirling in my stomach says otherwise, but I nod for him to lead the way. Around the corner, a set of tired-looking kitchen cupboards are stacked against the wall and the worktops are grimy with grease, topped with a layer of dust. It looks like the place has been empty for years.

'Everything'll be refurbished, obviously,' Jude says, turning to look at me. 'You'll probably even be able to choose the kitchen you want, too.'

I follow him through the rest of the flat. The bedroom at the back of the building is surprisingly bright with big windows, and a smaller room right next to it could be designated as a nursery. The bathroom is a decent size with a standalone sink and bathtub.

'Gosh. I haven't seen one of those in years,' I say, smiling at the rubber hose attached to the taps in the bath.

After having a power shower installed in the house we'd lived in before the divorce, it had taken time and a fair amount of frustration getting used to the improvised shower system we'd had to adapt to after moving. The hose attachment for the hot water always slipped off, leaving cold water to run through the showerhead. When the council finally refurbished the bathrooms and kitchens in our block, I'd stood under the new power shower for half an hour and swore never to take it for granted again.

'I'm pretty sure we can swing it so you get a new shower,' Jude replies with a wink.

The separate toilet reminds me of the loos at school, with its cold-looking black seat and overhead tank with a pull chain. I stand behind Jude in the narrow room with the smell of ancient pine-scented cleaner and an undertone of ammonia hanging in the stale air.

I pull a face. 'There's no window?'

He looks up at a small box on the wall. 'Just an extractor fan. It probably hasn't been used for ages though.'

The idea of stale toilet air being stuck in such a small space for who knows how many years makes my stomach flip and I quickly shove Jude out of the way to reach for the toilet.

'Oh, shit. Are you okay?'

I wave a hand at the sound of his shocked but concerned voice to try and shoo him away as I retch into the bowl. The toilet is beyond grimy, with discoloured limescale and God only knows what else. It makes my stomach heave again and when I hear Jude leave, my groan is as much one of relief as it is the nausea. My only saving grace is that, thanks to skipping breakfast, there's not a massive amount to throw up. When I'm finished, I slam the toilet lid down to avoid looking back into the disgusting bowl and stand up with a weary sigh to pull the chain.

'What the?' I frown as the chain does nothing.

'There's no water,' Jude says from behind me and I turn to see him handing me a bottle. 'It's mine, from the van. Hope that's alright?'

I nod gratefully and take it from him. 'Thank you. God, I'm so embarrassed.'

'At least you've got an excuse,' he says as I rinse my mouth and spit into the sink.

'Oh, God. If the toilet doesn't flush, then—'

'Don't worry, I'll sort it out,' he replies, as if he's used to cleaning throw-up all the time. 'On one condition.'

I frown. 'What's that?'

'You take the flat.'

Despite the rawness of my throat, I laugh. 'I need some air.'

'Oh, good. That means I can show you the best bit then,' he smiles. 'Besides, you've already seen the worst now.'

We leave the toilet and I close the door behind me. He's right, it definitely can't get any worse than that. Jude opens a door at the end of the corridor and we step onto the flat roof of the extension of the dentist's surgery below. I draw in a gulp of a breath of air and tilt my head back.

'Better?' Jude asks.

'Much.'

The sky is pale blue above the row of terraced houses opposite and the traffic noise is considerably lower back here. The extension is longer than it is wide and covered with grit.

'You could use this as a terrace,' Jude suggests. 'It would look great with wooden decking and a fence for privacy.'

He stands with a wide stance and his hands on his hips. He has good vision, I'll give him that. So far all he's done since we've got here is see the potential behind the grimness of it all. Then again, maybe it's part of his job to be able to do so. I look at him in his thin, long-sleeved fleece and workmen's trousers with a couple of pens sticking out of one pocket and a metre-stick from another. The sunlight makes the sprinkling of brown freckles on his face look more pronounced and he looks pleased with himself, as if he knows this is a done deal. I turn to look up at the back of the building. The bricks are old and brown and the white window frames are grey with years of grime. The whole place needs a good, thorough clean-up.

'What's the deal with this place? It's clearly been empty for a while,' I grimace. 'Nobody died here, did they?'

Jude laughs. 'No. The guy who owned it moved abroad and just never rented it out. He died – not here – and his nephew inherited it. The nephew's a friend of mine, and that's how I know about it.'

'How much is the rent?' I ask with an apprehensive wince.

He gives me a number and I'm pleasantly surprised. This place needs a lot of work, but pretty much everywhere with an SE1 post-code is an up-and-coming area these days. It won't be long before a Sainsbury's Local and a Franco Manca pop up on the road outside.

'I've already told him about you and it's yours if you want it.'

'Really? Without references or anything?'

'I'm the reference, obviously. Plus, my mate is much nicer than the guy you'd be renting from in the other place. He doesn't even really need the money, he just doesn't want it sitting empty. I'm telling you, this place has way more character than the other one. Look.'

Jude beckons for me to follow him inside where he crouches down on the living room floor. He peels back the carpet to reveal dusty floorboards.

'This is original parquet floor. You don't even want to know how much it would cost to buy that new.'

He shakes his head and runs his hand across the wood with so much affection, I can't help but smile at his geeky passion.

'Why anyone would cover it with carpet, I don't know,' he continues. 'But once it's sanded and varnished, this place will be unrecognisable. You'll be able to choose some of the stuff we'll fit, which means you won't have some off the shelf boring flat to live in. It would be a travesty if you ended up somewhere like that. You were never boring.'

I grin. 'Really?'

'Come on.' He fixes me with a look. 'The girl with the chunky boots and jewellery? You were like something from *The Matrix*. Remember that leather jacket?'

I cringe at the memory. 'Oh, God. I loved that thing.'

I'd begged and begged for an ankle-length jacket like the one Carrie had worn in what used to be my favourite film, and I'd got one as a Christmas gift. It must've cost a fortune. It's embarrassing now but I'd been so into that whole tech-chic vibe which, considering I'd switched from law to web design and coding, kind of makes sense. For the last few years, I've either lived in guesthouses or rentals with Airbnb vibes. Massive plants, wall hangings with motivational statements like *live, laugh, love* and macramé hanging baskets were invariable aspects of the interior design. Even the apartment I'd just left in Sydney was an example of cultivated boho-chic. When had I moulded myself into that life? These days, I don't dress in head-to-toe leather, wear bug-eyed sunglasses or transparent butterfly clips in my hair – thank God – but Jude's right. A clean-cut, brand new, shiny everything home isn't really my style.

I'm surprised, in a good way. The Jude I'd known as a young man wasn't passionate about very much. His mum had worried about him drifting from job to job or worse, getting mixed up in gangs which were a real thing to worry about around Peckham at the time. And he definitely wouldn't have been so caring about me throwing up like that. We didn't have smartphones back then, but if we had, he would absolutely have been the type to film me vomiting and upload it to YouTube or TikTok and make it go viral. I smile with the realisation that, even though I've known Jude for so many years, in some ways I feel like I hardly know him at all.

'You've changed,' I say. 'You used to be obnoxious.'

Jude scratches the back of his neck with a sheepish shrug. 'Yeah, well. Life has a habit of kicking you in the nuts and bringing you down a notch.'

That's certainly true. I glance around the room again, trying to look past the hideous carpet, rotting windows and peeling wallpaper. The skeleton of the building is good. It's big. And it will be mine and mine alone – at least until the baby comes along. I walk over to the window and peer through the almost black net curtain.

'Can you believe it'll be my first time living alone?' I ask, watching an elderly woman pushing a tartan-printed shopping trolley on the street. 'At thirty-eight. It feels kind of lame.'

Jude crosses his arms and leans his tall frame against the door jamb. 'I only moved into my own place after Rachel left. If she hadn't gone, I'd probably always have lived with someone else. Most people can't afford to rent alone in London.'

'It *would* be the first thing off my list,' I say with a smile.

'What list?'

'After what you said at the barbecue, Nina and I made an unsexy bucket list of things to do before the baby comes.'

Jude chuckles. 'What's so unsexy about it?'

I perch myself gingerly on the windowsill. 'Moving into a flat, baking bread . . . it's a little different to the stuff people would normally put on a bucket list.'

'Well then, congrats on striking the first thing off. Because there's a toilet full of puke back there, I kind of feel like you owe it to me.'

'You're never going to let me live that down, are you?'

'Unlikely.'

I shake my head with a laugh. Even though I've left everything behind to come back to London, moving to a new place will be a real fresh start. Like wiping the slate clean. I'm well aware of the privilege I have. If it weren't for Jude, I'd never have the connection to the owner. So far, all I've received since coming back is support. Nobody's blamed me for ending up alone or told me I'd made a mistake in leaving. If Sam would've been happy with the pregnancy, I'd probably have stayed in Sydney. But now that I'm here, I couldn't imagine doing this anywhere else. A wave of nerves hit me, quickly followed by a flash of excitement as I walk over to Jude.

'Alright,' I say, holding out my hand for him shake. 'It's a deal.'

Pregnancy week: Fourteen
You're the size of a: Lemon
Today, I feel: Impatient

Hello, Little One . . .
Well, you're the size of a lemon and you've already got a collection of clothes that's bigger than everything I had in my childhood put together. Now that we're past the twelve-week mark, Mum's been bringing back Babygros and bibs every time she leaves the house. You'll need a walk-in wardrobe if she carries on!

I know our new flat was in a state of chaos yesterday, but I'm glad you didn't make me throw up again. I'm taking it as a sign that you're warming to the place. Jude's working evenings and weekends to get it ready for us and I can't wait to be there with you.

It's the strangest thing to be so close to you without knowing what you look like. Or what your voice will sound like. The journal says you're starting to grow your fingernails and you might be sucking your thumb. You're already pulling my heart strings, Little Lemon! I think you'll probably have me eating out of the palm of your hand when you get here.

Love, Zoe

xx

Chapter Ten

'I can't believe you're making me do this,' Nina groans as we walk through a set of enormous revolving doors. 'You do know this is my idea of hell, don't you?'

'I know,' I reply with a smile, linking my arm through hers. 'But who knows what I'd walk out of here with if I let Mum come with me.'

Nina laughs. 'Fair enough.'

Mum and I have wildly different tastes. I'd known a furniture shopping trip with her would be out of the question when she'd shown me a floral print three-piece suite online. IKEA isn't exactly individualistic, but at least it's modern and within a reasonable price range. I pull out the piece of paper I'd scrawled my list on as we walk up the stairs, leaving the glorious May sunshine behind us. After a little to-ing and fro-ing between sunshine and rain, Mother Nature seems to have finally made her mind up. Feeling the warm air on my skin and golden rays on my face after so long has been like waking up from a dream and it's as if the spring weather has brought my inner state into balance too. Today, I woke up feeling well-rested and upbeat. My shower had felt luxurious, as if I'd somehow developed a more delicate sense of touch overnight. I'd stood in the mirror and looked at the tiny but visible bump above my knicker-line and grinned. I don't look podgy anymore – I look pregnant.

'Alright, where's the list?' Nina asks, and I hand it over. 'Bloody hell. Your credit card'll be in for a bashing.'

'Tell me about it.'

But what else can I do? I have a whole flat to kit out and it's not like I can borrow someone else's furniture.

'I've already looked online and made a shortlist, so all we're really doing is checking the real-life versions out,' I say.

As it turns out, spending so much time trawling through the website first has been worth it. From the five sofas I'd shortlisted, only one lives up to its looks and comfortability in real life, and it looks like the same is going to be true for the mattresses, too.

I plonk myself down onto the third one we try and run my hand across the grey fabric. 'This one feels good.'

'Actually, it is. It's way comfier than mine,' Nina agrees, sitting next to me and bouncing up and down. 'I might get one myself.'

'Have you worn yours out already?' I ask with a grin.

'Not quite, but it doesn't hurt to think about things in advance.'

She laughs, adjusting the long fringe she's cut into her hair. The way it falls into her eyes makes her face look softer. Then again, maybe that's down to Luke, the guy she's been dating for the last few weeks. These days, Nina has a coyness to her smile, like she's hiding a secret, even though I know pretty much all there is to know about her very own version of Jamie from *Outlander*.

The upbeat, springtime vibe I'd woken up with this morning has stuck with me, despite the inevitable tiredness that comes from being in an airless, artificially lit room and taking in a hundred different objects and smells. But as I look over to one of the other display beds and see a heavily pregnant woman lying on a mattress and chatting to the man standing next to her, my throat tightens. And when he helps her stand up, it's like the balloon of my world has just been violently popped with a needle. I lay back on the mattress with a sigh and stare up at the fluorescent lighting before turning my head to look at Nina.

'Do you think he ever thinks about me?'

Nina raises her eyebrows. 'Who? Sam?'

I nod. I know I'm asking the wrong person, considering how little she thought of him to start with, but I can't help it.

'Maybe,' she replies. 'Probably.'

'It isn't fair, Neens. Not on me, or the baby. I know I made the decision to do it all alone so it's my own fault but, fuck . . .' I shake my head and will the tears building in my eyes to stay put. 'It isn't fair.'

'It's not your fault he's too weak to face up to his responsibilities,' Nina says, turning her body to face me better. 'It takes two to tango, Zo. If he can be happy with putting things in your vagina, he should be happy with the things that come out of it.'

I can't help but laugh at that.

'It's *true*,' she insists. 'He can't just keep on having his cake and eating it.'

The thought of Sam in Sydney, living essentially the same life he always has, pushes the tears from my eyes. I'd made compromises and stretched my tolerance in ways I'd never have imagined I could for him. Why couldn't he have done the same for me? Being pregnant has been a distraction from the break-up, but at times like this the truth of it feels as strong as ever. I wipe my eyes with the heels of my palms and take a breath to compose myself.

Nina puts a hand on my shoulder with a small smile. 'I'm sure he'll get in touch at some point once he's accepted it.'

Her words are kind and her voice is sympathetic, but I know she doesn't believe a word of what she's just said. She's simply doing what has to be done in this moment to take the edge off and I love her for it.

'Thanks, Neens,' I say, sitting up and wiping the rest of the dampness from my cheeks.

'So,' she replies. 'The mattress? Yay or nay?'

I appreciate the change in subject and nod. 'Yay. You?'

'Not sure yet. Where are you going to keep all this stuff until you're ready to move in anyway?'

'I'll keep the small stuff at Mum's and have the rest delivered straight to the flat.'

'And who's going to help you build it all? Because you know me and flatpacks don't mix.'

I laugh and sniff the last remnants of my tears away. 'I know. Jude's offered to help. He's got all the tools and it'll take half the time.'

'Good idea,' Nina says. 'It goes against my feminist principles to say it, but that's something I'd happily delegate to a man.'

'I hear you. Though I do think it'd be good to know how to do it myself.'

I take a picture of the mattress's item number on my phone before we continue down the fixed path.

'He's been really sweet,' I continue. 'I don't know how he's managing to do a day job *and* my place in his spare time. He's a machine.'

'He always has loads of summer plans. He probably wants to make sure he's free for that so nothing gets in the way of holidays and festivals and stuff.'

I nod. 'Yeah, maybe. I was thinking I should get him something to say thanks. I know he's being paid to do the work but still.'

'Good luck with that. He's the *worst* person to buy for unless you're buying him power tools.'

I stop in front of a wall of mirrors and take the opportunity to check my reflection while checking out the different frames. Although my belly looks less fat and more pregnant, I'm still not quite ready for maternity clothes. The vintage 501s I'd ordered on Depop are a good fit, though only if I wear them with a hairband around the button to fill the gap I can't close. My oversized, sleeveless t-shirt hangs down to my hips and I've liberated one of Mum's ancient leather handbags. I flip it open to take out a mint. The morning sickness has thankfully stopped, but the habit of keeping mints with me has stayed.

'Rachel leaving really did a number on him, didn't it?' I say, handing the pack to Nina.

Her face flares with disapproval. 'You have no idea. It makes my blood boil just thinking about it. I'll kill her if I ever see her again.'

She takes a mint and drops it into her mouth. I don't doubt that she would. I know what an angry Nina looks like, and it is *not* pretty. Jude's her younger brother and, even though they tussle and drive each other nuts, they're family, and that isn't to be messed with.

'But,' Nina continues with a loud sigh, 'if she hadn't shagged around behind his back, he'd never have been depressed and if he hadn't been depressed, he probably wouldn't have got so deep into his work.'

'Yeah, I was really surprised about how serious he is about it. And how good. Everything in the flat looks amazing so far.'

'Every cloud, right?' Nina sighs as I take a picture of the item number of a big mirror in a vintage-style gilded frame.

When I look back on my life as a whole, I can totally get with the saying. Every cloud does have a silver lining, even if it doesn't make sense at the time. I know there has to be one to this current cloud above me, aside from the baby of course. All the upheaval, the collapse of a relationship, financial stress – and no doubt the pain when the time comes – will be worth it. But still, it doesn't make being under it feel easy all the time.

A few days later, I glide my stick of gloss across my lips in front of the mirror. I've spent the last two evenings reading Reddit forums about single motherhood and pregnancy and one thing that's sparklingly clear is that opportunities to spend quality time by myself will probably reduce even before the baby comes. I'd read posts from women who'd had debilitating back pain and could barely get out of bed. And then there were those with complications who ended up in hospital, especially those in my over thirty-five age bracket. On the one hand, it was comforting to read stories of women who'd laboured without a partner and managed to look after themselves alone. But on the other, it started planting worst-case scenarios in my head of all the things that could go wrong. Today, I've resolved not to let myself get sucked into those kinds of thoughts and decided to take myself off on a date to enjoy a day alone instead.

My 501s are still holding up and I've teamed them up with a long, white shirt. With the jeans turned up at the ankle and my shirtsleeves by my elbows, I feel summery and feminine. My plan is to jump on the bus to Trafalgar Square and take a good wander through The National and Portrait Galleries before treating myself to a solo lunch at Wagamama's for some brainstorming about how to bring in some more money.

I put my phone and Kindle into my handbag and sling it over my shoulder before closing the door to my bedroom behind me. I go into the kitchen to grab an apple in case I get peckish and frown at the sound of the door opening.

'I thought you were at work today?' I say, putting the apple into my bag as I turn to Mum.

'I had a doctor's appointment.'

She shrugs her jacket off and rolls her head back as if her neck is tense.

'Everything okay?'

'Oh, fine. Well, it will be.'

I look at her and frown. 'What does that mean?'

It will be? Her choice of words means that even if everything would be fine, right now it wasn't.

Mum looks back at me with a smile that's so small, it doesn't get anywhere close to her eyes. I know that smile. It's all tight around the edges. It's the kind of smile she gives to people when she's hiding the truth. She gives it to one of the neighbours who likes to pop over under the guise of needing something but inevitably starts launching into gossip and doesn't have a kind word to say about anyone.

'Mum?'

'It's nothing serious,' she says, bustling past me to put the kettle on. 'But I went in a couple of weeks ago after some sudden bleeding.'

I feel my face blanche. Mum is years past menopause. I don't know much about female reproductive health, but I know bleeding after menopause isn't normal.

'And?'

'It's cancer.'

My breath leaves my body as forcefully as if someone's just winded me, and I grip the back of the chair in front of me.

'What?'

'It's not serious.'

'What do you mean *it's not serious?*'

'I mean, it's not serious. It's very early stages. I went as soon as the bleeding started.'

Her calm tone of voice jars against the reality of what she's just said. It's as if she's talking about what to cook for dinner instead

90

of the fact she has cancer. Just repeating the word in my head makes my body feel cold with fear. Nobody close to me has died yet. Mum's dad died way back when I was a baby and both of my dad's parents are still alive. The only people who'd had cancer in my family were distant grand-aunts and third cousins I'd never met.

'I can't believe it.' I shake my head, trying to dislodge the images that fear is creeping into it.

'Zoe, listen to me. They've caught it early. It really is going to be okay.' Mum pulls a chair away from the table to sit down and I do the same.

'You can't know that, Mum,' I shake my head, feeling my eyes well with tears.

'I've got an appointment in a few days with a specialist, but I might not even need chemo. It's the best possible news I could have in this situation.'

I shake my head again. This has to be the most surreal conversation I've ever had, and it isn't helping that Mum is being so nonchalant about it.

'I know it's a shock,' she says, dragging a thumb across my cheek to wipe away my tears. 'But it really will be fine.'

She hasn't done that since I was a kid. The memory of it only seems to make the news drop deeper into my belly and a fresh wave of tears fall. Mum tuts in a way that says, *silly girl*, and pulls me in close. It's an awkward angle that means I'm barely even sitting on my chair, but I don't care. I cling to her in a way I probably haven't ever done before.

'Come on, Zoe,' Mum says. 'It's not good for the baby for you to get upset.'

I pull away from her and wipe my face with my palms. 'But what if—'

'There is no 'what if'. I know everything is going to be just fine.'

'How? How are you being so calm about this?'

'I knew what it was from the moment I saw the blood. I've had time to get used to it and the prognosis is really good. And anyway, it's in God's hands.'

I bite my lip. I want to argue that it's in our hands, to make sure she gets the care she needs, not God's. Mum stopped going to church years ago but she's always had a strong faith. It isn't something I can relate to. I like to think that things unfolded in an organic, unplanned way. I'd hate to think there could really be a god who would plan for people to have cancer. On the other hand, now that this is happening, I can already feel myself hoping there is one who can take it away.

◆ ◆ ◆

Before this year, I barely knew anything about a uterus. I'd imagined it was somewhere by my belly button instead of low down in my pelvis. Or, as the ancient Egyptians believed, it wandered around the body, causing hysteria. And I had no idea that it's one of the strongest muscles in the body. While Mum's been carrying on as normal, going to work and acting as if nothing out of the ordinary is happening, I've spent the last few days browsing websites and reading up all I can on uterine cancer. I look at the doctor sitting on the other side of the table. It's been a huge relief to hear him repeat what she'd told me. It was very early and treatable with surgery. It's unlikely to have spread, but she's been scheduled for more tests and, if they come back clear, she won't need any chemotherapy.

'You'll be in recovery for some time, around four to six weeks,' he says with a kind voice.

'So, it's not the time to take up weightlifting, then?' Mum laughs gently and he returns it.

'Not unless it's lifting the TV remote.'

I wonder how many times a day he has these meetings and how many of them are with patients who can make light of such a serious situation. I look over at Mum who's sitting there calmly, as if she's making plans for a holiday. I've had interviews for part-time bar jobs at university where I was more nervous than she is right now.

'See?' Mum says, looking at me. 'I told you I was in good hands.'

I look back at the doctor. Would he have such a look of ease and warmth in his wrinkle-framed eyes if things were really bad? When we leave his office, I sneak a look at Mum to see if her mask slips but, if she is wearing one, it's fixed on tight. I link my arm through hers and she looks at me, surprised. I don't think I've ever done it before.

'I'm going to speak to Jude,' I say as we walk down the corridor. 'I'm sure the landlord can find someone else in time.'

Mum shakes her head. 'What for?'

'You just heard him. You'll be in recovery for weeks. You're going to need someone to look after you.'

'Zoe,' Mum replies, shaking her head. 'You're not giving up your flat.'

'But you can't do this alone.'

'I know. I've been talking about it with Barry, and—'

'Barry?' I splutter. 'You've only just started seeing him. And I'm family.'

'Yes, and you're also pregnant,' she replies, lowering her voice as we get to the lifts. If there's one thing Mum hates, it's airing her business in public.

'So?'

She sighs. 'So, you need a place of your own, where you can prepare for the baby in peace. Barry and I have already spoken about him moving in. This would just speed things up a bit.'

'Speed things up?' I reply, whispering loudly. 'Mum, you've known the man two minutes.'

'We've known each other for a long time. We're not kids, Zoe.'

She cuts the conversation as we step into the lift. I know this isn't about me. I know it's about Mum and what's best for her, but really? How does she know that Barry will be up to the task of looking after her? It's post-surgery recovery. She'll need help getting washed and dressed, not to mention help around the house.

'Look, Zoe,' she says as we step out of the lift. 'This is *such* a special time. You're already getting that pregnancy glow and you're going to start feeling great. You need to be building memories and enjoying it. Not looking after me.'

'It's my responsibility to look after you,' I reply.

She turns to face me, shaking her head with a little smile. 'No, it's not.'

'But you're my mum,' I point out.

'And you're my daughter. Soon, you'll understand.' Mum squeezes my arm. 'And Barry's a good man. He's caring and kind. And he cooks a mean soup.'

'But—'

'No buts, Zoe.' Her voice is firm. 'You're not letting that flat go, and that's the end of it.'

I want to protest. I want to talk sense into her, but she has that *because I said so* vibe about her. It used to annoy the hell out me as a teenager because I knew there was no getting around it.

'But thank you,' she says. 'I love you, Zoe.'

She links her arm through mine and I swallow the lump in my throat. 'I love you, too.'

Pregnancy week: Eighteen
You're the size of a: Bell pepper
Today, I feel: A bit overwhelmed

Hello, Little One . . .

I'm trying not to let myself worry too much that I haven't felt you move yet. At least, I don't think I have. The midwife assured me that you're doing well and you might just be shy. Shy. I loved that. My journal says I should start to feel you between weeks 16–22, but so far all I'm feeling is hunger and gas rumbling around in there. It does also say I'm more likely to feel you move in quiet moments and, let's be honest, there hasn't been too many of those!

Between Mum's operation and getting the flat ready, it's been a lot. In theory, it'll all calm down once we move in this weekend, but I wish I wasn't leaving her behind. Being a daughter and a mum-to-be at the same time has definitely given me another perspective on it all. I know she's been worried about me through it all because I'm sure that, if I were in her situation, I'd be worried about you. I already do. I worry about you and your life and the things that haven't even happened yet and might not happen at all.

Maybe that'll calm down when we move into the flat and I can feel like I've got some proper roots put down for you to be born into. Mum is practically kicking me out, but Barry's actually been really good with her. Seems like he's one of life's good guys. Which reminds me, I need to get something for Jude to say thanks for basically being a machine and working so hard to get things ready for us.

Oh, and we're almost halfway there! Is it going as quickly for you as it is for me??

Love, Zoe

xx

Chapter Eleven

ZOE, AGED 22

Zoe grinned as a much-needed blast of dry ice whooshed over her body and a plane flew low, right above her head. She felt *alive*. The pressure of university was done, she'd bagged her Bachelor's and she was free. Zoe laughed as Nina flung her arm around her shoulder and plastered a kiss somewhere on the side of her face.

'Argh, this so epic!' Nina laughed, pushing a pair of Day-Glo rimmed sunglasses from the bridge of her nose to her head and grabbed Steph's hand. 'Come on, it's top-up time.'

Sun, sea and unashamed fun. A ball of happiness fizzed in Zoe's stomach. She was at a legendary beach club on Ibiza with Nina and Steph, her two best friends, and they still had five days of bliss in front of them.

'Oh, that smells so *good*,' Steph said as they made their way to one of the bars dotted around the vast space.

The scent of barbecue wafted through the air and Nina nodded. 'I could eat.'

'Me too,' Zoe said, feeling the grumble of an empty stomach. Steph grinned. 'Me three.'

'We might as well before we get wasted,' Zoe said, looking down at the neon-pink band around her wrist.

A flash of it gave them access to an all-you-can-eat grill, free drinks, the jacuzzi at the far end of the beach club *and* a taxi back to the hotel. The ticket had cost more than the return flight from Gatwick, but the all-star DJ line-up was worth it. It was a massive upgrade from the overcrowded bar they'd gone to after their flight had arrived late last night. The drinks had been cheap and the music listenable, but at least today her shoes wouldn't be sticking to the floor. The sun was still high up in the sky, beaming its concentrated rays down onto Zoe's skin and hundreds of people filled the spaces between the three bars and two swimming pools. Everyone was having a great time and, because it was a day party, it felt like they had all the time in the world.

Nina and Steph went over to the grill to order some hot dogs, and Zoe turned to lean on the bar to order the drinks. As expensive as the tickets had been, they were still saving a fortune. It cost eight euro for a tiny bottle of Evian here and otherwise the cocktails they'd been sipping since they arrived were most definitely more.

'That looks lethal.'

Zoe turned to face the direction the deep, male voice had come from and found herself looking into a pair of brown eyes. They glinted with more than a hint of mischief and she looked down at her glass with a grin.

'Rum, vodka and tequila. It's called a Headbanger.'

'Sounds like it should be called the Hangover from Hell,' he grinned back. 'I'm Jerome.'

'Zoe.'

He blatantly looked her up and down, taking in the white mini sundress which set off the brownness of her skin and the hint of fluorescent-pink bikini underneath. He clearly wasn't shy, and she liked it. With his calf-length board shorts and full tattoo sleeves, Jerome looked a bit rough around the edges. He wasn't her usual type and was different to the guys she'd dated at university. Somehow, it only made him seem even more attractive.

He turned to signal the topless man behind the bar. 'Five Headbangers, please.'

'Five?' Zoe raised an eyebrow 'Bit ambitious, don't you think?'

Jerome laughed and raked a hand through his dark hair. 'I love a drink as much as the next guy, but even I wouldn't try and sink five of those. They're for my mates. Who are you here with?'

Zoe looked over to the other side of the pool where Nina and Steph were flirting with the men behind the grill.

'Those two,' she said, pointing towards them.

The music was too loud for her to possibly hear it, but the sound of Steph's trademark cackle rang in her ears when Zoe saw her friend throw her head back with laughter. The place was full of other groups of friends that, if asked, would probably be adamant that their friends were the best. But Zoe knew otherwise. Because hers really were.

'We've got a cabana and some loungers over there,' Jerome said, nodding to a row of beachfront wooden structures. 'You should join us.'

Zoe grinned and pulled her sunglasses down over her eyes.

'Sorry,' she said, using the skills she'd gained in her part-time bar job to pick up all three cocktail glasses at once. 'It's a girl's night, tonight. No boys allowed.'

Was she mad? Probably. He was gorgeous and clearly interested. But the three of them had been looking forward to this for months and had made a pact to enjoy it, together. Jerome laughed as she blew him a kiss and left, swinging her hips as she went. There was something satisfying in saying no and leaving the tension untouched. Besides, the island was small enough. She was sure that, if it were meant to be, their paths would cross again.

◆ ◆ ◆

Three days later, Zoe giggled, swinging her legs to and fro from her seat on the rickety table. Two nights after meeting Jerome in the beach club, they'd bumped into each other on the street. Nina had decided that fate was dealing Zoe a hand and, instead of going out clubbing, they'd taken the party to the room he was sharing with three of his friends where alcohol had been flowing in abundance.

'How do I say, "I'm a little bit drunk" in French?' Zoe asked.

Just when she'd thought Jerome couldn't get any hotter, he'd told her he was half French.

'*Je suis pompette.*'

She looked up at him with a grin and repeated the words. '*Je suis pompette.*'

'Hey, Zoe, remember that song?' Steph asked from across the kitchen. 'You know, the one from *The Little Mermaid*?'

Zoe frowned. 'Which one?'

'You know, when Sebastian almost gets caught by the chef?' Steph skipped over and jumped up to sit next to her on the counter.

Zoe tried to concentrate her mind as she thought through all of the songs from what had once been her favourite film until she got it.

'I remember,' she giggled. '*"Les poissons, les poissons, hee hee hee, haw haw haw."*'

The boys watched as they gave a full rendition of the song, swaying and flailing their arms for the big finale before giving into fits of laughter.

Jerome shook his head and laughed. 'You girls are crazy.'

'Yep, craziness guaranteed,' Steph grinned before jumping down from the counter. 'You haven't seen anything yet.'

Zoe nodded, wiping her eyes as she tried to catch her breath while Steph danced across the room. She was wild. She was like one of those crazy college girls she saw in films – always up for anything. Zoe and Nina had an off-button and generally knew when to stop, but not Steph. There was *always* a story to tell after a night out with her.

'So, you can sing in French but you can't speak it?' Jerome asked as the others went back to the sofas to carry on the drinking game they were playing.

'I can say "*Où est le gare?*" Does that count?'

'Only if there's a train station nearby.'

Zoe shrugged and laughed before hopping down from the counter. 'Be right back.'

As the night had worn on, she'd been more and more drawn towards Jerome. The attraction between them was undeniable and she didn't want to break that, but she desperately needed the toilet. In the bathroom, Zoe looked in the mirror above the sink as she washed her hands.

'Zoe, it's us. Open up.'

She flicked the water off her hands and unlocked the bathroom door to let Steph and Nina in. At least she wasn't the only one looking a bit of a mess. Steph's lipstick had faded, leaving pink stains behind and Nina's eyes were red from night after night of too much booze and not enough sleep.

Zoe grinned. 'You look smashed.'

'You don't look so grand yourself,' Nina replied.

The girls laughed and crowded around the mirror, retouching make-up and fixing their hair.

'So, we're going to hit the beach and watch the sunrise in a bit,' Steph said.

So far, they'd watched sunsets at the iconic Café Del Mar and on their one cultural excursion to Ibiza Town, but with all of their late nights, the sunrise was something they hadn't yet specifically set out to see.

'Cool, that sounds good,' she replied.

Nina snickered. 'You're not coming.'

'Why not?' Zoe frowned.

Her friends turned to face her and Steph stood with a hand on her hip – a sure sign that she was about to go into leadership mode.

'Look,' Steph said. 'It's nearly five in the morning. If you want something to happen with Jerome, you have to do it now.'

'She's right,' Nina said. 'If you wait much longer, the moment will be gone. You two have been huddled together all night, he clearly likes you.'

'Come on. Look at the state of me. I'm not wearing a hint of make-up and my hair's ridiculous.' Zoe sniffed her armpit. 'I'm sweaty and I didn't bother shaving this morning.'

'As if he'll care,' Steph laughed. 'You look fine.'

'Please,' Zoe replied, deadpan. 'I look like a deranged scarecrow.'

Steph tutted. 'A touch dramatic, don't you think? Just freshen up in the sink and away you go.'

Zoe laughed as if it were the most insane thing she'd ever heard. She'd had one-night stands before. But this felt different.

'Do you really want to go back to London wondering what could've been?' Nina asked, raising her eyebrows.

'Well, what about you two?' Zoe said. 'I can't leave you to go off with a bunch of random blokes.'

'They're not random and we'll be fine.'

Zoe shook her head with a smile. Nina and Steph were strong personalities on their own, but together they were formidable.

'I hate it when you're right,' Zoe said, and Steph laughed before they left her alone in the bathroom.

She stood in front of the mirror and checked her reflection again. She'd known this was coming all night. How could she not have? And she was sure Jerome knew it too. So why was she suddenly so nervous? Her stomach leapt at the thought of him out there, just a few feet away. Maybe she actually, really liked him. It would explain why she'd pretty much dragged Nina and Steph from bar to bar over the last few days, hoping to catch a glimpse of his tattooed arms or dark hair.

Zoe shook her head and squared her shoulders with more bravado than she really felt. Thinking about the way she'd existed on bated breath over the last few days in anticipation over seeing him again would only make her even more nervous than she already was. If she didn't do it now, she never would and Nina was right. Zoe would hate going home wondering, *what if?*

Zoe left the bathroom and closed the door behind her, just as Jerome emerged from one of the bedrooms.

'A little accident with the beer,' he laughed, tugging on a t-shirt that was different to the one he'd been wearing before.

'They're going to watch the sunrise in a bit,' Zoe said, looking at his face and taking in his features – the faded scar on his jaw, the light coating of stubble and his full lips.

He nodded. 'I know.'

Her heartbeat went into overdrive as she slowly closed the gap between them in the hallway. He stood with his face less than an inch away from hers and Zoe hooked a finger under the top of his jeans, pulling him towards her.

◆ ◆ ◆

The next morning, Zoe, Steph and Nina walked out of the boys' hotel with their heels in their hands and the sun in their eyes.

'Sooooo,' Nina said as they set off down the yellow-paved street. 'Details.'

Zoe grinned. 'Amazing.'

'I knew he would be. He's got that look about him.'

'As if you can tell if someone's good in bed from the way they look,' Zoe replied.

'Of course you can. It's in the way they carry themselves. Right, Steph?'

'Yeah, sure,' Steph replied curtly, shielding her eyes with her free hand. 'I can't talk right now or I'll puke.'

Zoe and Nina laughed. Her own hangover wasn't nearly as bad but, then again, being with Jerome had probably taken the bite out of it. Her body pulsed with the memory of his body on hers. If he weren't leaving today, she'd probably have made plans to go back for more.

'Oh, you've got that smitten look on your face,' Nina said with a grin.

'We've swapped numbers. I think I like him,' Zoe admitted. 'Thanks for the nudge, guys. I'd have been too chicken otherwise.'

'Why are there so many people up this early?' Steph said with a groan as a couple walked past with a screaming toddler in a pushchair.

'It's almost two in the afternoon, Steph,' Zoe replied.

Steph groaned again. 'Then why do I still have a hangover?'

'Because you haven't had a drink yet,' Nina laughed.

So far, their holiday breakfasts had been part food, part hair of the dog. Zoe was secretly craving a fresh fruit salad and a week's detox, but they only had one day left and she was certain it wasn't going to be a quiet one, despite the lack of sleep.

'Oh, God,' Steph groaned and bent double, throwing up onto the side of the road.

Nina immediately grabbed Steph's long hair to keep it back from her face, and Zoe made a lunge for her shoes and bag – a tag-team move that had been perfected over the years.

'All done?' Nina asked as Steph stood back up.

Steph spat onto the ground and nodded gingerly before taking back her bag and shoes. 'Thanks guys.'

Zoe shrugged and Nina laughed as they stood on either side of Steph and each hooked an arm around hers. What else were friends for?

Chapter Twelve

I stand by the window, directing the two men who've somehow managed to haul my new sofa up the narrow staircase. They position it to face the wall with the closed-up fireplace that, somehow, I'd missed on the first viewing. The flat has been a hive of activity all day and the doorbell has rung so often with deliveries, that I've simply left the door to the street wedged open. The new dishwasher has been plumbed in, Nina's at the supermarket getting some essentials and, now that the sofa's here, the last major job for today is building the bed.

'All set,' Jude says, handing me the television remote.

After not having a television for years, I'd got right back into it at Mum's. I don't know how much it says about soaps, but I've managed to pick up the storylines to my old favourites with so much ease, it's as if I've barely taken a break from watching them at all.

'You're a genius,' I say with a smile.

'All in a day's work,' he replies and frowns as I rub the small of my back. 'Back ache?'

'A little.'

He shakes his head with a little smile that says *I told you so.*

'It goes with the territory,' I explain, looking at my bump.

'Maybe, but I'm sure carrying all those boxes didn't help.'

'I'm pregnant, not disabled,' I reply softly.

I'd been told not to lift a finger, but there was no way I could sit around like a useless lump all day. And who was to say the twinging isn't just from being pregnant? When I consider the fact that my body has to make space for a baby which is now the size of a bell pepper, it makes total sense.

'Yeah, well. If you were *my* girlfriend, I'd have had you sitting on the sofa with your feet up. But hey, what do I know?'

'More than some, apparently,' I reply.

Jude's words hit me unexpectedly in the chest with a thud and it's like being in IKEA, watching that couple all over again. When it comes to feminism, I'm not quite as radical as Nina but it's a given in my world that I ought to be able to live the life I want, earn a wage that isn't reduced because of my gender and not be treated as a possession. But pregnancy has, if not changed that, then softened it. Now, I find myself wanting to have doors opened for me. I appreciate it when a man offers his seat on public transport and, even though the choice to lift and move stuff around today was my decision and Jude *had* told me to take it easy, I can't help but wish it would have come from a partner.

I sigh and Jude looks at me, taking a swig from a cup of tea that was made so long ago it must be stone cold by now.

'Why are you looking at me like that?' I ask, my eyes narrowing with suspicion.

He tilts his head from side to side. 'I'm wondering if I'll put my foot in it by mentioning *he who shall not be named.*'

'You mean Sam?'

'It was Nina's name for him. She's been *very* clear about not bringing him up.'

I laugh. 'In case my water breaks early with the trauma of it or what?'

'Something like that,' he laughs back and shrugs. 'I'm just wondering how someone could let their pregnant girlfriend fly halfway around the world and do all this on her own.'

I cup the top of my belly protectively, as if it can somehow block out the conversation from the baby's ears.

'That makes two of us,' I reply.

'Well, for what it's worth, I think you're really brave.'

Why couldn't Sam have been more like Jude? It's a thought that feels guilt-ridden, as if it's some kind of betrayal, but he's bent over backwards getting this place ready, and it's not even his baby. Not to mention, he knows his way around a toolkit – something Sam was hopeless at. I've never considered myself as brave, but it gives me a warm burst of happiness and a little nudge of confidence. A fluttering feeling blooms in my belly and I gasp, moving my hand further down my bump towards my groin.

'What is it?' Jude asks, putting his cup down quickly.

I shake my head with a little laugh. 'I think I just felt the baby move.'

It's the most surreal feeling I've ever had, and it most definitely was *not* wind. I shake my head again as relief floods through my body.

'I've been a bit worried it hadn't happened sooner,' I say, giggling with the excitement of it and the slightly alarmed look on Jude's face. 'You look totally freaked out.'

'I'm okay,' he smiles uneasily, shaking it off. 'I was just wondering if you were going to throw up again, that's all.'

I roll my eyes. 'Thanks for the reminder.'

'I'll go get on with the bed,' Jude says, picking up the small toolkit on the windowsill.

'You don't have to finish it today,' I say as my phone rings. I look down at it and see Mum's name flashing on the screen.

'Do you really want to sleep on the floor?' he asks with a raised eyebrow.

'Well, no, but—'

'Exactly,' he grins. 'I've done most of it already anyway.'

He turns to leave me to it and I slide my finger across the phone to take the video call.

'Hi, Mum,' I smile into the phone. 'How are you?'

'Not much has changed since you saw me this morning, Zoe,' she replies with a laugh. 'How's it going?'

'Good,' I nod. 'Everything's been delivered, Nina's grabbing some shopping and Jude's putting the bed together.'

I look at her on the screen, propped up on the sofa where she's set up camp since the operation two days ago. I'd felt like the worst child in the world saying goodbye to her this morning, as if I were abandoning her right when she needs me the most. Except, Barry had been there and, just as Mum had said he would, he'd assumed the role of primary carer with ease. He'd been tactful enough to be mindful of not shoving me completely out of the way. He's good natured, with a lot of patience and when he'd cooked a huge pot of pepper-pot soup, I'd known Mum would be well looked after. Especially because he'd gone out of his way to get the exact blend of spices Mum likes.

'Show us around?' Mum asks, moving the phone a little to include Barry in the call.

I wave at him before taking them on a tour of the flat with Mum oohing and aahing as we go. It's all absolutely warranted. The flat couldn't look any different to how it did when I'd first seen it. The floorboards are, as Jude had promised, beautiful and light, giving the rooms a golden hue. The kitchen is compact but the reflective surfaces and bright lighting make it look and feel bigger than it is. A shower has been installed in the bathroom and thankfully the awful toilet has been replaced and a new extractor fan fitted.

'He's done a good job hasn't he?' Mum says. 'Debbie would be proud.'

'She would,' I agreed, returning to the kitchen.

Nina's come back from the supermarket with what looks like much more than just the essentials she'd been tasked with buying.

'Is it your mum?' Nina asks and when I nod, she takes the phone for a chat.

She wanders into the living room, leaving me to unpack the shopping. It seems that being pregnant hasn't only kicked in my own maternal response, but Nina's too. Then again, she's always been the friend to hold your hair back after one too many shots. I think back to the last girls' holiday we'd had as a trio in Ibiza and my smile at the memory of Nina doing just that with Steph. I wipe the insides of one of the empty cupboards with a cloth before putting in bags of rice, couscous and pasta. At one time, the idea of Steph not knowing when something as major as pregnancy was happening in one of our lives would've been unthinkable. It was funny how quickly we'd adapted to life without her.

When I finish unpacking the shopping, Jude walks in with his toolkit.

'That was quick,' I say, raising my eyebrows.

'I told you it would be,' he smiles, rubbing his eye with his free hand.

'You. Are. A. Legend,' I smile.

Jude isn't overtly muscular to look at, but as he runs his hand back and forth over his shaved head, his tattooed bicep looks huge. I don't know why I'm surprised after seeing the machines, tools and bits of furniture he's carried up and down the stairs all day with ease. He blows a raspberry and shakes his head as if he's trying to wake himself up.

'You look exhausted,' I say gently. 'I was just about to make something to eat. Nothing fancy, just some potatoes and veg. Want some?'

The skin around his eyes crinkles as he returns my smile. 'I'd love to, but I've got plans already.'

'Big night?'

'Bigger than I'd like. I'd rather crash in front of the TV but I can't really cancel.'

Of course. It's the weekend and he probably has a date or a night out planned with his mates.

'I bet you're glad to finally have your weekends back,' I say with a grimace.

'You say it like it's been awful spending them here.'

'I know I've said it before but, thanks. I really do appreciate it. You have to let me know how to repay you.'

'I hate to break it to you, Zoe, but I haven't been doing this for free,' he says with a laugh. 'Besides, it was either now or in August and I want to keep that clear.'

'Holiday?'

'I'm going to Portugal for a couple of weeks.'

'Nice. I spent some time there a few years back. I loved it, Lisbon especially.'

'I'll be surfing mostly if I've got anything to do with it, but maybe I can get some tips a bit closer to the time?'

'Absolutely. The coast is gorgeous too,' I reply with a nostalgic smile. 'We did the whole van-life thing for two weeks before I gave out and demanded a place that wasn't on wheels and had a flushable toilet.'

Jude laughs. 'You're not a camper, then?'

'Living with your partner in a tiny van for days on end gets crowded. But for a weekend thing, like a festival? I could do that.'

'Fair enough.'

'Actually,' I say, tilting my head to one side, 'Nina said you'd be a good person to speak to about festivals and which might be a good one to go to.'

'It depends what you're looking for,' he replies as Nina comes back into the kitchen. 'I'm only going to Solar this year.'

'Oh, yeah,' she says, handing my phone back, 'I totally forgot to tell you, I checked Solar out too and it looks perfect for your list. Don't you think, Jude?'

He raises his eyebrows and shrugs. 'I mean, it's a festival. It'll be loud and crowded. I don't know how much fun it'd be for a pregnant woman.'

Nina pulls a few grapes from the bunch she's just bought. 'If you can have kids there it can't be that bad. When do tickets go on sale?'

'They already are,' Jude replies. 'They might have even sold out by now.'

I might not have been to a big festival before, but I know plenty of people who have and it always sounded like a pain to get tickets. It had put me off which was probably why I'd always found myself watching coverage on TV with envy instead of actually being there in person.

'Maybe I'd be better off at a day festival instead,' I say. 'Wireless, maybe?'

'But then you won't have the camping experience you wanted,' Nina replies.

'That's okay,' I say, and Jude shakes his head.

'Nina's right. A day thing's great and all, but it's a different experience to camp for the weekend.'

'I'll be almost seven months gone by then. Can you imagine me waddling around a festival with a bump?' I shake my head and break the green stem from an orange bell pepper. 'It was a silly idea to start with.'

'I think,' Nina says, 'you should check out the website and *then* decide. We could all go together. I mean, how fun would that be?'

When I'd put it on my unsexy bucket list, I'd had no concept of what life with a belly would feel like. Now I do. The sickness has gone, but my centre of gravity has left with it, leaving me off-balance. Then there's the ridiculous regularity with which I need to pee which will probably mean spending half the time in skanky Portaloos. But, as I put the pepper on the draining board, I realise Nina and Jude aren't wrong. I'd made that list for a reason. It feels important to have the full experience and, let's be honest, this is probably the closest I'll get to a holiday this summer.

'We could even camp together,' Nina suggests. 'We'd have our own tent, obviously. It could be cool, right, Jude?'

A look flickers across his face that says it would be anything but as he picks up his toolbox from the counter. 'Why don't you look at it first, and then we'll talk? I've got to get going.'

'I'll see you out,' I say quickly, leaving Nina to rinse the rest of the vegetables. I pull a face as we got to the front door. 'I'm sorry. I feel like we've just hijacked your plans.'

He smiles wryly. 'Don't be. I'm used to it.'

'So, we *would* be hijacking then?'

His smile turns into a laugh. 'Like I said, let's talk if it looks like it's happening.'

I get it. That's the nice thing about having known someone for so many years – he doesn't have to try and cover up his discomfort about his sister and her friend tagging along to a festival. He hadn't even said who he was going with. It could be a group of friends but it could also be someone he's seeing. A breeze carries up the stairs from the door that's been wedged open and I catch the scent of London in late spring, a mix of warm tarmac and greenery.

'Let me know when you want to finish putting the other stuff together,' Jude says, taking his van keys from his pocket.

There's still half of IKEA waiting to be assembled in the bedroom and nursery, but I'm in no rush.

'How can you sound like you're actually looking forward to it?' I ask, shaking my head with a laugh. 'Assembling furniture is the worst. I can't even put up shelves.'

'It's not hard if you know how.'

'It's your job,' I smirk. 'Of course you'd say that.'

'I mean it. Add it to your list and when you've got time, give me a call. I'll show you how it's done.'

His brown eyes hold mine in a friendly challenge and I grin. 'Alright, I will do. And thanks again, for today.'

He smiles again and uses his free hand to wrap me in a hug. A base layer of the type of shower gel marked as *for men* mixed with a hint of sweat and the earthy scent of wood settles around my shoulders. It's a masculine combination that I've somehow missed without even knowing it until now.

'Enjoy your first night in the flat,' he says, pulling away.

'I will.' I wrap my arms around myself as he starts down the stairs. 'Have fun tonight.'

Jude turns for a second and grins. 'I will.'

A burst of longing flames in my chest as I close the door. Suddenly, I miss that feeling of the weekend stretching out with possibilities ahead. Dinner, drinks, going to a club, meeting people. Life with Sam meant always having people around. Now, I'm living on my own in a world that feels like its reducing and expanding at the same time. On the way back to the kitchen I rummage in the box containing my laptop and work things to retrieve my journal. I pull out a piece of folded paper, read the list I'd made at Nina's and strike a line through the first item.

Pre-baby unsexy bucket list
~~Find a flat~~
Make money!
Have a spa day
Go to a festival
Make a fire from scratch
Learn to bake
Do a belly cast

I add a new line:

Learn DIY/flatpack

I smile at the last item and take the paper along with a roll of tape from the box to the kitchen.

'Nice,' Nina says as I tape it to the fridge. 'Already smashing it.'

'It does feel kind of nice to have some goals over the next few months,' I reply before turning to look at her with a wary smile. 'Remember that holiday in Ibiza?'

'Which one?'

'The last one.'

Nina's forehead flickers. 'Sure. What made you think of that?'

I pick up a jar of mixed herbs and pull the tray of chunky chopped vegetables that Nina's prepared towards me.

'I don't know,' I reply, sprinkling oregano, marjoram and rosemary on top. 'Just reminiscing I guess.'

We'd all been such good friends. I'd thought Steph would be in my life forever. Then again, I'd thought the same thing about Sam and look where we are now – on opposite sides of the world with not so much as an emoji conversation between us. When you felt so strongly for someone, where did all those feelings go when things ended?

'It feels weird that Steph's not here sometimes, don't you think?' I ask. 'Do you ever think about her?'

'No, I don't,' Nina replies curtly.

But that little sliver of a flashback from our last girls' holiday together is stirring up memories that had been buried a long time ago and not without effort. I've trained myself not to think about her over the years. Did I miss her? Sure, sometimes. But the betrayal is stronger than that loss. Maybe the feelings that once existed between people are simply eaten up with time, leaving only raw facts when you looked back on it all. Steph had always needed to be centre of attention. She'd take things that didn't belong to her with a sense of entitlement, just because she could. She'd been a great friend, and the worst of friends. Maybe it would be the same with Sam. Maybe, one day, I'd look back and see that his way of relating and the need to keep his options open were more to do with selfishness than being forward thinking. Maybe.

Nina and I settle into the brand-new sofa with our feet propped up on a couple of boxes as we eat. An intermittent breeze carries in the sound of traffic from the road but after so many nights at Mum's with the idiot midnight racers, I barely even hear it.

'I lied before,' Nina says, biting into an almond Magnum ice-cream.

'About what?'

She rolls her eyes as if it pains her to say it. 'Steph.'

'Oh.'

I'd thought as much. Steph might be persona non grata, but Nina isn't as harsh or heartless as she can make herself sound.

'So, you *do* think about her?' I ask, unwrapping my ice-cream.

'Not often, but sometimes.'

'Same,' I reply as I tentatively bite through the chocolate coating.

I've never liked ice-cream. It probably goes against every law of life there is, but I've never cared for the texture and coldness of it. For the last week though, it's all I've been able to think about and I'd surprised myself by actually popping into the corner shop on my way back from the doctor's the other day and buying one.

After a few moments of nibbling at the chocolate shell of my ice-cream, I laugh. 'Remember how she used to convince bouncers she was on *Geordie Shore*?'

Despite coming from Kent, Steph had put on a perfect Newcastle accent and got us into countless clubs pretending to be a reality TV star.

'Yeah. She had that bullshit-ability,' Nina replies.

'I was thinking about Ibiza earlier. It was a great holiday, wasn't it? I remember thinking how lucky I was to have two such amazing best friends.'

'Aw, shucks,' Nina replies with mock shyness.

'It's true though. And it's so nice to be back because it's only now that I realise how much I've missed *this*. Hanging out in real time, in person. Life with Sam was about new experiences and places and people . . .' I shake my head. 'But wow. There's nothing like being with people you really *know*.'

'There's no place like home.'

'Exactly. Being back here and remembering how things used to be is making me think about things with a different perspective. I mean, if you'd have told me a year ago I'd be living alone in a flat above a dentist's in Peckham . . .'

The little flutter I'd felt in my belly earlier comes back and I smile, dropping a hand onto my bump. Surely it can't be a coincidence that my baby's saved her first movements to be at the exact moments when I've been talking about being here, in this place, with my people around me. If that isn't a sign of being on the right track, I don't know what is.

Chapter Thirteen

Cool water glides across my skin as I swim, making wide leisurely circles with my arms and legs, just like Dad taught me. A couple of days ago, I'd made the mistake of coming earlier in the morning to swim in lanes. After years of swimming in the wildness of the sea, it had felt too narrow and my pace had been slow. I'd felt flustered, certain that I was getting in the way of people who'd wanted to put serious laps in before work. I'd wanted to apologise, to insist that I was a very strong, confident and competent swimmer who could be left to go way out at sea, even in choppy conditions. But then I'd thought, *who cares?* and come in later today.

It's no longer rush hour and the leisure centre is living up to its name. The lanes are gone, leaving the pool free for everyone to go at their own pace. A group of seniors are in the shallow end doing water aerobics and, apart from a couple of other swimmers, I'm alone as I make my way along the length of the pool. The weight of my belly is surprisingly non-existent in the water, and I like the idea of my baby floating around in there while I'm in the water, too. The leisure centre has been majorly overhauled since the days when Dad worked here, but still, it feels familiar. The smell of chlorine and the bright lights belong to a part of my childhood just as much as the ritual of getting chips after a swim does. Running was never my thing and I've always hated the gym, but being in the water has always been my happy place. It's a place where I can let my mind go, which is exactly what I need today.

As I slice through the water, I turn the idea I've come up with to increase my income over in my head. I went self-employed for a whole load of reasons, one of which was to be able to live the kind of lifestyle I wanted – a lifestyle that has no space for working when I should be focused on life as a new mum. I need to earn some serious money before the baby comes. Putting my prices up isn't enough, and ideally I don't want to have any clients at all past month eight. The idea that had come to me when I'd first ducked under the surface half an hour ago was: what if I could find a way to get a bunch of clients before then and do the work in much less time? The most time-consuming thing about my job is people changing their minds about the design of their site, or wanting added, fancy extras. I turn at the end of the pool to change directions. Imagine if I could do the work that normally took weeks, in just one day? There must be a bunch of people who are just starting out with their business, or don't need something with bells and whistles. They might be happy for something with a quicker turnaround.

By the time I leave the leisure centre with my damp hair wrapped up in a headscarf, I've fleshed my idea out some more and feel galvanised by the rush of a new project. Swimming again after such a long time was like getting an MOT. I feel clearheaded and motivated. I've mentally assembled my to-do list for the week and decided on a concept for the roof terrace to chat through with Jude. It's a gorgeous June morning and my bump is poking out between the lapels of my light blazer. I cross the road, feeling the hard tarmac beneath my thin-soled espadrille shoes, and duck into a greasy-spoon cafe to get a roll and hot chocolate before walking the few minutes to Mum's.

The sun is in full force as I walk through the courtyard towards the main door of the block. I'd really hated this estate at first. All I'd wanted was to go back to the house we'd lived in before, where there'd been a garden instead of a square of concrete with signs that read, *no ball games, no cycling* and might as well have said, *no fun*. I'd adapted quickly though, probably because I still had my friends around me. Our old house is just a few streets away and I hadn't had to move schools. At least Mum and I hadn't had to find new friends just because of a philandering man. Anger quietly boils under my skin as I think about Sam, even though, technically, he hadn't cheated. I shake the thought of him away. I've had a gorgeous start to the day and don't want to lose it thinking about things I can't change anyway.

I use the brass knocker on the door and smile when Mum opens it.

'Why don't you use your key?' she asks.

'Because.'

'It's still your home, you know.'

'I know,' I reply with a smile.

But it isn't. Not really, not anymore. And I don't mind at all, because for all my protesting, it's how things should be. I follow her as she walks slowly back inside. The wall-hanging coat rack that Mum had bought ages ago but never got round to putting up is now where it should always have been, and the tap in the kitchen no longer dribbles. It isn't that Mum doesn't know how to do those things. It's thanks to her that I know how to change a fuse and a toilet seat (which was much trickier than it looked). Mum had done everything when I was a kid because she'd had to, but it's nice that she doesn't *have* to do these things alone anymore. She has Barry to take some of the maintenance from her hands.

'Do you want some breakfast? There's some fried dumplings in the microwave if you want them.'

'Ooh, yeah,' I grin, ducking into the kitchen. I take three of them in my hands. They've cooled down but the dough inside is still fluffy and they coat my fingertips in a light coating of oil.

'Why don't you make some beans or something to go with it?'

'It's fine, I had a roll on the way over,' I reply with a full mouth. 'How are you doing?'

'Great,' she replies, muting *This Morning* on the television as we settled into the sofa. 'With any luck I'll be back at work in a week or two.'

'Already?' I raise my eyebrows.

'You know me. I hate being idle.'

I'd be surprised if Mum even knows what being idle really means. It was totally normal when I was a kid for the aroma of our Sunday dinner to be wafting through the flat before I'd even opened my eyes in the morning. I'd heard song lyrics once that said if you were poor, you were never bored. And while we hadn't been poor necessarily, there'd definitely been no time for boredom.

'I was thinking of redecorating the hallway,' Mum says.

'*Mum*,' I groan and shake my head.

She's always been a spontaneous decorator, changing wall colours and furniture arrangements on a whim, especially right before Christmas. I've lost count of the number of times I'd come home from school to find the living room had had a facelift in the few hours I'd been gone.

'You're supposed to be resting,' I say.

'Well, Barry would be doing most of it and I can't just lie around all the time, it'll do more damage than good the doctor said. I have to start moving.'

I take another bite of my dumpling. I suppose I can't argue with that.

'You've been swimming?' Mum asks, and I nod back.

'When are you going to come with?'

'I'm supposed to be resting, remember?'

It's a smart way to avoid answering. Mum's as strong a swimmer as I am and I'd thought it would be a great way to spend time together while keeping fit. But whenever I've brought it up, I've been stonewalled. As far as I know, she hasn't dipped even a toenail into a pool since Dad left.

'Well, she loves it,' I say with a smile, rubbing a hand across my belly.

Mum looks at me quizzically. 'She? How do you know it's a girl?'

'Just a feeling.'

'Are you going to find out?'

'Maybe,' I shrug. 'I'm not sure yet.'

I've got my twenty-week scan next week and as much as I want to be one of those people who says the sex of the baby doesn't matter as long as it's healthy – which is of course true – I know myself. It'll be next to impossible to say no to knowing.

'It'll make buying things easier when you know,' Mum reasons.

I laugh. 'I'll have everything neutral anyway. I'm not buying into that whole pink is for girls, blue is for boys rubbish. And I've already got the paint for the nursery. I went for oatmeal.'

'Why do they have fancy names for things now? Before, it would've just been called beige.'

'Probably so they can charge five times more for it?'

'Speaking of,' Mum says, readjusting herself slowly in her seat. 'How are things on that front?'

'They're okay.'

I'd been under no illusion that moving would be expensive and everyone has been so generous. Nina gifted me that first grocery shop, stocking my fridge and cupboards with a mix of essentials and treats, and Mum and Barry have taken care of practical things like tea towels, cleaning products, glass food containers, towels and bedsheets. And of course, Jude had given his time and energy with work. But still, there are things I hadn't planned on, but needed. Like pots and pans and a brush for the toilet that weren't expensive by themselves but still added up to a substantial amount of money. And of course, there are things I still need for the baby – bottles, a steriliser, nappies – a cot and a pram at the minimum.

'Do you need some help?' Mum asks.

'Thanks, Mum, but it'll be fine,' I reply. It isn't like she's got a pot of gold stashed somewhere. 'Actually, I had an idea this morning that I think will bring in a fair bit of money.'

'What's that then?'

'Instead of working with a client for three months to build a website, I'm going to offer simpler versions that can be done in a day. Not everyone needs something fancy.'

'Sounds reasonable. How much can you get for that?'

'Not sure yet. I've got to calculate some stuff, but a grand. Grand and a half, maybe?'

I can tell by the sceptical look on her face that it sounds ridiculous, but the more I think about it, the more I think it'll work.

'Will people really buy it?' Mum asks, pulling a face.

'Sure. People usually want something done *yesterday*. It means I can give them what they want without having to lock myself in for three months at a time. If I can get ten people in before the baby comes, that's ten grand at least, and I don't think that's an unreasonable guess.'

Being self-employed comes with a lot of perks, but the downsides are: no work equals no income. I don't want to have to juggle a newborn and clients. At least this way, I can give myself a cut-off date to go on maternity leave without working myself into the ground before the baby comes.

'I was thinking I should also look into life insurance and stuff like that,' I continue.

I catch the look on Mum's face and it's as if I've just been given a glance of this new me in a mirror. I've never been an insurance type of person. Car and travel insurance, sure. But life insurance? Pensions? I'd never thought about any of that until the flutters in my belly had begun.

'Wow,' I say and take a bite from the last dumpling. 'I guess I officially just became an adult.'

◆ ◆ ◆

Later that week, I swear under my breath and throw the instruction manual I'm holding onto the floor. After a few days of feeling capable and motivated, I'd decided to try and tackle the double length drawers I'd ordered from IKEA that have been propped up in their flat-pack box behind my bedroom door. I know Jude had offered to help, but there's a part of me that wants to be able to do these things myself and besides, how hard could it be? I sigh and swear again. It might not be hard to put together, but for one person alone, it's impossible. I go into the kitchen and pour myself a glass from the pot of mint leaves I boiled earlier before grabbing my phone.

I hover over the message thread with Jude. We haven't spoken since the day I moved in. After all his hard work I hadn't wanted to put any pressure on him to finish the bits and pieces that still needed to be done. Especially because I'd told him there was no need to rush. And I'd meant it too, until a few hours ago when I'd almost lost it searching for a pair of maternity shorts I'd bought just yesterday and could no longer find. At twenty weeks I'm too big now for the elastic band trick and the thought of having my legs covered in this heat had almost sent me over the edge. I *have* to get some order in the flat. And it would be nice to cross the flatpack construction off my list.

I take a long glug of my drink, letting the coolness of the mint help calm my nerves and go back to the bedroom. I take a photo of my furniture assembling attempt and send it to Jude.

Zoe: Apparently building these things is a two-man job . . . SOS?

I add some wacky emojis to make it sound less sad as irritation adds to the heat flushing my skin. There's nothing like failing at flatpack furniture to make you feel down yourself. After a few minutes without reply, I go into the room next door. Soon, it'll be a nursery, but right now, it's being used as storage. The parquet floor doesn't reach to the bedrooms and despite having the windows open almost constantly, it still smells of the fresh carpet that's been put in. I go into the living room where I lie, splayed on the sofa in front of the TV until my phone vibrates. I open the reply from Jude, prefaced with a row of laughing emojis.

Jude: Well, good on you for trying. I'm free now if you are?

Zoe: Lifesaver. Yes please!

Jude: Give me an hour.

I heave myself up from the sofa and go back into the bedroom to rifle through my growing selection of bras. My breasts feel enormous – much too big now to get away without being safely contained behind a barrier of cloth and wire. And even though I've known Jude forever, there's no need to let him be exposed to that. It'll be almost seven by the time he gets here and, while I don't know if *he'll* be hungry, I know I will be. I throw a salad together before marinating a couple of chicken breasts. The thought comes into my head that I really should've done it this morning when I'd known it was what I'd wanted for dinner, and I hear it with the sound of Mum's voice. The fact that pregnancy seems to be literally turning me into my own mother makes me laugh as I put the chicken back in the fridge along with the salad dressing for later.

When the buzzer rings, I stand holding the door to the flat open with my foot and grin at Jude as he comes upstairs with a small tool bag.

'The cavalry has arrived,' he says, grinning back.

I tiptoe to hug him hello and am again greeted by the scent of wood and fresh sweat that seems to be his own personal brand of aftershave.

'I hope I haven't disturbed you from something?' I ask, closing the door behind him.

He shakes his head. 'I'd just finished football when I saw your message.'

'Did you win?'

'Of course.'

It feels like he's brought a different kind of energy with him that somehow makes the flat feel more occupied than before.

'So.' He lifts the toolkit. 'Where's the scene of the crime?'

I giggle and take him to the bedroom, sweeping my arm extravagantly to show him my handiwork, or lack of it. Jude crouches his tall frame down to the ground and has a quick flick through the assembly instruction manual.

He looks up at me with a little tug of his eyebrows. 'You know you could've just called, right? I did say I'd help you with this stuff.'

'I know.' I sit on the bed crossing my legs. 'But you were busy.'

'How would you know? You don't call, you don't write . . .' He smiles playfully. 'If I were the sensitive type I might read all sorts into it.'

'I didn't want to bug you,' I reply with a small laugh. 'And you know, I'm a modern woman. I wanted to try it myself without having to have you come rescue me.'

'If it's any consolation, it looks like you almost succeeded. It's just too heavy to lift alone in your condition.'

'I don't want to just assume I can click my fingers and you'll come running because we're friends.'

'Good. Because you can't,' he laughs, 'but I said I'd help and I meant it.'

People always have plenty of bad things to say about boys who are raised without dads around, but Jude's clearly positive proof that a single mum can bring up a boy to be a good man. That and the fact that I'm not just some random person he can give promises to and not uphold. I let a puff of pride chip away at the inept frustration I'd felt earlier. I'd actually done really well. If it were smaller and I didn't have to avoid heavy lifting, I might well have been able to finish it myself after all.

'Did you get the email about the festival?' Jude asks as he hammers a nail into the thin board at the back of the drawers.

'Yeah, I saw it this morning,' I reply. 'I still haven't decided yet.'

'Well, I wouldn't hang around, they sell out really quickly. We've already got ours.'

'Who are you going with?'

'Couple of mates. It's not a big group.'

'Ah, I thought we might be gatecrashing a romantic weekend.' I pick up a stray t-shirt from the floor and fling it onto the bed.

'I don't know if I'd class a festival as a romantic weekend, but whatever floats your boat.'

I laugh. 'Me neither, to be fair. Won't your mates mind your sister and a pregnant woman invading a boys' trip?'

'One's a girl, one's a guy. It's not a "bros' trip",' Jude replies with a small smile. 'Any other wild guesses you want to make?'

'Nope, not right now,' I smile back, hiding the embarrassment creeping under my warm cheeks.

He shakes his head with the smile still lingering on his face. 'To answer your question, no. They won't mind.'

'Awesome.'

Have I been wrong for assuming that if he hadn't been going on a date then he had to be going with a group of guys for a messy weekend? I must admit, I'm relieved. I've looked at the festival website and watched videos of the previous years, and I actually really want to go. It looks like the perfect combination of live music, nice people and workshops. And they have a swimming lake. I'd take that over a field full of mud any day.

Jude puts the hammer down. 'Alright. So, where do you want it?'

'Just here, against the wall.'

I go to take the opposite end but he shoos me away before manoeuvring the furniture into place.

'Happy?'

He looks at me and I nod. 'I am. It looks like a proper bedroom now.'

'You mean the bed didn't do that already?'

He's clearly in a playful mood and I decide to let it wash away the funk I'd got myself into earlier. He's right. I should've just called and asked for help instead of trying to do it all myself. I could've kept myself on the high I'd been on all week.

'Hungry?' I ask.

'Why are you always trying to feed me?' he replies, picking up his tools. 'Do I look like I need fattening up?'

'God, no.' I shake my head. Jude's height matches his build perfectly. 'I just eat a lot these days. Food is on my mind pretty much constantly at the moment. I've made some salad and I'll put some chicken in the oven. You'd be more than welcome to join.'

'That'd be great,' Jude replies, patting his lean stomach. 'I didn't eat yet.'

We go through to the kitchen and Jude looks at the list taped to the door of the fridge as I open it to take out the chicken and salad.

'DIY/flatpack,' he reads. 'You were *so* close.'

'I know, right? Now you see why I was so reluctant to call you,' I smile.

Jude looks around at the kitchen. 'So, you're feeling all good and settled here then?'

'I am,' I smile, handing him the bowl of salad. 'It was nice at Mum's but I have to admit, it's nice to have my own space.'

He crosses his arms. 'How's she doing?'

'She's good. I'm just glad she didn't need chemo.'

'Yeah, I bet. Chemo's a nasty business.'

The easy lilt to his voice drops for a second and I guess he's remembering the short battle his mum had had with the same disease. I turn the grill on and despite the door to the terrace being open, the air in the flat feels still. I consider putting the radio on but there's something about the current calmness that I don't want to disturb with music.

'How do you feel about onions?' I ask.

'Raw?' He raises his eyebrows and I nod. 'I will if you will.'

'Awesome. You finish the salad and I'll fry the chicken.'

He takes an onion from the bowl next to the cooker before re-mixing the dressing I'd made earlier.

He tastes it and frowns. 'Have you got any vinegar?'

I point to one of the cupboards, blinking against the stinging building in my eyes as I thinly slice the onion.

'Is that something you picked up from food tech?' I ask with a little giggle.

When Jude had chosen food technology at school for GCSE, it had caused quite the stir. Back then, food and textiles were for girls while the boys went straight for design and technology or computer science.

'Yeah, yeah.' He rolls his eyes. 'Everyone laughed but who's the one who actually knows how to make a salad dressing?'

I set about frying the marinated chicken breast. 'Seems like a waste of a couple of years, given your job now.'

'Oh, I don't know. I learned how to cook and all my mates were jealous because I got to know all the fit girls in our year better than they did.'

'Ah. Now it all comes out.' I shake my head. 'That makes much more sense.'

'I didn't expect to like it much but I learned a lot,' he shrugs with a hapless grin. 'You can't say that doesn't taste better now.'

He hands me the glass and I take a sip of the dressing. The apple cider vinegar has added a touch of sharpness that had, in hindsight, been missing.

'It'll do,' I reply, sounding deliberately unimpressed and he simply laughs.

'Mostly I just wanted a lesson where I could hang back and not have much expected of me. Nobody thought I'd be any good at cooking. It was like having a bit of freedom in the schedule.'

I frown. 'Really? I didn't know that.'

If we'd have gone to school in America, Jude would've been the one crowned homecoming king. He played football, rugby and lacrosse, and he was smart. I remember how Nina had always hated having to study for hours just to scrape by, but Jude could skim read the night before an exam and fly through.

'I thought you loved being the centre of attention,' I say. 'Being Mr Popular and having all the girls on your case. Didn't you go out with a girl from my year?'

'Yeah. Sarah something,' Jude laughs, shaking his head at the memory.

Is it just me, or is he cringing a little? Sarah was one of the *it girls* in our year. Going out with her must have only added to his reputation.

'Nina was *pissed* that we went out together.'

'Didn't you all used to be friends?' he continues. 'Or is my memory skewed?'

'No, we were,' I reply, taking two plates from the cupboard. 'Until Year Eight, anyway. Can you grab some cutlery from the drawer there?'

Jude pulls open a drawer and I see him in my mind's eye, putting this whole kitchen together, building the cupboards and screwing in the drawers. We take the food through to the living room and he pushes the coffee table closer towards the sofa.

'So, what happened?' Jude asks as we sit down. 'How did she go from friend to the devil?'

'Oh, she earned those wings. I had a crush on a boy in our year. Nathan Clarke,' I laugh. 'He used to have his hair in curtains, you know that boyband style? Anyway, I had the not so smart idea to write him a love letter.'

'Why not so smart?'

'Because I basically wrote that I'd never even kissed a boy until then. Which, at fourteen was pretty lame. Anyway, I wrote this letter, dropped it into his backpack in biology class and somehow, the next day, it was all around the school. Literally.'

Jude's eyes widen. 'Oh, shit. That was *you?*'

I nod slowly. 'Someone highlighted the parts about me never having kissed anyone before, wanting to lose my virginity to him and basically being a pining mess, photocopied it and stuck it everywhere.'

I can still remember that awful sinking feeling in my belly when I came in the next day and felt everyone's eyes on me. I'd walked through the main doors as people snickered, pointing and laughing behind their hands. I'd never been so mortified in my whole life.

'And it was Sarah who did it?' Jude asks.

'There were rumours. Apparently, she'd fancied him too and felt threatened, I don't know,' I shrug. 'She denied it when I confronted her, but not before telling me I was basically delusional for even thinking Nathan would be interested in *someone like me.*'

'Ouch.'

'I know. She said I tried too hard to be something I wasn't. I was just *too much*. Whatever that meant.'

I can see the memory so clearly in my mind, it's as if it's playing out in front of me. We'd been in the classroom before Latin class and I can see the green board behind Sarah's head now, dusty with years of accumulated chalk. I'd stood there, stunned as the friends I'd had since primary school started shunned me from the group. Latin had always been my least favourite class, but on that day, it had been almost intolerable. I'd sat on my own, feeling embarrassed, small and like an outcast.

'That was the end of our friendship.' I look at Jude and shrug, smiling lightly as if to say, *what can you do?*

'Do you know what?' Jude says. 'I wouldn't go back to those days if you paid me. Too many hormones and not enough self-esteem.'

'Same.'

I do wonder what I would tell myself if I could go back though. How my life might be different. It was a throwaway comment from a fourteen-year-old girl who didn't know any better, but it had stuck. It had been like saying, who did I think I was, to go after someone like Nathan? Being told I was too much meant I've kept myself quiet at times when I should've been loud. Maybe, if I'd felt differently about myself, I'd have told Sam right from the start that I didn't want to close myself off to a life with children. Or that I'd prefer to have a boyfriend that was mine and mine alone, not a boyfriend who sometimes *needed more*.

'So that's my sad little story,' I say with a laugh, feeling strangely naked and vulnerable in front of Jude.

'Kids can be arseholes,' he replies. 'Here's hoping yours won't be one.'

'I'm pretty sure you're not allowed to say stuff like that.'

'So, sue me.'

I smile and shake my head. After never really giving him much thought for so many years, I'm seeing Jude not just as Nina's little brother, but a man in his own right. I look at him sitting on the other side of the sofa and smile.

'You know, you're actually pretty cool,' I say with a grin.

'I'm trying not to be offended that you're only just figuring this out now.' He shakes his head with mock distaste.

I laugh. 'There's a lot I'm only just figuring it out, it seems.'

'You know what they say,' he replies. The knowing smile on his face is accentuated by his brown eyes looking at me as if he knows something I don't. 'Better late than never, right?'

◆ ◆ ◆

Pregnancy week: Twenty
You're the size of a: Banana
Today, I feel: Amazing!

Hello, Little One . . .

I knew it!!! You're a girl!! I would have been this excited if it turned out you were a boy but YAY! A girl! How amazing is this? There's no way I could've said no when she asked if I wanted to find out. You're going to be one in a long line of strong women, little one. It's a pretty good tradition to be born into.

So, we're halfway there. And now I can start thinking about names. Any ideas? I cannot wait to see your little girl eyes :)

Love, Zoe

xx

Chapter Fourteen

'Is it weird to be annoyed by people constantly wanting to touch my belly?' I ask.

'Course not,' Nina replies. 'It's an invasion of privacy.'

'I suppose. I just feel a bit of a cow if I say not to.'

'Your body, your rules. Imagine if you went up to random people asking to feel *their* bellies. You'd probably get arrested.'

I laugh and stretch my legs out along the grass, letting my frilly rah-rah skirt skim my thighs. 'True.'

Tell that to the old ladies in Sainsbury's this morning. It feels as if being pregnant in public in summer is an open invitation to ask when it is due, if I know the sex and, *oh, can I have a feel?* I tilt my face to the sun and sigh. Still, it isn't messing with my contentment. Despite the rivers of sweat my body seems to be producing, I feel fantastic. My bump is perfectly neat and round and, somehow, I feel like pregnancy has settled me into my curvy body in a way I'd never felt before. For someone who's always been extra conscious of my body shape, that's a good, good thing.

Nina swears and swats her hand in front of her face. 'Since when do we have so many mozzies in London? And why are they all coming for me?'

'Maybe they can smell the sweet nectar of love,' I reply with a grin. 'He's cool, I like him.'

I look over at Luke, who's officially been given the title of being Nina's new boyfriend. He's sitting over on the other side of the blankets hidden under a selection of supermarket-bought picnic food, chatting with Jude.

'I don't know if I've ever seen you look at someone like that before,' I say.

'Can you blame me?' Nina laughs. 'He's delicious.'

He couldn't be any more different to her ex, who'd had that kind of banker look about him. Luke looks more rough and ready, kind of like Jude. He's an electrician so maybe it's something to do with them both having hands-on careers. He's definitely striking, with his red hair and piercing blue eyes. Sitting next to Jude, they make a head-turning pair.

'I'm glad you're happy,' I say with a smile. 'I know you were happy before but you're different now. You're a bit softer and gooier.'

Nina sighs. 'Good sex will do that.'

'I wouldn't know.' I roll over as much as I can and point towards the pack of cherry tomatoes. 'It's been so long I could compete with Mary for the title of virgin mother.'

Sex with Sam feels like a long, long time ago. In all the time that's passed since, I'd barely even thought about it. And then two days ago, I'd woken up with an internal feeling of needing *something*. I hadn't known quite what it was at first. I'd booked in for a haircut on a whim and managed to get a last-minute appointment. After years of relying on extensions to get by while abroad, I've had my natural hair temporarily straightened and cut into a bob that skims my jawline. I'd walked out of the salon with the forgotten high of a new hairstyle and the feeling of amazingness that it brought, but still. That feeling of needing something hasn't gone away.

'Maybe you need to go on a date?' Nina suggests, handing me the cardboard tub as sunlight glistens through her hair, creating a pink halo.

'God, no,' I shudder and pop a tomato into my mouth. I bite on it and a burst of tangy sweetness floods my mouth. 'Small talk with some random guy? No thanks. Plus there'd be a pretty big elephant in the room and the last thing I want is to have to talk about my ex-boyfriend who's probably shagging half of Sydney as we speak.'

'Screw him.'

'Right now, I would if I could,' I reply grimly.

It was only when I'd walked into the park earlier that I'd cottoned onto what the feeling I've been experiencing is. My body feels hypersensitive. Even now, I can feel the sun permeating every inch of my exposed skin. My breasts are enormous and my pelvis feels full of a zingy and, somehow at the same time, heavy energy. From groups of teenagers flirting with each other to couples kissing on benches and families with toddlers stumbling in the grass, the pursuit and result of sex seems to be everywhere around me. Even the trees are in full bloom, with their bright-green leaves splaying out and providing respites of shade from the sun, and the air is full of pollen waiting to be caught and fertilised.

Jude crawls across the blanket and takes a pack of pineapple chunks from the pile of food. I can't help but notice the way the muscles of his arms flex as he moves. Bloody hell. I shake my head and blink the image away. I need to get a grip.

'It must be the hormones,' I mutter. 'I don't think I've ever been so turned on in my life and here I am, single. You couldn't make it up.'

'You could do a casual hook-up kind of thing?' Nina suggests and I flinch.

'Ew. You mean have sex with someone who's not the father of my baby? Gross. Is that even allowed?'

It sounded more than gross. It sounded wrong. Surely there has to be a rule that if you're going to have sex while pregnant, it should at least be with the guy who got you there in the first place.

'Would *you* do it?' I ask.

Nina thinks it over for a second. 'I don't know. Maybe. I mean, it might not be culturally accepted but . . . I'm sure it happens.'

I raise my eyebrows. It probably did. I'm not the first single pregnant woman in the world and I definitely won't be the last. There's probably a Reddit thread on it somewhere – I make a note to look it up later on tonight.

'And I think I'd be curious about how it feels to have sex with a bump,' Nina adds with a laugh.

'Awkward, I'd expect.'

The baby moves and I put a hand on my belly. I've got used to the strange, fluttery feeling but it still takes my breath away each time.

'Remember the belly casting I wanted to do for my list?' I ask. 'I saw a DIY kit online the other day. Would you do it for me?'

'Of *course*,' Nina grins. 'Ooh, maybe I can do one too. Of my boobs. Or my vulva.'

I laugh, wrinkling my nose. 'Really?'

'Yeah, why not? I saw a photo of one on Instagram once and she'd painted it gold. How cool would that be?'

'I don't know if I'd want to see my vulva hanging on the wall every day,' I reply. 'Imagine if you brought a guy back and he saw it.'

'He'd be seeing it anyway. At least he'd know what he was getting into beforehand.'

I laugh again, shaking my head. 'What would Luke think?'

'I reckon he'd be into it. Hey, Luke,' Nina says, turning to face the guys and raising her voice a little. 'What would you think about me getting a vulva cast done?'

'Really?' Jude wrinkles his nose and shakes his head as I snicker into my hand.

He's always been a pretty open-minded guy – he's had no choice with a sister like Nina – but he clearly has his limits.

Luke shrugs with a little laugh. 'Why not?'

Nina grins and, when the guys return to their conversation, she looks back at me. 'See?'

I get the feeling that Luke's just unknowingly sailed through a test on two counts – being up for anything *and* knowing the terminology for the female anatomy.

'Alright,' I say with a nod. 'I'll do my belly and *you* can do your vulva. If that isn't a postcard for women's empowerment, I don't know what is.'

'Equal pay and an end to femicide?' Nina counters. 'But yeah, this'll do, for now.'

I wriggle my toes in the sunshine. I've got little splodges of varnish on some of the skin around my nails. I'd felt like a contortionist, bending and twisting to reach them with the varnish brush. It looks like home pedicures are now another thing to add to the list of things I used to be able to do with ease. It's a list that's increasing in direct proportion to the rate my belly is growing. Lying on my back is a no-go now and I have the distinct feeling that soon, I'll have to book myself in for a bikini wax instead of getting by with a shave in the shower. I suppose I could just let it all grow out. It's not like there's going to be anyone apart from doctors and midwives looking down there for months now anyway. Years maybe, even. It's too sad a thought to occupy myself with on such a gorgeous day, so I shuffle my body to rest my head on Nina's lap and lie down on my side.

I yawn quietly as the thud of someone kicking a football echoes through the air and mingles with the faint rhythm of reggaeton in the distance. Today has been one of those summer days where time feels like it's stretching endlessly, filled with good company, laughter and a ton of food. Nina had gathered us all under the pretence of taking advantage of the weather, but I know it was also a way of bringing Luke into the fold without making it a huge deal.

The breeze has a slight chill to it and, as it lands on my skin, it reminds me of one time when I'd fallen asleep on a beach in Thailand with Sam. It had been a day that wasn't much different to this one – sunshine, friends, food. I'd felt happy. So happy. I was in paradise, with the man I loved, living a lifestyle most people aspire to. The memory feels like a dream and, when I feel a hand shaking my shoulder, I realise that I've fallen asleep.

'Come on, you. We're making a move.'

I squint through one eye and look up to see Nina's face, framed by her pink hair.

'I must've fallen asleep,' I say with a yawn, slowly sitting up.

'I'm surprised you didn't wake yourself up with the snoring,' Jude says with a laugh.

I frown. 'I don't snore.'

'How would you know?'

'Don't be mean, she's pregnant.' Nina throws a scrunched-up paper bag at him. 'Ignore him, he's a moron.'

'This moron's the only one with a car and it's about to chuck it down,' Jude says. 'So be nice.'

I look up at the sky. Big, grey clouds are looming, making it darker than it normally would be at this time of the late afternoon. The park has already emptied out in comparison to how it had heaved with life earlier. Now there's just a few dog walkers and stragglers left.

'We're going to Luke's, it's not far,' Nina says, ducking as he slings an arm around her shoulder. 'Why don't you take Zoe home? You've only got two seats anyway.'

A breeze blows and my skin reacts, raising goosebumps on my arms. I cross them over my chest and shake my head. 'It's alright, I can get the bus.'

'Don't be daft,' Nina says. 'You're pregnant.'

'You keep saying that like it's an excuse for everything.'

'Isn't it?' Nina raises her eyebrows. 'It won't last forever; you should milk it while you can.'

'She's right. Besides, you can't walk around in those things in the rain,' Jude says, looking down at my flip-flops.

'I've lived in pretty much nothing else for years, I think I'll be okay,' I reply with a gentle laugh as we set off towards the path.

'Do you know how many people suffer flip-flop-related injuries in a year?' Jude asks and I smirk.

'Flip-flop *what* now?'

'Two hundred thousand.'

'Really?'

'Really.'

'I won't even ask how you know that,' I smile and nod towards Nina and Luke walking a few paces ahead of us. 'So, what's your verdict?'

He nods. 'Seems like a decent guy.'

'Really, that's it?' I laugh. 'You've spent all afternoon with him and that's all you have to say.'

'Would it matter if I *didn't* like him?'

'Of course it would. You're her brother. She listens to what you have to say.'

'That's news to me,' Jude chuckles.

A cyclist whizzes past us on the path sending another bout of cool air across my skin. I shiver, rubbing my arms. I clearly still have some acclimatisation to life in London to do. My optimism at the British weather had overridden the common sense and experience that had told me to bring a jumper, or a pashmina at the very least.

'Cold?' Jude asks.

I nod and he pulls out one of the blankets we'd been sitting on from his bag. The soft material lands on my skin like a sigh as he drapes it over my shoulders and my internal shivering stops.

'Thanks,' I smile. 'That'll teach me for not being better prepared.'

A fat droplet of rain splashes onto my forehead and within seconds, the tarmac is darkening as rain falls. The dramatic sky feels positively apocalyptic as the clouds draw nearer and I'm guessing it'll more than likely turn into a storm. We rush towards the street where Nina pulls me in for a quick hug goodbye before they set off.

'Where did you park?' I ask, holding the blanket back from my face so I can look up at Jude.

'Couple streets away. We'll be there in a minute.'

We walk in the opposite direction to Nina and Luke as the rain drops in heavy pellets, ricocheting back up from the slick pavement. As we turn off the main road and into a side street, my heel slides off my flip-flop and I stumble. My hand instinctively cups my bump as I anticipate falling, but I'm stopped by Jude clutching my arm.

My heart gallops in my chest. 'Bloody hell.'

I'd barely fallen. It had only been a slip, but still, it could've been much worse. We both look down at my feet, glistening with rainwater and specked with flecks of dirt and grit.

'I get your point. No more flip-flops,' I grimace, and grip his arm for support as I take them off.

'Come on,' Jude replies. 'The van's just up the road.'

At least he has the good grace not to say I told you so. I carry the flip-flops in the crook of my fingers and let the wet blanket lie around my shoulders as we walk at a normal pace. There's no point rushing anymore. Even if we hadn't been soaked already, we would be now. I haven't seen rain like this outside of the tropics and, with the heat rising from the pavements and a kind of clamminess in the air, if I close my eyes for a moment, I could probably tell myself I'm on a road in Malaysia instead of London.

When we get to his van, Jude takes the blanket from my shoulders and opens the passenger door, holding my hand to help me climb up. The air in the van is humid after being in the sun all afternoon and the seat is hot under my bare thighs. It's a delicious juxtaposition to the cool water on my skin and makes me shiver as my chest peppers with goosebumps.

Jude jumps in and blows a puff of air through his mouth. 'Well, that was intense.'

His grey t-shirt clings to his skin and I catch myself staring at the broadness of his chest. I actually swallow at the way his nipple pokes against the material like a bullet. I snap my head away and reach for the sun visor. Having *those* kinds of thoughts about Jude is inappropriate to say the very least. I've known him most of my life and he's Nina's younger brother.

I pull down the visor and frown. 'There's no mirror?'

'It's a work van,' Jude replies, pulling his seatbelt across his chest.

'So that means you don't need a mirror?'

I raise my eyebrows. The back of the van is enclosed so there was no rear-view mirror either. I unwind the window and peer at my reflection.

'Bloody hell, Jude.' I use my fingers to help tidy my hair. 'You could've told me I look like this.'

'Like what?'

I point to my head. '*This*.'

The wetness and humidity has reduced my temporarily straightened hair to less than half its natural length, leaving a head full of shrunken curls.

Jude starts the engine and makes a face as if he doesn't get it. 'It's just hair.'

I roll my eyes. It's such a boy thing to say, especially because he barely has a centimetre of it himself to worry about. Warm air flushes in through the open windows as we drive down the street which, after such a sun-soaked day, now looks like a myriad of shades of grey. Judging by the number of people in sodden clothes, we weren't the only ones who'd been caught out by the downpour. We chat easily as we drive the few minutes to my flat where he parks in a technically illegal space. I look up at the two windows of my living room.

The facade of the dental surgery downstairs has been repainted and the faded cream it used to be is now a light shade of pastel green to match the side door that leads to my flat. The building looks much smarter and prouder. The brickwork still looks ancient and there are cracks all over the place, but still, it looks loved and lived in. It looks safe.

'Want to come up?'

I cringe inside as soon as the words come out of my mouth. It sounded so . . . corny, like a line from a bad TV soap.

'I mean, for . . .' I tail off.

Adding *coffee* to the end of that sentence would only make it worse and I don't have anything else he'd need. Unless he wanted one of my oversized hoodies to drive home in. My hormones have taken over my brain and God this is embarrassing. I glance at him and he looks completely normal. Maybe I'm overreacting and he hasn't picked up on anything strange. The calm smile on his face doesn't say he's offended or worse, disgusted.

'I should be getting back. I've got plans later,' he says.

'Sure, of course.'

'Actually.' He twists in his chair to look at me and rests his arm on top of the steering wheel. 'I've been thinking about what you told me earlier. About your website building stuff?'

I nod. After a few solid days of writing a sales page and putting my offer together, I'm all ready to go and have already had two enquiries come back. If they sign up that'll be enough money to pay my rent for two months and will only take two days to complete.

'Mine's a complete mess,' Jude continues with a sheepish look on his face. 'I made it years ago and with business picking up like it has been, I think it's time for an update. I wondered if you'd be interested in doing it?'

'Sure,' I reply, my face lighting up with a smile. 'What did you have in mind?'

'Nothing over the top, just something simple and clean.'

Of course. It's his style all over, right down to the wet clothes on his back. He wears skate brands I've never heard of and if he isn't in his work trousers, he's nearly always in a pair of faded jeans.

'We can do that,' I nod.

'Cool.' He smiles with what looks a little like relief. 'I'll text you and we can talk a bit more about it.'

I smile back and sling my handbag over my shoulder as he jumps out of the van. I shake my head with a laugh as he opens my door.

'We can't have you slipping again.'

I put my hand in his and step down with my bare feet onto the wet, warm pavement. 'Yep. This is precious cargo right here.'

My bump sticks out proudly between us as I reach up for a hug. His broad hand seems to fill the entirety of my lower back and I quickly peck his cheek. Is it weird that we're hugging goodbye? Or that I've just kissed him? We've never done this before. Then again, everyone does it these days, it hardly means anything special.

I flick a strand of wet hair back from my forehead and look up at him as we pull away.

'Thanks for the lift,' I smile, lifting the flip-flops in my hand as a salute.

'Any time.' He grins at me before closing the door and leaning back against it.

'What are you doing?' I ask, eyeing him with a frown.

'Waiting till you get inside. Like you said – you're carrying precious cargo.'

'Right,' I reply, nodding. 'Bye, then.'

It's impossible not to feel self-conscious, knowing he's watching me as I turn and walk towards my front door. My already substantial bum has got bigger, my thighs have grown and my hair is a mess. But there's something thrilling about having his eyes on me. When I put the key in the lock and push the door open, I turn and wave before I go in. He returns my wave and pushes himself away from the van to walk around to the driver's side. I close the door behind me, hearing his engine start. And as I go up the stairs, the grin is still on my face.

◆ ◆ ◆

Pregnancy week: Twenty-three
You're the size of a: large mango
Today, I feel: Like dancing!

Hello, Little One . . .
So, it seems you like a bit of Whitney :) Seeing you move about like that under my skin was WILD! I'll consider you as being in training for the festival, but I'm pretty sure you won't get many 90s ballads there. I can't wait. It'll be like

a mini holiday! And speaking of holidays, I read about babymoons in a magazine yesterday and it sounds like a great idea. What do you say to a little break, just the two of us before you get here? I've always wanted to go to a little cottage for a weekend and even with all the travelling, it's still something I haven't done yet. It could be really nice being out in the countryside in the autumn :) And there'll be enough money too if things keep going the way they are.

Let's keep it going.

Love, Zoe

xx

Chapter Fifteen

The scent of wood and coffee fills my nose as I sit on a chair in Jude's office. My laptop is sitting amidst a sea of papers and letters with the mock-up of his new website up on the screen. I've always been a neat freak but looking at Jude's desk makes me want to sit on my hands to resist the urge to sort through the pile of papers. It feels criminal that such a gorgeous oak desk isn't able to bathe in the sunlight fighting its way through the dusty windows. Come to think of it, they could do with a clean too. I turn away from the chaos of his desk and look through the doorway to his workshop where he's taking a call on his mobile.

It's less chaotic than his office. An assortment of chisels, saws and other tools are hanging on the wall as if they're being displayed in a gallery, and the opposite wall is filled with labelled rows of drawers and cupboards. Assorted planks, chunks and boards of wood are stacked against the other walls and a couple of big machines dominate the far end of the large room. Jude puts his phone back in his pocket and comes into the office.

'Sorry about that.' He pulls a face.

'Don't worry about it,' I reply as he sits back down in his chair.

The office is small already and with him in it now, it feels even smaller. While travelling over the years, I've come across a lot of people who like to talk about energy and auras. I'd never really bought into it. Of course, everyone has their own feel to them, but the idea of people walking around with a colourful bubble surrounding their bodies always felt like a bit of a stretch. I'm not so sure now. I can't see a swathe of colour around Jude, but he *does* seem to have something about him that makes me sit up and take notice. His familiarity is a safe haven and his energy, for lack of a better word, actually feels tangible. He doesn't have to say anything when he's in my vicinity. I just seem to know he's there.

I turn back to my laptop screen, away from the weirdness of energy and auras to the familiar ground of web design. 'So, we were talking about images.'

'Right, yeah. I've got a few we could use from past projects,' Jude replies. 'Hang on.'

Somehow, he manages to find the computer mouse on the chaos of his desk and he furrows his brows as he navigates his files. Something feels off with him. I'm not sure what, but his light-brown eyes look dull and he has a tightness around his full lips.

'Damn it,' he tuts and squints his eyes making the skin around them crease. 'I was sure I'd put them there.'

I let one of my hands rest on top of my bump and use the other to tuck my hair behind my ear.

'Don't stress about it,' I say after a few seconds of clicking. 'We don't need them today.'

Jude nods. 'I'll get onto it this week.'

I tilt my head and scan his face with my eyes. 'Are you alright? You seem a bit . . .'

He grimaces. 'Ehh, just one too many last night. My head's killing me.'

'Hungover on a weekday?' I playfully raise an eyebrow. 'Isn't that what they call burning the candle at both ends?'

'I don't make a habit of it, trust me. There's not much worse than feeling crap with a full load of physical work on top.'

'It feels like an absolute age since I even had a drink, let alone a hangover,' I smile with nostalgia.

'So, there's no point in asking you for cures then?'

I nod to the window where a shaft of sunlight is illuminating what looks like a whole galaxy of dust motes. 'Fresh air? Sunlight? Opening a window?'

'And risk a gust of wind messing up my intricate filing system?' Jude spreads his palms across his desk and lifts an eyebrow. 'That would only add to the headache.'

'Intricate? Really?'

'Fuck no. It's a mess.' He shakes his head. 'Look at the state of it.'

'I *did* wonder,' I reply with a laugh. 'I don't know how you find anything under there.'

'You and me both.' He leans back in his chair, letting it roll away from the desk a few inches. 'It's time to get a secretary or something, I guess. As well as a hired hand for the work coming in this autumn.'

'You can advertise on your new website. We just need a picture of you on there.'

'Do I really need one? I haven't until now and it's been alright. Can't I just have pictures of my work instead?'

He crosses his arms and runs a hand across the light coating of stubble on his jaw with scepticism clouding his eyes.

'What, and hide that face of yours?'

Jude raises an eyebrow and lifts the corner of his mouth into a lopsided grin. If there was ever a moment where I wished the ground would open up and suck me into it, this might be one of them.

'What I mean is, people like to see who they're dealing with,' I say, fighting the heat creeping into my cheeks.

He tilts his head back and laughs before looking back at me with amusement in his eyes.

'Damn. There I was thinking my hungover self was getting a compliment.'

'No such luck I'm afraid,' I reply with a slight curl to my lips.

Jude pulls himself back in towards his desk. 'I just don't want to buy into that whole carpenter look.'

'What carpenter look?'

'You know. Plaid shirt, slicked back hair, faded jeans . . .'

I laugh. 'You don't have to unless you're trying to be a lumberjack from somewhere in Canada.'

'You laugh, but that's what people think when they hear, *carpenter.*' He shakes his head. 'The girl I was out with last night was devastated when I said I have no plans to grow a beard.'

So, he's hungover because he'd been out on a date. It makes no rational sense but hearing that lands in my chest with a little sting. Why shouldn't he be dating? He's single, successful and, alright, I admit it, very attractive. I suddenly feel frumpy in my light, long-sleeved shirt and maternity leggings. My last date had been all those years ago with Sam, back when I could fit my feet into high heels and my hips into skinny jeans. Technically, I could have gone on plenty of dates when we'd opened things up. It was *allowed* within the confines of our relationship, but I'd never wanted to. I'd wanted to be seen by the man I'd planned to spend the rest of my life with, not some random stranger. I have no idea who Jude was out with last night, but I'm pretty sure she wasn't wearing leggings and carrying haemorrhoid cream in her handbag.

'I promise, you don't have to pretend to be a lumberjack,' I smile weakly. 'It can be a simple headshot taken on your phone.'

I reach for the laptop and pull it a little closer. Being at the mercy of hormones is like being in uncharted territory, but websites aren't. I'm mad at Sam and missing having someone to be close to, but I know how to will the feelings into submission because I'm not here to give in to a flood of irrational tears. I'm here for work.

◆ ◆ ◆

I turn and pummel the pillow under my head back into shape before readjusting the one between my knees. I sigh heavily, reluctantly opening my eyes. The amber digits on the clock on my bedside table read 04:50. There's no point trying to sleep anymore when my bladder is threatening to burst. Again. My legs feel like they're filled with lead as I swing them off the bed and pad to the toilet.

For the last few nights, I've tried not to drink an hour or so before bed, and I've made sure to go to the toilet right before tiredness takes over, but it's no use. It feels like my bladder has shrunk *and* developed extra sensitivity at the same time. At least the coolness of the toilet seat helps to take down the heat in my body and, I suppose, all the broken sleep means it shouldn't be too much of a shock when my daughter comes. My daughter. A frisson of fear and pressure runs through my body at the thought of it.

Am I really going to be a good mum to a girl? I think about it as I make a cup of herbal tea. Why do I feel like a boy would be easier? They seem to be so much more resilient and able to get on with things when they grow up. Then again, it was probably easy to be when the world was created for you. After all, it wasn't that long ago that a woman was technically the property of her father and then, if she was lucky, her husband. I think back to last week when Nina had tested Luke's knowledge of the female anatomy. I've never done that. I've never been vocal about my periods like she is. Or attended a march for women's abortion rights in the US. Am I really prepared to raise a daughter? For hormones and tears over girls at school who tell her she's too much? For worries about breast and dress size and heartbreak?

I take my tea back to bed and sit up with my back against the wooden headboard. Did I really just wish that the baby I'm growing, nurturing and carrying would be a boy instead of the girl she is? A wave of guilt floods my body in the near silence of my room, quickly followed by anger. Why is it okay for those thoughts to even enter my head? Why is it okay to feel like my child's life would be easier if only she'd be born a boy?

I know where this is coming from. The flash of jealousy I'd felt hearing that Jude had been on a date, combined with my hormonally increased libido, had made me feel unattractive. It had undone the high I've been on for the last few weeks. It had undone the pride I'd felt for blitzing my way through my list of things to do – opening a savings account, signing a life insurance policy, recruiting a part-time virtual assistant, creating a service that was selling so well that I even *needed* part time assistant . . . they'd simply paled into insignificance. Because the reality is that Sam is still living his life as he always has done, and I am not. And even though it had been my choice to keep this baby and leave him, it makes me angry. Last night, my back had hurt so much I'd cried and they weren't just tears of pain. There was nobody here to hold me and tell me it would be okay. Nobody to schlep to the bathroom to fetch the tiger balm or massage it into my skin. It was yet another reminder that I'm in this alone, for the long haul.

I reach for my phone and scroll through my photos, past the ones from the last few months with Nina, my mum, random snapshots of London and the progress of the refurbishment of the flat until the colour palette changes. The backs of my eyes sting at the last picture I have with Sam. We'd spent New Year's Day on the beach, and in the photograph we're grinning, squinting against the sun. His blonde hair is covered with sand after celebrating a goal in an impromptu game of football and the sides of his eyes are squished and crinkled with his smile. I'm struggling to reconcile this image and memory of him, with the reality of how things are now. Where was the guy who'd emptied the vomit from my bucket while I'd been in bed after eating those crooked oysters? The one who used to say I love you, every night before going to sleep, without fail? How had he been replaced by someone who couldn't even be bothered to reply to a WhatsApp message?

I look out at the dawn sky. Five in the morning means it's around two in the afternoon back in Sydney. Before I can think twice about it, I press the call icon and pin the phone to my ear. He's probably working right now or grabbing a sushi lunch from the place around the corner we used to love so much. A flash of nerves dries my mouth as the ringtone beeps down the phone. Why exactly am I calling him? I'm not entirely sure. To tell him I'm angry at him for not reaching out? For leaving me to deal with this alone? But then I look back at my clock and a reality check hits me square between the eyes. Sam didn't leave me with anything. *I* was the one who left *him*. If there wasn't a baby involved, there'd be no expectation for him to return my messages or calls at all. I'm just about to hang up when the call connects.

My bedroom feels as silent as a monastery as I hear what sounds like shuffling filtering through to my ear.

'Zoe?'

'Are you sleeping?' I ask. After waking up to him for so many years, the tell-tale sleepy croakiness of his voice is embedded into my brain.

Sam clears his throat. 'I was.'

'In the middle of the afternoon?'

'It's almost one in the morning. I'm in New York.'

I blink with surprise. 'New York?'

A pang of jealousy hits me as I picture him crossing busy roads, dodging yellow cabs, walking streets lined with green signposts and taking the subway, no doubt with his camera, recording everything. I've always wanted to go to New York. America, in fact. I've dreamed of doing a road trip across the States since I was a little girl. I'd seen myself on Greyhound buses and overnighting in motels with neon-lit signs and empty swimming pools until I reached California. I'd been planning my trip and comparing flights, but then, Sam happened. And he'd got a contract shooting for a magazine in South Africa, so we went there instead. And then to Greece, and then Portugal. America slid way down the list until it barely got a mention anymore. Knowing that he's there now, seeing the things I've always longed to see, brings a bad taste to my mouth.

'I got here a couple of weeks ago. For work,' he adds.

His Gold Coast accent is as familiar as the image of him in my mind. I picture him sitting up against the headboard of his bed like I am, in a t-shirt and boxers, with his ruffled bed-hair and the sheets around his waist.

'Are you alone?' I jut my chin out a little in preparation for his answer.

'Yes,' he replies evenly. 'Are you?'

I roll my eyes. 'What do you think?'

'I wouldn't dare to presume.'

'Would it bother you if I *were* with someone?' I ask. His reasonableness irritates me like a scratchy wool jumper on bare skin. 'I *am* pregnant with your child.'

'I know you are,' Sam replies.

His voice has the tiniest hint of strain in it, and I picture him running a hand through his blond hair.

'So, no Charlotte, then?' I reply, hating the words as they come out of my mouth. I feel like a child poking a sleeping dog – it'll probably only end in tears.

Sam sighs and I consider hanging up. This wasn't the point of the call. Now that we're talking and the thousands of miles between us has condensed to the nearness of a phone call, I can't quite remember what the point was. But I'm pretty sure it wasn't this.

'No, I'm not with Charlotte,' Sam says heavily. 'Nothing happened with her.'

It shouldn't matter, but relief drips down my shoulders. I'd had a bad feeling about her from the moment we'd been introduced, and even though it makes no sense at all, I'm glad she hasn't been intertwined in the story of our relationship.

I run my thumb around the rim of my teacup. 'Why not?'

'You left.'

He says those two words so simply, as if I ought to know that my leaving would've stopped him from going to bed with another woman. It's ironic really, seeing as it was no problem when I *was* there. I want to reply that I couldn't have known anything since he'd ignored my messages but I don't. Instead, I drape the soft wool blanket I'd thrown off during the night over my feet.

'How are you?' he asks.

I put my cup on the bedside table, look down at the bump protruding from my body and shrug. 'Good.'

A few seconds pass and I hear him moving around in bed again. 'And the baby?'

'She's fine. It's a girl.'

'Yeah, I know,' he replies with another sigh.

'So, you *did* see my message then.'

As much as it has annoyed me, until now, I've been able to stay in blissful ignorance about his silence. Knowing that he'd seen it but just hadn't bothered to reply makes furious tears well behind my eyes.

'You really don't care, do you?' I ask, pulling my eyebrows into a deep frown.

'Come on, Zoe. That's not fair.'

I don't know why it surprises me that he's been able to keep himself at a distance. He'd been clear about not wanting to be involved after all, which means my irritation and anger probably isn't justified and that only makes the cluster of feelings intensify.

'I don't know how to navigate this situation, Zo. I mean, put yourself in my shoes for a minute.'

'It looks like things are pretty good from where I'm standing,' I reply hotly. 'You're in New York, living life how you always have.'

'No, Zoe. I'm not,' Sam says in a challenging tone. 'I've moved continents, my relationship ended and I have a daughter on the way that I didn't even . . .'

He tails off, leaving the word *want* hanging in the air. I can hear the scratching sound as he runs a hand across his beard and he sighs.

'My life is nothing like it was before, Zoe.'

I swallow. He isn't saying it's been terrible these last few months, but he's not saying it's been great either. The strangeness of having once known pretty much everything about his life, to now not knowing anything feels heavy and sad. Because, apart from the updates I've sent about the baby, he knows nothing about my life either. He doesn't know about Mum's surgery, or that I've been ordering from the Indian takeaway down the road almost daily to satisfy my curry cravings. Sam and I used to be lovers. And best friends. And now we're . . . I don't even know what.

'You know what, this was a mistake,' I say.

'Zoe—'

'You've been clear about how you feel. I shouldn't have called.'

I'm the one carrying her, growing her, feeding her. I'm the one who'll love her. Maybe I'd needed to hear him tell me that, even with all the updates I've been sending, as far as he's concerned, I really am doing this alone. I hear an intake of breath on the other end, as if he's considering saying something but doesn't know how to phrase it.

'It's fine, Sam,' I say, nodding to myself as if it's somehow sealing the knowledge into my skin, muscle and bone. 'Really.'

I hang up the phone and look down at the illuminated screen in my hands. I'd wanted him to acknowledge me. To acknowledge her. I rub a hand across my belly and feel a strengthening of my resolve because the truth is, I've managed without his acknowledgment until now. I've managed without him. I'm building a life for me and my daughter. Because despite leaving everything behind and starting again, I'm standing on my own two feet.

Pregnancy week: Twenty-six
You're the size of a: Aubergine
Today, I feel: A little freaked out . . .

Hello, Little One . . .
I had a dream about the festival last night. It was absolutely chucking it down and my wellies got stuck in the mud. You poked your head out of my belly and told me it was a terrible idea to have gone, and then flounced back inside, zipped my belly up and refused to talk to me. I hope it wasn't your way of telling me you don't want to go . . . I can't think why that would be though, because I have the feeling it's going to be amazing.

I promise not to keep you up too late (who am I kidding, I'll probably fall asleep before nine!) and make as much use of the lake as possible. You'll be a lake-water baby before you know it.

I'll be honest with you, it wasn't easy chatting with your dad, little aubergine baby. I know I haven't told you much about him, but I will one day (I promised that and I meant it). But I feel like this festival weekend has come at the exact right time for some fun and quality time with friends.

Let's do it!

Love,

Zoe

xx

Chapter Sixteen

I drain my glass of water and set it down on the windowsill where I've been perched for the last few minutes. A big ray of golden sunshine streams onto my thigh and even though the morning rush hour's only just slowing down, it's so hot outside that I can see the subtle shimmer of heat rising up from the tarmac below. It's a gorgeous summer's morning and perfect festival weather. I took my time this morning to clean the flat. The floor's been vacuumed, the bathroom is sparkling, and fresh sheets are on the bed, ready to welcome me back after four days of festival life. I wince a little at a pain under my ribs. There's still three months to go, but I'm honestly starting to wonder how there could possibly be any more space left in there.

My phone rings and Nina's face looks up at me from the screen. I laugh as I answer it. 'There you are, late as usual. I was beginning to think you weren't coming.'

'I'm not.'

'Yeah, okay.' I roll my eyes. 'Sure.'

Sometimes I think she forgets how long we've known each other. It wouldn't be the first time she's pretended to drop out of something only to crease into laughter and say *jokes* right afterwards.

'I'm serious,' she says, and the smile falls from my face as I hear the tone of her voice.

'What's wrong?'

'I'm sick. I've been puking for the last hour, non-stop.'

'So, bring a bucket,' I suggest, injecting a little smile into my words.

'I'd need one for the other end, too.'

'Oh.' I pull a face, remembering how awful I'd felt after eating those oysters back in Sydney. 'Food poisoning?'

'I don't think so,' Nina replies with a groan. 'It sounds like the same thing my assistant called in sick with yesterday. It must be a bug or something.'

'Damn.' I lean back against the window frame. There must be a way we can still rescue the weekend. 'Maybe we can drive up tomorrow instead? It might be one that only lasts a day.'

'But I might still be contagious. I'd feel awful if I passed it on, especially to you.'

My heart sinks in my chest. She's right, of course. Getting sick in my condition would be a nightmare, not to mention dangerous for the baby.

'It's a good thing you didn't come last night after all, I guess,' I say, getting up from the window ledge.

She was supposed to spend the night here so we could drive up to the festival first thing, but because her assistant had called in sick, she'd had to work later than expected.

Nina groans again. 'I am so *pissed*. And sorry.'

'Hey, come on. Don't worry about it, it's not your fault,' I say, waving my hand in the air and rocking my hips from side to side against a twinge of pain. 'Is there anything I can do?'

'It's alright, Luke's here, poor thing. Talk about a relationship initiation.'

'Is he passing?' I ask with a little laugh. Nina sounds exhausted and I figure she'll need all the cheering up she can get.

'With flying colours,' she replies with a sigh. 'What should we do about the car? It's still booked. If you want it, we'd just have to switch you to the main driver.'

I shake my head. 'Let's cancel it. It's probably best I don't go anyway. It feels like I've got a bowling ball pressing down on my hips.'

'Absolutely not,' Nina replies. She sounds suddenly very firm and strong for someone who's lying in her sickbed. 'You are *not* missing out on this weekend.'

'But it won't be as much fun without you there. I'll be in our tent alone and I won't know anyone.'

'What are you talking about? It'll be amazing and hello, you know Jude.'

'You know what I mean.' I rub the underside of my belly and shrug. 'And I don't want to drive alone.'

'So, take Jude. Or drive with him and his mates. Just please. Don't. Stay. At. Home. I'll feel even worse than I do right now.'

'Is that even possible?'

'I bloody hope not. Don't make me have to find out.'

I take a few paces around the living room. It won't be the same without Nina, that's for sure. She's the gregarious, outgoing yang to my more reserved yin. We used to meet so many interesting people on nights out but it was always down to her and her ability to strike up conversation with everyone and anyone. And while Jude and I have become friends in our own right, it's different. But when I think about the weekend going by without me, I feel actual FOMO. The fear of missing out is so strong that it makes me stand a little more on my tiptoes, as if I'm getting ready to sprint away from a weekend of finding other things to do instead. Sure, I could go to the park, for a swim, visit Mum or do some yoga. But I can do those things any time. There'll only be one chance for this festival, and it's now or never.

'Alright,' I say with a nod. 'I'll see if I can get a lift with Jude.'

'And I'll cancel the car. I really am sorry,' Nina replies.

'You can't help being sick. But I'll miss you.'

'Same. Have fun for me,' she says, following up with a groan. 'Ugh, I've got to go.'

She hangs up immediately and I grimace, picturing her on the other end. She must be feeling awful and not being able to use the ticket that had cost three hundred pounds probably won't help. I scroll down to Jude's number and press call, looking at my little suitcase waiting by the door. With any luck, they won't have left already. It's still early. Nina and I had wanted to leave after breakfast to take full advantage of the rental convertible Mini. The plan had been to take the scenic route there and stop off for a countryside pub lunch.

'Hey, Zoe,' Jude says, answering the call in a cheerful voice. 'How're you doing?'

'Good,' I reply. 'Better than Nina, anyway. She just called to say she can't come to the festival. She's sick.'

'Really? I haven't heard anything from her, what's wrong?'

'She only just called me. She thinks it could be a bug and doesn't want to pass it on.'

'Aw, man. That's crap,' Jude sighs with disappointment. 'I'll give her a call and make sure she's alright.'

'Luke's with her,' I reply and twist my lips feeling a tinge of nerves. I know he'd said he was happy I was going and his friends would be too, but now that Nina's not coming, I can't help feel like a bit of a gatecrasher. 'I don't suppose I could get a lift with you guys?'

'Yeah, of course. I was just about to suggest the same. We'd planned to leave around eleven. That work for you?'

'It's perfect,' I reply with a smile.

'We'll swing by and pick you up.'

I'm gutted Nina can't go but as I hang up, I feel a thrill of excitement and anticipation. It'll still be a couple of hours until they get here, so I take the magazine I'd bought to read in the car, chop up some fruit and take myself out to the terrace. Jude's idea of decking the flat surface has been put on hold due to an astronomical rise in the price of wood. Even the cost of cheap offcuts made my eyes water and with my due date coming ever closer, I'd decided it simply wasn't a priority. But Jude did come over last weekend to attach a bamboo fence to the tiny walls of the flat roof. It had taken less than an afternoon, but now I have what feels like an almost truly private space. Once I get some big plants and furniture it'll be complete, but for now I'm happy to unfold the camping chair I bought from the second-hand shop down the road. I skilfully wedge an umbrella into the frame to provide some shade and put my feet up on an upturned crate.

I already have my email out-of-office responder on but, after reading an article in my magazine, I go a step further and delete my social media apps. I've followed a load of pages and profiles about pregnancy and motherhood, but recently I've come off the apps feeling a certain sense of pressure. It hadn't bothered me before, but seeing women with neat bumps and not an ounce of excess body-weight was making me look in the mirror with a more critical eye. And while I know it's weight I need for the baby, it seems to have all piled on in a short space of time, filling my already substantial bum and the tops of my arms. I decide to take my social media detox through to the end of my pregnancy and it already feels like a huge relief. By the time the buzzer goes, I've read the magazine from cover to cover and I'm already waiting by the door with my suitcase and a bag full of snacks for the drive. Jude takes the steps two at a time with a smile that's so wide and infectious, I can't help but return it.

'Ready?' he asks, taking my suitcase as I close the door.

'*So* ready,' I reply, and I really am.

'Still in flip-flops, I see.'

I roll my eyes playfully. 'They're for the car, smartypants. I've got trainers in my bag.'

We walk around the corner to where a woman is leaning against a white VW Golf smoking a cigarette.

'You must be Zoe?' she asks, wafting the smoke away from me with her hand as I nod. 'I'm Tasha, that's Tyler.'

As Jude puts my suitcase in the boot, I drop my head a little to wave at the man behind the steering wheel before looking back at Tasha. To say she's gorgeous would be an understatement. Her legs are long and thin in her high-waisted shorts, showing off a tattoo on the front of both thighs.

'Thanks for letting me tag along with you all,' I say, trying not to feel frumpy in comparison.

'No worries, the more the merrier,' she replies, dropping her half-smoked cigarette onto the pavement and stubbing it out with the toe of her chunky ankle boots. 'Come on, jump in.'

I manoeuvre my way into the car, holding my belly as I go, feeling more awkward than I'd like to. There are certain things that I just can't do with the same ease as before. The trainers I've brought don't have laces and I'm pretty sure the woman at the beauty salon down the road thought she was waxing the bikini line of a gorilla when I went yesterday.

'How far along are you?' Tasha asks, chewing on a piece of gum and twisting around in her seat as I fasten my seatbelt.

'Six months.'

'So cute,' she replies with a smile. 'And I *love* that dress.'

I laugh as Tyler pulls the car out of its illegal parking space. With her expressive face and tone, she reminds me of Nina, which both relaxes me and makes me wish she were here with us. I get the feeling Tasha thinks everything is cute but instead of brushing the compliment aside, I look down at the orange dress I'd bought on Depop especially for this weekend. The colour pops against my skin and, in this seated position, the V-neck shows more than a hint of cleavage. Maybe it does look cute after all. I look across at Jude and he simply grins back with a shrug as if to say, *duh, of course you do.*

'Jude said it's your first festival?' Tyler asks, catching my eye in the rear-view mirror. I nod and he laughs. 'Fair play to you for diving in with a baby on board.'

'But you lived in Australia, right?' Tasha asks, scrolling through the phone attached to the dashboard looking for music. 'They have some *amazing* festivals over there.'

'I know,' I reply with a nod. 'I just never managed to get to one.'

It sounds like a lame excuse really, but there was always something else to do that came first.

'Better late than never, right?' Jude says with a smile.

I smile back but, as Tasha presses play and music fills the air in the car, I can't help but feel annoyed at myself. From the outside looking in, someone might look at my life over the last eleven years and mistake me for someone who lived it to the full, creating one unforgettable experience after another. But the truth is, if I hadn't gotten pregnant and had Nina's pushy influence behind me, I probably wouldn't have prioritised getting to a festival any time soon, despite it being something I've always wanted to do. It's not that I've just gone along with life in the last few years. I just don't think I've played much of an active role in it or fought for the things I wanted, until reading the pregnancy test back in February.

'Anyone want some crisps?' I ask, opening my snack bag.

'Wow,' Jude laughs. 'What's with the lifetime supply of Hula Hoops?'

'Craving,' I reply, laughing back. 'They make up about ninety per cent of my suitcase.'

We all giggle as I hand out packets of beef flavoured crisps and we fall into easy chitchat. The atmosphere is light, and it's a nice drive on the motorway. I'm pretty sure they could've made it there much faster without having to stop all the time to accommodate my weak bladder, but they make no fuss about it. Between the familiarity of Jude, the laidback reserved nature of Tyler and the gregarious fun vibe from Tasha, it feels like I've always been part of their group. They've been going to this festival for years and have given me so many tips I could probably navigate the weekend alone if I wanted to. We come off the motorway and veer around tiny country lanes for what feels like an age. I'm just starting to feel a bit carsick when we slow down, joining a queue of cars that stretches for at least another mile.

After spending the whole journey chatting, the slowness of the car creeping along seems to quieten us all down, as if we're being given a last bit of quiet time before a noisy weekend. As we inch closer to the entrance, Tasha flicks through a magazine, Jude dozes next to me with his head leaning against the window and I stare out at the countryside, with a hand resting comfortably on my bump. There really is nothing like England in the summertime. To my left, fields of barley shimmer like gold under the sun while on my right, an army of trees provide a green canopy of shade. I smile, picturing my little girl being as relaxed as I am right now. She's been quiet on the drive and has barely moved at all. With any luck she'll be the kind of kid who sleeps as soon as she gets into a car.

Once we've traded our tickets for wristbands, we drive through a field, find a space and park up. I get out of the car with the stuffy heat of the late afternoon sun on my skin and Jude yawns loudly, stretching as he does so. He raises his arms way over his head, pulling the hem of his t-shirt up, revealing the smooth brown skin underneath. I look away and take a deep breath of clean countryside air as I open up the boot.

'Here, I'll take it,' Jude says, reaching for my suitcase.

'It's alright,' I reply with a smile. 'I can wheel it.'

He raises his eyebrows and looks over my shoulder with a nod. 'It's a good twenty-minute walk. Thirty, probably with a baby. And there's no tarmac.'

I remember what he'd said on the day I moved into the flat, protesting that if I were his girlfriend, I wouldn't be lifting a finger. I'm sure I could easily wheel my suitcase to the campsite, but do I really *have* to? I'm reminded of what Nina said at the picnic – that I should take the offer of help while it's being given and throw Jude a smile.

'In that case . . .'

He grins and lifts my tiny suitcase from the boot before slinging his backpack on. The festival doesn't officially start until tonight, but already there's a distinct and energised party vibe in the air. I quickly swap my flip-flops for trainers before we set off on the long walk to the campsite. Tyler and Tasha walk arm in arm a little ahead of us, and I try to figure out if they're a couple. They have that comfortable, jokey ease that says yes, but there's something that hints at an underlying tension between them.

I glance up at Jude. 'Are they together?'

'It's complicated,' he replies in a whisper, bringing his head towards mine. 'They're kind of off and on. Right now, they're on.'

'They look cute together,' I say, and they really do, if a little mismatched.

Tasha looks like the epitome of a blonde bombshell, with her long hair, full make-up and knock-out figure. Tyler, on the other hand, is a little unremarkable. He's funny and friendly, but he looks like that nerdy boy in school who never really got the girl. Maybe they're a living embodiment of opposites attract. Either way, there's something about the idea of them being together that makes me smile. Like it's the natural order of things.

'Yeah, they do,' Jude agrees. 'Who knows, maybe this weekend Cupid'll get it right.'

'Maybe,' I reply with a laugh. 'Stranger things have happened, I guess.'

We take our time, ambling along under the shade provided by the trees with a steady stream of other people. The crowd is completely mixed, from groups pulling carts of beer behind them to couples walking hand in hand and families with toddlers running ahead. I take a few snaps of the landscape and grab a quick candid shot of Jude, Tyler and Tasha to send to Nina. The girl in front of us is dressed in sequined hot pants with a halo attached to her headband and I nudge Jude's arm.

'I hope you've packed your halo too?'

He clicks his fingers together and tuts dramatically. 'Damn. I *knew* I'd forgotten something.'

'Have no fear,' Tasha says, pointing to her enormous backpack. 'The festival fairy godmother is here.'

'If you're not up for getting doused in glitter and face paints, this is your last chance to turn back now,' Tyler says with a laugh.

'Oh, I am definitely up for it,' I reply.

Ever since I saw pictures of Burning Man for the first time, I've dreamed of wearing an outrageous costume at a festival. I might not have the outrageous part down, but it sounds like this will be close enough and who knows when or if I'll get to do it again.

'I knew I liked you,' Tasha says, falling out of step with Tyler to link her arm through mine.

Birds are tweeting in the trees around us and I can't help but compare how easily I've been accepted into the fold here with the difficulty I'd faced in Sydney. It wasn't that Sam's group were unfriendly, but they hadn't exactly tripped over themselves to welcome me either. The Sam I'd met in London was a man who surrounded himself with artists and designers. He'd lived in a warehouse in Dalston with seven other people – all of whom treated me like one of their own. No small talk, no insider jokes. I'd expected the same when we moved to Sydney, but his crowd were a strange mix of boho chic freelancers and marketing creatives, and it was clear from the outset that I wasn't one of them. I didn't have the shared history and couldn't get in involved in the *remember when* stories. The ease with which I've been slotted into the festival weekend plan is like another pro for being here, against a con for being there, in supposed paradise.

We finally arrive at the campsite and I blink, a little stunned. The dense woodland curves at the bottom of the field to create something like a cul-de-sac and a sea of white bell tents cover the grass.

'Jeez,' I push my sunglasses up onto my forehead and wipe a trickle of sweat from my hairline. 'It's huge.'

'Oh, this is only the half of it,' Jude says, hooking his thumbs through the straps of his backpack.

'There's another campsite way over the other side of the lake for the people who actually want to pitch their own tents,' Tasha explains with a laugh, as if the idea of putting up your own tent would be madness.

I'd almost forgotten about the pictures of the glistening lake I'd seen online. My skin prickles in the heat and I can almost feel the water calling me, wherever it is. I can't see it from here, or the music stages, which means this place is vast. A little wave of tiredness creeps over me and doubt flickers in my mind about being here instead of back at home on my sofa where I can rest whenever I need to with access to a clean, functioning toilet I don't have to share with hordes of other people. I shake it off and drop my sunglasses back down onto the bridge of my nose. I'm here now, and as I resolved to, I'm going to have fun.

We make our way through the labyrinth of tents and it's actually like landing in a new city for the first time. What looked confusing on first glance is in fact quite simple, with the tents all numbered and organised into rows. I take note of where things are for landmarks. The toilet and shower area is over in one corner, a fire pit with log benches is in another, and a first aid tent is pitched at what looks like a walkway out of the accommodation site. Luckily, we'd been able to have our allocated tent close to Jude, Tyler and Tasha's when we'd booked and when I spot my tent number, I almost wilt like a dried-out flower.

'Aw,' I chime, noticing that Jude's tent is on the opposite row and a few units down from ours. 'You'd have been all over there on your own if I wasn't here.'

I throw him a playful smile, as if I'm doing him a favour by being here after all.

'Hardly,' Tasha snorts. 'You do *not* have to worry about him. Jude's never alone for long in this place – some woman will have attached herself to him before dinner tonight.'

'Yep, thanks, Tasha,' Jude says, rolling his eyes and practically shooing her into her tent.

'Right,' I say slowly. 'Looks like it'll be *me* playing gooseberry then.'

'Don't listen to her,' Jude says, pulling his eyebrows together in a frown. 'She says really dumb stuff sometimes.'

If I'm not mistaken, a hint of embarrassment is lurking behind his chocolate brown eyes.

I shrug and smile nonchalantly. 'Hey, it's none of my business. We're here to have fun, right?'

'Yeah, right.' He scratches the back of his neck and nods. 'Want some help getting yourself set up?'

I nod gratefully and duck under the flap to the tent. Honestly, I'd been shocked at the cost of the accommodation. When I'd pictured what a festival weekend would look like, it included bringing a sleeping bag and my own tent that would probably be pitched in the rain. In fact, it would've been someone else's tent, because I've never owned one in my life. It was Nina who'd insisted on booking a pre-pitched one. Why faff around wasting precious time, energy and nerves putting it up, when you could simply arrive, dump your belongings and enjoy the festivities.

'I'm really glad I listened to Nina about the tent thing,' I say.

'I've always done the traditional camping thing and brought my own tent but I have to admit, this is just so much easier. Must be getting old,' Jude jokes, crouching down to fit himself under the roof. The long drive, constant conversation and sun have seeped into my muscles and bone, and I put both of my hands on my belly before yawning loudly.

He pulls the airbed from its box and fixes me with a curious look. 'Ready for bed already?'

'I *am* a little bushed,' I admit. 'Which is super lame considering we only just got here.'

'Well, I'm not pregnant and I'm tired, too. I almost always have a party nap once my tent's sorted.'

'A party nap,' I grin. 'I like that.'

Jude laughs and gets to work on blowing up the airbed with a foot pump. I literally couldn't be any more grateful for every puff of air that goes into it because, if I'd have to pump it up myself with this level of tiredness creeping over me, I'd probably end up just sleeping on the floor instead.

'So, what's the plan for tonight? Apart from the party nap,' I ask.

'Food, a few drinks and then catching some music. And then rinsing and repeating for the weekend.'

I nod and yawn again, shaking my head at the end of it and try to wake myself up. I'd felt fine the whole way here but now that a bed is in my sights, all I can think about is lying down on it. It's a bit like needing the loo for ages and being able to hold it easily until you put the key in the door and the urgency magnifies a hundred-fold.

'Maybe we can go down to the lake too?' I suggest, imagining the coolness of the water soothing my skin. I yawn again, breaking it with a laugh. 'But first – a nap.'

Chapter Seventeen

When I open my eyes, I immediately know my nap must've evolved into a full-blown sleep. The brightness shining through the white canvas of the tent is brighter than it had been when I'd laid on the airbed for a short doze. I yawn and stretch my legs before sitting up. As soon as I do, my bladder screams at me and I wince. I can't remember the last time I slept through the night without getting up at least once for a pee, let alone the whole evening too. I must have been completely wiped out. A quick glance at my phone tells me it's just approaching seven a.m. I pull the dress I fell asleep in over my head and reach into my suitcase for my bikini, deciding to look for the lake after I've had a pee. With my bikini on and a new dress over the top, I pack my phone into my toiletry bag, grab my towel and step outside.

The air is cool and crisp with a hint of heat building behind it as I make my way to the shower block. A few tents are unzipped and there are a few people around, but the camp is mainly quiet. I soak in that magical feeling of being awake in that liminal time before activity takes over. The dewy grass tickles the tips of my toes in my flip-flops and when I get to the toilet block, I'm surprised to see that they're compost toilets that actually look pretty decent. I've seen and used much, much worse over the years. I take a couple snaps for Nina, including the witty handwritten sign explaining how to use the loo and then freshen up.

I've never really been a camping type of person. I'm much more at home in a hotel, guesthouse or Airbnb, but there's something nice about stripping back to basics and having a view of the woodland to brush my teeth to. And while I'm not exactly stuck out in the wilderness of Alaska, it still adds up to the feeling of independence that's been building steadily throughout my pregnancy. Look at me, here, camping at a festival, with a big pregnant belly under my dress. It might sound silly to some, but I'm proud of myself for being here.

After brushing my teeth, I set off to find the lake. It can't be that far away and as soon as I'm behind the treeline of the woodland surrounding the camp, I can see there's no danger of getting lost. There are signposts every few metres and soon enough, I emerge through the trees to a stretch of water that looks so enticing I almost want to run into it as if it were the sea.

The surface is still and as I step beneath it, the water glides over me like velvet. Apart from another woman taking a slow breaststroke, nobody else is here. I'm certain it won't be this way for long. It might have been the music line-up that made most people book their ticket, but for me it was this. The chilled water takes the weight of my belly as I swim gently, taking in the pale-yellow tint of the sky and the special algae smell that only lakes have. I feel instantly at home and if it weren't for the hunger building inside, I'd happily stay here all day. But I haven't eaten since lunch yesterday, and if I'm hungry, the baby must be too.

With my towel wrapped around my shoulders, I make my way back to the campsite. There are more people up and about now and outside our tents, Tyler and Tasha are setting up a camping stove. She looks up at me with a grin.

'Ah, Sleeping Beauty's awake. How'd you sleep?' she asks, piling her blonde hair up on top of her head and securing it with a band from around her wrist.

'Like the dead,' I laugh with a hint of embarrassment.

'Yeah, we tried waking you up,' Tyler says. 'You were totally wiped out. Didn't you hear the music?'

'I dreamed some,' I shrug, 'but clearly it wasn't enough for me to wake up and join the party.'

I unzip my tent, sling my stuff inside and bring out my foldable chair, lowering myself into it. I smooth the baby hairs at the back of my neck that got wet during my swim with my hand. I didn't bring a swimming cap and now that I don't have the ease and protection of my braids I have to be careful not to get my hair wet, or I'll end up with a mess of tight, tangled curls.

'What did I miss?' I ask. 'I'm gutted I slept through the first night.'

'Not much,' Tasha says with a wave of her hand. 'Not enough food and too much booze. Are you hungry? We've got vegan sausages and beans.'

'Oh, that sounds so much more appealing than muesli,' I admit. 'Is there enough?'

'Of course. It's kind of like a first morning tradition,' Tyler explains, right when Jude emerges from his tent with a foldable camping chair just like mine.

He's wearing a pair of soft-looking jogging bottoms, the hood of his hoodie is pulled up to cover most of his head and his eyes are hidden behind a pair of dark sunglasses.

'Ouch.' I pull a face. 'That looks painful.'

'Ah, I just need a coffee.'

'And a new head?'

'It's not that bad. See?' He lowers his head, drops his glasses a couple of inches and looks at me with a raised eyebrow. 'Good morning.'

'Morning,' I smile back as he flops himself down into the chair and produces a glass jar of instant coffee. 'The lake could probably do just as a good a job as that.'

'You found it then?'

I nod with a dreamy sigh. 'It was gorgeous. So clean and super quiet.'

'Isn't it hard swimming when you're pregnant?' Tasha asks, ripping open the packet of sausages.

I shake my head. 'Just the opposite.'

'I don't do lakes.' She shakes her head and shudders so visibly her bare pale shoulders tremble. 'You can't see the bottom. It freaks me out.'

'She can't swim,' Tyler explains.

'I *can*. I'm just not a strong swimmer and I hate going out of my depth. I always panic that I'll drown.'

The admission of her not being able to do something and even being afraid of it, makes Tasha even more likeable than she already is. Steph hadn't been able to swim either. I remember the time we went to Portugal for a week and she took a surfing lesson, only to tell us afterwards that she couldn't swim. Nina had lost it. Surfing without knowing how to swim wasn't the brightest of ideas – anything could happen. But that was typical of Steph. She always acted first and thought of the consequences later. Tasha's personality reminds me a lot of Nina, but her looks conjure up Steph, from her long legs to her blonde hair, to her skinny fingers and high cheekbones. In a parallel universe, Steph would probably be here with us. I blink the image of her away. She'd made her choice and I resolve not to think about her, or Sam, or anything other than having a good time for the rest of the weekend.

◆ ◆ ◆

'Am I allowed to say I'd never have expected this to be your kind of place?' I say to Jude with a smile.

We're sitting at the edge of the crowd at one of the music stages where a band I've never heard of are playing something that sounds like a blend of Björk and eighties synth pop.

'Oh, yeah?' Jude's hangover has eased enough for him to put his sunglasses away, and he looks at me with amusement in his brown eyes. 'Why's that?'

I shrug, looking around us. 'I didn't think you were into the boho-artsy scene.'

The festival is decidedly middle-class, with stands selling chai for a fiver and kombucha for double that. After a long and lazy breakfast, we'd taken a tour. The food stalls had everything from kebabs and chips to venison burgers, eggs benedict and raclette. I'm glad I brought my muesli and a few other bits to balance the cost or it would end up being much more expensive than I'd bargained for. The crowd is diverse – I'm not the only Black person here by far – but if I were to compare it to places in London it would be less Hackney and more Hampstead.

Jude shakes his head as I open a pack of Hula Hoops. 'How many of those things can you eat in a day?'

'A lot,' I grin, looking at the crowd dancing just a few feet away. 'Honestly, if I had to guess, I'd have thought you'd go to something a bit more . . . urban?'

He takes a couple of crisps and leans back on his elbows, stretching his long legs in front of him. The jogging bottoms have been swapped for more weather appropriate board shorts that show off his shapely calves.

'I learned a long time ago that life is much simpler and way more fun when you can feel good in most places,' he replies. 'Plus, if you never try something new, you'll never know if you like it. It's like always ordering the same thing in a restaurant.'

'Oh, God!' My cheeks flush as I laugh. 'I can't believe I'm admitting this, but I am *that* person. I order the same thing every time.'

The people at the Indian takeaway on my street can probably predict my order just from seeing my number flashing up when I call.

'You do?'

I nod. 'Ninety-nine per cent of the time. I hate to say it, but when I order something different it's usually a disappointment.'

'You like what you like?' he asks, with a look of knowing on his face.

'Exactly.'

The band on stage finish their song and even though I've barely been listening, I clap anyway.

'What do you think of the band?' Jude asks.

'They're actually pretty good. Not my usual thing, but . . .'

He grins as if his point has been made and it takes me a moment to catch onto why. I roll my eyes before tilting my face towards the sun.

'It was actually my ex who got me here,' Jude says, and I open my eyes to look at him. 'This was her favourite festival.'

'Rachel?'

He nods. 'She's one of Tasha's closest mates. It was Tasha who turned her onto it and then me in turn.'

'Aren't you nervous about bumping into her?'

'Not really. I mean, I'm not exactly seeking her out but no, it'd be fine. Besides, I'm pretty sure she isn't here. Tasha would've told me if she were coming.'

I frown, looking out at the crowd where Tasha and Tyler are embedded in the throng. 'Isn't it awkward for you that they're still friends?'

Jude shrugs. 'Not anymore. I don't see her and Tasha doesn't speak about her. I became really good friends with Tyler and Tasha. It would be a shame to lose that because of what happened with Rachel.'

'True,' I concede.

'You're not still friends with anyone in Australia?'

I pull a face. 'Nope.'

Wasn't that just how things went? Mutual friends rarely stayed mutual after a break-up, at least, not from what I'd seen. And, not that I'd really expected it, but not one of Sam's friends have reached out to me since I left. I've swapped a couple of messages with Adele, my old co-working buddy, but generally it's been a case of out of sight, out of mind.

'Anyway,' Jude continues, crossing his ankles. 'I like it here. It's chilled, the people are mostly friendly and the music's pretty decent too.'

I smile, shaking my head. Somehow, being around Jude makes me feel a little shy. It's nothing I can really put my finger on. It's more of a recognition of how strange it can be to know someone for pretty much your whole life, and not really know them.

'What's that goofy smile for?' he asks.

I look at him and squint one eye against the sun that's shining from behind his head. 'I was just thinking that it feels like I didn't really know you before.'

'Well, you didn't.'

'How is that possible? You're my best friend's brother. I've known you almost my whole life.'

'So?' he laughs. 'I mean come on. Nina and I fought like hell as kids. The last thing we'd be wanting to do is hang out with each other's friends.'

'Yeah, it was pretty brutal for a while there I remember,' I nod. 'But you've been close for ages since then.'

'And you've been away for ages,' he replies, raising an eyebrow.

I nod. He's right of course. Trips home always meant making sure to see and spend time with Nina, but Jude? Less so.

'Well, I'm back now,' I say with a smile.

'You are.' He nods and the skin around his eyes wrinkles as he smiles back. 'And you're at your very first festival. Yet another thing to strike off your list.'

I think about the piece of paper stuck to my fridge with a sense of accomplishment. I feel proud of all the things I'm doing. I look down at the bump and rub my hand across it. It's odd to think there'll be a time in the not-too-distant future when it won't be there.

'Can you make a fire?' I ask, and Jude laughs.

'Okay, that was random.'

'I've never built a fire from scratch before,' I explain.

I don't know how many fires I've sat in front of, from beach fires to ones in accommodation Sam and I lived in over the years. Before we'd moved into our Sydney apartment, we'd house-sat for one of his friends and they had a huge woodfire oven in their living room. It feels bizarre to me that I never built one. It was one of those things that automatically fell under Sam's list of responsibilities, like checking the oil in the car. Of course, a relationship is about teamwork but I do wonder if I'd handed the reins over more than I ought to have done.

'Isn't that weird?' I ask, shaking my head again.

'Not really. I think most people don't know how to do it either.'

'I can do something as huge as making a baby, but I can't make a fire. Can you?'

'I can *help* make a baby,' Jude replies with a laugh and I swat his arm. 'And yes, I can make a fire. I learned it on the Duke of Edinburgh at school. I can show you if you want, there's a firepit at camp. We just have to get there early enough before someone else gets to it.'

I nod. 'That would be awesome.'

I don't know why it feels so necessary to do this, but it does. It's like a primal thing that's embedded in my DNA and needs to be remembered before I'm responsible for the survival of another human being.

'Nature calls,' I say with a sigh.

'Again?'

I shrug. I seem to have spent half the day walking to and from the toilets. There are plenty of them at least and there seems to be an army of people keeping them clean. Considering it's a festival, I'd expected much worse. I'm just gathering my will to get up when Tasha emerges from the crowd with a huge grin and what look like very glassy eyes.

'Oh my God, they're *so good!* Why aren't you dancing, you're missing it.'

'I'm still recovering,' I reply with a laugh.

I'd managed to dance to couple of songs but, honestly, it felt like effort. I didn't know the songs and I was afraid of getting jostled in the crowd.

'Oh, sure. Not you, obviously. But you.' She kicks Jude's foot and he groans.

'I'm still hungover,' he replies.

He doesn't look hungover – at least, not quite as bad as this morning.

'I've got a cure for that,' she says in a sing-song voice.

'All sorted.' Jude holds up the same bottle of beer he's been nursing for at least an hour. There can't be anything left in there and, if there is, it definitely can't be drinkable.

Tasha swizzes the sparkly purple bumbag she's wearing around her hips and unzips the front pouch. She pulls out just a sliver of a sealed plastic bag.

'Maybe you want a dab?'

'What is it?' I ask.

'MD.'

'MA?' I raise my eyebrows and Tasha laughs.

'What other kind is there?'

Jude sits up and shakes his head. 'I'm good, Tash.'

He says it with a laugh, but there's a hint of irritation there, just like when she'd insinuated that he'd be getting laid left, right and centre over the weekend. He lets his bottle fall to the ground and, as I suspected, nothing spills out of it.

'Oh, well. More for us then,' she shrugs before looking at me and tilting her head to one side. 'Loo break?'

'I'm going to go wander around a bit,' Jude says, rubbing his hands together as if he's dusting them off.

I nod and Tasha loops her arm through mine as we set off. Her footsteps are a little heavy and while she doesn't quite stumble, she's not exactly sure-footed either.

'Moo-hoo-*dy*!' she giggles, taking a little peek over her shoulder.

'Who, Jude?'

She nods and her upper arm bumps into mine, leaving a little patch of sweat that feels cool on my skin.

'He's normally totally off his head by now.'

'Really?'

'Oh, yeah. Festivals plus Jude equals madness. It's *so* not like him to be sober.'

An out-of-control Jude is a version of him I haven't heard of since he was a teenager.

'I don't think I've seen him wasted in a long time,' I reply.

184

'He doesn't do all this stuff usually,' Tasha says, wrapping a thick strand of hair around her finger. 'Except at festivals. It's like, at festivals, normal rules don't apply.'

'What happens on tour, stays on tour?'

'Exactly,' she laughs. 'It's so nice that you're here. Since he split with Rachel it's always just been us three. Festivalling with two guys . . . ugh.'

'He's never brought anyone else?'

'And ruin the—' Tasha shakes her head and pulls her lips into her mouth as if she's literally keeping the words inside. 'Anyway. It's fun that you're here.'

Curiosity scratches at the back of my throat. I want to ask what her hesitation was about and whether it was to do with her comment last night about him never being alone for too long.

We walk past a burrito stand and my stomach flips with nausea. The sensitivity to food smells I thought I'd left behind in the first trimester seems to be back in full force here. Between the constant weed and cigarette smoke, which I've tried my best to avoid, the air is filled with a cloying mix of incense, food and alcohol. A couple of guys walk straight towards us, so absorbed in their joking laughter that I'm sure they don't even see us. I unlink my arm from Tasha's to protectively wrap it around my belly as we dodge them and they saunter right through the space we'd just occupied.

'God, men. Sometimes they're just *so* oblivious,' Tasha says with a sigh.

In fairness, it isn't just the men. It's a part of the festival experience I hadn't really banked on, but the constant worry about someone accidentally jabbing an elbow into my belly hasn't been far from my mind since I got here. By the time we get to the toilets, my bladder is bursting and my legs are tired from the walk, but if I'd have thought there'd be preferential treatment for being pregnant when it comes jumping the queue, I'd have been mistaken.

Most people are too busy chatting, drunk or high to even know where they are, let alone notice my belly and the ones that do are inevitably with children themselves. We join the queue and while Tasha strikes up conversation with the people in front, I go back to people-watching and settle in for the wait.

◆ ◆ ◆

It takes a day and a half to acclimatise to festival life. I've become a pro at learning how to beat the crowds to the toilets by going when the main acts are playing the most popular songs, and my nose has desensitised to the assault of smells. I've probably walked the equivalent of John O'Groats to Land's End, have seen what looked like at least two break-ups and had a hormonal cry when I witnessed a marriage proposal. It looked completely substance induced and spontaneous, but still, I cried like a baby. I'll admit there was more than a hint of sadness at how far away I am from that, but at least ninety per cent of the tears were happy ones.

The sun has been so strong that the grass has turned crisp, and last night I'd had to sleep with the tent flap open to get more air. Today's the hottest it's been so far and, with Tyler and Tasha being so hungover, we've spent most of the day by the lake. It feels bizarrely like a beach holiday. The four of us have been laid out on towels, trailing like ants from the grass to the water and back again. Even Tasha ventured in, going only as far as her feet could touch the pebbly ground.

'This is the life,' I say, dipping my body back down until everything up to my shoulders are underwater.

'I had no idea you were such a water baby,' Jude replies.

'Always have been. Especially when it's natural water, like the sea or a lake.'

A dragonfly skims the water and I catch a few bars of a song floating over the trees from the big stage. The lake is busy with children splashing about in their special kids' section over on the far side and a few people are sunning themselves on the floating platform in the middle. Laughter occasionally pierces the air and somewhere overhead is the sound of a propellor plane flying over the fields. A wave of contentment washes over me and Jude's eyes catch mine as I smile.

'You're glad you came?' he asks.

'Absolutely.' I nod. 'Thanks for chaperoning.'

He pulls a face. 'What makes you think I've been chaperoning?'

I raise my eyebrows up to my hairline. 'You've had, what? Three beers or something since the first night?'

'So?' he shrugs with a nonchalant smile. 'I don't feel like drinking.'

'Right,' I reply with a small laugh. 'From what I've heard you're a festival party animal. And I saw the amount of booze you brought with you.'

Jude rolls his eyes and, with a shake of his head, the tiniest of flushes creeps across his freckled, light-brown skin. Or maybe it's a hint of sunburn. He dips his head under the water for a second and, when he comes back up, he shakes it from side to side, sprinkling me with droplets that land on my face. Is it self-centred to think he's been chaperoning me? Why else would he be behaving in a way that, by all accounts, is the complete opposite to how he normally does when he's here? Jude scrubs his hands over his short hair and rivulets of water stream down his toned inner biceps. My eyes are drawn to the tattoo of interconnected triangles on the side of his ribs and even in the coolness of the water, I feel my skin ripple with goosebumps. I tear my eyes away. The first near-naked man I've had this close to me for months and my body's overreacting. I'd laugh if it wasn't so sad. Or inappropriate. I scoop a handful of water from

187

the surface and splash my face before adjusting the light scarf I've wrapped around my hair to protect it.

'I'll have a beer tonight,' he says with a hint of defiance on his face.

'Ooh, push the boat out, why don't you.'

I laugh and squirm as he splashes a bunch of water towards me. I feel like a giddy teenager at the leisure centre on a Saturday afternoon.

'What do you think about building that fire tonight?' I ask.

Jude looks up at the sky with his face twisting in apprehension. 'I don't know. Those clouds don't look promising.'

I look up and have to agree. I'd thought today would be just like yesterday – dawn-to-dusk sunshine and gratitude for shade – but clouds have crept in so stealthily it's as if they've sprung up from nowhere. It's only making a fire. It's hardly a life-or-death situation, but I'm suddenly filled with fear that if it doesn't happen today, it won't happen at all. I shake my head as if trying to dislodge the feeling when a fat drop of rain lands in the water between us so heavily it leaves a little crater behind that ripples out in a perfect circle.

'It might just be a shower,' Jude says. 'It's so hot that everything will probably dry out before it gets dark anyway.'

A sharp gust of cold air cuts through the cloak of humidity, brushing against my shoulders and making me shiver as it disappears as quickly as it came. A second later, rain falls all around us as if someone has unzipped the bottom of the clouds and the almost heavy, calm vibe around the lake is disrupted.

'I guess that's that, then,' Jude laughs, squinting his eyes against the downpour.

On both sides of the lake, people are gathering their blankets, towels and clothes and I can't help but laugh at Tasha's loud shriek.

'We should go,' Jude says, speaking a little louder over the noise of the rain splashing against the surface.

'Come on,' Tasha shouts, cupping her hands to make the sound travel faster.

'I'm staying in,' I shout back.

Jude turns to look at me as if I've gone mad. 'Seriously?'

'Why not?' I shrug with a grin. 'I'll be just as wet in here as out there. Plus, everyone will be rushing to the stage and food stalls now. It'll be a muddy mess. I'd rather be in here than risk slipping and falling over.'

Jude nods his head as if he hadn't considered it. 'Makes sense.'

'But you can go. I'll be fine here,' I say, and laugh when he frowns. 'Seriously. I'm in my element.'

As if to prove my point, I swim a little half-circle around him, grinning playfully. He laughs and looks back over at Tasha and Tyler.

'I'll stay too.'

They shake their heads as if we've lost our minds before scurrying up the incline with almost everybody else.

'And before you say anything, I'm not chaperoning,' he says. 'I've just never swum in the rain before.'

I consider it for a moment and realise I haven't either. 'You know what? Neither have I.'

Our grins widen as if we've just shared a secret, and I look around at the three other people who've decided to stay in the water. We might be in the countryside somewhere in Yorkshire, but with pellets of rain spraying a fine mist around us, the greenery of our surroundings and the humidity in the air, it feels like we could be in a rainforest. The rain intensifies and neither of us say a word as we swim out a little deeper. It's as if we both want to soak up the experience of listening to the sound of the rain bouncing up from the surface, the sluicing of water across our skin and the faint hint of music from the main stage.

I find myself staring at Jude's shoulder muscles as he swims just a half a meter in front of me. Maybe it's okay to notice the dusting of dark freckles across his skin and the deep, almost ravine-like inward curve between the muscles on either side of his spine. He is a man, after all. And it's never been a secret to me that he's a good looking one at that. But it feels a little inappropriate. Firstly, because I'm pregnant with another man's baby, and secondly because he's Nina's brother. And Nina feels like a sister to me, which means . . . I pull a face at the thought and rip my eyes away from Jude's back just in time to notice he's stopped swimming. I stop myself from smashing into him and we both tread water, making arcs in the water with our arms.

He looks at me and smiles. 'I've got a confession to make. Well, two, actually.'

'Oh, this sounds good.'

'I've actually never been in this lake before.' He frowns a little and then laughs. 'At least, not that I can remember.'

'How is that even possible?' I laugh back.

'I was always too hammered.'

'So, the stories about you are all true?' I raise my eyebrows playfully and he pulls a face.

'Not all of them, I'm sure. But why, what have you heard?'

I pull my fingers across my lips and mime turning a key in the lock. I don't know any nitty-gritty details, but I don't need to tell him that.

'What is it about festivals that gets you so . . .' I tail off looking for the right word. 'Hedonistic?'

'I don't know. A lot of my best memories are at festivals. It's kind of like keeping the spirit alive or the trend going . . . I don't know.'

I wonder if the memories he's talking about are to do with his ex. The curious part of me wants to ask while the other part, the part that's feeling an unexpected wave of electricity as his eyes look back at mine, doesn't want to know.

'So, how's it been being sober?' I ask, deciding some things are probably best left unsaid.

'You know what, it's actually been good,' he replies, sounding more than a little surprised. 'I don't think I've managed to see so many acts before. We normally end up wasted in someone's tent and miss everything.'

'You're getting your money's worth then,' I say with a wink. 'To be fair, our girls' holidays used to get messy too.'

He nods and laughs. 'I know. Nina always seemed so destroyed afterwards.'

'We all were.'

'And there I was thinking you were the nice, cute one who never got wild.'

My cheeks blaze and my stomach jumps so hard I wonder if the baby can feel it. 'Cute?'

Jude shrugs it off with a laugh. 'Yeah, compared to Steph.'

The blazing in my cheeks dies down. 'I'm not sure that's much of a compliment.'

'Oh, it is. She was a *lot*,' he laughs. 'To think I almost had something with her. If it wasn't for Nina being so bossy about not dating her friends – I'd have probably only regretted it.'

I remember how Nina had gone mad when she'd heard that Jude and Steph had kissed. I wonder if she'd have done the same if it had been me instead. It's a stupid thing to think, really. I don't know why I've suddenly decided to develop a teenage crush on my best friend's brother. I can only put it down to being here, away from the real world with a feeling that anything might happen. I quickly remind myself that while I might still have the libido of a twenty-year-old, I'm really six months' pregnant and in no position to be thinking about such things.

I clear my throat. 'So, what was the second thing? You said you had two confessions.'

'I lied about not chaperoning you.'

'I knew it,' I reply with a laugh. 'Did Nina put you up to it?'

'Yeah. Well, not really. I'd have done it anyway,' he replies. 'Someone has to be the responsible one and make sure nobody does anything stupid. I figured this could be Tyler's year off.'

I laugh again. 'You're a terrible liar, you know.'

'I know,' he shrugs with a smile. 'I've been told that before.'

A rumble of thunder rolls across the sky and I feel a gentle nudge in my belly. We've been in the water for a while and even though I could probably stay here forever, the water feels colder now. Another clap of thunder rings out, a little closer this time and Jude and I nod at each other, knowing it's time to make our way out. If there's lightning coming then a lake is the last place we should be. We glide across the surface with our movements matching like synchronised swimmers until we're able to touch the ground with our feet. He reaches a hand out and I take it, steadying myself with his grip against the slippery pebbles.

'Woah,' Jude says, his eyes widening and fixed on my belly.

I look down as the baby nudges against my skin again, creating a visible pulse. I laugh and rub my hand across it.

'She's been doing it on and off all day. Maybe its hiccups.'

'They can get hiccups before they're born?'

'I've read about it, yeah. Maybe she's hungry,' I smile. 'I know I am.'

'Mad.' He shakes his head. 'A few of my mates have kids but I've never really spent much time around a pregnant woman.'

I tilt my head to one side and widen my smile. 'Do you want to feel?'

He looks unsure for a moment and then shrugs. 'Yeah, sure.'

Jude puts his hand right on my belly. I've hated random people touching it and, thankfully, not one person has done that here. But it feels different with Jude. She kicks almost straight away, right under his hand and as he gasps with surprise, I laugh at his reaction. For a second, it feels like the most natural thing in the world. By now, she can hear and recognise my voice – the voice of her mum. It's a strange thing to realise that she's heard the tone of Jude's voice multiple times but has never heard Sam's. The man who's actually her dad. The realisation of it lands squarely in my chest and dampens my laughter so abruptly that Jude takes his hand away, leaving a patch of cold skin behind.

I shake my head in what feels like an apology as he crouches down to pick up our sodden towels.

He bunches them up in his arms and looks at me. 'You alright?'

'Yeah,' I reply with a little forced lightness. 'Just hungry. And cold.'

I wrap my arms around myself as if to prove the point and he looks over towards the treeline.

'Come on, it's only a couple of minutes to the tents.'

The rain has cooled the air substantially and it doesn't take long for me to start shivering. I feel ridiculous and, despite there being hardly anyone else around, I wonder what they'd make of me – soaked and half-naked in my bikini with a pregnant belly. The ease and contentment I'd felt earlier has gone, replaced by a weighty feeling of being irresponsible.

'Still cold?' Jude asks, catching the tremble of my shoulders.

I nod and he wraps an arm around me. His skin feels warm and I let myself melt into it, snuggling my shoulder into his armpit. He smells of lake water and the remnants of sun cream, and I sigh as the shivers leave my body. As predicted, the ground has become slick with mud and I'm grateful for the support of Jude's arm around me. The mud squelches under my feet and squeezes between my toes, and I can feel the tired muscles in my calves protesting as I try to hold my centre of gravity against the full weight of the baby in my pelvis.

When we get back to our tents, Jude drops his arm from my shoulder and I look up at him.

'Thanks, by the way,' I say. 'For looking out for me. I know it's not what you expected when you booked your tickets and I *definitely* feel like I've hijacked your weekend. But I really appreciate it.'

'It's all good,' Jude replies with a smile. 'Do you want to grab some food?'

I grin widely. 'God, yes. Just as soon as I've got some dry clothes on.'

I pull the string around my neck with my padlock key over my head and unzip my tent, but no sooner have I stepped inside, am I drawn back out again by the sound of Jude swearing.

'What is it?' I ask, opening the flat to his tent. 'Oh, no.'

The coconut matting squelches under his feet and a steady stream of rainwater pours in through a rip in the canvas, high up and close to the central pole. I step inside and my heart sinks for him. Everything is soaked.

'Shit.' He shakes his head again, bending down to pick up a piece of clothing.

'Should we call someone?'

Jude shakes his head. 'For what? We're leaving tomorrow anyway and it's not like there'll be a spare tent for me. The tickets were sold out.'

He sighs and his shoulders deflate like a pierced balloon. I feel awful. If he hadn't had to chaperone me, he'd have probably come back to the tent as soon as it started raining for some clothes. He might not have been able to do anything about the rip, however that had happened, but he'd have at least been able to move his things. Jude picks up one of his Vans trainers and a stream of water runs out of it.

'You never know,' I smile weakly, 'it might go back to blistering heat and everything can dry off.'

'Yeah, maybe.'

We both know it's unlikely. Even if the rain does stop, the hottest part of the day is over and it'll be moist overnight. Tomorrow we'll wake up to dew-beaded everything, just as we have for the last two mornings. Jude reaches for his sleeping bag. It's totally sodden and there's no way he'll be able to use it. I look back out through the tent flap as a group walks past in wellies, clearly better prepared for the gloriously unpredictable British summer. I look back at Jude, wringing the top end of his sleeping bag between his hands.

'Hey,' I say, feeling oddly nervous. 'Why don't you stay in my tent tonight? You can't sleep in here.'

Jude's eyebrows flicker into a frown. 'Thanks, Zoe. But your airbed takes up pretty much all the floor space there is.'

I swallow and use having a bump as an excuse for something to busy my hands with. 'I know. But it's a double and I mean, you can't sleep in that thing.'

Jude looks at the sleeping bag and shakes his head a little. 'Really? I mean, I can ask Tasha and Tyler. I'm sure they won't mind.'

'I think they're very much in that *on* phase you told me about,' I reply with a cheeky smile. 'I'm pretty sure you'd be gatecrashing their party.'

Maybe it's the booze or the drugs, or simply being in a tent together, but they haven't exactly been quiet about their relationship status if the moans and groans have been anything to go by. Jude and I catch each other's eyes again and we both fall into fits of giggles. I hide my face in my hands as I laugh, feeling the bounce of my belly as it contracts. We're both adults, so why do I feel like a fifteen-year-old? I drop my hands and our laughter turns into long sighs.

He looks at me. 'Are you sure?'

'Of course. It's the least I can do.'

'Thanks, Zoe. I really appreciate it.'

'Just let me get changed and you can bring your things over.'

He nods. 'I'll leave most of it here. The wet stuff, anyways.'

I duck out of his tent and cross the little walkway to my own. I know it's stupid to be excited about it, but there are butterflies in my belly as I root through my suitcase. I take the compact mirror from my bag and hold it far away from me so I can see as much of my face in it as possible. I take in a deep breath and fix myself with a stern look.

'Alright, Zoe,' I say to myself in a whisper. 'This is Jude we're talking about here. This weird crush is silly. Beyond silly. But God, he's hot, isn't he?'

I shake my head and laugh at myself before snapping the mirror shut. I have clearly lost my mind. I grab my phone from the, thankfully, waterproof casing I'd left it in under my mattress and find my chat with Nina. The screen is full of the pictures I've been sending and while she's over the worst of it, she's still not back to full health.

Zoe: We've had the maddest rain today! Jude's tent is completely flooded :(I've offered for him to stay with me . . . at least we're coming back tomorrow so he doesn't have to live in his swimming shorts LOL.

I put the phone down. Telling Nina brings the whole thing back down to the level it should be at: normal. It's just me helping out a friend – a lifelong one at that. I fish out jogging bottoms from my suitcase. It's hardly the trendiest of festival looks but the weather's cooled considerably and there'll be legions of mosquitoes around now. But, as comfortable as they are, they don't do a very good job of making me feel attractive. After Jude brings in a change of clothes for tomorrow, we make our way to the main area, both wearing jogging bottoms. There is a part of me that laughs at the fact that we actually look like a matching couple, especially with our grey hoodies. It's one of life's ironies that you probably couldn't plan, even if you wanted to.

It's the last night of the festival, but it feels like the rain has washed some of the mojo away. Now that it's stopped, the place feels more chilled and less frenetic. Even Tasha and Tyler seem a little subdued. As I chomp away on a delicious burger, I decide to let myself feel the excitement flickering like a lightbulb in my belly. I know it's sad. But really, what harm can it do? It's not as if anything's going happen between Jude and me. And it has been *months* since I've had even a hint of flirtatiousness with a man. So, we'll share an airbed, it's not really a big deal. I can totally let myself enjoy having close company and tomorrow, we'll drive back to London and it'll be back to situation normal.

Once I've decided to let myself play out this weird fantasy, I find myself relaxing into the rest of the evening. There's no self-built fire to sit around which is sad, but there is plenty of nice conversation to make up for it. I find myself swaying gently to an acoustic folk act on stage. With bulbs strung up overhead and a half-moon right above us in the thankfully clear sky, the feeling of contentment I'd had in the lake comes back. For a while, I stifle my yawns until I see that Jude is doing the same. And because it's my sad fantasy, I tell myself it's because he's nervous about being the one to suggest we call it a night, so I do it. After hugging Tasha and Tyler goodnight, we walk back to the tents talking easily about the bands from the weekend. We keep talking as we brush our teeth and carry on the conversation after using the toilet. And even though we haven't agreed to sleep fully clothed, once we're inside, we keep our hoodies and jogging bottoms on as we get into bed.

In the darkness of the tent, our conversation falls away and we simply lie there listening to the sound of crickets and the occasional person walking by, squelching in the mud outside. It's the easiest silence I can remember being in for a long time. If ever. I can tell by Jude's breathing pattern that he's not sleeping. At least, I don't think he is. I imagine what it would be like to see someone's breath as a colour, and picture it floating in and out of his body, hovering in the air above us, along with mine. Soon, there's the light pitter-patter of rain on the canvas and it slowly lulls my eyelids to slide and stay closed.

At some point, I hear Tasha and Tyler coming back, giggling as they unzip their tent. I roll over, turning away from Jude to lie on my other side, falling promptly back asleep. Sometime later, I feel him turn and wrap his arms around me, spooning his body around mine. I know it's a sleep reflex and simply the very human need to reach for another warm body, but I don't shake him off. Instead, I snuggle in a little deeper and let myself go back to sleep.

◆ ◆ ◆

Pregnancy week: Twenty-seven
You're the size of a: Cauliflower
Today, I feel: Magical

Hello, Little One . . .
Wasn't that a great weekend? Since you didn't rip my belly open and shout at me like you did in my dream, I'm guessing you enjoyed it too :)
I'm actually glad it wasn't a massive festival with super-famous acts and humungous crowds. I'm

still dreaming about swimming in the lake with the rain falling . . . just divine. I hope you'll be a water baby too, like me. If you come on your due date, you'll be a Scorpio which is a water sign, so fingers crossed!

What would you like to be called? Names say a lot about a person . . . it feels important to choose the right one. I've always liked mine, but I'd hate for you to hate yours. Harper, Ava, Lily, Emilia . . . I looked online and those are some of the most popular. I don't like the idea of an obviously made-up name, but I don't think you'd want a common one either. Maybe I'm overthinking it. Maybe I'll see you and just know what you're supposed to be called . . .

In the meantime, we've got our first antenatal class next week! Mum says they're a good way to meet other mums-to-be with babies being born around the same time and I have to admit, now that the due date is getting closer and closer, I feel a bit dubious about what to expect. It can only be a good thing, right?

Love,

Zoe

xx

Chapter Eighteen

I close the pregnancy journal and lay it on my outstretched legs. It's two days since we drove back from the festival, and the deluge that had drenched us so dramatically there has slowly followed us home. The portion of sky I can see from my position on the sofa is a layer-cake of grey on grey. Fat, heavy drops of rain are bouncing back up from slick pavements instead of the gorgeously green lake, and the earthy smell of mud and wet grass has been replaced by the whiffs of engine exhausts and wet tarmac. But listening to the downpour is like being right back there again. I'd felt a huge surge of satisfaction when I came home and crossed the festival off my list. It even eclipsed the fact that learning to make a fire hadn't happened.

I look at the ever-growing curve of my belly. I don't know why I didn't mention Jude in that last journal entry. It feels like lying by omission, but this isn't a journal where I write down my deepest, darkest innermost feelings. It's a way to document my pregnancy so that, one day, she can read back on it and see how her life started. So really, if I'm going to talk about a man in those pages, it really ought to be Sam. Her dad. Not Jude.

I wiggle my feet against the weird creepy-crawly feeling that's set in since the festival and the endless amount of walking we seemed to do. I'd spent the whole drive home dreaming of a long, hot shower followed by an evening with my feet propped up. Instead, I'd struggled to keep my restless legs still. I shake my head. I've lied again. I hadn't spent the drive back dreaming of my evening at home. I'd relived the feeling of Jude's arm around me in the tent, and the easy way his hand had rested on the curve of my belly. And the way I'd let myself melt into it without even a hint of resistance, because wasn't that what I should've had all along? Someone to wrap their arms around me, holding me and my baby as we slept? It had felt normal and natural and not at all weird, despite the fact that it was *Jude*. That's when I'd stopped and replaced thoughts of him with ones of a shower and an evening on the sofa instead. It shouldn't have felt so good to lie there with him. If Jude knew that he'd snuggled up to me in the tent, he'd made no mention of it the next day. I have no idea if the charged air between us was real or a figment of my over-stimulated imagination. But I do know that having a man look out for me and my baby, putting our needs above his, has only highlighted Sam's absence.

I drop my head to the side, resting it on a cushion. After days of eating out, I've kept food over the last couple of days bland, but even after a lunch of plain noodles with chicken, my throat has been stinging all day with heartburn. After a period of intense moving around and a stint of hiccups, the baby's quietened down too, so I close my eyes to take advantage of it and catch a nap. My mobile vibrates on the coffee table and my heart lurches in my chest as I fight the urge to open my eyes and check it.

Jude texted when he landed in Lisbon yesterday. He'd decided to stay and check it out for a couple of days before heading off to surf, and we'd spent about half an hour messaging back and forth. It was all nice and light and easy, friendly and familiar. An image of him walking those same cobbled streets as I'd done flashes up in my mind. The message that's just come through could be from him. I wish I could say I haven't spent today checking my phone to see if he'd got in touch, or that it doesn't matter whether he reaches out or not.

But I can't.

◆　◆　◆

'I have monkey feet,' I say, looking in the mirror in front of me a week later.

'Don't be silly,' Mum replies with a tut.

'I do.' I point down to them. 'Look.'

My toes have spread apart and the soles of my feet have widened. They feel like blobs of plasticine that someone has pressed down with their thumb, and after trying to squeeze them into my shoes yesterday, I'd decided enough was enough. I needed some new ones to accommodate the lumps my feet have become.

'You're pregnant, Zoe. It's normal.'

'Yes, thanks, Mum. I do know that.'

She inhales loudly as if I'm getting on that one last nerve of hers. She picks up a shoe from the wall in front of us. 'What about these?'

She holds up a hideous pair of beige shoes that look like they ought to be worn by a ninety-year-old woman called Maude.

'Absolutely not,' I reply firmly, and she bustles away from me.

It goes without saying that I'm beyond grateful she's well and recovered enough to bustle, tut and kiss her teeth again. But it's also safe to say that my nerves are frayed. It's not her fault though, and being squished on a bus with humid air and condensed windows thanks to the non-stop rain on the way here didn't help. I sigh and look at my reflection in the mirror. What happened to the glowing, clear-skinned, gorgeous-haired version of me that had sat in the park feeling connected to everything and hyper sensual? The version I see today is an enormous, frumpy, unattractive mess. My breasts don't look bouncy and full now – they look like udders with skin that's lightened enough to see the faintest hint of veins under my brown skin. A thick, vertical dark line has appeared from my bellybutton down to my now completely untamed pubic hair. My lips are constantly dry, my hair is an unruly mess and now I have feet that have widened to what feels like twice their original width. I don't want to complain. I am so in love with this little being and am fiercely protective of her already. I haven't even met her yet and I already know I'd literally die every single day, over and over again to protect her. But, wow.

I miss my body.

And I can't wait to have it back. Until I remember that getting it back means giving birth which just thinking about makes my skin prickle with fear.

Mum holds up another monstrosity and the look on my face is enough to make her put it straight back again.

'Well, you choose then,' she says with a sniff and raised eyebrows.

'I'm not going to find anything in here, Mum. I mean, look.' I pick up the nearest shoe I can find. 'Velcro?'

'It's a lot easier than laces,' she replies. 'They have to be practical.'

'I know,' I mumble. 'I just don't know why practical has to mean hideous. It's like anything that isn't standard automatically becomes drab.'

Mum sighs. It's a sigh that, as a kid, always let me know I was skating on thin ice and her patience was wearing thin.

'Come on,' I say, perking myself up a bit. 'There's a sports shop down the road. I'm sure I can find a pair of comfy trainers without laces or Velcro fastenings made for five-year-olds.'

We step out onto the street, temporarily popping open our umbrellas until we duck into a shop with bright lights, intense dubstep music and staff dressed like they're about to do a CrossFit class. In what feels like a mere matter of minutes, I've found pull-on trainers with material that accommodates my broadened feet, supports my ankles *and* actually look good. Mum purses her lips when I hand over my credit card to pay one hundred and thirty pounds for the privilege, but it's worth it. My offer of creating websites in a day is going down well and I've had another sign up for it this week. I can afford this, and leaving the shop with my new shoes on and the old ones in a bag feels like walking on billowy, springy clouds.

For the first time in days, the rain actually stops as we make our way to Wardour Street. It was my idea to come to the West End. I'd wanted to spend a nice mum-and-daughter afternoon, shoe shopping followed by lunch at a little Jamaican restaurant she loves, but all I've done is moan. As we step inside the restaurant, I decide to stop complaining and start enjoying. The restaurant is busy, as always, with a queue out of the door for takeaway orders. I think the baby can already recognise the familiar smell of Caribbean spices, because she starts waking up as we sit down at one of the tables. After ordering, I try to imagine being here with my daughter – first in her pram, then as a young, inquisitive child and finally, as a petulant teenager. I dab the rainwater on my arms with a napkin from the table and laugh to myself.

'What's so funny?' Mum asks, using a napkin to wipe the rim of her can of Ting.

'I just looked fifteen years into the future and pictured myself with a daughter complaining about not being able to find the right shoes.' I shake my head. 'I'm sorry. I've been a complete pain today.'

'You forget I've been there.' She takes a sip of her drink. 'It's normal to feel emotional.'

'From one day to the next?'

'I did,' Mum replies.

'Really?'

'Of course. It wasn't like I'd been pregnant before and it was before the internet. I couldn't just Google things to see what was normal or not. I was terrified and excited at the same time for almost the whole pregnancy.'

I take a sip of my carrot juice. 'But at least you had Dad by your side. When I think about being in labour alone . . .'

Mum chuckles and raises her eyebrows, smoothing her napkin out on the table with her fingers. 'Well, honestly, sometimes I wonder if it would've been easier if he hadn't been there.'

My eyes widen. 'Mum! You can't mean that.'

'It's true,' she replies, lifting her shoulders to her ears. 'I mean, it was beautiful to see how he just fell in love with you from the moment he clapped eyes on you. And he was really helpful in the beginning stages, massaging my back, helping me move around and making tea. But when it got messy and more intense, he didn't really know what to do. I remember swearing at him to get a grip.'

'*You* swore?' I shake my head in amazement. 'It must have been bad. But I always remember Dad being unflappable in an emergency.'

As I remember it, it was always Dad who'd rush to the ready with a fully stocked first aid kit, like the time I went over the handlebars of my bike when I was ten.

'*After* you were born, yes,' Mum smiles. 'Maybe watching it all spurred him into motion.'

'How long were you in labour for?' I ask, suddenly aware that I know nothing about my birth at all.

'Twenty-nine hours.'

'Jesus,' I mutter, before catching the look on Mum's face. 'Sorry. I just . . . twenty-nine hours?'

I'm almost ashamed to admit it, but all I know about birth is what I've seen on TV and in films. Until now I've avoided reading birth stories or watching documentaries, telling myself it was a bad idea to scare myself. This week, my journal suggested I start thinking about a birth plan, pain intervention and having a bag packed in case of an emergency trip to hospital and I realised, I can't ignore it anymore. I'm twenty-eight weeks. It's like being afraid of flying but being excited about going on holiday. You know the *going* part will scare the life out of you, so you busy yourself with the vision of *being* there instead until it's time to pack your suitcase, get to the airport and get on the plane.

'Well, it wasn't twenty-nine hours of excruciating pain if that's what you're worried about,' Mum explains. 'At first it wasn't really too bad. It was almost like a painful period, if I remember rightly. It was only towards the end when things got worse.'

'And then? On a scale of one to ten?'

'Not even close to the love that came afterwards.' She smiles and squeezes my wrist. 'It's the world's best painkiller with a memory suppressant.'

'It has to be, otherwise nobody would have more than one child. I must be mad,' I say with a sense of panic rising. 'What if something goes wrong?'

'It won't. Labour is like teenagers. Ninety per cent of them are normal, but the terrible ten per cent make up the ninety per cent of the ones you hear about.'

My face pulls into a puzzled frown as my foggy brain makes sense of all those percentages.

'You'll be fine,' she insists. 'The antenatal classes will help.'

I nod. Having information given to me in a setting in context will be much better than getting lost in forums and reading about horrific birth stories. And even though I'm a little nervous about everyone else being there with a partner, Nina will be a great plus one. She always thinks about questions I never even consider.

I look at Mum and feel a mixture of shame for being so snappy with her over a pair of shoes, and love because, she's my mum. I wasn't a terrible teenager by any means, but still. She's put up with it all and somehow *still* has patience.

'Would you be with me?' I ask. 'When I'm in labour?'

Mum smiles widely and nods. 'Of course.'

Even though I've got a great midwife who I trust completely, I have to admit that knowing Mum will be there is already making the waves of fear feel that bit less intense.

It's a predictably lengthy wait for our food, but we stay away from the topic of birth.

'How's Barry?' I ask between mouthfuls of rice and peas.

'I think he's going to propose,' Mum replies with a little smile, pulling apart a piece of tender mutton.

'Wow, really? How do you know?'

'He's been a bit skittish and one of my rings went missing from my jewellery box for a few days.'

I grin. 'You think he took it to get measured?'

'Maybe.' Mum looks at me critically. 'You don't know anything about it do you?'

'Your ring?' I reply cheekily.

'You know what I mean.'

'He hasn't asked my permission, no.' I shake my head with a smile. 'Will you say yes?'

'That depends.'

'On what?'

'On you.'

I laugh and put my knife and fork down. 'Mum, come on. I'm not a kid anymore. I don't live at home. Why should it matter what I think?'

'Because you're my daughter.'

'I think he's lovely,' I reply, holding my shoulders up to my ears with a smile. 'I mean, how many men would volunteer to move in and look after you after something so major as surgery for cancer? Even if I didn't approve, you deserve to be happy.'

She really does. I try to consider what it must have been like to be single for twenty-four years and it feels impossible. At least, I think she's been single that whole time. She certainly never brought anyone home to meet me and considering she was always working, I'm not sure where she'd have even found the time to date.

'I do approve, by the way,' I add. 'Totally.'

'He is a good one, isn't he?'

The relieved smile on Mum's face is enough to bring a lump to my throat as my phone vibrates on the table.

Jude: S.O.S . . . I can't seem to leave . . .

I can practically feel the sunshine beaming from the selfie of him in front of a cafe with an espresso and pastel de nata. His face is pulled into a silly *uh-oh* expression that makes my throat bubble with a giggle as I write back.

Zoe: That's the power of Lisbon! Glad you're enjoying it so much <3

Jude: I'm going to the fish place you told me about tonight and then tomorrow – SURF!

Zoe: Lol, sure. Maybe I should put a bet on that you'll still be there this weekend

Jude: If you were here . . . maybe ;)

My fingers hover over my screen as I try to decide how to respond. I'm sure he means that he'd still be there because I'd be showing him all the things I'd discovered in my time in Lisbon, but still. There's something about the winking emoji that's making a swell of excitement build in my chest.

'Who's that?' Mum asks.

I look up at her and shrug nonchalantly. 'Nobody. Just a friend.'

Why didn't I tell her it was Jude? It's not like they don't know each other.

'Friends don't make you smile like that.'

Mum raises her eyebrows and slowly spoons some rice into her mouth as I laugh, despite the flush creeping across my face.

'Like what?'

'Like I'm sure I did just a few seconds ago about Barry.'

I blink and shake my head quickly as if she's said the most ridiculous thing I've ever heard.

'Mum, come on.' I look down at my belly. 'Like you said earlier: I *am* pregnant.'

'I know you are.'

'Exactly,' I reply firmly before clicking my phone shut and turning it to lie face down on the table.

◆ ◆ ◆

Two days later, Nina and I walk through the revolving doors of a plush central London hotel. She'd told me to meet her with a bikini so I'd assumed we were going swimming, until she grinned and declared we'd be striking my spa day wish from my list. I gape at the gorgeousness of the space we're in.

A huge bouquet of expensive looking flowers sits in a round, glass vase on top of the vast walnut desk, and the air is scented with expensive, barely there diffuser perfume. A perfectly preened receptionist books us in and hands us a fluffy Terry bundle of dressing gown, towel, disposable slippers and an eye mask. When we open the door to the locker room, I look at Nina and shake my head. Calling it a locker room is like calling Lambrusco champagne. It's all white-washed wooden counters, plants and expensive looking Moroccan tiled walls.

'Neens,' I say, 'you can't be serious. This must be costing a fortune.'

I've stayed in some pretty luxurious places over the years. Whenever Sam had a corporate gig that required travel, we'd book a suite and he'd put it on business expenses, but I always knew how much things cost. And this place is right up there with the five-star hotels Sam had taken us to.

'Relax and thank Coleman.'

I frown. 'The footballer?'

'Yeah. I called in a favour and he was happy to hook a girl up.'

'Awesome,' I grin and open the door to my assigned locker with the chipped wristband from reception.

'Right? Although, even if it wasn't thanks to him, I'd have booked it anyway,' Nina replies. 'At this point, I need it more than you do. Being sick was bad enough but having so many clients booked in on top is killing me.'

I throw her a sympathetic smile. Her symptoms might have gone, but that stomach bug has left her looking completely washed out, with her pale skin exacerbated by her bright-pink hair.

'I'm telling you, that was *the* worst experience I think I've ever had. I'm surprised I can even still call Luke my boyfriend after the things he saw.'

I nod as I peel my maxi dress down over my bump. 'Oh, I hear you. Just be careful now because if you're not, you'll end up with one of these.'

'I can't believe how big you've got in such a short space of time.'

'I know. I feel like a whale.'

She rolls her eyes and pulls her t-shirt over her head. 'You're about as far away from a whale as you can get. And I was talking about your belly. Your bump looks different.'

'She's moved. The midwife says she's pretty much head down now.'

'Crikey,' Nina grins. 'That sounds serious.'

'Don't,' I warn her, sitting on the smooth wooden bench to thread my legs through my swimming costume. 'I'm already trying not to freak out as it is. I'm anxious to get on with the antenatal classes.'

'Don't worry, there's no space for freaking out today. Today is all about much needed R and R.' Nina puts a hand on her heart in a promise before unhooking her bra. 'So, come on. How was the festival? Your photos made me so jealous.'

I sigh happily. 'It was really cool.'

She pulls on her bikini and frowns at me, clearly waiting for more while I readjust my balloon-like breasts in my costume.

'Really? That's it? *It was really cool?* She shakes her head. 'After wanting to do it for years, that's the only thing you've got to say?'

I hesitate. Of course there's more. So much more. Like the fact that, the festival feels like a pivotal moment in the last few months. That being up there, on that campsite, in that lake, in that tent feels like the first time I've truly felt *at home* since coming back to London. But I can't say that, because then she'd ask why and I can't exactly tell her it's because of Jude. She'd think I've lost my mind and probably go nuts at him for crossing the boundary they'd established and taking advantage of me. Which of course, he hadn't. Even if I kind of wish he had.

'Well, the place itself was gorgeous.' I say, shoving thoughts of Jude from my mind. I know she wants to relive her lost weekend through me, so I flick back through the reel of memory footage.

Since I can't go into the hot tub, we start off in the pregnancy-friendly version with body temperature water. The place is quiet so I don't have to feel like I'm disturbing the peace as I fill her in. I tell her about the music acts, but not that I'd hardly paid attention because I'd spent most of the time chatting with Jude. I tell her about that magnificent rainstorm while I'd been in the lake, but I don't mention the way that being alone in that body of water with him had felt strangely intimate. Or how sharing a bed with him has been playing on repeat in my mind ever since.

Nina seems satisfied though, so we quieten down and enjoy the bliss of our surroundings. I've positioned myself perfectly to aim a strong pulse of water into the precise place where the muscle around my hip has been bugging me since the festival. Between this and the massage we both have booked in, I'm hoping it'll finally be gone by the end of the day. We've been chilling for a good fifteen minutes in silence when Nina lifts her head from the edge of the tub and looks at me with a frown.

'So, you didn't do our flirt challenge then?'

I laugh and shake my head. 'No, I didn't.'

She nods and tilts her head back. The flirt challenge had been her idea – a way of having no-guilt fun to remind myself of the fact that I'm still a fully functioning, sexual being despite also being single and pregnant. Her words, not mine. Technically, it's not a lie. I didn't really flirt with Jude. That only happens in my daydream replays.

She looks back at me again and I sink down into the water a little more. 'So why do I get the feeling something happened that you're not telling me about?'

The thing about Nina is, she has a knack for being able to pull things out of people. She's one of the best secret keepers too and, if Jude were someone else's brother, I'd have shared my little crush with her already. But she can sense there's something I'm holding back and if there's one thing Nina can't stand, it's knowing that there's something she *doesn't* know.

I swallow down a flicker of nerves but try to conceal it with a nonchalant shrug of my shoulders. 'I mean, there was someone . . .'

'I knew it,' Nina grins. 'Come on, spill. Who was it?'

'Nobody. We didn't talk or anything. I just saw him around a lot.'

I feel like the worst friend in the world for lying to her, but I know that this is the easiest way for the subject to be dropped and forgotten about.

'What did he look like?'

'Umm. Well, he was tall. Short hair and well built,' I reply easily. At least I didn't have to make up that part. 'And he had a nice smile.'

'Shame you didn't get to chat,' Nina says and I shrug.

'I've got a totally different set of priorities right now.'

'I know, I know,' she replies quickly. 'You deserve to have fun and a treat now and then, that's all I'm saying.'

'Which is clearly why I have you,' I smile. 'Thanks for this, Neens. It's amazing.'

I look around at the beautifully tiled space set in low lighting and sigh with a pleasurable feeling that comes right up from my toes. After the pool, we grab a snack from the bar which, anywhere else would probably be a tuna and cucumber sandwich but here is a slice of sweet potato toast topped with bananas and blueberries. Our massages aren't for another half hour yet, so we wander over to a recessed area with even lower lighting and loungers for a nap. I sit on the comfortable padding and readjust my dressing gown, sending a piece of fluff right into my eye. After a few seconds of blinking and trying to rub it out, Nina perches on the edge of my lounger, bringing her face inches away from mine to blow it out.

'Oh, goodness. Sorry.'

Nina turns and we both look at a woman standing there with a book in her hand.

'I didn't mean to interrupt a romantic moment,' she says.

Nina gets up and we both laugh.

'You're not,' I reply. 'I just had something in my eye.'

'Oh, good. I wasn't sure.' She moves from her place at the door as if she now has permission to enter and sits herself down on the bed next to mine. 'Not that it would've mattered if you were gay, of course. I like to be "inclusive".'

'Right.' I raise my eyebrows and nod slowly before catching Nina's eye as she sits on her lounger.

Judging by the quotation marks she'd mimed around the word, I have the feeling this woman is anything but.

'How far along are you?' she asks, noticing my belly.

'Twenty-eight weeks.'

'I'm fifteen.' She puts a hand over her lower belly and smiles. 'I swear, with every pregnancy I come here earlier and earlier. It never hurts to get the pampering in early. We're hoping it'll be fourth time lucky with a girl.'

I nod as if I can relate to her having three children and spending what must be thousands on spa days. Unless, of course, she's here thanks to a Premier League footballer too. Which, judging by the big sapphire on her ring and clearly expensive honey highlights in her hair, she might well be.

She looks past me at Nina. 'Gosh. You have a lot of tattoos.'

'I certainly do.'

'Didn't they hurt?'

'Not as much as pushing a baby through your vagina, I'm sure,' Nina jokes.

'I almost got one once, but my husband wasn't keen. He thinks its un-lady-like.'

I can feel Nina bristle from her lounger. 'Mm, yeah, I've heard the same. The world is unfortunately full of patriarchal, patronising morons.'

I flash her a warning glare. It's a topic that gets her hackles raised and the last thing we need in such serene surroundings is a spat but the woman either ignores it or doesn't get it.

'Well,' she says with a little laugh, 'I know you're here with your friend, but they do a great couple's package for next time.'

I nod and pick up one of the magazines I'd taken from the bar. 'Thanks for the tip.'

'I must say though, sometimes it's nice to be on your own, am I right?' she says in a conspiratorial way, leaning across from her lounger. 'At least until the five-month mark when all you want is a man. Can I give you a bit of advice?'

'Sure,' I reply, just about managing to hide my resignation. I'm guessing she'd probably give it whether I want it or not.

'If you're still in that little hormonal surge, take advantage of it now before it disappears and you're too huge to even think about having him near you. Believe me, you'll be too sore after birth to think about it for weeks.'

'Well thanks for the tip,' I reply, straining to keep my voice even. 'But I'm not actually *with* the dad so I don't think I'll be needing it.'

'Oh, gosh. You poor thing.' She pulls her eyebrows together and the sides of her mouth down. 'It must be hard doing it all alone, especially as a woman of colour.'

I draw in a breath and see Nina sit up in her lounger from the side of my eye. Her extreme, unfounded sympathy smacks of privilege and it makes the space under my skin boil.

'Actually, it's been a walk in the park,' I say frankly, opening my magazine and lying back in my lounger to signal the end of the discussion.

'I didn't mean anything by it,' she says apologetically. 'Just that it must get lonely.'

'What was it you were telling me earlier, Zoe?' Nina asks loudly. 'About the guy you met at the festival last weekend? The hot one with the amazing body?'

She grins at me and I return it. 'Oh, Jude? God, yeah. It was heaven. Being single and pregnant is just *great*. I had the time of my life – men can't resist me at the moment. Must be the hormones.'

'Well, people do all sorts,' the woman says, bristling at the sound of it. 'If it were me, I think I'd have more important things to think about than sleeping with a man who's not the father of my baby.'

'God, that is such a double standard,' Nina says, grabbing her dressing gown. 'Would you be saying the same thing to the guy who got her pregnant in the first place?'

'Exactly,' I say with a heap of indignation. 'Am I allowed to have a social life, or should I just be sitting at home reading parenting books and knitting baby clothes? I think I'd rather be pregnant and single than married and having to take myself to an expensive spa to escape my husband.'

My heart thumps in my chest and the baby moves in my belly, stretching against my skin as if she's joining the protest. The backs of my eyes are close to stinging but I refuse to blink as I glare at the woman on her lounger, sitting with her mouth gaping open. She huffs and shakes her head, gathering up her things as if we're the ones who have overstepped the mark before sniffing loudly and leaving. As soon as she's gone, I remember to breathe and swallow against the lump in my throat.

'God, what an awful cow,' Nina says. 'Are you okay?'

I nod with a trembling breath and put a hand on my chest, feeling the thrum of my heartbeat. 'Did I really just say all that?'

'Yeah, you did,' Nina chuckles, 'and it was epic. That'll teach her for butting in with her outdated morals. The world does *not* need another Karen.'

'We're going to have to try and avoid her now, you know.'

'Screw that. She should be the one avoiding us. The pink-haired, tattooed thug and the single, slutty, pregnant Black woman.'

'Lesbians, too, don't forget.' I burst into nervous laughter. 'Can you believe the nerve?'

'Sadly, yes. I hope you meant every word of what you said.'

I can't deny feeling weird at the idea of being pregnant and sleeping with someone. When I think about it, I can't recall it ever being portrayed on film or television apart from Miranda in *Sex and the City*. Why is that? Why is it fair for Sam to go on a date and have nobody question his character, but if I dare to do the same, I'd be seen as a bad mother in the making?

'You know what,' I reply, 'I think I did mean it.'

'Good. Except for the bit about Jude,' she replies, pulling a face.

I hadn't even realised I'd used his name in my fiery response but I guess it made sense given that I was technically there with him.

'God, Jude?' I laugh and shake my head, trying not to overdo it. 'Of course not. He's your brother.'

'Exactly. So gross,' Nina says with a shudder.

I laugh again and pull a face similar to the one she'd made to show how turned off I am from the idea.

'Yeah,' I repeat with a self-conscious laugh. 'So gross.'

Chapter Nineteen

Zoe, aged 25

Almost two and a half hours after setting off from London, the train slowed on its approach to Leeds and Zoe pulled down her bag from the overhead shelf. After so many trips north over the last three years, she barely needed to bring anything with her anymore. She had spare sets of everything at Jerome's place – underwear, clothes, make-up and even shoes. The train squeaked over the rails as she slung her little canvas duffel bag across her shoulder. She liked travelling light to Leeds. It made the journey feel more normal, like it was one she made every day instead of only once or twice a month. Zoe winced as the squeaking got louder before the train jolted to a halt. She hopped down onto the platform, automatically turning left. She'd made this journey so many times now that she didn't even need to look for signs of where to go; up the stairs, over to the arrivals hall and then to the bus stop for the number 47 bus that would take her pretty much to Jerome's front door.

It was a sunny day for October, but the platform was windy and a gust of it whipped the back of her neck. She zipped her jacket all the way up to her chin and made her way up the stairs. Halfway up, as the crowd thinned a little, Zoe stopped. There Jerome was, standing like Ryan Phillipe at the top of the escalators in *Cruel Intentions*. He grinned and skipped down the stairs to meet her.

'What are you doing here?' Zoe asked with a shocked laugh. 'I thought you had to work?'

He kissed her full on the lips in that way of his – the way that made it clear how little he cared about what other people find appropriate.

'I told them I had an important appointment,' he replied, lifting her bag right off her shoulders and slinging it over his head.

'And they just let you go?'

'Of course,' he replied with a laugh that says, *why wouldn't they?*

Their work environments couldn't be any further apart. Zoe spent her time in front of a computer engrossed in HTML coding, fuelled by acidic coffee from an awful machine, and with her colleagues Alan and Tim for company. Jerome, on the other hand, worked for a skate brand which apparently meant he got to spend his days either skateboarding or filming other people doing it to upload onto the internet. Zoe looked at him, in his baggy jeans and blue checkered shirt. His sleeves were rolled up to the elbows, showing off his tattooed arms. Even after three years, he still made her stomach flip as he draped his arm around her.

'So, what are your plans for this important appointment?' Zoe asked as they left the station.

'Sex, drugs and rock 'n' roll.'

She laughed back with a thrill of anticipation. 'I'm in.'

She still found it amazing that they were even together at all. If she'd have gone to get the food instead of the drinks that day at the beach club in Ibiza, she might never have met Jerome. From Ibiza to Leeds – it felt like something from a romance novel, and she had Nina and Steph to thank for talking her into making the first move with him.

'I was thinking we could do something with Steph this weekend?' she said. 'It's always a pain trying to split myself between the two of you when I'm here.'

'Yeah, sure, whatever,' Jerome replied nonchalantly.

Steph had got a job in graduate recruitment here a few months ago and Zoe loved the coincidence of it all. She'd pictured the three of them hanging out together on her Leeds weekends, but neither Steph nor Jerome seemed thrilled with the idea of spending time with each other. Jerome argued that he wanted as much alone time as possible since they barely saw each other, and Steph said she'd rather not have him around while they were catching up because it changed the girly dynamic. Which meant schlepping from one end of the city to another for a night. Still, it had been an age since Zoe had seen either of them, so she wasn't complaining.

They sat at the back of the bus and she let herself sink into Jerome's shoulder. Now that she was with him, she felt relieved. Everything felt normal, as if they'd been in their usual rhythm of being together every other weekend instead of the reality. The last time she'd come to Leeds was almost two months ago. And it had been even longer since he'd been to London. The company he worked for had been going through a rough patch – probably because they paid people for having fun as opposed to actually working – and Jerome had been reluctant to make too many plans. He'd been having sleepless nights and was stressing out about it and said he didn't want to make their time together all about him.

Zoe understood and, in all fairness, work was busy on her end too. But lately, their emails had felt . . . weird. They didn't call each other as much and text messages weren't as instant as they had been.

And then, Jerome had dropped off the grid completely. She'd started to get that feeling. The *it's not you, it's me* feeling. She'd tried not to think in terms of *well if it were me* . . . Because if it *had* been her, Zoe would want to see and talk to the person who she claimed made her feel better. She would want something to look forward to and move heaven and earth to make a visit happen. Zoe had worked herself up with worry and stress to the point where her stomach had ached and she'd probably driven Nina and Steph to insanity in their WhatsApp group about it. And then, as if nothing had happened, Jerome had reappeared. He'd said he'd been busy filming some new up-and-coming skaters and sorting out his CV to start job hunting in case things continued to decline at work.

Zoe looked at him as he told her about a new bar that'd opened and how he wanted to take her there tomorrow. She was happy nothing drastic had happened, that he hadn't lost his job and nobody had died, like she'd feared. But she had the strongest urge to say something. Surely just disappearing without contact for a week at a time wasn't normal relationship behaviour? It was already hard enough that theirs was a long-distance one. The miles between them magnified everything, making the good things feel amazing and the bad things dire. She'd been genuinely worried about him. Anything could have happened. He could've come off his skateboard and cracked his head open for all she knew. All it would have taken was a simple message to say *I'm busy, will catch up with you in a few days*. Zoe took a breath. It didn't matter now anyway. She was there and they were together, and everything was just fine.

The Victorian terrace he shared with two colleagues was empty when they got there and Jerome dropped her duffel bag onto the floor as he closed the door behind him. Zoe sighed contentedly. She was happy to be back in her home away from home.

'Beer? Rum? Wine?' Jerome asked.

Zoe laughed in reply. 'Maybe a tea to start with? It's not even three yet.'

'As you like, but I'm having a beer.'

'And I'm going to freshen up,' Zoe replied, picking up her bag.

She made her way up the steep, narrow stairs. How he could navigate them in darkness or while drunk without falling over was a mystery to her. Zoe went into the small bathroom. For saying it was shared by three punky skateboarding men, it was surprisingly clean. Or at least it always had been when she'd been there. After having a super quick wash in the sink, she went into Jerome's room. She smiled. He'd clearly just tidied it. The sheets on his bed looked fresh, the floor was clear of laundry and there was even a small vase with two pink carnations on the windowsill. Zoe pulled her jumper over her head and turned to throw it onto the chair in the corner when she saw writing scrawled on a whiteboard tacked to his wall.

Je suis au supermarché ma belle. x

She'd always been terrible at languages and almost failed GCSE French. But Zoe remembered enough to understand that it said he was *at the supermarket*. That part was fine. But a frown flickered across her face at the term of endearment attached to the end of the sentence. If her recollection of Madame Laurent's classes were right – and she was sure it was – the note was addressed to a female. A close female at that. One who wasn't likely to be just a friend.

Zoe sat on the bed, sending a whiff of fabric conditioner into her nose. She'd only just got there. Jerome was downstairs, not at the supermarket. Maybe he'd been planning to go later and was thinking ahead when he wrote it? But that didn't make any more sense, especially because he never spoke French with her. She chewed the inside of her lip with the feeling of unease crawling on her skin. She scratched at her arm. There had to be an explanation for it. He was her boyfriend and she trusted him. Besides, if he *had* done something, he wouldn't be so stupid as to leave it there for her to see. But if it wasn't meant for her, then who was it meant for? She tore her eyes away from the whiteboard and tried to act normal when he came through the door.

'Are you sure you want tea?' he asked. 'Or do you want to skip to the good stuff?'

'I'll take the tea,' she replied, reaching out for it.

Zoe held the cup in both of her hands and her eyes flicked back to the whiteboard again as he sat next to her and dropped a kiss onto her shoulder.

She blew on her tea and nodded towards the whiteboard. 'What's that?'

'What's what?' Jerome replied, slipping a hand under the back of her t-shirt.

'That note on the whiteboard.'

His hand paused for a moment and from the corner of her eye, Zoe saw him look at it before he flicked the clasp of her bra open.

'It says I'm at the supermarket.'

Zoe scrunched up her face. It was basic French. He had to know that even she could translate that part herself. It was the *ma belle* she was after an explanation for. She thought about digging further, but Jerome took the cup from her and put it on the floor. He seemed so unfazed about it, it had to be nothing. They hadn't seen each other for such a long time and she didn't want to cause a fight by sounding jealous or insecure. So, she let him pull her t-shirt over her head and said nothing, but she couldn't stop thinking about that sentence. Even though it had been forever since the last time they'd slept together, Zoe couldn't concentrate, but Jerome didn't seem to notice.

Afterwards, as he laid next to her on the bed rolling a cigarette, his phone vibrated on the floor. He didn't hear it over the music playing through his speaker and Zoe ignored it, focusing instead on the warmth radiating onto her legs from the sun shining in through the window. Jerome stuck his cigarette between his lips and pressed repeatedly on his apparently empty lighter.

'Damn it,' Jerome said. 'I'll be back in a sec.'

He pecked the side of her head before hauling himself out of bed and swinging his door open. Zoe heard the stairs creaking as he made his way down them and his phone vibrated again. She turned her head to look at it, plugged into the wall. It was just sitting there, right within reach. Maybe . . . she frowned at herself and pushed the thought away. Looking at someone's phone was a bad road to go down. And she *did* trust him. A long-distance relationship couldn't work without trust, especially not for three years. But then she read that note on the whiteboard again.

Zoe rolled over onto her side and leaned forwards, just a little. Jerome's iPhone was his most prized gadget. Did it even count as snooping if she couldn't unlock it? She'd never used an iPhone before and didn't know his passcode. He was only getting a lighter downstairs – he wouldn't be gone for long, but she picked the phone up and pressed the button at the bottom, illuminating the screen.

Stephanie: I can't do this anymore!

Stephanie: I'm serious.

The phone trembled in her hand as she read the messages stacked on the screen. Can't do what anymore? And who the hell was Stephanie? Her heart throbbed in her body, so hard she could hear it in her ears. Zoe pulled the phone from its cable and sat cross-legged on the bed. The phone vibrated again as another message slotted onto the screen.

Stephanie: If you don't tell her, I will.

A pain ached in Zoe's chest, so physical that it took her breath away. She shook her head trying to make sense of it. There had to be an explanation, but she couldn't think of one. It was as if someone had switched the channel in her mind and all she could see was a blank screen. When Jerome came through the door with his lit cigarette, he saw her sitting on the bed and stopped in his tracks.

'Who the hell is Stephanie?' Zoe demanded, surprising herself with the firmness of her voice.

He shook his head an inch, as if he'd never heard of the name before. 'What?'

'*If you don't tell her, I will?* Tell me what?'

'I don't know what you're talking about.' His eyes flicked from Zoe to the phone and back again.

She tossed it to him and he fumbled to catch it, dropping his cigarette. 'That's what I'm talking about.'

Jerome hesitated and Zoe realised that she was holding her breath, controlled by the part of her that desperately wanted to believe she'd somehow got it all wrong. He stood with the phone in his hands, and she waited for him to look at the screen and read the messages. He didn't. He picked up his cigarette and stared back at her. Zoe could practically hear his brain turning over as he tried to find a way to explain it, but he didn't have to. His silence said it all and the pressure building in her chest pushed her to leap up from the bed and grab her jeans.

'Zoe, wait,' Jerome said, taking a step towards her.

'How long has it been going on? Is that why you dropped off the face of the earth two weeks ago?'

'I can explain.'

Zoe yanked the jeans on, jamming her leg through the denim. 'I'm such an *idiot*. I was so worried about you and all this time, you've been sleeping with someone else?'

'It's not like that.' He grabbed her arm. 'Will you just stop a minute?'

'Don't touch me,' Zoe shouted, shaking him off. Her breath left her body in short, sharp bursts and she roughly wiped the tears from her face.

'Zoe, I'm sorry.' His face contorted and he shook his head. 'I just . . .'

'You just *what?*'

She glared at him with what felt like the most amount of anger she'd ever felt before. Her body burned with it. She could feel it in her blood and under her fingernails.

'How could you do this? To me. To *us*.'

'I didn't mean to.'

'Oh, so it was an accident?' Zoe scoffed, grabbing her t-shirt as a wave of fresh tears scalded their way down her cheeks.

'No. Yes. God, I don't know.'

'How long?' She pulled the t-shirt over her head before glaring at him. 'And don't lie to me.'

Jerome sighed, as if he was accepting the fact that he'd been caught out. 'I don't know. A couple of months, maybe.'

'Why?' she asked, her voice cracking.

'Because I'm an arsehole. And I just . . .' He sagged his shoulders and looked away. 'It's hard, being in a relationship like this. I needed someone . . .'

'For sex?'

'I guess. The whole long-distance thing just got to me.'

Zoe shook her head with disgust etched onto her face. 'Bullshit. We live less than three hours away from each other. I'd have seen you as often as you wanted. I'd have moved here and uprooted my whole life for you. The only reason we've hardly seen each other lately is because of *you*.'

'Look, I was messed up, okay?' he replied, running his hand though his hair. 'It was a really rough time and she was there. She helped.'

'And I couldn't? Me, your *girlfriend*? That's for her, isn't it?' Zoe looked at the whiteboard but didn't give him time to answer. 'Remember when I told you I was feeling insecure? And you told me I was the only woman in your life? The *only* one?'

'Yes.' Jerome rubbed a hand briskly over his eyes.

'And remember when you said you would always be honest with me? It was all *bullshit*.' Zoe laughed bitterly, feeling the anger push upwards to her throat. 'Do you know how many times people ask how I deal with trust in a long-term, long-distance relationship? And how many times I've said I trusted you without a shadow of a doubt?'

'Fuck. Zoe . . .' Jerome's eyebrows knitted together and he shook his head with his face flaming red. 'I'm sorry.'

'Yeah, well, so am I. I'm sorry I've wasted three years of my life on a complete and utter wanker.'

The word felt harsh coming from her lips. She'd never sworn at him before, but right now she wanted to call him every disgusting word she could think of. Zoe opened the drawer filled with the clothes she'd left here for her visits and started pulling them out.

'Zoe, come on. We can talk about this.'

'And say what?' she replied, tossing her clothes into her bag.

Her face was flooded with tears and snot was coming out of her nose, but she didn't wipe it away. She wanted him to see. She wanted him to see how much he'd hurt her. She wanted him to see himself how she did right now – a lousy, cheating bastard.

'Where will you go?'

'I don't know. Why, what do you care?'

'Of course I care.'

Zoe's insides shook as she snatched her bag from the bed and hooked it over her shoulder.

'Zo, please. Wait.'

She ignored him and ran down the narrow stairs as quickly as she could, holding onto the banister so she wouldn't fall and break her neck. She shoved her feet into her boots and swung the door open before walking quickly from the house. Zoe hoped he wouldn't try and follow her. It wasn't her neighbourhood, but she didn't want to have her humiliation exposed in public. She wiped her tears and nose with her hands and followed the quiet residential street towards the main road where she knew a minicab office was. Her hand trembled as she dug her phone from her bag and called Nina, wondering how she was able to do something as normal as walking when it felt like the world had just shifted under her feet.

'Jerome's been sleeping with someone else. I just found the messages on his phone,' she said, speaking to Nina's voicemail. 'I'm on my way to Steph's, I'll call you later.'

She hung up before firing a message to Steph, telling her she was on her way over and needed to talk. Thank God she was here. She couldn't think of anything worse than having to sit on a train for over two hours feeing like this, surrounded by strangers. What she needed right now was the comfort of a friend who would have her back and a stiff drink.

Within minutes of reaching the minicab office, she was sitting in the back of a Ford Mondeo being taken across the city. Jerome had said it had been going on for a couple of months, but it could've been longer for all she knew. There could have been others, too. He'd clearly had no problem lying to her and she couldn't trust a word he'd said now. Zoe swallowed against the sickly feeling of betrayal in her stomach.

She felt like an idiot. What would've happened if he'd have switched his phone off, or if she'd have fallen asleep after they'd had sex? She could have gone the whole weekend and never known the truth. He would have continued to lie, pretending that everything was as it always had been and she would have been none the wiser. He must have laughed to himself at how easy it was to keep her happy with a text here and a phone call there, when all the while he'd been seeing someone else. Zoe sniffed and the driver looked at her through the rear-view mirror. She turned her head and stared out of the window, shielding herself from his eyes. She didn't know what hurt more – that Jerome had slept with someone else or that he'd been so good at lying to her.

The car turned into the cul-de-sac where Steph lived and Zoe's emotions come bursting back up to the surface when she saw her friend waiting outside her block. Zoe paid the driver and got out, dragging her bag behind her. Steph stood with her arms crossed over her chest and her face set into an expression of pure worry.

'God, Zoe,' she said shaking her head. 'I'm so sorry.'

Steph's eyes were filled with tears and Zoe let her bag drop to the floor. This was exactly what she'd needed. Someone who could see her, understand her and be there for her while she tried to make sense of it all.

'I don't know what to say . . . I wanted to tell you,' Steph said, tightening the grip around herself.

'What? I don't . . .' Zoe tailed off, letting the sentence hang as her eyebrows creased together.

It took a moment for Steph's words to land and Zoe shook her head, confused. How did Steph know why she was there? Zoe hadn't told her in the message – she'd only said she was on her way over. She replayed the argument with Jerome in her head. She'd asked who Stephanie was, and he hadn't replied.

'Oh my God,' Zoe exclaimed as her face pulled into a frown. 'It was you?'

She never called herself Stephanie. Zoe had never heard her introduce herself to anyone using her full name. She'd always said she hated the pretentious way it sounded which was why she only ever went by Steph. Zoe's stomach lurched and she turned, bending over as it physically cramped. The cab was still standing there with the engine running and she put her hand on the roof, taking shaky breaths.

'You? And Jerome?' She looked up at Steph, willing it not to be true. 'You wouldn't.'

Steph's face was pale and her chin trembled as she blinked back tears. 'We didn't mean to.'

If it felt like the world had shifted under her feet before, now it felt like it was being pulled away altogether. Steph was one of her best friends. She was going to be the joint maid of honour at Zoe's future wedding – one she'd thought might actually be to Jerome – and godmother to her future children. She was like a sister. Zoe's brain scrambled to put things together, creating a timeline of it all.

The three of them had a night out together when Steph had first moved to Leeds, but it had never been repeated. They'd clearly found their way to each other since and she felt stupid for not having made the connection sooner.

A barrage of tears built behind Zoe's eyes and she quickly grabbed her bag before yanking open the back door of the cab.

The driver twisted around in his seat holding his phone to his ear with his face set into a scowl but when he saw her, he seemed to change his mind.

'Train station, please,' Zoe said, trying her best to keep her voice steady.

'Zoe, I'm sorry,' Steph called through the open window.

The driver looked at Zoe and she nodded, wiling him to start the engine.

'I love him, Zo.'

Tears erupted from Zoe's eyes at Steph's words but she stared straight ahead as the driver pulled away and she didn't look back.

◆ ◆ ◆

Why is it that the moment you're not allowed to think about something, it becomes the *only* thing taking space in your mind? Since my outburst at the spa two weeks ago, I've been playing a mental game of whack-a-mole except, instead of a mole, I'm trying to obliterate thoughts of Jude. A song I'd never have paid attention to before comes on the radio and I'm taken back to the festival, sitting on a sunburnt bank of grass with him. I whack it away. I'm at the antenatal class with Nina, practising a breathing exercise and I'm back in my tent, imagining coloured streams of our breath intertwining. I whack it away. I open a drawer in my bedroom and remember him being here helping to build it. I whack it away. What started as a schoolgirl crush is developing into a full-on attraction, which would be fine if there were even a basis for it in the first place. And if it were anyone else but Jude.

'Are you *sure* you don't want a baby shower?' Nina asks as we wander around the nursery section of John Lewis.

'Only if I'll get a pram. I can't believe the prices of these things; I could buy a car for less.'

Nina grimaces. We're only here for research so I can scour eBay afterwards. Apparently, buying a pram isn't just about transporting a baby from A to B. It's also about weight, foldability, storage and whether I want a cup-holder or not.

'Besides,' I add. 'I'd rather have a get together after the birth when I'll really need the adult company.'

'Fair enough,' Nina replies. 'I love your soon-to-be-born daughter, but I'm officially strollered out.'

I nod in agreement. 'Same. Coffee and cake?'

'I'm thinking more about an Aperol. There's a place not too far from here where we can get both.'

After a solid hour of looking at buggies and prams – and still not understanding the difference – we step back outside into the sunshine. The temperature is still high, but the intensity has changed in a subtle way that says these are probably the last hot days of the year. We head to a little cafe-bar, where I can have a decaf frappe and Nina can eke out the last of the summer feeling with her bright-orange Aperol Spritz. My belly sticks out wildly in front of me as we sit at a tiny table outside. It feels like a lifetime ago when I couldn't imagine having one. I remember the woman I'd seen on the bus after my first maternity appointment and how freaked out I'd been about the size of her belly. I reckon I can't be that far off from where she was now.

A white van drives past advertising plastering services and I look at Nina sitting opposite. 'Oh, yeah, before I forget, I've ordered that DIY plaster casting set. Do you still have time to do it?'

'Sure, but not this weekend,' she replies.

'Neither can I, it's nursery painting day.'

'Oh yeah. Sorry I can't help. Are you doing it alone?' she asks with a little frown.

I shake my head. 'Jude's already offered.'

'Really?' Nina raises an eyebrow. 'My brother hates painting. It was like pulling teeth getting him to help at mine.'

'He didn't say anything to me about that when he dropped by a couple days ago.'

He'd been passing through the area and brought me a multipack of beef-flavoured Hula Hoops which, of course made me giggle like a shy teenager. It was an incredibly thoughtful thing to do with great timing because I had actually just run out. When I'd mentioned my plan to paint the nursery, he'd offered to help straight away – not a hint of coercion needed. Why would he do that if it was something he hated? Butterflies flicker in my belly at the possibility of it being something special and on offer only to me before I realise the reality.

'Maybe he felt like he couldn't say no to a pregnant woman,' I say.

Nina snorts. 'Jude has no problem saying no to anyone, pregnant or not. Then again, you are practically family so . . .'

The butterflies crackle and wither one by one at the reminder of my relationship to Jude. I sip my cold coffee through my bamboo straw, thankful that my aversion to the taste seems to have worn off as my pregnancy has progressed.

'Okay, so for the casting . . .' Nina frowns at her phone. 'How's Thursday? I'll be free after four-ish.'

I nod with a tug of excitement. I've never done anything like this before and I'm intrigued about the result. I lean back in my chair and pull the collar of my jacket up as a cold breeze winds down the street and a pang of nostalgia hits me for the summer that's almost over. Autumn will bring with it my daughter, and I am excited about that. But this summer has been . . .

'What are you smiling about?' Nina asks.

I laugh, shaking my head a little. 'Just that this has been such a great summer. Moving into my flat, the festival, ample time with my loved ones, standing on my own two feet.'

'Yeah,' Nina grins. 'It's been pretty epic on my side too.'

'So? Has Luke officially moved in now then?'

'Well, he stayed when I was sick and basically never left,' Nina grins. 'It's nice. I could get used to it. Unless he starts leaving stinking socks around the place.'

We laugh and I feel such a warm glow inside that the cold breeze barely registers on my skin anymore. I skim my gaze across the street, watching the people walking past – the Londoners who clearly know their way around, striding purposefully while multitasking on their phones, and the tourists with their cameras. And then my eyes widen at the blonde woman walking in our direction.

'It's Steph,' I say, sitting up a little in my seat.

'What?' Nina frowns. 'Where?'

'Behind you – don't turn around.'

She tuts as if I've just said the most ridiculous thing ever and cranes her neck to see. It's been years since we've seen each other, but there's no denying, it's her. The warm glow in my chest is extinguished like a bucket of water putting out a fire.

'Yep, that's her alright,' Nina says, and in that split second, Steph sees us, literally stopping her stride.

'Oh, fuck,' I say. 'She's seen us.'

Nina looks back at me. 'So? You're not the one who should be uncomfortable right now. She is.'

'I know, that. I know. But still. In a city of ten million people, how is it that we just happen to be on the same street at the same moment?'

I've lost count of the times I've rehearsed what I would say to Steph after the humiliation and devastation of finding out about her and Jerome. But right now, I can't remember a single word. Part of me wonders if she'll just walk on by and pretend she hasn't seen us, but of course, that was never Steph's style. I take a deep breath and sigh it out loudly, gathering my inner strength as she stops right at our table.

'Zoe. Wow.' She shakes her head with a little smile. 'It *is* you. I wasn't sure for a moment.'

My words are caught in my throat so I simply tip my head a little in response.

'Neens, you look so different,' she adds before the smile quickly drops from her face.

Nina crosses her arms with a hostile look in her eyes and Steph's unease comes off her in waves. The memory of my fourteen-year-old self being shunned by my group of friends in that dusty room before class jumps into my mind. The line dividing Nina and I from our former best friend is invisible but as clear as if someone painted in on the pavement in neon pink.

'Congratulations,' Steph says, looking at my bump. 'How are you?'

'Good,' I nod again. 'You?'

Nina huffs a small laugh at my question and rolls her eyes.

'I'm fine, yeah.' Steph tucks a strand of her long hair behind her ear. 'I'm just on my way to a meeting.'

'Not in Leeds anymore then?' Nina asks, raising an eyebrow.

'No.' Steph shakes her head and her green eyes flick down to the ground. 'Jerome and I split last year. I moved back here, bought a place in the Docklands, got a new job. You know how it goes.'

All I can do is blink. I've often wondered if they'd made it as a couple, or if the very nature of the way they started always spelled a bad ending. Part of me hoped they'd still be together. That it would have been worth everything that it had cost. But the other part prayed that they'd burnt out quickly in an act of the universe righting itself.

'I don't know what you want me to say,' I reply simply with a small shrug.

I can't say I'm sorry to hear it like I would if she were anyone else, because I'm not. But I'm not jumping for joy about it either.

'I know. I just, well . . .' she shrugs back. 'I want to say, I'm sorry. It was such a shitty thing to do to you and I've regretted it every single day.'

'Not so much that you couldn't stop yourself from letting it happen in the first place, or continuing to let it happen, right?' Nina says.

'I really did love him,' Steph says, shaking her head.

'Well that makes two of us,' I reply sharply.

'But you were my best friend,' she continues and looks at Nina. 'You both were. I just wish things were different.'

She looks older, of course. But that isn't all. She looks . . . like an adult. Like she's less of a loose cannon than she used to be. Like life has got its claws into her now. The memory of that moment outside her flat when I realised she'd been sleeping with my boyfriend rears itself inside of me so strongly, it's like having a blade driven into my heart. And I realise for the first time that it wasn't Jerome who'd broken it. Steph had.

She glances at her watch. 'God, I can't believe this, but I'm late for my meeting. I really would love to explain myself. Maybe we can meet for a drink?'

Nina looks at me with a deeply unimpressed expression on her face, and all I can do is shrug my shoulders.

'I'll message you,' Steph says before leaving the table as if she's being pulled against her will.

'Can you believe the fucking nerve of her?' Nina seethes, shaking her head. 'I can't remember the last time I've wanted to punch someone so badly.'

I squeeze the tips of my fingers across my closed eyelids and pinch the bridge of my nose.

'You okay?' she asks in a much softer tone.

'Yeah,' I nod, releasing my hand back down and take a long exhale. 'I'm fine.'

◆ ◆ ◆

Later that night, when I'm sitting at home alone and replaying the encounter with Steph in my head, my phone beeps with a Facebook message.

Steph: Hey, Zoe,

There's so much I wish I could've said earlier but I was so shocked to see you like that. I really would love to meet up and talk. I've always regretted how things turned out. Jerome and I . . . we might have broken up but it really was real. I just wish it hadn't happened the way it had. We often spoke about you and we both wanted to put things right. I tried to explain so many times but I totally understand that you didn't want to hear it. I don't know that I could have either if the tables were turned. Anyway. I just wanted to say again – I truly am sorry. And if you'd be up for meeting just let me know . . . And congrats again, btw. You'll make a great mum.

All my love,
Steph xx

I've been in a daze all evening, trying to process the way seeing her earlier felt, but all I feel is numb, just like I did on the long train ride back from Leeds. The hurt has lessened over the years in the way that time does. But it's still there. And I don't know what to do with that.

For the first time since Jude and I started exchanging messages after the festival, I turn my phone off and go to brush my teeth before bed.

Chapter Twenty

'Are you alright?' Jude asks.

I look at him and blink. 'Yeah, why?'

He shrugs. 'You seem a bit . . . off. And you've been painting that same bit of the wall for the last five minutes.'

I look at the small square of oatmeal on the wall in front of me and shake my head. 'Just daydreaming, I guess.'

'Everything good with the baby? You're not getting high on the paint fumes are you?' he smiles, and I laugh.

'It's organic, silly. And I think there's more chance of getting high off a marker pen these days than paint,' I grin, and I point my roller at his handiwork. 'Not bad for someone who hates painting.'

'Who told you that?'

'Who do you think?'

Jude rolls his eyes as if Nina was just being a pain-in-the-butt sister, but the look behind them is the same as when he'd denied deliberately missing out on the festival. This time though, he doesn't deny it. Instead, he nods at the wall behind me, raising one of his eyebrows.

'You missed a spot.'

My mouth twists as I try, and fail, to hide the smile tugging at my lips before turning back to the wall. I feel hyperaware of myself as I dip the roller back into the paint. It's ridiculous really, but I feel his eyes on me. Music is playing on the speaker, and the window is wide open, blowing in gentle brushes of cool breeze. I sneak a peek at Jude as I move onto a new patch of wall. Maybe it's my imagination, or maybe it's an outcome of paddling into the surf every day for the last week and a half, but his shoulders look bigger. The spray-back from my roller has created a sprinkling of cream, freckle-like dots on my brown skin, and I remember the ones I'd seen on his shoulders as we'd swam in the lake.

I'd learned a lot about him that weekend and one of the questions that's been popping up in my head since is, why had his ex cheated on him? Had she loved the guy she'd left him for, like Steph had loved Jerome? What had his ex not been getting, or had been so unsatisfied with, that she'd looked for it elsewhere? From what I can see, Jude's a good guy. He does what he says he will, is successful, kind, handy with tools and, of course, it helps that he's very nice to look at. And that's all from a purely objective point of view, even without my little crush.

'Do you think one coat will be enough?' I ask once all the walls are covered.

'I don't know, that puke green was pretty strong,' he replies with a laugh. 'It might be. We'll see in an hour or so I guess.'

If the man in the shop I bought it from is to be believed, it will. It's apparently guaranteed to only need one application and, along with it being organic, was the reason I'd been willing to spend more than I ever thought I would on a tin of paint.

'Drink while we wait?' I ask.

'Sure.' Jude looks at the list on the fridge. 'You've made pretty good progress with that.'

I look at it and nod. 'I have, haven't I? I have wondered if I've cheated with the flatpack one though. I did have to call you for help.'

'Yeah, but you did most of it yourself. I'd pass it,' he grins. 'Shame we didn't get to make the fire though.'

I shrug and take the jug of sorrel juice I'd made from the worktop and pour it into glasses. 'There's still time.'

It felt so urgent before the festival, but now it feels less so. I've accomplished a lot from my list and every time I look at it, I feel a surge of pride.

Pre-baby unsexy bucket list
Find a flat
Make money! – 15K
Have a spa day
Go to a festival
Make a fire from scratch
Learn to bake
Do a belly cast
Learn DIY/flatpack

The rest are in progress and the most important – making that fifteen grand goal – is within reach. Just a couple more clients and I'll be able to relax for a few months after the baby's born. I lean against the worktop and look at the kitchen. It feels like it's been such an epic journey since the first time we were here, when the flat looked tired and shabby and nothing like it does now.

'Isn't it crazy how different this place looks now compared to when you first brought me here?'

Jude nods. 'It was awful.'

'Ah, now you admit it was awful. You were trying to sell it to me like it was a luxury penthouse.'

'I was selling the *potential*,' he replies with a grin. 'Which has been totally realised. I mean, look at it. It's hard to believe it was so bad it made you throw up.'

I roll my eyes. 'You're never going to let that go are you?'

'Nope. There aren't many girls I'd hold hair back for.'

'With your partying ways? I doubt that for a second.'

He tilts his head in acceptance. 'Fair enough. There aren't many girls whose hair I'd hold back and still stick around for afterwards.'

'Well, gee. I am well and truly honoured.'

We both laugh and, I'm sure it's not just me with a hint of coyness in the smile that's left behind.

'Anyways,' he says eventually. 'I think those party days are over since the festival.'

'No, really?'

He nods. 'Really. It was nice to not feel like death afterwards. I've got you to thank for that.'

'I think, technically, you should be thanking your sister.'

'Maybe I can make her responsible for the damaged tent too, then,' Jude replies with a laugh.

'Oh, she laughed pretty hard at that.'

'I bet she did. You did send her all the photos, right? She's been on at me about wanting all the info from the weekend.'

'Sure,' I reply. 'I sent them pretty much right as I took them.'

'Hm. Weird.'

We look at each other for a moment and, if I'm right, we're both thinking the same thing. It's not weird at all. It's Nina on her quest for the information she doesn't know. Jude looks down into his glass and takes a long sip. If I'm right and he *is* thinking that, then it must mean he's holding something back from her too. The memory of his arm around my waist and the softness of his breath landing on the skin of my neck jolts through my body so fiercely I can feel it as strongly as the Braxton Hicks cramps that have come and gone in the last couple of weeks.

'How's things with the baby?' he asks. 'Not long now.'

'Nine weeks . . . it's gone so quickly.'

'Nina told me about the woman at the spa.'

I raise my eyebrows. 'Since when did you two get so close?'

'It came up in conversation, that's all.'

I nod before remembering that I'd called my fictional, festival fling Jude and hope to God that Nina wouldn't have passed that bit of information on.

'Yeah, that was intense,' I say, feeling a flash of anger as I recall the awfulness of that woman. 'But it does open up the question though. I mean, I'm pretty sure that nobody's telling Sam he shouldn't be dating. Which I'm sure he is. I don't really get why it should be different because I'm a woman.'

Jude nods back, but we both know it's not only a question of gender. It's part of a bigger question around society and the limitations it likes to place on the pursuit of pleasure for women.

I look at Jude in his paint-splashed Volcom t-shirt that's clearly mainly used for jobs like this. It's old and a little tatty and should make him look like an unkempt mess. Instead, I have the feeling it's a t-shirt he's loved since the moment he got it.

'Would you ever date someone who was pregnant?' I ask.

Jude sucks in a breath and looks away, as if he's really considering his answer before nodding slowly. 'I never really thought about it before but . . . yeah. I think I would, with the right person. But that goes for any relationship, right? I wouldn't want to have kids with just anyone.'

'Sure, but it would be easier to leave someone who's pregnant with one that isn't yours.'

'I don't know . . . My dad left. Your dad left. Maybe it's the other way around. When you meet someone who's already pregnant, you have to actually decide to stick around,' Jude shrugs. 'It's probably easier to make the baby than to raise one.'

'Yeah,' I nod, letting his words sink in. 'Maybe.'

'But, you know. People are people. Relationships change,' he says pragmatically.

'If you'd have told me that Sam and I wouldn't be together a few years ago, I'd never have believed you,' I reply. 'I used to think he was *The One*.'

I laugh a little and cringe at sounding so corny, like a hopeless romantic. But it's true.

'But not recently?' Jude says. 'You said if you'd have been told a few years ago.'

'Yeah.' I drag the word out slowly. 'Things changed a lot towards the end.'

'Don't they always?'

I nod and look down at my feet. 'Sam slept with other women. And I knew about it.'

'He cheated?' Sam asks. 'Or were you polyamorous?'

I look back up with surprise. 'Most people wouldn't ask for a clarification. They'd assume I just knew about the cheating and ignored or put up with it.'

'I'm not most people,' Jude smiles.

'No, you're not. And, to be fair, I guess since Will and Jada came out about their open marriage, it's not exactly fringe anymore.'

'So, you were?'

'Not really,' I pull a face. 'Sam didn't really believe in monogamy but he didn't want to break up either.'

'And what about you?'

'Once I got past the initial shock and read up about it, I could see how it could theoretically make sense. I never doubted that he loved me.'

'But . . .?'

'I don't know, it didn't feel right for me, I guess. I mean, don't get me wrong. I didn't become blind when I met Sam. There were always men I'd find attractive, I just . . .' I shrug. 'They say that men go outside the relationship for sex but women do it for love. I never really felt like I needed to look outside of what we had.'

'Sounds about right,' Jude replies. 'I think I'd have preferred it if Rach had just had a one night thing instead of a whole affair.'

'Jerome – the guy I was with before Sam – cheated too. His excuse was that being in a long-distance relationship was *too hard.*' I laugh sarcastically and fold my arms. 'And Steph said she was in love with him, so . . . it must be true.'

'Wait, Steph?' Jude frowns. '*Steph*, Steph?'

I nod. 'The very same.'

He shakes his head. 'But you guys were . . .'

'Best friends. Yeah.' I nod again. 'We were.'

'Jeez. That's . . . I'm sorry.' His frown deepens. 'It explains a lot though. I just assumed you'd fallen out but I've never seen Nina hate on anyone so badly.'

'Oh, the hate is very much still there.' I chew the inside of my lip. 'We bumped into her last week. Or she bumped into us. Nina was *not* impressed.'

'You're surprised? That girl can hold a grudge.'

I laugh. 'She's loyal. The very definition of a ride or die.'

Jude tilts his head and probes me with his eyes. 'So. How was it seeing her after all that time?'

'Awkward. Sad. Confusing,' I shrug. 'She messaged asking to meet up so she can explain herself.'

'Are you going to do it?'

'I haven't replied. I mean, I'm not sure what the point is. It won't change what happened.'

'Maybe she wants closure,' Jude suggests and I pull a face. It sounds so . . . American.

'Would you want closure if Rachel asked for it?'

'Well, I didn't know the guy she ran off with, but she was clear about her reasons. We'd drifted apart, our bridge had collapsed with all the water that went under it . . . and so on.' The muscles in his jaw twitch as he throws me a smile that says, what can you do? 'Who knows. Maybe it's also a chance for you to really put it all behind you, too. Closure works both ways.'

I groan and shake my head. 'Maybe Sam had the right idea all along. At least if you're poly or open or whatever, you skip this part.'

'Hey, monogamy isn't all bad. It has its advantages.'

'Spoken like a true advocate,' I reply with a small smile, and he laughs gently.

'Well, it does. Sure, it might not be riveting all the time, but I don't know. There's something kind of special about committing yourself to one person.'

'You know that makes you pretty much the perfect guy, don't you?' I grin. 'Monogamous, would date a pregnant woman and knows his way around a toolbox.'

'Sounds like one of those *would like to meet* ads people used to put in the paper.'

'It's true though. You wouldn't be single for long.'

'And give up my amazing bachelor lifestyle? She'd have to be pretty special.'

'Ahh, so you're waiting for the perfect woman.'

'Nah. I said special.' Jude shakes his head vehemently. 'I thought Rachel was perfect and it didn't get me very far. I'd rather have someone real.'

'I thought men weren't attracted to real these days.'

'You need to stop reading those crappy magazines,' Jude replies with a smile. 'Men want to be happy, same as women do. And honestly, I've found out it's easier to be happy with someone who can deal with a little rain than someone who panics at the sight of a grey cloud.'

His eyes hold mine for a second and, there it is again, that crackle in the air. It could've been a generic comment. Or it could've been a reference to the festival and everything the rain brought with it. Am I really imagining this? Maybe it's a weird trick of my hormones making me think that this is anything more than a friendly chat.

The loud, almost aggressive buzz of the intercom rings through the flat, tearing through the charged air, making me jump. It cuts through the tension so completely that Jude and I both laugh in that nervous way you do when you've just escaped from something unscathed.

I point my thumb over my shoulder towards the door. 'I should get that.'

'You should,' Jude replies with a nod and an embarrassed smile.

'It'll probably be the nappy changing station.'

I don't know why I needed to say that, or why I don't move. It feels like my feet are glued to the floor.

'I can get it. They'll probably be happy not to have to lug it up the stairs.'

We smile awkwardly at each other again and when the buzzer rings a second time, it springs Jude into action and he pushes himself away from the kitchen counter. I watch him leave and put a hand on my forehead, shaking my head at the ridiculousness of it all while taking a big breath. I leave the kitchen feeling like a doe-eyed fourteen-year-old and go to the toilet. My nerves are on edge and my stomach feels giddy as I sit down, and then my breath stops, caught right in the middle of my throat.

My knickers are red with blood, as is the inside of my shorts.

'Oh, God.'

My heart rams in my chest as I shakily stand, pulling my shorts back up. My legs seem to have detached from my body as I head back towards the kitchen where Jude is holding the two big, oblong packages in his arms. He stops dead in his tracks when he sees me.

'Zoe? Are you okay?'

I shake my head. 'I'm bleeding.'

Saying the words makes it seem even more serious than it already is, and my eyes sting with tears of panic.

'Shit.' Jude puts the boxes down and rushes to my side. 'How bad is it? Should we call the doctor?'

I don't know how bad it is, but I know enough to know that bleeding when pregnant isn't anything good.

I blink, swallowing the panic back down. 'My midwife's on holiday. She won't be back until next week.'

The tears spill over and I swipe a hand across one of my cheeks.

'Hey, everything's going to be fine, okay?' Jude says calmly, leading me to sit on one of the chairs round my small dining table. 'We'll call NHS Direct and if we need to I'll drive you to the hospital.'

I nod, squeezing my eyes shut and picturing my little girl, remembering the advice we'd been given at my antenatal class in case any emergency happened – breathe and try to stay calm. Which is easier said than done when you know you're bleeding through your clothes and onto the chair.

Has the baby been moving less than usual, or in a different pattern than normal? Have I been moving rigorously? Have I had sex? Is the blood heavy and continuous? Do I have any pain? The operator's questions are simple, but my brain stumbles over them as I try to keep calm. The weight of Jude's hands on my knees as he crouches in front of me along with the calmness of the operator's voice anchors me a little. The advice is to go to the hospital to get myself checked out, and it creates a pulse of panic around my ribcage.

'I don't have a bag packed,' I say to Jude once I've hung up. 'I've been meaning to do it but I thought it'd be too early to really need one.'

I shake my head and a fresh wave of tears hit my eyes. I feel like the worst mother in the world, and I've not even given birth yet.

'It's all good, I can do it. Where can I find a suitcase or a bag?' Jude asks.

He stands up, ready to take charge of the situation and I thank God that he's here. I can't even think about how I'd be clear enough to even know what to pack. All I can think about is the blood, and my baby.

'In the bottom of my wardrobe,' I mumble, and he nods.

'Alright. Give me a minute.'

Breathe. Try to stay calm. Breathe. Try to stay calm.

The baby needs me calm. When I'd heard that at the antenatal class, I'd laughed to myself. The idea of being able to keep calm in the extreme pain of labour felt like asking a snail to run a hundred metre sprint. But now, I get it. This isn't about me. If I let myself freak out, she'll feel it too. So, I do something I haven't done since the day my dad moved out. I put my hands on my belly and I pray.

◆ ◆ ◆

Pregnancy week: Thirty
You're the size of a: Large cabbage
Today, I feel: Relieved

Hello, Little One . . .
Thank God. It was SUCH a relief to hear your heartbeat at the scan. I don't think I've ever been so scared in my entire life. Ever. The nurse had joked that you just wanted to get a peek of the

place you'll be born in ahead of time. I figured that if she was joking, it really must mean everything's fine – like being reassured on a bumpy flight that if the attendants are behaving normally there's probably nothing to worry about. So, here we are. It's no presidential suite but I have to admit I feel better being here for the night, just in case. If you're still doing fine in the morning, we'll be able to go home.

Once we do, I promise to slow down. No more festivals, no more swimming, no more DIY. All you have to do is stay in there until it's time.

Love,

Zoe

xx

Chapter Twenty-One

'Here's some shepherd's pie and spag bol,' Nina says, holding up a couple of glass containers. 'Don't get up, I'll put them in the fridge.'

'Thanks,' I reply from my position on the sofa.

I've barely moved since getting home from the hospital yesterday afternoon, even after hearing the baby's heartbeat, seeing her on the scan and reassurances from the doctor. I'm terrified something else will happen. I used to be obsessed with the Tudor era for a while, devouring TV shows, films and books about it, and could never understand why the queens were confined to bed while pregnant. Now, I do. And even though the doctor said some light movement would do me good, I still want to rest a little longer.

Nina comes over and drops a kiss onto my forehead. 'How are you feeling?'

'Exhausted. I was too wired to sleep.'

'You gave us all a fright there, girlie.' She puts a hand on my bump. 'Do you need anything? I can put a wash on, clean up a bit?'

I shake my head with a grateful smile. 'Mum did all that earlier. The machine's been going all day getting all the Babygros and bibs clean, just in case.'

'It's wild to think she could come already.'

'I'm keeping my legs tightly crossed, trust me.'

'I bet you are,' Nina replies. 'Jude's been asking after you. He said you haven't returned his messages?'

'Yeah, I just . . .' I swallow, hesitating for a moment. 'I guess I just felt a bit embarrassed. I made such a fuss over what turned out to be nothing.'

Nina frowns. 'It wasn't a fuss, he knows that. Better safe than sorry, right?'

'Yeah,' I mumble. 'Right.'

I feel awful for lying to her, again. I don't think I made a fuss, not in the slightest. But I can't tell her that, despite what the doctors had said, I still feel like it was my fault. I'd been painting the wall – who does something as vigorous as that when they're this heavily pregnant? And I'd been swimming that morning. I avoid Nina's eyes. Maybe all that had already been enough without adding on the giddiness I'd felt with Jude just before the bleeding had started. I know it sounds stupid, but maybe that woman in the spa had been right. Maybe, I should've been concentrating more on my baby, and less on some guy.

'He's worried about you,' Nina says.

'Really?'

'Of course. He was pretty shaken up afterwards. She was nowhere near as far along as you, but Rachel had a miscarriage, remember?'

I frown. 'God, yeah. I'd completely forgotten . . . He was so calm when it was happening, I'd never have guessed.'

'He was a mess when they lost the baby and did a first aid course after that,' Nina says with a sad smile. 'He tries to say it was for work because of being on building sites and stuff, but I know it was because of the miscarriage.'

My heart lurches. Jude had given me such a convincing speech about not wanting kids at Nina's barbecue that it had overwritten the memory of hearing about their miscarriage years ago. It can't have been more than a year after that when Rachel had left.

'Just drop him a message, let him know you're okay?' Nina prompts and I nod.

'I will. I was lucky he was here,' I smile. 'From now on, no more excitement.'

Nina laughs. 'You have to be the first person I've ever heard who calls watching paint dry exciting.'

I roll my eyes. 'You know what I mean. I've been doing too much. Working, the festival—'

'You deserve to have fun, Zo. And you needed that weekend.'

I chew the inside of my cheek. 'Maybe it was karma. For that guy I told you about?'

Nina frowns and her face blanks for a few seconds before recognition sets in and she sets me with a frank stare.

'That's the most ridiculous thing I've ever heard. You can't really believe that?'

I readjust myself on the sofa and shove a cushion between my knees. 'It was really scary, Nina. All kinds of stuff when through my head. And the woman at the spa said—'

'That woman chatted absolute bullshit. She had no idea what she was talking about,' she interrupts. 'You're fine, the baby's fine and none of it was your fault.'

'I'm alone and pregnant, though. That's my fault.'

'Girl, I don't know what kind of stuff they pumped you with at the hospital, but this has got to stop. You can't blame yourself for any of this. You'll drive yourself nuts.' She sighs with frustration. 'It's Sam's fault that you're dealing with this alone, not yours. It should have been him here, not Jude.'

She's right of course. I throw her a grateful smile. 'God, I love you.'

'I know. I love you, too,' she grins. 'Now are you *sure* you don't need anything else? I can tell Luke to go without me.'

'No way. You look great, go have fun.' I shoo her away. 'If they'll let you in with Converse.'

'It's Ministry, they'll let you in wearing a bin bag.'

'You, maybe. Anyone else? Not a chance,' I laugh. 'Have a dance for me while I'm deep in sleep.'

'Alright,' she says, getting up. '*Call* if anything happens. Promise?'

I draw a cross over my heart. 'Promise. Have fun.'

She drops another kiss onto my forehead before leaving with a hint of perfume trailing behind her and I try to take in what she'd said. Maybe being a mum is like Catholicism and comes with guilt as a matter of course. Sam chose not to be here and of course we don't live in a universe where a single mum-to-be gets punished for flirting a little. But the guilt is still there, pressing into the place where my ribs meet in my chest. It's not just about the choices I've made over these last few weeks or months, but in general.

I remember hearing someone say once that life is a culmination of all your choices and experiences. It's hard not to look back and wonder if I've made the right ones when I'm weeks away from giving birth and have just been scared out of my mind. How far back would I have to go to find the place where things could have turned out differently? To the night when Sam told me he wanted to open our relationship, the dinner when he'd told me about not wanting kids or the party where I'd met him? To the moment I'd seen that note on Jerome's whiteboard that day, or the night I'd slept with him back in Ibiza? Or does it go even further than that? To the time I'd been told I was too much and felt like I needed to keep myself smaller than everyone else? Maybe, everything would be different if I'd have made different choices. Or, to be more accurate, if I'd have made a choice and stuck to it, instead of simply going along

254

with things. If I'd actively said yes, I want this, or no, I don't want that. If I'd let myself take up space.

I reach for my phone and hitch myself up to rest against the sofa cushion. I still haven't replied to Steph's message. I ignored every single text, email and letter she'd sent after I'd driven away from her in that cab. I hadn't been interested in hearing her side of the story, any more than I had been in hearing Jerome's and it had taken a long time to stop feeling so raw and wounded. The only way I managed it was to try and pretend neither of them existed. When I'd met Sam, I was sure it had been buried. Clearly, it hadn't. The scars are obvious to me now – agreeing to Sam seeing other people and a future without children was all a way to stop him from swapping me for someone else. Just like Jerome had done. Calling it closure, like Jude suggested, feels a little too neat. As if by meeting up with Steph and hearing her reasons why could make up for the betrayal or the loss of a friendship. It can't. But making a choice to respond and close the chapter? That feels better.

I open up her message and read it again. It sounds sincere. And even though Nina would tut and sigh and call me gullible, I do believe that Steph is sorry. She might have got Jerome, but she'd lost me and Nina. And that had to hurt.

Zoe: Hi Steph . . .

I bite my lip as my thumbs tap against my screen. Do I really want to meet her? Do I want to hear her side of the story? To be told about the life she'd had with Jerome? What she'd done was unforgiveable in a hundred different ways, she had at least made a choice. Now, it's time to make mine.

Zoe: Hi Steph,

Thanks for your congratulations on the baby. It was a big shock to see you too. I understand you had your reasons for doing what you did and even though I'll never understand it, I'm sure it wasn't an easy choice to make. But meeting up isn't going to happen.

I've learned this year that life happens. We make choices every single day that affect the rest of our lives. For a long time, I've wished things could have been different. But the truth is, if things *had* been different, I wouldn't be where I am now. And where I am, is happy. For the first time in my life, I can really say that – I'm happy. What happened between us still hurts. It'll always hurt. But I want to let it go. I don't want to carry you and Jerome around with me anymore. And I hope you can let go too.

I really do wish you all the best, Steph.

Zoe

xx

I press send and let out a deep breath. I don't know if I'll ever really be able to forgive her for what she did, but I already feel as if a weight has been lifted from me just by saying what I needed to say and, most importantly, realising how I truly feel. Because I am happy right now, even if the road to get here was difficult.

I lock my screen and put my phone down with a smile before settling back down into the sofa.

Pregnancy week: Thirty-one
You're the size of a: Coconut
Today, I feel: . . . Not sure

Hello, Little One . . .

You've been moving around a lot these last couple of days since our little scare. I'm taking it as a sign that you're over all that poking and prodding and I am happy for every kick you make. But when you're asleep, I wonder if you dream and, if you do, what it is about. Some internet article said it would likely be your experiences of being in my womb until now, and I've been trying to imagine what it must be like to have such a blank canvas.

It's got me thinking about the things you'll experience in your childhood and as an adult. I wish I could say you're only going to have moments that are beautiful and make you smile, laugh and feel good about yourself. I wish I could say that every person you'll meet will have your best interests at heart. That you'll never get hurt. I wish I could but I can't.

The truth is, there'll be things that feel hard or impossible at the time. You'll have your heart and trust broken. I can absolutely promise that I'll do my best to lessen the impact of all that but, the truth is, I think it's all just a part of being human. I've heard before that some people think we choose where and into which family we'll be born, so we can learn the things we need to. I'm not sure what my lesson is, but it's sure got me thinking about yours. Why you might have chosen me and this little corner of the world.

I spent yesterday afternoon reading about different parenting styles. Should I be an attachment-mum, keeping you close at all times, co-sleeping and carrying you around in a sling to protect you from the world? Or should I take the lead and encourage you to adapt to life as you go, learning by trial and error? I have no idea which way is best. What I can say is I've always been thankful to *my* mum for being honest about life. So that's what I'm going to do for you.

I'll protect you as much as I can, and I'll be here for you, always.

Love,

Zoe

xx

Chapter Twenty-Two

'How's the patient?' Jude asks.

I smile, stepping back to let him in. 'Better. Sorry I dropped off the radar for a bit there.'

'Doesn't matter. As long as you're both doing alright,' he replies, handing me a huge canvas shopping bag.

'No, it does. It was rude and you've been so helpful.' I take the bag from him and take a look inside.

'I went to three different shops and cleared the shelves.'

'You're amazing.' I shake my head with a smile at what must be dozens of bags of beef-flavoured Hula Hoops. 'And I'm sorry for worrying you.'

'Honestly, don't be,' Jude replies. 'It was a scary thing to go through. I get that you needed some time.'

'It was,' I reply, feeling his compassion even more now I remember what he'd been through with Rachel. 'Anyway, I wanted to say thank you. For being here and taking charge of things. It helped. A lot.'

'You're welcome.'

'Do you want a drink or something?' I ask, moving towards the sofa, but he shakes his head.

'I'm on my way back to the workshop. I've got a ton of work to do. That mess of papers on my desk isn't clearing by itself. I just wanted to check in and see how you were doing. And I was wondering if that wall needed an extra coat after all?'

'Nope, it's good. It did what it said on the tin,' I joke.

'And what about the cot? I can still help with that if you need?'

My face fills with an apology. 'Barry did it yesterday . . . but thank you.'

'Ah, right.'

If I'm not mistaken, he sounds disappointed and it makes my heart lurches a little.

'Mum got a bit worried that the baby would come early and the nursery wouldn't be ready,' I explain. 'There was no stopping them.'

Jude stuffs his hands into the pockets of his work trousers. 'Yeah, sure, I totally understand.'

His dark eyebrows pull close together above his brown eyes and my chest fills with warmth. It had been nice with him, until the bleeding had started. It had felt easy and comfortable and, despite telling myself that it was somehow to blame for what happened and putting a little distance between us, the truth is, I've missed him.

'What are you up to this weekend?' he asks.

'I'll probably be here, chilling on the sofa and wrapping things up for work. Maybe I'll go for a walk or something.'

'Did they put you on bed rest?'

'No,' I reply. 'But I am taking things a lot easier than I have been. What about you?'

'Am I on bed rest?'

I laugh, shaking my head. 'No, silly. What are your weekend plans?'

'A friend of mine is opening a cafe a few streets away. I said I'd swing by. Maybe you want to come with? If you're feeling up to it, I mean.'

A flicker of a smile tugs at my lips at what sounds like a hint of uncertainty in his voice.

'And it's also fine if you're not. I probably won't go for long,' he adds.

His eyes are restless and he shifts from one foot to another. He's nervous. Jude is normally in complete control of every situation, and my smile widens at the hint of vulnerability that I'm sure hadn't been there before.

'Sure, sounds great,' I reply with a grin. 'As long as you know that having a heavily pregnant woman in tow will probably get people talking.'

'I can handle it,' he replies with a smile. 'Let me know on Sunday if you're feeling up to it.'

'I will.'

I nod and we say our goodbyes while my body fizzes with an anticipation I haven't felt in a long time. Not since Sam and maybe even further back than that. I close the front door and I put my hand on my massive belly, running it over the fabric of my t-shirt and the unfamiliar stub of my now outward facing bellybutton.

'I hope this is okay with you,' I say, speaking to her. 'I'll totally understand if it isn't.'

I put both hands on my stomach as if I'm waiting for a sign, but at this time of the afternoon she's usually asleep. Is it wrong to be excited about going to a coffee shop with a friend? It's hardly a date, even if he had sounded nervous which, he probably wasn't. I blow a raspberry and go back to the sofa, telling myself not to be so superstitious. If it were any other person, I wouldn't even think twice about it. Then again, if it were any other person, I probably wouldn't be sitting here with a large grin on my face. I shake my head and push the thought from my mind.

By the time Saturday rolls around, I feel back to normal. Well, as normal as I can being thirty-two weeks pregnant. Thirty-two weeks. That leaves just seven until the due date if all goes to plan. I have my birth plan sorted out and after toying with the idea of going *au naturelle*, I had to admit to myself that I'm a total wimp with pain. I figured that me being under stress will mean the baby being under stress, so I won't be saying no to pain reducing measures, except for an epidural.

These last few days have been about tying up loose ends. I've handed everything over to my virtual assistant and deactivated all my calendar booking links for the next few months. It's as if the change of seasons outside is reflecting a change inside. The start of autumn is bringing with it a slowing down and need to be cosy. Normally, September is a busy time for me workwise. The back-to-school energy of new starts usually means a fair few bookings but this year, all I'm wanting to do is snuggle under a blanket on the sofa with a TV series or a book.

The door buzzer goes and I waddle over to answer it because that's what I do now, I waddle. My belly sticks out in front of me and I hold my lower back like a caricature of a pregnant woman. I'm pretty sure I can't get bigger than this, which is good because today my bump is going to get immortalised in a plaster cast.

'If you're planning on moving in, I should warn you that you'll soon have a roommate who screams at multiple intervals in the night and poos a lot,' I joke as Nina lugs a suitcase up the stairs.

'Ha, ha,' she replies and kisses me hello before wheeling the suitcase in. 'Are you excited?'

I laugh back, closing the door. 'Yes, I'm excited. I know it sounds weird because it's my body and I've been walking around like this for months, but I'm curious about how it's actually going to look.'

'Okay, don't be mad,' Nina says, shrugging off leather jacket. 'But I did something.'

'What?' I frown.

She kneels on the floor and flips the suitcase to unzip it. Nina takes out a deflated gym ball, some towels and a smaller bag which she hands to me.

'You bought crisps and booze-free gin?' I raise an eyebrow. 'Shocking.'

'I've had that in the back my cupboard for ages and haven't tasted it yet, so it might be.' She smiles before pulling the sides of her mouth down into a grimace. 'But that's not what I mean. I already did my casting.'

Nina unwraps a pile of newspaper and pulls out a mould, turning it to face me.

'Oh, wow,' I laugh with surprise and put my hands over my mouth.

She grins, looking at a life-sized replica of her vulva. 'What do you think?'

'I . . . yeah.' I try to find the right words. 'Well, it's a vulva.'

'I hope you don't mind,' she says. 'I thought it was a good idea to know what to do and, well. I know you. Somehow, I didn't think you'd want to be stuck between my legs for half an hour.'

'And that's why we're best friends. So, you did it yourself?'

'Nope, Luke did it.'

'Well, just in case him looking after you while you were sick wasn't a clear enough sign that he might be The One, this should be.' I shake my head with a laugh. 'I'm impressed.'

'Me too,' Nina replies with a grin.

I reach for the mould. 'Here, let me have a look.'

She hands it over and I find myself having to resist the urge to giggle like an embarrassed kid in sex education class. Although,

I'm pretty sure we didn't even see an image of a vulva, let alone a real-life replica.

'It's really pretty,' I say after the giggles die down.

'Why, thank you.'

Nina and I have seen each other naked multiple times from sharing changing rooms to drunken skinny dipping. But this is different. It's intimate and, actually, it's pretty powerful.

'It kind of looks like a flower,' I say, handing it back. 'I wonder if mine does too.'

Nina stares at me and drops her jaw. 'You've never looked at yourself with a mirror?'

I shake my head.

'Not even since you've been pregnant?'

'Especially not since then. Then I'd have to think about how this,' I point to my belly, 'is going to come out of it.'

Nina laughs a little. 'I'm not sure avoidance is really going to help with that but hey, I hear you.'

'For what it's worth,' I continue. 'I would have done the mould for you. You know that, right?'

'And that's why *you're* my best friend,' Nina winks before clapping her hands together. 'Right, I say we should get started. It's going take a good hour or so. And you'd better go for a pee too, because you won't be able to once we've started.'

'That'll be a challenge,' I reply with a big dose of scepticism.

'You've got an air pump right?' she asks, picking up the deflated gym ball.

I nod and go to the storage cupboard in the hallway to get it. The box is right next to the manual foot pump I'd taken to the festival. The memory of Jude pumping up my airbed makes me smile as I hand it over to Nina. After going to the toilet twice, just to be sure, I come back into the living room where she's laid out newspapers and towels on the floor.

'How messy does it get?' I ask, closing the living room blinds.

'Not too bad, but I'm not about to get in Jude's bad books for ruining the floor,' she replies. 'Alright, ready?'

I grin and nod. 'Let's do it.'

I smother my belly with cocoa butter, making sure to heed Nina's strict advice to put it absolutely everywhere or else risk some serious pain when the cast comes off. When it comes time to sit on the ball, Nina dons a pair of marigolds which are, of course, bright pink to match her hair. She dips the first strip of plaster wrap into a bowl of warm water and I squirm as she lays it on my skin.

'I replied to Steph,' I say abruptly, and Nina looks up at me with a look of intrigue.

'And?'

'And I told her I don't want to meet up.'

She smooths the piece of plaster, pressing it onto my belly. 'What else did she expect? She can't seriously have thought you'd *actually* want to meet up with her after what she did.'

I'm about to shrug before remembering I'm supposed to be sitting still. 'I don't know. I just know that I don't have the energy to care anymore. It happened, and it was shit. But look at where I am now. Maybe it was all worth it, in a weird kind of way.'

Nina raises her eyebrows. 'You're a better person than I am.'

'It's not like she got off scot-free though, is it? She's lost us, and Jerome.'

'Did she tell you what happened between them?'

'No. And I don't want to know. I just said the door's closed and wished her well.'

Nina prepares another strip of plaster. 'Good for you.'

We grin at each other before switching the topic to *Outlander* and my body gets used to the tickling sensation. Over time, it becomes quite calming as Nina works the strips over my belly with the ease of someone who handles other people's bodies on a daily basis.

'Let's hope the baby stays still while it's drying,' Nina says once she's finished a good twenty minutes later. 'Otherwise you'll have a lumpy bump.'

I look down at my covered belly and, since I'm in the decision-making mood, I throw caution and my inner critic to the wind and ask Nina to do my breasts too. It would look odd without them and if this whole thing is to commemorate my pregnant body, it feels weird to leave them out. They've changed too, after all. Another ten minutes later we're done, and I concentrate on sitting still with the strange feeling of drying plaster around my torso. If I can make it for this next half an hour without peeing myself, I'll be impressed.

I look down at my fingernails as Nina clears up some of the mess and prepares our pretend gin and tonics. My toenails are clearly out of the question, but yesterday I'd sat at the table and taken my time applying two coats of varnish the colour of merlot. And today I'd stood in front of the mirror plucking stray hairs from my eyebrows for the first time in I have no idea how long. As the plaster hardens on my skin, butterflies flutter in my stomach. I know it's not a date, but I'd be lying if I said I wasn't excited at having been asked out.

'Ooh, what is *that* smile about?' Nina asks, raising her eyebrows with a knowing grin.

I didn't know I'd been smiling at all, but I quickly wipe it from my face, shaking my head. 'Nothing.'

'*Please*.' She perches on the arm of the sofa and crosses her legs. 'You're an awful liar. Come on, spill it.'

I glance at her and chew the inside of my lip. There's no way I can tell her about Jude, but this is Nina. I hate lying to her, not to mention the fact that I haven't been able to share a single iota about my increasing infatuation.

'I've got a crush and it's totally stupid,' I say with a touch of embarrassment.

She raises an eyebrow in surprise. 'On who?'

'Just some guy I see around sometimes.'

'Well have you spoken to him?'

I swallow and nod. 'A little.'

'So, tell me about him, what's he like?'

'He's . . . honestly, he's just kind of normal,' I smile. 'Not in an average way, but in a way that just feels like he's supposed to be there. He feels familiar, you know?'

Nina grins. 'How did you meet him, and why didn't you tell me sooner?'

'Because it's silly,' I reply with a nervous laugh. 'It's just been something to keep myself occupied.'

'Sounds like it's more than that.'

Does it? I picture Jude, with his gorgeous smile and deep, dark eyes. I think about the way he always looks like he's just pulled on the first bit of clothing he'd laid his hands on, and how he'd lovingly swept his hand across this floor, seeing its potential after it had been hidden away for years. And it makes my heart melt into a puddle in my chest.

Damn. Nina might actually be right. Maybe it's not something irrelevant. I think I might like him. Like, really like him – more than just a crush. Hearing myself admit to it in my mind sends a thrill through my body. It feels exhilarating and totally ridiculous. I know there's nothing in it, but it's such a relief to be able to share even just a little bit about how I feel.

'You might be right,' I say slowly, letting my mind process it.

Nina's grin widens. 'Aw, I *love* this.'

'Really? I'm not sure I do.'

'Because of the baby?' She fixes me with a look. 'You're still worried about it being wrong?'

'It's not just that . . .' I hesitate. 'He's . . . well he's not someone I should be interested in.'

Nina frowns. 'Why not? He's not married, is he?'

'No, no,' I reply quickly. 'He's single.'

'So, what's the problem?' Nina shrugs. 'As long as no one gets hurt, I say go for it. Why not? You're both adults.'

'He's probably not interested anyway. I mean, I *am* about to give birth.'

'Yes and look at you!' Nina says. 'You're a goddess.'

I look down at the white plaster covering my body. Goddess might be going a little too far, but still, I can't help smiling.

Chapter Twenty-Three

As far as Sundays go, today is near perfect. I lean back against the exposed brick wall, watching the world outside from my window ledge seat. It's a grey autumnal day and the tree outside is battling against the howling wind that's been buffeting the country thanks to a storm somewhere over the Atlantic. At least with this bump I'm in no danger of being blown away. I look down and rub my hand across my belly. I've spent years wishing it was flat and toned instead of soft and doughy, and I don't even know how many hours a day it had been sucked in on autopilot. I'd always seen my 32C breasts and wide hips an asset, but my belly? That was a place I didn't like very much. Until last night.

When I'd had the idea to plaster cast my belly, it had been to make a little memento. I'd expected it to be fun and something to show my daughter when she's old enough to understand the significance of it. What I hadn't expected, was for it to be so empowering. Nina's, I could get. She'd gone for an intimate body part that carries a whole load of shame and social taboo around it, but mine? Mine was a pregnant belly. It wasn't something hidden and, as I've found out, being pregnant meant becoming a medical patient. My belly had almost become public property. Being able to see it cast in plaster, removed from me and out of context, blew my mind.

There was nothing of my waist left and my cup size has more than doubled. But it all looked exactly how it was supposed to. It was the replica of a pregnant woman and a body that had stretched and shifted to grow, nurture and accommodate another human being. It was, in case I'd been in any danger of forgetting, a reminder of how amazing my body actually is. For the first time in the last few weeks, I'd fallen asleep with a lot less fear and woken with a surge of confidence. Not a bad return on a DIY plaster kit that cost less than thirty pounds.

I turn my head to see Jude coming back over with our drinks and a smile grows on my face. This might not be a date, but that extra dose of self-appreciation and confidence hasn't hurt. His faded light-grey t-shirt and slightly ripped jeans hang on his body like an afterthought, as if he'd pulled them on at the last minute for the sake of decency. Which of course makes my own thoughts completely *in*decent. It's a look I'm sure many men try to perfect, but with Jude it just seems natural, as if he's got far more important things to think about than choosing which clothes to wear.

'I kinda wish I'd ordered a hot chocolate now,' he says, putting our drinks on the table. 'Yours looks great.'

'We might actually have to share it,' I reply, looking at the huge cup topped with whipped cream, marshmallows and a dusting of cocoa powder. 'I'm still stuffed.'

'Wait, you mean you don't have space for dessert?' He raises his eyebrows and we laugh for what feels like the hundredth time today.

After a delicious and massive spinach, feta, pumpkin and cashew nut salad, I'll be coming back for the food, never mind the coffee. I've never been the type to get full on a plate of salad until getting pregnant, but Jude had suggested we get another drink and honestly, I'm not ready to go home yet.

'What did you get?' I ask, looking at his tall glass of foamy, milky liquid.

'Chai latte. Want to try it?'

He hands me the long spoon from his saucer, so I do the same and we sample each other's drinks before tasting our own.

'Damn. I really should've gone for the hot chocolate,' he says.

'And I was just about to say I like yours better.'

'Swap?'

We slide our drinks across the table and I smile, much happier with the cinnamon and ginger spiced latte that doesn't look like a second meal. The decor in the cafe is perfect for an autumnal day like this, with its exposed brick walls and chunky wooden tables. Our window seat is covered with faux-sheepskin rugs and big cushions with chunky knitted covers. It's only mid-afternoon but the candles on the tables are lit and the feel is utterly cosy, with chilled, soul music playing low in the background.

'I predict big things for this place,' I say, holding my glass in both hands as I look around at the other people in the space.

All of the tables are occupied, and a few people stand at the bar. Jude cranes his neck, looking at the big square of moss in different shades of green encased in a wooden frame and pinned to the wall. The moss looks so soft and bouncy and only adds to the warm, inviting vibe of the cafe. My eyes drift from the living wall art to the side of Jude's neck, taking in the contour of the muscle that runs from his jaw and disappears into the collar of his t-shirt.

'It's cool, right?'

He turns to look back at me and I quickly avert my eyes, glancing around again.

'It is. And I love that a good ninety per cent of the people in here can probably remember life before mobile phones.'

Jude laughs. 'Ah, yeah. Back when life was simple and the only thing that mattered was hanging out with your mates all day.'

'And Saturday mornings in front of the TV,' I reply, smiling with nostalgia. 'They were my favourite.'

'Same. Remember that show, *Live and Kicking*?'

I nod enthusiastically. 'Of *course*. It was the official start of the weekend. I used to call every week trying to get onto their game shows.'

Jude snorts a laugh, leaning his shoulder against the window. 'What a con. It was always some kid from the middle of nowhere who got through.'

'I still remember the number too. 081 811 8181.' I sing the number out with the melody, laughing at the memory.

'Well, that's impressive,' he says.

'Or lame. How can I remember a phone number for a TV show from thirty years ago but can barely remember my own?'

'Send the answer on a postcard when you find out.'

I scrunch my nose with a giggle at his reference. 'I never was much of a *Blue Peter* fan.'

'Me neither, but it would've been cool to get one of those badges.'

I'm pretty certain his smile is as wide as mine is. If this were a date, I'd be thinking that things are going very well. The easy flowing conversation and shared nostalgia would make me feel like we were getting close, like this was someone I'd known forever. Which, of course, it is. Unlike a date though – or at least how I remember them to be – there's not one ounce of self-consciousness. I'm not preoccupied with worrying about what Jude thinks of my dungarees and stripy long-sleeved top outfit, and my mind isn't racing ahead to think of topics to bring up if the conversation dies out.

Jude pulls a face and covers his nose while looking at me and I frown until I catch the smell and do the same.

'Tell me that wasn't you,' I say, laughing through my hand.

He shakes his head and we look down at the floor where a cute little dog is lying asleep on a rug.

I raise my eyebrows and drop my hand. 'How convenient that there's a dog to blame it on.'

Jude laughs back. 'Hey, if it was mine I'd claim it.'

We giggle like teenagers as a man comes over to our table, smiling at Jude.

'You made it,' he says, and Jude gets up to greet him, doing that hug-slash-handshake thing men do.

'Of course,' Jude replies before turning towards me. 'This is Zoe. Zoe, this is Finn, one of the owners.'

He reaches out to shake my hand, looking at me with big green eyes and a wide smile.

'Nice to meet you.' He looks down at my belly. 'Congrats. When are you due?'

'Thirteenth of November,' I reply. 'Not long now.'

'My girlfriend's due in January,' he says, his face lighting up.

'How is Jess?' Jude asks. 'I haven't seen her yet.'

'She's asleep, hopefully. We had a late one last night getting everything ready for today, so she'll come later.'

'This place is amazing, and the food was divine,' I say with a smile.

'Thanks,' Finn replies, putting a hand on his chest. 'We've got a good chef and a great team, so fingers crossed.'

'Well, I'm a local so I'll be coming back.'

I can already see myself sitting here with my laptop and a cappuccino. And a baby, of course.

Finn looks at Jude. 'I should get back, there's tons to do. If you've got time maybe we can catch up before me and Jess head back to Cornwall?'

Jude nods. 'Sure, I'm sure I can make it work.'

'Great. And congrats again, buddy. Here's to fatherhood, right?'

Finn slaps him on the shoulder before leaving, and I can barely disguise my smile as I lift my latte in a toast.

'To fatherhood?'

'Ha, funny.' Jude rolls his eyes and sits back down. 'It's an easy mistake to make, I guess.'

'But you didn't correct him.'

I suppose that, to anyone who might be watching us, we look like a young couple, about to embark on a shared journey of parenthood. It's an image that sparks a warm glow in my chest.

'No,' he laughs. 'Didn't feel the need to, I guess.'

I smile, allowing the glow to grow a little bigger because, why not? It adds to the boost that the belly cast has given me and I'm happy to bask in it for a while.

After almost four hours of chatting, laughter and a very close game of Scrabble, we decide to leave before we start to feel bad for hogging a table for so long.

'It's on me,' Jude insists when I reach for my purse. 'Seriously. Think of it as a maternity present.'

I smile at him, shaking my head. 'Only if you're sure.'

'Course I'm sure. I'll be back in a sec.'

I watch him as he makes his way to the counter. I don't get it. When you speak to single women who date awful men, they always want to know why the good ones are either gay or taken. Yet here I am with one who's single, straight, well-mannered, a nice human, attractive and makes a decent living. He leans against the counter on his forearms and I don't even try to pretend not to look at his bum in his jeans. If anything, he seems to get more attractive every time I see him. When he gets back, I stand up and Jude holds my denim jacket out for me to thread my arms into. The wind is still relentless as we step outside and set off on a slow but short walk back to my flat.

'I'm beginning to think you're some kind of bad weather charm,' I joke, wiping a wind-induced tear from my eye. 'Every time I'm with you there's some extreme weather system going on.'

'Oh, you mean you didn't know it's a superpower of mine?' Jude laughs. 'No rain today, though.'

I look up at the sky before shooting him a grin. 'Not yet.'

'I kind of like the extremes. It's a reminder that the world's a wild place instead of this concrete jungle.'

He gestures to the street we're walking on. Apart from the trees sprouting up from the pavement every now and again, there's not much of Mother Nature to be seen. Buses and cars roar past on the road and the street is lined with shops selling everything from newspapers and fried chicken to mobile phones. It's about as urban and inner city as it gets.

'You sound like a country boy,' I say with a laugh.

'Never,' he replies, fixing me with a look of mock horror. 'But it's nice to unplug now and again and be out in it, you know?'

'I do. I think that's one of the things I loved most about Solar. Being in the lake while it was raining like that,' I smile. 'One of my all time ever highlights, I think.'

'Yeah, that was something,' Jude replies, nodding in agreement. 'Having my tent trashed though? Not so much.'

I grimace. 'Next time you'll have to check the strength of it first.'

'Next time I'll take my own,' he jokes, and we laugh as we amble towards the corner of my street. 'Still, I did get an upgrade from a crappy camping mat to an airbed, so . . .'

The memory of being held in his arms spreads warmth around my body, shielding me from the persistent wind.

'Between the rain falling on the tent and a notorious pregnant snorer, I'm surprised you slept at all,' I say.

'I didn't. Why do you think I was so dead on the drive back?'

My face flickers and the skin around the collar of Jude's jacket turns a little red. I'd been sure that he'd been asleep, lying next to me on the airbed. I'd heard his steady breathing and he hadn't said a word. But then again, neither had I after a while. The silence had been enough. And if he really hadn't slept, then he must know that we'd huddled together like we did. The breeze blows on the back of my neck, reminding me of the way his breath had landed on my skin as he'd laid behind me. Jude clears his throat as I burrow my chin deeper into my scarf, taking advantage of being able to hide my mouth because, try as I might, I can't help the grin fighting its way onto my face.

We round the corner to my flat and I fish out my keys. Despite the Sunday traffic on the road, the jangling sound jars loudly and I squeeze my fingers around them as we stop in front of my door. I look at it, remembering how cynical I'd been when he'd first brought me here all those months ago. He'd stood right here, one hand with the key in the lock and the other on the peeling painted door and had told me to trust him. He knew me, and he knew this would be a place where I could feel at home.

'So,' I say slowly, glancing at him. 'This is me.'

I cringe a little inside, giving myself an internal face palm. Why did I say that? It's not like he doesn't know where I live.

'Yep,' he replies with a nod. 'This is you.'

His hands are jammed into his jeans pockets as he looks at the door, and we exchange a smile before he seems to see the silliness in the situation and laughs. He shakes his head, takes his hands from his pockets and I automatically lean in for a hug, tilting myself forward ever so slightly to accommodate the bump. His woody scent envelopes me as his arms wrap around my body. It feels so good to be held and I let myself melt into it as we stand there for a few seconds with my head nestled in the crook of his neck. We pull apart and I look up at him. His face is centimetres away from mine and his arms are still looped around my shoulders. His brown eyes skip across my face and I let myself do the same, taking in the shape of his eyebrows, the fullness of his lips and the freckles on his skin. My heart trips in my chest and a hundred things run through my mind at once.

It feels like we've been here for an age. Who'll be the one to break away first? Or will he kiss me? Will I be the one to kiss him? *Can* I even kiss him, this man I've known since forever but have only just got to know properly? Is this appropriate, given the circumstances? His Adam's apple bounces as he swallows and I can tell he's weighing up the same thing.

I don't know who moves first, but the gap between us closes and as our lips meet I feel myself soften. It's a gentle kiss. A slow kiss. A kiss that starts with the tentative contact of his mouth on mine, becoming deeper and firmer. There's a part of me that wants this to feel wrong. But it's completely overshadowed by the fact that everything about it feels right. His hand cupping the back of my neck, the taste of him on my tongue. It feels like we're being held in a bubble, shielding us from the outside world, suspended in a doorway on a busy Peckham street until our lips part. We stand there for a moment with his forehead pressed against mine and his breath rushing onto my lips in short bursts. My body feels alive and my heart is beating loudly in my ears, but my insides feel the sort of calm that's like being back on land after hours out on a choppy sea.

'I should go,' Jude says slowly.

His voice is quiet, but he doesn't move away. He stays where he is with his fingers teasing the back of my neck.

'You don't have to.'

'No,' he replies, shifting his head from side to side and pressing his forehead into mine. 'But I should.'

He takes a step back and drops his hand down, catching the tips of my fingers in his and glances up at me with a look on his face that says, *did that really just happen?* The kiss could only have lasted a few seconds at most, but with the distance between us my body feels acutely aware of the absence of him.

'I'll call you.'

'Okay.'

He nods and takes a few backward steps before turning around and my smile widens into an enormous grin as I turn towards the door. I put my key in the lock and step into the stairway where it's calm and sheltered from the crazy wind. I'm not entirely sure what just happened, but one thing I do know, is that everything has changed.

◆ ◆ ◆

I lie in bed the next morning, listening to the torrential downpour and howling wind, remembering the way my skin bloomed when Jude's lips touched mine and recounting our conversation. It feels like I've reached for my phone a hundred times since waking, and every time I see the lack of a message from Jude, I start to wonder if I've imagined the whole thing. I try to remember who made the first move, freezing the moment like a screenshot and trying to look at it from all angles. Truthfully, I think it was the both of us, at the same time, pulled together like magnets.

And then I tell myself to get a grip. It's Monday morning and he's probably already busy at work. It's pure madness to expect a call first thing.

I lie with my hands on my swollen belly and count the number of kicks I can feel as instructed by my midwife.

'What do you think, Noemie?' I ask, trying out the name.

I shake my head. She's not a Noemie, I can feel it. I reach for the tub of cocoa butter on my bedside table and rub some on the stretched skin of my belly. I've still not settled on a name yet and can't seem to find one that fits the feeling I have of her. Once I've counted the kicks, I haul myself out of bed and make myself a bowl of thick, sweet porridge. When my phone rings, I almost drop my spoon as I lunge for it, expecting to see Jude's name. Instead, I blink, stunned when I see the picture of Sam I'd taken years ago staring back up at me.

This is the first time he's initiated any sort of contact since I left. Can it really be coincidence that it just happens to be the day after Jude and I kissed? Or is the universe playing some kind of twisted game? I slide my thumb across the screen and take a breath.

'Sam,' I say. 'Hi.'

'Hey, Zoe.'

His voice is so achingly familiar that it throws me for a second, taking me from the autumnal cosiness of my surroundings to the lush Sydney summer I'd left behind.

'How are you?' he asks.

'I'm good. How are you?'

'I'm in London.'

I blink, shaking my head. 'You are? Since when?'

'I just landed. I'm on my way to Istanbul for a last-minute job and thought . . . well I hoped we could maybe meet? I've a few hours until my next flight.'

'I . . .' I raise my eyebrows with shock. 'You're kind of catching me off guard here, Sam.'

'I know. I just . . . I think we need to talk, and I guess it'd be better in person.'

So now he wants to talk, after months of silence. Isn't this what I've wanted all along? Hasn't the point behind messages with pregnancy updates been for us to talk? So why do I feel pressured now?

'I can catch the Tube and meet anywhere you want. Even if it's just for ten minutes.'

My eyebrows flicker at the sound of his voice. He sounds uncertain and insecure. I don't think I've ever heard him like this before.

'Okay,' I nod.

I give him my address. The last thing I want to do is go out in this storm and I have the feeling this isn't a conversation I want to have in public. Besides, this is Sam, the father of my unborn child. We've got too much history to meet in a museum or other neutral setting.

'I'll be there soon,' he says, and I hang up, stunned.

Of all the conversations I'd been expecting to have today, that wasn't one of them. Then again, I tell myself that it's normal in Sam's world to hop on a last-minute flight somewhere. It had been normal for me too, once upon a time. I tap out a message to Nina, telling her what's just happened, before getting showered. I dress in a pair of maternity skinny jeans and an oversized jumper that I would never normally wear around the house, and I apply a little lip gloss and mascara. It feels important to show Sam that I'm doing well in my new life, because I am.

'You're going to meet your dad,' I say out loud, looking down at my belly.

It's a sentence that feels bizarre after resigning myself to the fact that it would probably never be said. When my buzzer goes a little under an hour after Sam's call, nerves flicker as I let him in. I don't wait at the top of the stairs like I usually do when someone comes over. I can't. Instead, I wait inside the flat, holding the door open and the anticipation builds, creeping across my chest as I hear him coming up the stairs.

My heart lurches when I see him standing in my doorway. He looks just like he always has. His sandy hair flops into his face and the skin around his mouth wrinkles as he gives me a lop-sided smile.

'Hey,' he says.

'Hi,' I reply.

I hadn't expected to feel this way. His voice had sounded so familiar on the phone and he looks like he always has. But somehow, he feels like a man I don't really know anymore. His eyes flick down to my belly and an unreadable look passes across his face.

'Wow.' He raises his eyebrows.

'Yep,' I nod and stretch my arm out for him to come in.

He puts his umbrella on the hallway floor before stepping inside. The shoulders of his jacket are specked with rain and his skin is tanned. I catch the scent of that aftershave he'd doused himself in on that fateful night in Sydney and close the door.

'Do you want a drink? Some tea or something?'

He nods. 'That would be great, thanks.'

'Where's all your stuff?' I ask as he takes his jacket off.

'Airport locker.' Sam hangs his coat up on the stand by the door and follows me into the kitchen.

I flick the kettle on and drop teabags into cups as he looks around at the flat. It feels distinctly mine, reflecting my tastes and mine alone. From the furry covered cushions on the sofa to the reclaimed lamps, there's nothing from the apartment we'd shared in Sydney. I wonder if it's as strange for him to be in a space with me in it that's completely separate from him as it is for me. I open the fridge door to get the milk and he notices the list.

'You've been to a festival?' he asks with surprise.

'Yeah. About a month ago.'

His face registers this and I pour the milk in, remembering exactly how much he likes as I wait for him to voice his disapproval.

'Who'd you go with? Nina?'

'Her brother, Jude.'

I hand him his cup and he struggles to meet my eyes. I get the feeling there's a lot he wants to say about that but is thinking better of it. It's a smart move. After being disinterested he can hardly come in and start throwing his opinions around. I put the milk back in the fridge, knowing that he's probably checking out the rest of the list. I wonder if he's noticed the one about needing to make money to support our baby and a swell of irritation rises in me.

'How's the baby?' he asks and I put a hand on my belly.

'She's fine.'

We take our teas into the living room and sit at opposite ends of the sofa. He holds the base of his cup in one hand and clasps the handle with the other before looking at me.

'Why are you here, Sam?' I ask gently.

'Where to begin?' He shakes his head and furrows his brows before releasing them again. 'I want to say sorry. For a start.'

I raise my eyebrows. 'Oh.'

'I've been thinking about what happened a lot. I acted like a complete and utter moron.' He shakes his head again. 'I should never have let you just leave like that.'

I pull a face, trying to take in his words. 'It's fine.'

But no sooner have I said it, I know it's a lie. It wasn't fine and it's like a piece of a jigsaw has been slotted into place because I see the pattern I'd been stuck in for so long. I'd never fought for what I believed in with him. Not about wanting children, or a one-on-one relationship, or even going to Australia. I'd coasted, happy to be swept along with the romanticism of a life of travel. How many times had I said *it's fine* to something that really wasn't?

'Actually,' I say with a firmer voice. 'You know what? It wasn't.'

Sam's face flinches as I say it. 'I know. And it's no excuse, but I was just terrified about becoming a dad. I still am. I thought if I just ignored it, it would go away but apparently that's not how this works.'

I raise my eyebrows. 'Yeah, no shit.'

He puts his cup down and faces me. 'I'm confused, Zo. Things were good with us. I mean, I know now that you had reservations about our open relationship and I feel like a tool for not seeing that at the time, but we were good, right? If I'd have said yes to the baby when you'd told me about it, we'd still be together, wouldn't we?'

His blue eyes search mine and I puff the air through my cheeks. 'I guess.'

'I'd be the world's biggest prick if I pretended she didn't exist. And if I pretended you didn't either. I miss you.'

'Sam . . .' I sigh, shaking my head. Why now, when I've made peace with his absence? 'Things have changed. *I've* changed.'

The crazy thing is, that even though Sam and I are long since over, there's a part of me that feels a bit guilty for kissing Jude. How mad is that? Especially because it would've been completely allowed within the confines of my relationship with Sam. There's a part of me that feels like I've done something wrong for kissing another man.

'I know,' he replies quickly. 'I didn't mean we should get back together, I just . . . I don't know. I guess I'm feeling confused. I want to be part of this, I just don't know how. We should be some kind of family, shouldn't we? I don't know if I should be moving here or . . .' he shrugs. 'I don't know what to do.'

I look down at my belly. He wants to be involved. They're the words I've been waiting for since the moment I'd taken that test. It would mean not having to do this alone. Having someone to share the sleepless nights and school runs. He *is* her dad. She'd grow up having two parents in her life, like she deserves. But moving to London? What would co-parenting even look like anyway? Sam lives for his work, which means things like today – lots of travel, sometimes last minute. How do I know that he'll actually be around in the grand scheme of things?

'What do you think?' Sam asks. 'What should I do?'

'I don't know, Sam,' I reply, shaking my head again. 'I can't tell you what to do. You have to decide that for yourself.'

'Yeah, I know,' he admits and runs a hand through his hair.

'What I can tell you, and I'm sorry if it sounds harsh,' I say, 'but I've been doing fine. I'm settled here and we've got a great support network. So, if this is a way to relieve your conscience, you can relax. But if you're really interested in being a dad, then you should do what you feel is right.'

I feel strong as I say the words and I know I really mean them. A few seconds pass and judging by the look on Sam's face, he knows it too.

'Will she have a nursery?' he asks, and I nod.

'Do you want to see it?'

We go through to the small room at the back of the flat, with its oatmeal covered walls painted by Jude and I, the cot and nappy changing station that Mum and Barry put up and the adorable illustration prints on the walls that Nina bought. It's a room that's been created with a group effort from people who love me and my baby. Sam stands in the middle of the room and I try to feel into the space he'd occupy in that group. It's the strangest feeling to realise that, after a decade with someone, there can be simply empty space left where love used to be. I mean, I guess I'll always have some love for him – he's the father of my baby. But it's nothing like what was there before. I remember the intense crushes I'd had on boys at school as a teenager – including the one that had led to the humiliation of having my love letter plastered all over the halls. I think about Jerome and how hard I'd fallen for him. There'd been such a feeling of need. If you'd have asked me at the time, I would have sworn that I couldn't live without them. I'd have definitely said the same thing about Sam. And yet, here I am. Very much alive and, dare I say it, happy. It's reaffirming to know that my life didn't just stop because my relationship did. In fact, it feels like it's only just beginning.

'It's nice,' he says, turning to look at me, 'and it must have cost a fortune.'

'A small one, yeah.'

'I'll transfer you some money today.' He shakes his head before rubbing his palms down his face. 'It was shit of me to let you pay for it all yourself.'

I smile gratefully but this conversation feels so awkward. I wouldn't say there's been a power struggle in our relationship, but *if* the balance of it were in anyone's corner, it would've been Sam's. I show him the rest of the flat. It feels strange now to be in a position where he's on the back foot even if it is of his own making. We finish our tea, sitting on the sofa as we catch up. I tell him about Mum's surgery and he tells me about his Dad's Alzheimer's diagnosis. It's hard not to feel sad that I didn't know about it earlier because there was a time when things like that would have been shared in an instant.

'I should get going,' he says, putting his empty cup on the coffee table. 'My luggage is in a different terminal and it's a tight schedule, so . . .'

'Thanks for coming,' I say as we get up. 'It means a lot.'

He grabs his jacket and we hug. It feels both familiar and awkward and we both laugh self-consciously. I close the door behind him and put a hand on my belly as I go to the window. Did that really just happen? After waiting and wishing for Sam to show some interest in his baby, I feel stunned. I blow a big puff of air through my cheeks and my heart stops as I see Jude's van parking up in the loading space by the bus stop. The universe has a twisted sense of humour today. As Sam ducks under the shelter, Jude hops out of his van and even though the two have never met, I know Jude will recognise Sam from pictures I've posted on social media over the years. On the other hand, Sam has no reason to know who Jude is because I don't think I even had a single photo of me with Jude in it until the festival. I catch Jude's double-take as he walks past the bus stop but, thanks to the rain, his hood is up so I can't see his face. I hadn't expected him to show up unannounced and for a moment I wish he'd have called first, just so I could gather myself again after Sam's surprise visit. Instead, the door buzzer goes and all I can do is run my fingertips through my hair and rub my hands across my face as Jude comes upstairs.

As soon as I see him, I know. I know that our kiss wasn't a mistake, or wrong, or immoral. I can feel it in the way my heart feels like its expanding in my chest, and the way my first instinct is to seek the warmth of his arms. But I also know from the guarded look in his eyes that I was right. He did see Sam, and he knew who he was.

I pull the sleeves of my jumper down over my hands and step back, inviting him in. He brings that woody scent with him and, just in case there was any doubt in my mind, I know, one hundred per cent that even if Sam had begged for us to get back together, I couldn't have done it. Not when just being in the same room as Jude feels like this.

I close the door behind us and my heart jumps in my chest and a strange, almost sickening feeling rises in my belly. I feel like I'm standing by the side of the road watching the traffic whilst knowing there's about to be a nasty accident.

'Do you want a cup of tea, or coffee?' I ask and Jude shakes his head.

'I can't stay long. I was just on my way to a job and was driving past, so . . .'

I look at him in his work clothes, remembering how he'd stood on the terrace after showing me around the flat. He's looked out for me in such a supportive way these past few months and even though it was just one kiss, I feel myself craving more of it.

Jude looks at me. 'How've you been?'

'Good,' I reply with a nod.

He returns it and my eyebrows flinch together at the feeling of distance growing between us.

'Zoe, about yesterday . . . I think it was a mistake. I shouldn't have kissed you.'

'I think technically, we kissed each other,' I reply.

'Yeah, maybe.' He smiles a little before stuffing his hands into his pockets and looking down at the floor. 'I really like you, Zoe.'

A smile flickers around my lips. 'I like you too.'

'But I don't know if this is a good idea.' He looks back up at me with his face pulled into a deep frown. 'I mean, you're a friend. You're my sister's *best* friend. And then there's the baby . . .'

'Right,' I reply slowly.

His frown deepens. 'And I know this might sounds crazy but wasn't that your ex I just saw at the bus stop?'

I wrap my arms around my chest and nod. 'He just flew in today on layover. He wanted to talk about the baby.'

Jude nods with that guarded look still clouding his eyes, as if his thoughts have just been confirmed. 'Right.'

'We're not getting back together, if that's what you're thinking,' I reply. 'We're definitely over.'

'I don't know, Zo. It's a pretty complicated situation.'

'But you knew that when you kissed me. So why do it?' I ask, shaking my head.

'Like you said, I think we kissed each other,' he offers. 'It wasn't planned and I hadn't expected it to feel like it did . . . I just don't know if I can get into something like this right now. I don't know if I'm ready to be a dad.'

I wrap my arms tighter around myself, feeling suddenly exposed and vulnerable. If Sam had left a couple of minutes of earlier, I'd have been able to tell Jude he'd been here myself instead of feeling like I've been caught out. And I get it. Getting involved with someone who's about to give birth, with their ex-partner hanging around is taking a modern view on relationship models to a new level. Jude isn't a simple guy by any means, but he's not about complications. It feels like I'm being pulled right back to where I was eight months ago, like I'm a walking complication that someone else wants to avoid. I feel just like I had in Sydney.

'You're right,' I say. 'This isn't a good idea.'

'I really like what we have going on,' he replies.

'So did I. And it's been fun these last few months.'

It really has. It's been surprising and beautiful getting to know him, and he's come to my aid like a hero on multiple occasions, saving the day. He's literally put a roof over my head. But somewhere along the line, I'd got carried away with it all and let things go too far.

'Maybe we can just continue hanging out?' he offers.

I put my hand on my belly and look at him, shaking my head. The dull ache in my chest feels like it might be my heart literally cracking.

'I can't just date and see where it goes, Jude. I have a baby to think about.'

That woman in the sauna might have been awful, but she'd had a point. Sure, it's been fun getting to know Jude and reaffirming myself as a woman entitled to a life of my own, but there are more important things going on.

'I can't be someone's maybe.'

The baby kicks, pushing herself against my skin. I know it's my imagination, but it feels like a high-five. I hadn't been enough for Jerome. Or Sam. And I'm tired of making compromises. I'd always wondered why Mum had stayed alone since Dad left. I get it now. If I'm going to get involved with someone, they need to be in it, fully, with both feet. They need to be willing to take me *and* my daughter, and that might mean Sam to an extent, too. Sure, it makes things complicated, and it won't be for everyone, but after years of feeling never quite enough, I deserve it. My daughter deserves it. I could end up spending the next twenty-odd years as a single parent, just like Mum had done, but if that's the case, then so be it.

Chapter Twenty-Four

Pyjamas, slippers, toiletries, t-shirts and leggings for me, and Babygros and a pile of nappies for the baby. I go to close the suitcase before remembering my flip-flops. Years of using public showers in swimming pools has drummed it into my head to err on the side of caution, and the idea of walking barefoot in a hospital is enough to gross me out. I reach into the bottom of the wardrobe where I stashed them after their last summer outing. How many people injured themselves in a year because of flip-flops? I can't remember the number Jude had said, but I do remember the way I'd laughed at him for knowing something so obscure and the way he'd grabbed hold of me after the rain had made me slip on these rubber soles. I clench my jaw, stuff them down the side of the suitcase and zip it closed.

I'd meant it when I'd told him I didn't want to be someone's maybe. But God, do I miss him. I'd got so used to being in contact with him over the last few months, while he was working here on the flat and helping me build stuff up, not to mention the festival and almost daily contact we'd established since his holiday to Portugal. It's been a week since we kissed and week of silence. No messages, no calls, no random stops on his way home bearing Hula Hoops. I'd been right about the kiss. It changed everything.

It hasn't all been bad, though. Nina would hate it if she knew, but that awful woman from the sauna has become my own private Yoda – albeit a privileged, superior and assumption-making one. I've been focusing on what's really important – myself and my baby. I've slept in late and gone to bed early. I've let my nesting instinct take over and cleaned the flat, slowly, one room at a time. I've painted my belly cast and, even though I actually think it looked better without any colour, I've hung it up in the nursery. I've plucked my eyebrows, eaten soup and read yet more parenting books. It's not that I haven't been focused on myself and the baby until now but entering my thirty-fifth week has definitely brought with it a redirection of my energy.

I stand the suitcase up and leave it behind the front door, prepped and ready for when the time comes, which will hopefully still be another four weeks away. It's incredible to think that she's almost fully developed. If she came now, she'd more than likely be fine. One of the mums from the antenatal group gave birth early a couple of days ago and her son was perfectly healthy. The news had somehow reminded me of hearing about the first girl in class to get her period. You know it's going to happen to you, too. You just don't know when – and the same feels true for birth.

My phone pings from my bed, and I listen to the voice note from Nina.

Nina: 'I'll be there in five minutes. So you've got plenty of time to pee and get some clothes on.'

I look at my reflection in the mirror hanging on the wall. Do jogging bottoms and a hoodie constitute clothes? As much as I'd like to say yes, I'm not sure that they'll do much against the weather outside. I haul myself up from the floor to change into a pair of maternity jeans and a thick jumper. Honestly, I'm relieved that the scorching summer heat has gone. It was starting to get uncomfortable, feeling heavy and sweaty all the time. But the grey October sky and sideways rain is dismal, and I can't think why Nina's being so intent on getting me out in it.

'Remind me why we can't just watch a film again?' I say after trudging down the stairs to meet her when she buzzes to signal her arrival.

'Because movement is good for you,' she replies.

'It's not like I'm spending all day plonked on the sofa, and I am about to pop.'

'No, but you're not swimming like you used to, either.'

I open my umbrella. Since the bleeding scare, I've been too afraid to. The doctor had told me it was fine, especially because my body was so used to it already, but still. I've been opting for pregnancy classes down at one of those trendy yoga studios that have popped up and I'm enjoying it just as much. Well, almost. It's no substitute for that delicious feeling of being submerged in water, but it's keeping my body active and my mind relatively calm.

'So where are we going?' I ask, and she pulls up the hood of her bright-yellow raincoat.

'I thought we could just do a round at the park.'

I fight a grimace. The idea of walking around the park in this grisly weather isn't exactly appealing, but I decide to humour her. Brown leaves are scattered on the ground and the tree branches are almost empty, stretching up like spindly arms reaching for the sky. I think back to that summer's day in the park when we'd been introduced to Luke. Everything had felt so alive then. The air had buzzed with potential, everyone seemed to have a smile on their faces and there was such a feeling of optimism. It might be down to my renewed inward focus this week and the tangible loss of Jude's company, but the decline of autumn feels sharp. Even with the burnt orange hues of pumpkins, the promise of bonfires and toffee apples and cosy coffee shops, there's no denying that the last hurrah has well and truly gone.

'So, how've you been?' Nina asks. 'You've been so quiet this week.'

'Good,' I reply. 'I've just been nesting, I suppose.'

'I don't blame you with this weather. Imagine how strange it must be, going from a cosy womb to this.'

We walk through the gates to the park and I raise my eyebrows. 'I think I'd rather stay in the womb. At least it's warm in there.'

We laugh, but it strikes me that this will be my first autumn in the UK since . . . well, in a long time. Of course I've visited during the colder months, but I'd always known it wouldn't be for long. It had kept the romanticism of it all alive. A walk in Hampstead Heath on an ice cold, sunny day is a treat when it's once in a while and you know you'll be escaping back to a warmer climate again.

'I'm not sure I'm ready for this,' I say.

'The baby?'

'No,' I laugh. 'The baby I can deal with – I think. I mean *this*. The cold. Winter. England.'

'Well, you'd better learn because I'm not letting you leave again. We've only just got you back.'

'Where would I go?'

'I don't know. New York?' She links her arm through mine and I throw her an incredulous look.'

'Why would I go there?' I shake my head.

'I don't know. I guess I'm waiting for you to decide to take Sam up on his offer of getting back together.'

I roll my eyes. 'He didn't say that. He said he missed me which is understandable I guess. But we are *not* getting back together – no way. That ship has long since sailed. If he's really going to be back in my life, it'll be as the baby's dad and nothing else.'

We pass a man walking his dog and Nina pulls a face. 'At least you're only having a baby. I mean, I love dogs but imagine having to go out twice a day, every day to take your dog out in this.'

'Well, they do say having a dog is like training wheels for a small human.'

A crisp packet blows on the ground in front of us as we follow the tarmac path around the empty children's playground. It's pretty depressing but I do have to admit, getting out and having some fresh wind under my nose feels good. Especially because I feel like I can breathe again. The baby's moved down lower in my belly to prepare for birth, according to the midwife. It's meant reducing the capacity of my already overstretched bladder but I'm happy for it.

'What would you say if I said I got pregnant?' Nina says.

I stop dead in my tracks and grip her arm, widening my eyes. 'Are you?'

'No. But my period came a day late and when it did, I was disappointed for the first time ever,' she replies. 'Is it nuts to be thinking about it? I've only been with Luke a few months.'

'What does that matter? I was with Sam for almost eleven years and look at me,' I shrug. 'Does Luke want kids?'

'A whole troop,' Nina nods.

'You'd better get started soon, then. We're not exactly spring chickens anymore.'

'Speak for yourself,' she replies with a laugh, gently bumping into my shoulder. 'It would be so great though, wouldn't it? Having kids close together in age? Maybe they'd be like us.'

'And we'd be like our mums,' I smile.

I'd always found it special that my mum's best friend was the mum of my best friend.

'You're lucky,' Nina says with a hint of sadness. 'I wish Mum would've had a grandkid before she died.'

I squeeze her arm with one hand and readjust my umbrella with the other, letting the handle of it rest in the crook of my elbow.

'How is Jude?' I ask lightly.

'I don't know. He's been a bit pissy with me lately. I think he's stressed at work.'

'Well, he's a busy guy.'

'I know. I just worry about him sometimes,' Nina says. 'I wish he'd find someone and settle down. I thought he'd been seeing someone lately but I guess not.'

'What makes you think that?' I ask, keeping my eyes on the wet, grey tarmac.

'He was just acting different. You know how guys get all gooey when they like someone,' she laughs. 'Anyway. I have to remind myself that I'm his sister, not his mum.'

'Really? You are?' I reply with a sarcasm-laden tone because Nina's always bossed him around like a second mum, even when theirs had still been alive.

'Ha, ha,' she laughs in a deadpan tone. 'Isn't it weird that sometimes, the most awful people seem to find someone to live happily ever after with, but gorgeous humans like you and my brother have to deal with so much crap? Maybe you two should get together and put the world right.'

She laughs and I know it's a joke. I can hear the *ba dum tss!* of a drum kit in my head, but I can't laugh back. It's stuck in my throat and even though we'd only shared a kiss, I'm hit with guilt. I haven't told Nina the truth because I didn't know how she would react. I've crossed the clear black and white lines of honesty and entered a place that's murky and grey with her for the first time ever. After that horrific last trip to Leeds, Steph had bombarded me with messages, apologising because she apparently hadn't known how to tell me the truth. It makes me shudder inside to think I'm using the same excuse.

I stop and look at Nina's rain-speckled face. 'I kissed Jude.'

Nina blinks as her face draws into a frown. 'What?'

'Or he kissed me. I don't know anymore. We kissed each other.'

'Are you joking?'

I swallow and shake my head.

'You kissed *Jude?*'

The frown on her face deepens and I find myself wincing, waiting for her reaction once the shock is gone.

'Are you mad?' I ask.

She fixes me with a bewildered look. 'Are *you*?'

'No. I don't know, maybe a little,' I reply with a small, hapless smile. 'It just happened.'

I hear myself saying the words and remember how both Jerome and Steph had said the same thing. This is nowhere near the same level on the betrayal scale, but it still burns on my tongue.

'Say something?' I prompt, pulling a face.

'I don't really know *what* to say. I mean . . . you and Jude?' Nina blows a puff of air through her mouth. 'When? How?'

'Last week. We went for lunch and one thing kind of led to another. We didn't sleep together,' I add quickly. 'It was just a kiss.'

'Okay,' Nina replies slowly.

'The thing is . . . I've sort of had a crush on him for a while. Since the festival. Before it, maybe.'

'The festival?' Nina's eyes widen as the pieces fall together. 'Wait – the guy you told me about was *actually* Jude?'

I nod and, unexpectedly, she bursts into laughter.

'You're not pissed off?' I ask, raising an eyebrow.

Nina shakes her head and looks at me as if she's only just seeing me for the first time. 'God, no. Confused? Yes. But mad?'

She shakes her head again and I let go of the breath I've been holding. The rain has stopped so I drop the umbrella from my shoulder and press the release button to put it down.

'This makes *so* much sense now,' Nina says, and turns to start walking.

It does? I take a sideways glance and see her pierced eyebrows squeezed together in a look of concentration.

'I'd wondered why he'd started asking about you so much.'

'Really?' I reply. Nina nods and my heart takes a little skip. 'What was he asking about?'

'Oh, you know. How were you doing, what I thought about Sam and whether he was really leaving you to do the whole parenting thing alone. I just thought he was just being polite.' She looks at me with a grin. 'Now I know different. And him painting your walls makes so much sense too now.'

'I can't believe you're being so okay about this,' I say warily.

'Why wouldn't I be?'

'Because you'd drawn a hard line about it after he'd hooked up with Steph.'

'Yeah, because it was *Steph*. I'd never have wanted him to have ended up with her, and that was before she fucked you over with Jerome. But you? You'd be my sister-in-law. How awesome would that be?'

I blink, shaking my head as we walk around the children's playground, making a loop. Nina being so normal and even excited about the idea of me and Jude only makes me feel more guilty. We've been best friends for so long, I can't remember a time when she wasn't around. How could I have thought that she'd fly off the handle about it? I feel like I've done her a massive disservice.

'It was just a kiss,' I say.

'But you like him, right? You told me so yourself while we were doing your belly cast. And he clearly likes you.'

I sigh a little. 'It was *only* a kiss. We're not getting together or anything like that.'

Nina frowns, looking at me.

'I *am* about to have a baby,' I explain. 'It's a lot to ask of someone to jump into.'

'Did he say that, or you?'

'We're just better off as friends.'

'So, *he* said it?' She shakes her head with obvious disappointment.

'Actually, I said it. I know you think it shouldn't matter and I should be able to date who I like, but it does. And to be honest, I just want to focus on myself and the baby right now.'

'Oh. Well, that probably explains his crap mood the other day. I wish I'd have known. I could've spoken to him about it.'

'I don't want you to feel like you have to be in the middle.'

'I wouldn't be.'

I laugh. 'Yes. Yes, you would. I mean, imagine if we did date and things didn't work out.'

'I wouldn't take sides,' she insists and I laugh again. 'I mean it. You're both adults after all.'

I fix her with an unconvinced look and she rolls her eyes before linking her arm through mine. 'Okay, okay. Am I allowed to say I'm a bit gutted, though?'

'Only if I am.'

I swallow the lump in my throat. If she's right and this is the reason why Jude's been in a bad mood, then it made three of us. I'd known way back at the beginning that having this baby would mean making sacrifices and compromises. I guess this is just another reminder of that.

Nina takes her phone from her coat pocket and checks the screen. 'Come on, we should get you home.'

'Maybe we could go for a coffee? There's a lovely new place around the corner,' I reply, thinking about the chai latte I'd had with Jude.

'I'd love to, but I can't. I have to get back.'

We chat as we make our way out of the park and it feels like a huge weight off my shoulders. Telling her about Jude was like submitting a tax return. It felt like an impossible task in my head but, in reality, it was painless and made me wonder why I'd been so worried about it.

'I'll come up quickly,' Nina says when I put my key in the lock. 'I'm dying for a pee.'

As we head up the stairs, I dream about getting back into my comfy jogging bottoms and getting snuggly on the sofa with a book and a reheated bowl of the carrot and ginger soup I'd made yesterday.

'Surprise!'

I stand in the doorway, gaping with shock. Helium balloons are stuck to the ceiling, a pink, *It's a girl!* garland is tacked to the wall and Luke walks in from the kitchen holding a plate stacked with of pink-iced muffins. A couple of the women from my antenatal classes are unwrapping containers of food, Mum is pouring what looks like champagne into a coffee mugs and Barry is handing them out.

Nina squeezes my shoulders from behind. 'I know you didn't want a proper baby shower but we couldn't *not* do something.'

'How did you do this?' I ask, stunned, shrugging my coat off.

'Spare key, remember?' Mum replies, handing me the mug as Nina puts a sash over my shoulder.

'And your mum had the numbers for Liz and Sabrina.'

'You guys . . .' I shake my head, laughing. 'I don't know what to say.'

I'd really meant it when I'd told Nina I didn't want a baby shower. There's already so much stuff for the baby and, honestly, the idea of sitting around playing guess-the-name and having all the attention on me felt overwhelming. The decorations in my living room are minimal and it's a handful of people instead of a whole guest list, but as I'm hugged by each one of them, I can see the point. It feels like an important rite of passage for a transition from one life stage to another. I'm guided to sit on the sofa and Luke carries in a cardboard box.

'We know the baby's got loads already, so we decided the gifts today should be for you,' Nina says as he sets it down on the floor next to me.

'Sorry it's not all wrapped,' Mum says. 'It was all a bit last minute.'

I shake my head, so full of gratitude for there even being a box at all that my eyes start to well up.

'Don't be silly,' I say. 'This is amazing.'

Nina laughs. 'You haven't seen what's inside yet.'

I put my alcohol-free champagne filled glass on the table before reaching into the box.

'It's double insulated and will keep your drink hot for six hours,' Mum says as I pull out a boxed vacuum-sealed cup. 'I don't know how many times I tried to reheat cups of coffee when you were a newborn. In the end I gave up and drank them cold.'

I laugh. 'Why do I have the feeling that this is going to save my butt with all the night feeds?'

'Because it will,' she replies with a wink.

I pull out an Aesop bodycare gift set and Barry smiles shyly. 'It's not as lifesaving but I hope it comes in handy.'

I drop my shoulders with a wide smile. 'Are you kidding? This is great, thank you. I've been wanting to try their stuff for ages.'

'This is from me,' Nina says, handing me an envelope.

I open it up and drop my jaw. 'Oh no you *didn't*.'

'Hell yes I did.'

I laugh as I pull out an embossed gift card for the spa we went to a few weeks ago.

'Nina,' I say, tilting my head to one side. I'm pretty sure this wasn't another freebie from her Premier League connections.

'I thought you deserved another visit without some awful lady interrupting the peace. It's valid for a whole year so you can go whenever.'

My eyes well up again as I hold the card to my chest. 'Thank you.'

She smiles at me, crinkling her nose and I blow her a kiss.

Facemasks, a voucher for a company that delivers from restaurants, luxury bubble bath and a Fortnum & Mason giftset make up the rest of the boxed contents. I'm overwhelmed, in a good way. I remember sitting in Mum's kitchen when I'd told her about the baby. I'd been so worried that I'd be alone because I no longer had Sam. Looking at the gifts on the coffee table makes me realise I'm not. They say it takes a village to raise a kid, and even though I live by myself, I *do* have a village around me.

A couple of hours later, when there's only two cupcakes left and everyone else has gone, Mum pulls on her coat.

'Alright, that's the dishwasher loaded.'

'Thanks, Mum.' I smile at her from the spot where I've collapsed onto the sofa. 'And thanks again for today. It was really nice.'

'Good. I'm glad.' She kisses the top of my head. 'I'll see you tomorrow.'

I hoist myself up a little to look at her over the back of the sofa as she goes towards the door.

'Did you ever wish Dad stayed?'

She looks at me and laughs a little. 'No.'

I raise my eyebrows at how quickly she replied. She never even missed a beat.

'He didn't leave,' she explains. 'I told him to go.'

'But I thought . . .' I frown, trying to remember how it had gone on the day he'd left. 'I mean, he'd left us for another woman, right?'

Mum shakes her head. 'We were in a rough patch at the time. I'd probably have forgiven him for that, eventually.'

My eyes almost pop out of my head. 'Really?'

'He'd said he wasn't sure if he loved her, so yes. But then he'd said he didn't think he was cut out for family life anymore. He wanted to reclaim his youth. Maybe it was an early mid-life crisis.'

In my memory, Dad seemed to have fully embraced his role as a parent. He was hands on, always coming to my school plays and helping with my homework.

'I gave him a while to figure it out and he still wasn't sure, so I told him to go,' Mum says, picking up her bag. 'It's one thing to have an indiscretion. But to be a parent, you have to be *in* it. I didn't want to carry someone who didn't want to be there. I deserved better, and so did you.'

I rest my elbow on the back of the sofa and drop my chin into my hand with a small laugh. 'That's exactly what I thought.'

It feels like I'm in some kind of strange, ancestral storyline of repeating patterns. I'd used the same reasoning when I'd left Sam, and a week ago with Jude. Is it pure coincidence, or is it some kind of genetic passing down of values? I don't know the answer, but I do know that, even though it's not how I would have imagined it, I'm actually thankful for things unfolding as they have. It feels like this pregnancy journey has opened up a new channel of understanding between Mum and I that hadn't been there before.

'You're going to be just fine,' Mum says with a smile. 'You just do what feels right for you and the baby. You can't go wrong with that.'

She closes the door behind her and I sit back on the sofa, rubbing my hands across my bump, feeling perfectly content. Except, for the one thing – or person – that had been missing. Today had been clearly last minute. Maybe Jude already had plans. Or maybe he'd simply decided to stay away from the complicatedness of all of this. The thought makes me shiver and I brush it away at the sound of my door knocking. I frown, glancing around as I get up from the sofa to see what Mum might have forgotten. I waddle over to the door and click the latch open.

'What did you—'

The words dry up as I see Jude standing in front of me. If anyone has forgotten anything, it's my brain's capacity to think and my mouth to speak.

'Hey,' he says with a lop-sided smile that immediately brings up the memory of his lips being pressed against mine.

'Hey,' I reply. 'Do you want to come in?'

Jude's forehead flickers before he shakes his head. 'I can't. I know it was your baby shower today, so I wanted to bring you this.'

He hands me a little box and our fingers touch. The feeling of our skin connecting is nostalgic and familiar, and I wonder if going back to being *just friends* will get any easier than how it feels right now. The black cardboard box is simple and unbranded, and I frown as I lift the lid. Inside is a collection of things that, apart from a small lighter, I've never seen before.

'It's a fire-starting kit,' Jude explains. 'For whenever you want to strike that one off the list.'

My eyes water unexpectedly as the thoughtfulness of it, and immediately my mind goes back to the festival and the fire that never was. The memory of the closeness we'd built up and how easy it had been makes my heart ache.

'Thank you,' I say, holding the box to my chest, as if it might somehow ease the feeling of missing him, even though he's standing right in front of me. 'It means a lot.'

'I'm happy to help you with it.'

I swallow and nod. 'I'd like that.'

Jude jams his hands into the pockets of his faded jeans. He looks down at the ground for a moment and shakes his head before looking back up at me, his dark eyes boring into mine.

'Look, I know we decided what we decided. But I just wanted to say that you mean a lot to me. I don't want to lose you as a friend and I'd hate for things to get weird.'

His words wrap around me like a cloak and, not for the first time, I wonder how it is that he'd existed under my nose for so long without me truly knowing how great he is. He's right of course. Just because things can't work out in a romantic sense, I'd hate to lose him too. He's become inextricably woven into the fabric of my life.

'Me too,' I reply with a smile. 'Not to mention, it'd be pretty impossible to avoid each other.'

He laughs and nods. 'Exactly.'

We stand there for a moment, looking at each other as if we're sealing a secret pact.

'Are you sure you don't want to come in? I've got leftover muffins.'

Jude smiles and shakes his head. 'I can't. But I'll take you up on the offer another time.'

I nod, still holding his gift to my chest. 'I'll hold you to it.'

We grin at each other and, even though we don't hug goodbye as we usually would, I feel as close to him as ever. I'd be lying if I said I didn't wish things could be different, but despite the way my entire being feels soothed and somehow at home with him around, I know my mum was right. It had been the right decision to make, for me and my baby. I watch him trot down the stairs and take a deep breath before going back inside. I stand by the door, alone inside my flat. Of course, I'm not really alone. I've got my daughter inside me and the feeling of having been wrapped up in love for the whole afternoon.

The thought crosses my mind for the thousandth time that I have absolutely no idea what I'm doing. Even with the antenatal classes, I don't know how it'll feel to breastfeed, or even if I'll be able to. I don't know how it'll feel to actually hold her and make all the minute decisions that will affect her life. But I do know about the things I've done already to create the best possible life for her. Moving continents, building a home, increasing my earning potential and taking a stand for what's best for her.

And I think that, as much as I'd love to be handed an instruction manual when the time comes, I think I'm doing okay. Like Mum keeps saying, I'll do the best with what I have, just like she did and my nan before her. I snuggle down into the sofa with a contented sigh. I come from a line of pretty strong women, and I know it won't end with me.

Chapter Twenty-Five

Zoe: Introducing my little Halloween baby, Margot Elise Wright! After a frenetic Uber ride and with more drugs than a cartel, she's here. The both of us are wearing nappies and I'm as hungry as she is! Somehow, I'm still alive and she's doing great after tricking us by coming a whole two weeks early. But the treat? Just look at her 🖤 🖤 🖤

Chapter Twenty-Six

Things nobody tells you about becoming a mum:

1. Labour is messy. Really messy. I'm talking blood, sweat, tears, pee, poop and puke. And that's just you, never mind the baby.
2. All that is just training to prepare you for the relentless baby puke-poop-loop that goes on all. the. time.
3. Your baby will look like a squished cone-headed alien for a while. And you'll still think it's the most gorgeous being on the planet.
4. Nobody tells you how life changing it is. Well, they do, but not in a way that actually, really, accurately describes what it's like.

We all know about sleepless nights and stinky nappies, and even I knew about sore nipples and catching up on sleep when the baby does. Still, when I scrolled through Instagram or Pinterest before giving birth, I'd seen pictures of new mums who were of course tired, but still had a clean house, clean clothes and some semblance of routine. I'll be just like them, I'd thought. I'd thought wrong. These past two weeks have been intense. Even with antenatal classes, the internet and books, I've never felt so ill-prepared for anything in my life. But it's been worth it. So worth it.

Margot is stunning. Even when she's screaming like she is right now, for what feels like the hundredth time today for no apparent reason. I'm in awe about how I can love someone so much, despite the torture of living a life that bares zero resemblance to the one I had before while operating on one per cent of sleep. I pace the living room, holding Margot close to my chest as I bounce and walk at the same time, singing a lullaby of absolute gibberish. It's a wonder I haven't worn a path into the polished parquet floor. The doorbell rings and I frown. The supply train of support has already been through the house today. Mum's taken a load of washing and Nina brought over containers of soup and chilli. I don't bother to ask who it is – I wouldn't be able to hear them over Margot's crying anyway.

I poke my head around the door, shielding the baby from the cold air in the hallway and do a double-take.

'Jude? What are you doing here?'

'I told you I'd drop by, remember?' He gets to the top of the stairs and strokes a finger across Margot's back. 'Hey, what's all that noise about?'

'If she tells you, please fill me in,' I grimace as he closes the door behind him. 'She's been like this all day. I'm getting worried. She's been fed, winded and changed. It can't be normal.'

'Maybe she's tired?'

'Then it'll make two of us,' I reply as her cries get louder. Exhausted tears prickle the backs of my eyes and again I'm hit with the feeling that I am so very, completely out of my depth. 'Did we arrange something? I must have forgotten – sorry.'

I almost choke with laughter at how absurd that sounded – as if I'd been asking if we'd arranged to go for a drink or a bite to eat or something even vaguely resembling *normal*. Jude had come to visit with Nina when Margot had been born and he'd sent a couple of texts, but I couldn't even tell you where my phone's been for the last few days. Had he said he would come over? I can't remember if he did.

Jude shrugs. 'Hey, don't worry about it, you've got your hands full. I just thought I'd see if there was anything you needed help with.'

'That's lovely,' I reply with a smile.

I have no idea how single parents without a support network like mine do it. I go to tell him that between Mum and Nina, I've been taken care of. But then I look at Jude, standing in the middle of my living room. He smells fresh and zingy, like he's just got out of the shower and I try to remember the last time I'd done more than a quick freshen up in the sink. Thanks to social media making it look easy, I'd thought I could do the whole new mum goddess thing. The reality? Right now, I'm less goddess, more goblin. The sweat under my boobs is relentless and I've consistently chosen to skip brushing my teeth in the morning for two minutes of extra sleep. My left shoulder is covered with regurgitated milk that wasn't there before Jude rang the doorbell and I've been wearing these leggings for so long, they could probably walk away from me.

'Maybe I can take her for a bit and you can have a nap?' Jude offers. 'Or a bath.'

'Do I look that bad?' I pull a face and he laughs.

'I've seen worse.'

Even in my sleep-deprived state, I manage to crack a smile. 'A bath *would* be good.'

But even as he goes to the bathroom, I find myself protesting. Margo's been crying non-stop. If *I* didn't know what to do to calm her, how could *he* possibly have a clue?

'You said she's been fed, changed and winded, right?' Jude says, sitting on the edge of the bath with the hot tap running on full blast.

'Well, yeah, but . . .'

'So, we'll be fine. And if we're not, we're only in the next room.' He looks at me, waiting for more excuses to fend off.

I don't have any. Margot's cries are starting to quiet down and there's something nice about having a bath run for me. Jude pours in a generous squeeze of bubble bath and, not for the first time, I find myself looking at him and wondering why he's still single. I've never expected a knight to ride in on his white horse and save the day, but Jude's come close to doing just that so many times, I'm starting to lose count.

He gets up from the bath and I tentatively hand Margot over. My heart melts, just like it had when he'd visited after the birth and held her. She looks miniscule in his arms. But then again, she looks miniscule in everyone's arms.

'Cup of tea?' he asks and I nod gratefully.

'You're sure this is okay?' I ask.

'Absolutely.'

He walks slowly with Margot in his arms and I try not to feel guilty about the relief I feel at having a few minutes to lie back and do nothing. I hear the kettle boiling and picture Jude manoeuvring around the kitchen he built. For someone who'd said he didn't know if he was ready to be a dad, he seems to be putting himself into the vacant spot. I correct myself as I heap a healthy glug of some lavender-scented oil into the water. It's not technically vacant. Sam's been in contact more since I gave birth than he was the whole time I was pregnant, and if he does what he's planned to, he'll be flying in after his current job finishes next week.

With my tea sitting on the corner of the tub, I climb into the water, feeling the almost audible sigh of pleasure as my body takes in its warmth. It seeps right through to the bone and I tilt my head back, closing my eyes. Even now, when it should be a time to switch off, all I can think about is Margot. She's become my biggest love. Becoming a mum and actually seeing this new person who wasn't here before has made me start asking some big questions. Like, has she been born with a personality that's just waiting to be expressed, or is she a blank slate? If it's the former, then where did she get it from? What is there before conception and birth? And if it's the latter, then how can I make sure she'll be a thoughtful, compassionate, decent human? How can I make sure not to mess her up?

I strain my hearing, but the flat is silent. Maybe Jude took her out for a walk? It's a ridiculous thought. Stepping out of the flat with a newborn needs military style packing and organisation – he'd need more than ten minutes for that. And besides, I can feel them. They might be in another room, separated by walls and doors, but I can sense the two of them as easily as I can feel the water on my skin. Between the warmth of the water, the scent of lavender and days of interrupted sleep, my eyelids quickly grow heavy. And knowing that my baby is in good hands, I quickly fall asleep.

Epilogue

Margot gurgles, totally mesmerised by her foot, and I take yet another picture of her. My photo app is pretty much filled with images of her and it would probably take dozens of up-swipes to get past them to photos where I still had a bump, let alone life pre-pregnancy. I send the picture I've just taken to Sam without text, for him to wake up to over in Seoul. I look into Margot's brown eyes and my heart just melts. Her chubby toes are covered in drool and, as weird as it sounds, I could just eat her up. Of course I'm happy that Sam's decided to step up to the plate. But even without him, I've got enough love for this little girl for the both of us.

I squish her feet together playfully, grinning from ear to ear before picking up the enormous bag I carry with me nowadays. I give myself a quick look in the mirror by the front door. Braids in a bun, a long-sleeved t-shirt, a pair of jeans and my trusty biker-style boots – it's hardly winning any style awards, but these days I consider it a win to be wearing clothes that are clean. It's Nina's barbecue today. It barely feels like yesterday since the last one when

I'd been exhausted, numbed from jetlag and the end of the longest relationship I've ever had. They say a lot can change in a year. Whoever *they* are, they're not kidding.

I look like I'm moving out when I leave the house these days and it takes just as long too. Today, it's a new record. I haven't had to do a last-minute nappy change or forgotten anything, and it feels like progress once I've negotiated my way down the stairs and put Margot in her pram. Outside, the sun is in an epic battle with the clouds, and I wonder if this might be the year that sees the end of the good luck weather streak this annual barbecue has had. Still, the spring vibe is definitely in the air. Bright yellow daffodils are on display at the florist by the bus stop and the mini supermarket has an offer on hot cross buns. But by the time I wheel the pram off the bus twenty minutes later, the clouds have taken over and, when I get to Nina's, the party has already been moved upstairs.

'Can you believe it?' she says with a groan after hugging me hello. 'The one time we do it on a different weekend and it's a washout.'

Problems with the drainage in the building meant part of the garden had to be dug up and the work had gone a few days later than planned.

'Well, you had a good run,' I reply softly. 'And you know your mum. She would have winged it, just like you are.'

Sometimes I catch myself saying or thinking things and realising I'm a mother. It's not that I couldn't be tender or nurturing before, but now it feels like an automatism, like a tap that's been turned on and somehow doesn't quite turn off fully anymore.

'Anyway,' Nina says with a sigh and practically shoves me out of the way. 'I need some Margot snuggles.'

She scoops her up from the pushchair and Margot laughs, recognising her straight away. I fold the pushchair and stash it by the shoe rack as Nina takes her into the living room, showering her with kisses that make Margot squeal with delight. The feeling of loss is ridiculous considering she's only just a few paces away, but it's tempered by the internal relief of having both hands to myself again.

With the rain lashing down outside, the party feels a much more chilled and cosy affair. The music isn't as loud as it would be in the garden and because of the close space, it's easier to chat to everyone without the feeling of intentionally having to mingle – something I've always been hopeless at. I look at Nina and Luke with Margot and it's like staring into the future. He's good for her. Nina's still as bossy and fiery as ever, that'll never change, but Luke has softened her edges and I'm finding myself impatient for them to make a little playmate for Margot. She is, predictably, the star of the show and as I drink a mug of deliciously brewed coffee, I find myself thanking the universe for the millionth time for that dodgy oyster last year. I wouldn't change it for anything and as soon as she's back in my arms I hold her close, inhaling her delicious scent as she gnaws on one of my fingers.

'Is your mum not coming?' Nina asks with a frown.

I nod. 'She's on her way, just stuck in traffic. She had to stay a bit later at work.'

'Jude texted and said the roads are awful. Bloody rain. I bet he wishes he stayed in Majorca.'

'You know he'd never miss this.'

'Oh, I know. And I also know he misses you.'

I swallow and kiss the soft curls on Margot's head, using it as an opportunity to avert my eyes.

'I'm not allowed to have told you that by the way but . . .' she rolls her eyes and I sigh.

'You said you wouldn't get in the middle of this.'

'I'm not,' she replies with her voice rising an octave. 'I'm just saying.'

We sit in silence for a few seconds until curiosity gets the better of me. 'Why? What have you heard?'

Nina fights a smile. 'I think he's asked after you two every day in the last three weeks. In fact, it might be that he misses her more than you.'

I'd felt guilt-ridden when I'd fallen asleep after he'd come over and looked after Margot while I'd had a bath. I'd slept until the water had gone cold and woken up feeling refreshed with a brain that was decidedly less foggy than it had been. I don't know what he'd done, but Margot was asleep in her cot and he was knocked out on the armchair next to it. Seeing the two of them like that had filled me with more love than I knew how to deal with. Since then, he's popped over regularly, bringing fresh nappies and taking care of things like taking the rubbish out and sorting through my post. He's been a true friend and watching him with her has been both divine and bittersweet.

Have I regretted how I'd reacted after we'd kissed? Yes. But I'd done what I had to and even though we're not together, we're just as close as we were before. Even if we have less time for talking now that Margot is here.

'He really loves her, you know,' Nina continues.

'I know he does.'

Everything he's done, he's done voluntarily. He'd asked how to burp her properly. He'd learned how to put her nappy on in a way that was loose enough for her to be comfortable but not so loose that she wouldn't literally lose her shit. He'd kept me in supply of beef Hula Hoops for a long time, until I'd had to tell him that since giving birth, I couldn't even imagine eating a single one, let alone a whole packet. It's hard not to compare all of that to Margot's actual dad who's half a world away and knows practically nothing about what she needs in a hands-on way.

'I *know* you still like him,' Nina says. 'Honestly, I don't know what you two are waiting for. You'd be perfect together and you know it.'

I shake my head with a reluctant smile playing at my lips. It would be a lie to say that Jude doesn't make up a big portion of my fantasy life, now that I have the brainpower to do such things again. But there's a big difference between having someone there because they want to be there, instead of feeling like they have to be. The minute Jude and I become something more is the minute he'll start to feel obligated. I know him. And I don't want that.

I feel the distinctive gurgling sensation from inside Margot's nappy against my legs and a second later, Nina and I pull a face.

'Duty calls,' I say, getting up. 'We don't want any of the oldies to keel over with the nappy stink.'

Nina snickers and I grab my bag from the pram before ducking into Nina's bedroom. It's amazing how quickly you can become an expert in something. The first time I'd had to change Margot's nappy was an experience I'm not likely to ever forget, but now, four months later, I barely even blink – not even when it's a big one like this. I wipe her clean and wrap the messy nappy up, stashing it in a plastic bag. What happens next is so quick, I'm literally frozen in position, kneeling at the end of the bed. Margot giggles and gurgles as I blink and look down at the poop she's just projectiled all over my top.

'What the . . .' I shake my head, unsure whether to laugh or cry.

At least she's on a portable changing mat. As much as Nina loves her, I'm sure she'd be less than impressed to have her bed covered in baby crap. Margot laughs as I clean her up, completely oblivious to the fact that in a few years, the idea of pooping herself will more than likely come with floods of embarrassment. I'm just about to slide a fresh nappy under her when the front door opens and closes, and a second later the bedroom door opens.

'Oh.' Jude stands there with his hands on the lapels of his jacket and stares at me. His eyes flick down to the mess on my chest and he raises his eyebrows. 'I was just going to dump my coat but I'm thinking that might be a bad idea.'

'Yeah, no shit,' I reply and he laughs.

'Looks like you've got plenty of that already.'

Margot squeals, kicking her legs at the sound of his voice and I can't help but smile at the cuteness of it. Jude shrugs his jacket off and hangs it on the corner of the door.

'Why don't you go wash up?' he says, kneeling down on the floor next to me.

His skin is darker than it was three weeks ago, and his hair has grown out beyond the usual close cut he wears. His jaw is covered in short, light-brown stubble and he smells delicious – despite what's just happened. Maybe *because* of it.

'Hey, you,' he says, tapping Margot on the nose. 'What kind of a mess have you been making?'

My heart tugs in my chest as she giggles at him. Aside from a couple of very easygoing messages, I haven't heard from him while he's been away. Did Nina mean what she'd said, about him checking up on us daily? Rain flicks against the window and I'm taken back to that night in the tent. It was so long ago, but I can remember how my skin had bloomed with goosebumps as he'd laid next to me. How he'd wrapped his arms around me and we'd slept like that, as if it were the most natural thing in the world.

'Go,' he says, turning to me and nodding towards the door. 'I'll get her dressed. I can handle this.'

He grins and a jolt of electricity pulses between my legs as I remember the moment when we'd kissed in my doorway. It had felt like a natural progression of things and it feels the same now. It feels like the most normal thing in the world for him to have walked through the door, seen what was happening and roll his sleeves up to get involved. It's all he's done since the day Margot arrived. Heck, it's been like that from the moment we'd seen each other after so long at this very barbecue last year.

I go to say something, but as soon as I open my mouth I think better of it and lean forwards, firmly planting my lips on his. He pauses with surprise. The thought that it might all be a little too late for this crosses my mind, but a second later his hands are cupping my face as he kisses me back. As his tongue flicks against mine, I remember that moment after the picnic when I'd looked at him in his van and seen *him*. Not as Nina's brother, or someone I've known since childhood. I'd seen Jude for the man he'd become and as he pulls me in closer, I'm struck by the feeling that everything – the mortification at school for writing that love letter, the betrayal with Jerome and Steph and the split with Sam has been leading to this point. To me, being here with Margot and with him.

Margot babbles and we break away, pressing our foreheads together and my heart is racing so fast, it feels like it might jump out of my chest. Jude and I laugh a little before he shakes his head, turning it from side to side, just like after we had after our first kiss.

'You should go,' he says slowly. His eyes flick down to my top. 'You're still covered in baby poo.'

We both laugh and just like when Nina had put Luke to the test about her vulva casting, I feel like this is a moment where Jude's just passed the stepdad test with flying colours – in case I'd been in any doubt.

'You sure you can handle it?' I ask with a snicker.

Jude scoffs. 'Absolutely. Go. I'll be here when you get back.'

I look at them both – the girl I'm only just getting to know and the guy I've known since forever – and smile, feeling the warmth of contentment in my chest. It's just like Mum had said. The best thing is to go with what feels right.

I can't go wrong with that.

ACKNOWLEDGEMENTS

They say it takes a village to raise a child and it takes one to write a book too. The journey was full of twists, turns and actual tears until I found the story that needed to be shared and, like any birthing process, I couldn't have done it alone. Firstly, thanks to you, my readers, for the continued love, support and reviews (trust me, they help!). Big, big thanks goes to Victoria Oundijan for coaching and believing in me during the times when I wanted to give up and felt confused beyond measure. The story we ended up with is a billion miles from the one I thought it would be, and it's so much better for it! Thanks also to Celine Kelly, Sammia Hamer and the whole Lake Union team. I never lose sight of what a privilege this is. On a personal note, thanks to my Mum, Winsome, for being the best one there is despite the ups and downs and for showing me how to stand on my own two feet with confidence to go into the world. And last but never least, my own carpenter, handyman and biggest cheerleader, Simon. I literally could not have written this book without you and your support. You rock.

ABOUT THE AUTHOR

Natalie K Martin was born in Sheffield and grew up with a fascination for human relationships. After leaving her corporate career to travel and write, her novels became Amazon bestsellers on release.

Writing emotionally-led contemporary fiction about life, love and the tricky parts in-between, Natalie's books are relevant and relatable to the everyday woman and have been featured in the *Daily Mail*, *Woman's Own* and *Pride Magazine*.

A dedicated advocate for women's empowerment, Natalie also works as a Menstrual Cycle Coach. She lives in Bavaria, Germany, with her boyfriend and their rescue dog.